10:22pm

by

Ivor McKenzie

The fallen angel becomes a malignant devil. There is such a devil in all of us.

Be peaceful, be courteous, obey the law, respect everyone, but if anyone lays their hand on you, then send them to Hell.

Chapter 1

This was the early Seventies. The swinging Sixties were long gone, along with the hippies, their free love, long hair and unwashed bodies. Not that anybody who lived in Drumbrig, had experienced those carefree days of free love, and drugs.

Drumbrig nestled in the county of Fife, in the heart of farming country. Many people referred to it as 'The Land That Time Forgot,' minus the dinosaurs of course. Although, many of the residents would say that they weren't really sure about that. What they did know, was that Fife County Council had forgotten about their sleepy, small village. In fact it seemed that Scotland had forgotten about Drumbrig.

It was like it had been erased from the map. It wasn't that the sun never shone on them, but at times it struggled to get through the perpetual greyness that blanketed their lives. A pretty unremarkable town in anybody's eyes. It was only a mile off the main road to Dundee, but it might as well have been five hundred miles. Nobody ever came to Drumbrig. Life expectancy wasn't very high either.

Drumbrig was just one long main street, surrounded by rows of council houses, a lot of which were prefabricated bungalows. So small that they were quite unpleasant to live in. With constant rising damp and mould on most of the walls, it was a continual fight with a bottle of bleach and a scrubbing brush, but it often felt like you were fighting a losing battle. People long ago decided it wasn't practical to have anymore than two kids, and prayed they were of the same sex when they did have them.

There were always kids out playing at night for as long as they could. Nobody ever wanted to go home to be virtually sitting on top of each other in one small room. Invariably, either your dad or mum would smoke, making the air in your house very unpleasant. Your diet consisted of potatoes most days, along with anything your mother could put together. Cheap tins of spam and corned beef were life saviours. Most of the kids thought that kind of life was normal though. Although life was hard for the kids, they never knew anything different, until they started to get older.

In the main street there was the too expensive Co-op, which sold anything and everything, even doubling up as the chemist. People often said that if the Co-op closed, then you would be as well boarding up the houses in Drumbrig, as there were no other shops selling provisions. Many of the kids went to school in clothes which had been taken out on 'approval' from the Co-op, which gave the parents time to save up before buying them. After a good few weeks, a warning letter was sent to them asking to pay up or else. What the 'or else' meant, nobody was quite sure.

Naturally, the local pub, The Star, was 'bang' in the centre of the street, to catch the clientele from each direction. To a lot of people, it was where the wife and child beaters hid out. It was owned by Gerry Timson, or GT as he was commonly called. He was a small, weak man, who just stood behind the bar, chain smoking and drinking the odd 'half' of Bushmills whisky. If trouble broke out he would just sit on his high stool until it played out, or his wife would run through from the back wielding a piece of two-by-two wood, and the problem was soon sorted.

Discipline was still meted out with the father's leather belt, and their family suffered in silence as they didn't know any better. Some fathers seemed to revel in the beatings they handed out. With some families they suffered at the fists of a drunken father. Did it make the kids stronger? Probably not. Maybe they just ended up hating their fathers. The youngsters couldn't wait to grow up and leave the place.

Straight across from the pub was the police station. A two-cell unit with a one-bedroom house attached. Manned by PC. Harry 'Luggy' Burns, a very arrogant and hated man. He was a bully. Licensed to kick the 'crap' out of anybody he wanted to just because he was the police. Many of the men he had beaten up over time had vowed to get their revenge on him. It wasn't a matter of if rather than when they would. He had massive ears, hence the nickname. The kids used to joke that if ever aliens sent a message to earth, then Luggy would pick it up first.

Doctor Henderson's house and surgery were at the top of the street. A small man with constant blood shot eyes. He was always stinking of cigarette smoke, as was his so-called surgery. His teeth and fingers were badly discoloured with nicotine stains. None of the older boys wanted to go and see him, as no matter what ailment they had he always wanted them to masturbate into a bottle, with you hidden only behind a thin curtain. Invariably, he would poke his head around the curtain to see if you were finished, with a full-strength Capstan cigarette hanging from his mouth. Most of the boys never said a word about their ailments to their parents. They just put up with it.

The school, which was both primary and secondary, was set back from the main road. It was a pretty dismal, concrete building, run with a rod of iron. So, if you didn't get the belt at home, then you definitely ran the risk of getting it at school. The teachers never seemed to smile or have a good word for you. They didn't want to be there either. No encouragement was given to you whatsoever. You were destined to leave school with little or no qualification. Girls were to go on to be mums, but not necessarily wives, and the boys finding any job they could. Most times a dismal existence.

You couldn't miss the petrol station, with all the scrap cars lying around. Nobody could ever remember the owner, Bert Richardson, wearing anything other than greasy, oil-stained overalls which had never been in the wash. However, he could fix anything that had an engine in it. He was the unofficial taxi service for the community. Most of the time he never charged anybody for the local journeys, but it did cost them for the cleaning of their clothes afterwards. He was just a kind man.

There was a football pitch of sorts at the school, but you ran the risk of breaking a limb, due to the amount of boulders sticking up from the ground. That never seemed to deter the youngsters. Many a Friday night kickabout ended up with cut knees, and loud arguments about who had the biggest cuts on their legs. All cuts and bruises were worn like badges of honour. The local team played there on a Sunday, assuming they could organise an opposing team from some of the villages round about. Often, they had to get some of the lads from the pub to play for them. Many were full of alcohol, so invariably fights and arguments broke out, but nothing that sharing a few pints of the 'amber nectar' afterwards couldn't solve.

The only entertainment in the place was the cinema. It was pretty run down, with holes in the seats mostly from cigarette burns. It smelled, and never seemed to be swept from one week to the next. It did have a small balcony and the whole cinema held about one hundred patrons, although if you got fifty people in to see a film you were very lucky. It didn't help with the projectionist taking too much whisky while showing the film. When he screwed up with the continuity of the reels, lots of people would throw anything they had in their hands at his window. Most of the youngsters couldn't afford to get in so they used to club their money together, pay for one of them to go in and then they would open the fire door next to the toilets. Everybody would then pile in and spread out keeping an eye open for where the usherette was, although invariably, she was away having a cigarette somewhere.

Drumbrig had its fair share of characters, just like every other town. Noticeably the Olivers. Twin brothers. From a very early age they had struggled a bit with their mental health, but it was when everything about them started to become identical that people had become slightly wary of them. The same greasy receding hair style, combed in exactly the same way. Same colour and style of spectacles. They dressed the same, especially their duffle coats, with the same top toggle missing. When they ended up getting the same type of old push bikes with the same matching rust on them, then people gave them a slightly wider berth. Scary.

You came into Drumbrig over the Motray bridge which spanned the river Mot. In the summer, the kids had great times jumping off the bridge into the deep pool below. There was nothing much else to do in the summer months, just lazy days and nights. As much as living in Drumbrig was a pretty grim existence at times, the people there were mostly lovely folk. After all, they were Scottish, and as near to perfection as you could get. Unfortunately, they lived in one of the 'shitholes' of society.

Vinny, Billy and Barney were the best of pals from an early age. They called themselves 'The Three Amigos', although they probably never thought it was of any importance, other than sounding fanciful. They were inseparable, both in and out of school, especially the summer nights, weekends and school holidays. Like every young lad, they had dreams. Dreams that they used to often talk about. Dreams that got bigger and more expansive each time they brought them up.

What these lads were going to do with their lives was nothing short of wonderful. Nothing was going to stop them. Little did they know that life is never like that, and at some point, their lives would turn sour.

At this stage of their lives, they would say that nothing would change their friendship. They were to be 'Amigos' for ever. They even tried to be blood brothers by scratching their palms for blood to flow, before shaking hands. However, Billy fainted at the first sight of blood. So much for his aspirations to enter the RAF and be a war hero. They never stopped winding him up about it.

Vinny was born, Vincent McKenzie Hunter, to Eileen and Tam Hunter. He grew up in constant fear of his drunken bully of a dad. Many nights he would go to bed with big welts on his legs and backside from his dad's belt. His dad used to terrorise him by saying that he was going to give him a 'right good hiding' while taking his belt off. Most of the time Vinny never knew why he was receiving such treatment.

What hurt him more was the treatment handed out to his mum by his dad. He hated to see his mum being slapped and punched. If the tea wasn't on the table at an exact time, his dad would lash out at her. He knew his mum wanted to protect him, but she wasn't strong enough both mentally and physically.

Every day his hatred for his dad grew. Even to the extent that as Sunday was bath night he used to get in the tin bath before his drunken dad came home from the pub. Always shouting at him to get out as he wanted in, but Vinny would get up and empty his bladder into the bath, occasionally turning round and spitting into it as well.

He never knew anything different and thought that this was what life was supposed to be like. Anyway, he always had his two pals, Billy and Barney. Life seemed so different when the three of them were out playing. Not a care in the world. At least in the summer days swimming in the river the cold water helped with the pains in his legs after a beating.

Although he would mostly be out with his pals, Vinny on an occasion would want to be on his own and just wander down the river, find a quite spot, while thinking about everything and anything. Vinny was a great thinker. More than his pals were, who would often just act on impulse. He was a very intelligent boy, but would often hide it so as not to fall foul of his classmate's ribbing. He was a good-looking lad, and grew to just under six feet tall from an early age, but never thought of himself as good looking. No matter how much of a thinker he was, his thoughts never went to what he wanted to do when he would eventually leave school and move away.

The only thing that Vinny hoped for, was that he could transport through time for the next ten years. He would then wave goodbye to the dinosaurs forever. It was when he was about fourteen that he started to get the odd game for the local football team, and listened intently to the older boys stories about their sexual experiences from previous nights or last week, that he wondered about girls, and what other functions his penis had.

He made it his mission in life to find out what sex was about and take it from there. It got worse when Barney had found a load of 'scud' magazines in the bins at the back of the Oliver twins' house although he would never reveal what he was doing there. It became a bit of an obsession with him seeing these pictures, and he needed to find out more about why he felt the way he did on looking at naked girls in magazines. He often mentioned this to his two pals, but they would just shrug their shoulders and invariably change the subject.

One girl's name often came into the older boys boastings, and that was Big Irma. He knew there was an older girl at school called that, but she wasn't that big, just tall. During school days he noticed that the older boys tended to pay more attention to her than the rest of the girls. She always seemed flattered when they did this. Vinny didn't fully understand why, until he heard one boy recounting his experience with Big Irma, to his 'all listening' pals.

He knew there and then that he had to find out what sex was all about, but how? Several times, he had tried to casually speak to her, but she would just smile at him, and walk away. After weeks and weeks of his best efforts being ignored, he finally plucked up enough courage to ask her to go a walk with him. At first she was a bit taken aback by him asking her, but then she said, why don't we meet up on Wednesday night, and she would see him at the bridge at seven o'clock, but said there would be no promises as to what might happen.

That day he went through a range of emotions, from excitement to anticipation, to worry that she wouldn't turn up. Every possible emotion was going through his mind. There was nothing he could do about it, but just wait and see, and hope she would appear. He was oblivious to anything that was going on around him that day, and had been given several warnings in class for not paying attention, but nothing mattered to Vinny other than the walk that night.

On the Wednesday night it was as quick as he could 'shovel' his tea over his throat with his mother asking what was going on. He had forgotten how many times he had washed himself in the bath. Especially his genitalia as he was confident they could play a big part that night. After putting on clean underwear he was ready and told his mum he was off to see his pals. He was nervous, even more so when he couldn't see Irma. As he got near the bridge he saw her sitting on one of the seats. She stood up when Vinny approached her, and he was surprised when she gave him a hug and asked him to sit with her for a few minutes.

She then told him that she knew why he wanted to go for a walk with her, and with his face bright red, said to him not to be embarrassed. She took his hand, and they started to walk down the river with just some small talk between them. They walked to a large depression behind a couple of large oak trees, Vinny thought she had been here before. As they walked, Irma could sense he was getting too nervous, so she just squeezed his hand now and again. After all she didn't want it to be over too quick for either of them. Completely hidden from any prying eyes, Vinny was at a loss as to what he should do, so he just let Irma take the lead.

Irma started to take her clothes off, giving the impression that it was all a matter of fact to her. When he saw her naked, apart from her knee length boots, it was everything he could ever have imagined. Her breasts were shaped to perfection, well as far as he knew.

Irma took off his clothes, with Vinny feeling a bit nervous about that. They lay down on the cool grass and Irma showed him everything she knew about how to please her, with Vinny getting a throbbing erection. She then put her hand down, grabbed his penis, and put him inside her. There was a time during sex that she had started to moan, which grew louder while thrusting her hips into him before letting her hips drop down and her back arch with her head rolling back. Vinny hadn't been sure what had happened, but when he eventually climaxed he understood. This was the most wonderful feeling ever. If this was what sex was about, then he wanted more and more.

After lying beside each other for a while, Irma started to put her clothes on and suggested he do the same. They walked back along the river in silence and back onto the road. She gave him a kiss, and told him not to expect this all the time, but there was no harm in him asking her as she had enjoyed it. She walked up one of the streets to where she lived while he stood at the bottom, waiting to see if she would turn around. She didn't. Vinny walked home feeling like he was on a different planet, and never got much sleep that night.

Vinny had been in a bit of a daze for the next few weeks, which both Billy and Barney had commented on, but he refused to be drawn on why. Although, it was Billy who kept pestering him about why he was withdrawn, but Vinny had assured him he was fine.

He went the same walk with Irma a few times in the ensuing weeks. She would try and show him new sexual positions, but he thought it would have been better if he had been more supple so that he could have enjoyed them better.

It all went pear shape when the headteacher came into his classroom one day. He announced that Irma Ingles would no longer be coming back to school as she was expecting a baby, and although he didn't think that any of the young boys in this class were involved, if anybody knew of any other boys who had been seeing Irma, then they were to come and see him in confidence.

Vinny couldn't function for days after, and twice faked illness to get off school. He had been worried that Irma would give a list of the boys she had been with to the headmaster, and his name would be on it. It was two weeks later that he happened to bump into Irma at the Co-op. She must have seen the worry on his face. She took him outside and told him that she had no intention of naming him as one of the prospective fathers. He had thanked her, and wished her good luck with having her baby.

The relief that came over him that day was mind-blowing, and he made sure that from that day onwards he would always wear protection. After all, there was enough French Letters, as they were called, in the Co-op, and it wouldn't be the first thing that he had 'pocketed' from there. Although, he wondered how different they would make to sex. He had just had a massive scare, but was now going to get on with his life.

Billy 'Bomber' Clark was quite a 'lanky' lad who seemed to be smiling all the time. He came from a very religious family. It always seemed like his dad had wanted to be a minister, and whenever possible he would take the opportunity to be involved in church business and Billy and his mum just had to go along with it.

When Billy was young he was virtually frogmarched to the church every Sunday morning for bible class and later to the full service. Billy hated it, but at that age he couldn't do much about it. Every room in the house had a wooden crucifix up on the wall. His dad would sit beside the fire with his bible on a shelf next to him. The black and white television was never even plugged in on a Sunday, and often his dad would just pick up the bible, and give him and his mother a reading, boring the pants off Billy.

At his age, he could never understand what was happening, when every three weeks on a Sunday his dad would take his mum to their bedroom and lock the door. He just heard a lot of squeals and his dad's name being shouted out a few times. He thought that his dad must have been misbehaving, as when they finally emerged from the bedroom he would see him sitting reading the bible, looking a bit flushed. Years later when he realised what had been going on, he would just shudder thinking about it.

He got his nickname due to the number of times he would try and speak about the RAF to Vinny and Barney, much to their annoyance at times. At least he had a bit of ambition whereas the other two didn't have any. Billy was quite an accomplished dancer. Nobody knew about it, until they were old enough to attend the occasional 'record hops' held in the school hall. He was always the star dancer, and all the girls wanted him to dance with them, but he was never that interested, just happy to be dancing in a wee world of his own. He put his attributes down to dancing to the music in his bedroom from the small radio he had, but never on a Sunday.

Billy never seemed interested in school. In fact he was never interested in anything except the RAF, which seemed to put off a lot of people talking to him or even being around him. When the three amigos were together, and the talk got around to girls, both Billy and Barney didn't seem interested, and often Billy would just shrug his shoulders, which Vinny had found strange, but he never pushed the subject.

He was the one that got the other two interested in fishing. Many a night or weekend, they could be found with their home-made rods down by the deep pools, trying their luck on the Mot river. It didn't matter that they invariably came back empty handed as it had been a challenge. You versus the fish, with the fish mostly winning. Life seemed simpler when they were just sitting on the riverbank wiling the hours away.

Barney Anderson was a bit of an enigma. He lived with his Grandfather Jock, a decorated war hero, although he would never tell anybody about it, but nobody new where Barney's parents were or even if they were still alive. When asked about them he would just say that he didn't care as his grandfather was the only person who had been there for him from an early age. Barney was a stocky guy, with his lop-sided smile, who was as strong as a horse. Although mild mannered, people from an early age knew never to try and wind him up. Instead of intellectual he was more practical, and he had actually made the fishing rods for the amigos.

He was always arguing with the teachers at secondary school as to why he was learning a foreign language, or obtuse angles at maths, or even who won the 'bloody' Crimean War. He had no interest whatsoever in things like that, but give him something to mend or create then he was a genius at it. It seemed that he was always laid back, with an infectious laugh which would often set Vinny and Billy off. Nothing seemed to faze him. Always with money in his pocket, and he would often treat Billy and Vinny to sweets from the Co-op, assuming they couldn't 'pocket' any. When they had asked him where he got all the cash he was upfront with them. He stole it from his Grandfather's wallet while he slept. His Grandfather knew what he was doing, but Barney never took more than he needed so his Grandfather just let it go, sometimes only leaving a small amount in the wallet.

Barney was a perfectionist, and kept his Grandfather's house clean and tidy, while making good meals for them both. He loved his Grandfather very much, but always knew that some day he would have to leave him and go his own way. It bothered him, but his Grandad had survived two world wars, so he reckoned he would be fine when the time came.

It was when they were sitting down the Mot, Vinny came out with a profound statement.

"Hey lads, have you seen how the two Polish girls, Anka and Maja are developing? I think I might have to ask one of them out soon. What do you think? Maja's breasts seem to get bigger every week, but that's just wishful thinking on my part."

Maja and Anka were lovely looking girls, but due to the fact they were Polish, lots of the boys never went near them.

Billy and Barney looked at him as if he had two heads.

"Vinny, are you looking to lose your virginity? For God's sake we are only fourteen," asked Barney.

"Right you pair, let me tell you something. I lost my virginity to Big Irma months ago, and I tell you it was brilliant. I went out with her several times, and each time was better than the last. Maybe it's time you two started to think about it, or all the nicest girls will be taken soon."

"Vinny, could you be the father of Irma's baby?" said Billy.

"She said I wasn't Billy, and I was so glad when she said that. If I get the chance to have sex again, I swear I will use French Letters, which I can easily 'pocket' from the Co-op. After all, Mrs Stoddart at that counter is as blind as a bat. I don't know why you two aren't interested in girls."

"It's just that we haven't put a lot of thought into it Vinny," replied Barney.

Vinny wished he had never brought the subject up, as they constantly asked him about it for half an hour before Vinny had to say enough was enough. Over the next few months, both Vinny and Barney started to pay more attention to the girls at school. Any girl. However, Billy was still a bit shy about it. Barney and

Vinny thought it might have been his religious upbringings, but they never pushed him into anything.

Vinny spent a lot of his time getting to know Maja, and the inevitable happened. He took her down the river to the same spot where he had been with Irma. She was a bit frightened at first, but by the end of their love making session, she told Vinny she was madly in love with him. That scared the hell out of him. After all, it was just supposed to be a bit of fun. He had to sit her down and explain that to her after a few sessions down by the river.

She hadn't been happy, as Vinny had thought she had dreams of wedding bells. He wondered what was wrong with him as he couldn't get enough of sex. He had such a high sex drive that he was going out with any girl that he thought might be interested in lying with him.

One night, when Barney had come round to the house, they were both a bit taken aback when Vinny's mum had asked Barney who he was.

"Mum, you know who this is, it's Barney my friend. Don't you recognise him? You've even made him you're famous cottage pie."

"Oh, that's right son, I remember now." Both Vinny and Barney weren't sure she did.

They walked to Billy's house with their fishing poles in their hands. When the three of them were sitting on the banking casting their lines into a deep pool, Billy said, "Do you think we will ever catch anything worth taking home lads. Good job we aren't depending on what we catch for our supper." Barney started to laugh, which set the other two off. Life was good.

Over the next few months Vinny noticed a big deterioration in his mother. He had asked his dad about it, but all he said was that she was a daft old goat, which made Vinny very angry. He told him forcefully never to say that again. This had surprised his dad. Vinny decided he would try and find out what was wrong with his mum. He refused to go and ask the doctor, or it would end up with him masturbating into a bottle. Instead he went to the school library to see if he could get any information.

When he went in to the library, he was met by a beautiful young girl, who asked him if she could help him find what he was looking for. She was stunning, but he knew he had to concentrate on the task in hand, or at least until he had the information he needed. She was very helpful and directed him to an area under the heading, medical. She could see he was struggling a bit, so she wandered over and asked him what he was trying to find out about. When Vinny explained, she knew exactly which books to give him and asked if he would accept her help. He told her his name, and they sat down at a large table and spread the books out.

She introduced herself as Lori, and was the minister's daughter, but was only helping out in the library until she found out if her university application had been accepted.

"Where are you hoping to go?" asked Vinny.

"It looks like it will be either Aberdeen or Glasgow, but I don't have any preference. As long as it gets me away from this God forsaken place."

They spent about an hour pondering over the books, with Vinny finding it difficult to concentrate as Lori kept leaning over with her left breast touching his right arm. He had to ignore it as he needed answers about his mum.

"Vinny, after reading all this information, my opinion is that your mum is in the early stages of dementia. It's not nice as my grandmother had it, and your mum seems quite young to have it, but a doctor could confirm it."

Vinny agreed with her and thanked her for her help. Before he left he thought he would take a chance and see if she wanted to go on a date with him.

"I realise I am nearly sixteen, and might be too young for you, so don't be afraid to say, but I was thinking of a night at the cinema."

"I'll think about it Vinny. Come in and see me next week."

Chapter 2

Vinny struggled with the medical books he had taken home from the library. They were far too technical, so he wondered if he should go back and speak to Lori, but would she be thinking he was being too pushy about the date he had asked her for. He felt he had no alternative. As he walked through the library door, there was a look of surprise on Lori's face.

"Don't worry Lori, I'm only looking for some help. Did you say that you were hoping to study medicine at university? It's just I'm not sure that I am understanding some of the words with regard to my mum's condition."

"Bring the books over here Vinny, and we'll try and work it out together."

An hour later, Vinny had his head in his hands. Lori was just sitting there not saying very much. She felt a bit embarrassed.

"Lori, I knew she wasn't well, but never thought that she was as bad as this. This means that at some point she won't even know who I am. I'm not fussy if she never recognised my dad again to be honest but I just don't know what to do."

"She needs to see a doctor Vinny, although you may not want to take her to Dr Henderson on your own. How about I come with you. Not the first date you wanted. Can I ask you if it's true that the doctor gets all the boys to masturbate into a bottle, no matter what they are attending for? That's the rumour that has been going about."

" Unfortunately, yes it's true Lori, and I make no apologies if my face is red, as he tried to make me do it. I told him what to do with his bottle."

Lori started to laugh which eased Vinny's embarrassment.

"You should go and make an appointment at the doctors and try and explain to your mum that she should go with you, and then come and let me know so that I can arrange to come with you."

Vinny thanked her, and made his way up to the doctors to make an appointment for his mum. When he got home he saw his mum trying not to look him in the face. When he finally got her to look at him he saw two cuts on her cheek. He turned to see his dad lying on the couch in a drink fuelled sleep. Too much alcohol from the previous night had prevented him from going to work. Vinny wasn't a violent guy, but he had enough this time. He lunged at his dad and punched him as hard as he could on his face. His dad stirred briefly so Vinny smacked him again. His mum was shouting at him not to do that, as he was still his dad. Vinny sat beside her while holding her hand. He then explained that he had made an appointment for her to see the doctor about her memory loss.

"Don't be silly Tam, my memory is fine. Honest."

"Mum I'm Vincent. Tam is your sorry excuse of a husband, who was hitting you a wee while ago. Him lying there. Tomorrow I'll come out of school, and take you to the doctors at two o'clock. Don't worry you'll be fine."

Vinny moved a stool next to where his dad lay unconscious on the couch. He told his mum to carry on what she was doing before being hit. It was a while before his dad fully regained consciousness. When he did, Vinny grabbed him by the throat and sat him upright and told him to listen to him, so he fully understood.

"That was the last time you hit my mum or me. She is obviously ill, and I am taking her to the doctor tomorrow. If you come near either of us again, I will take a kitchen knife, and stick it up your arse and twist it. Got me?"

His dad could only nod his head, whereby Vinny shoved him back down on the couch. He walked into the kitchen and gave his mum a hug and told her that she wouldn't be hit again. He then left the house, and walked up to the Co-op hardware dept. to see if he could steal a bolt for his bedroom door, as he couldn't trust his dad and he needed to sleep sometime.

He met Barney walking up the road, when he told him what had happened, Barney wanted to go up to his house and give his dad more of the same, but Vinny persuaded him not to, although he could see Barney was angry. That night he heard somebody walking about but didn't know if it was his dad or his mum. Although he had put a bolt on his bedroom door, he wedged a chair up against the handle just to be safe.

Next day he told his teacher that he was leaving for a doctor appointment, but he felt she couldn't care less. Never even asked him if he was feeling unwell. He called in to the library and Lori said she would just be five minutes. When they both walked up the road, she told him not to get upset with what the doctor would say. As they walked into the house, Vinny's mum had a look of surprise.

"Don't worry mum, this is Lori from the school, she is going to come with us to the doctors. Is that alright?"

They set off to Doctor Henderson's clinic, for want of a better word. As they sat there Lori whispered in his ear that she would stay with his mum while the doctor examined her. Vinny took Lori's hand and squeezed it. While the examination was going on, Vinny had sat through in the small waiting room, until Lori shouted him through.

"Mr Hunter, I have done a thorough examination of your mum, and have come to the conclusion that she has the early onset of dementia. Although, I must admit she is quite young for this. To be honest, it will only get worse, so please get it in your head that at some stage she won't even know who you are. However, I would like to send her to see a specialist at Ninewells hospital in Dundee, if that is alright with you and your father."

"That's fine with me, but please leave that bastard of a father of mine out of this."

They thanked the doctor and walked home with Lori going back to the school library. He didn't know why, but before she left he gave her a hug and thanked her for coming. She had said she was glad to help, and he could pop into the library at anytime.

Vinny made a decision while walking home with his mum. He was leaving school. His mum didn't need constant looking after just yet, but that time would come. Anyway, school time was pretty crap. He knew he could get some part time work at the farm at the top of the valley. The owner was a kind old guy and had always treated Vinny well in the past.

He went into school the next day and told them. The head teacher wasn't too happy, but understood his predicament. He waited on Barney and Bomber coming out at lunch time, and explained the situation to them. They were far from happy, especially Barney.

"Vinny, do you think that all the battering's your dad gave your mum has caused her condition?"

"I don't know Barney, why?"

"I was thinking we should maybe lure him down the Mot and drown him, after giving him a beating."

Billy and Vinny just looked at Barney to see if he was joking, but apparently not by the look on his face.

"Don't worry lads, we will still have our times together, and Barney, no more thoughts of violence. Okay?"

"Yeh, whatever."

Vinny wasted no time in speaking to the farmer Mr Hamilton, who said he would be glad of the help. Vinny explained about his mum, and at times he might not turn up if she needed help. He had said that was fine by him.

Life for Vinny became pretty mundane. His dad would hardly lift a hand to help his mum, which made Vinny him despise him all the more. His time with the other amigos was beginning to become less and less. Lori had headed off to Aberdeen University, with the promise that she would look him up when or if she came back.

He always felt sexually frustrated, and had tried on occasion to ask Maja out, with the hope that sex might be on the menu at the end of the night. Not always though, as she knew he was really just using her. He knew that, but every night he would lie with an erection for hours at time. Times were hard for him in that respect.

By the time Vinny was approaching eighteen years, his mum was quite far gone. The lady next door came in each morning to bathe and dress her, with Vinny giving her as much as he could, despite her protestations. At that stage Vinny had no qualms about taking money out of his dad's wallet when he was lying drunk, which was often.

Vinny never thought his life was going to turn out like this. At times he really did just feel sorry for himself. Often, while working, he would just sit down and cry. He didn't want to, but he couldn't help it. After their second visit to the Ninewells, the specialist had told Vinny that it might be better if his mum was to go into a home.

On the bus home his mum had said she wasn't going into any home. No way. Vinny reassured her that he wouldn't let that happen. Life carried on as normal, until two incidents changed his life, and not for the better.

One night, while Vinny was going through his dad's wallet, his dad had woken up, and after grabbing the wallet off him had punched Vinny. He didn't hold back and started raining blows down on his dad's face, who ran out the door heading towards the police station with blood streaming down his face. After about five minutes Vinny looked out the door and saw his dad coming up the road with Pc Burns. His mum was crying hysterically, so he calmed her down, telling her he would put the kettle on.

He stood in front of his mum waiting for Luggy to make his usual dramatic entrance. The door burst open, and in came 'Luggy' Burns with a snarl on his face with his dad hiding meekly behind him.

"Right Hunter, I'm here to charge you with theft and assault and battery, after what your dad has told me. I want your full name and date of birth, and I want it now."

"Why don't you just fuck off Burns, and take these enormous ears with you, and I suggest you take your hand off that truncheon or use it."

"I'm going to lock you up and then give you a good hiding Hunter. Then we will see who the big man is."

"Your not going to do anything," came a voice from the doorway.

"Hi Barney. Nice of you to drop by," said Vinny

"Are these two cretins bothering you pal?"

Barney suddenly gave a straight right hand onto the chin of Vinny's dad's chin, dropping him onto the couch. Vinny's mum was hysterical by know, with Vinny trying to calm her down.

"I want the pair of you down at the police station with me now. You're going in the cells"

"I've already told you Burns, to get the fuck out of this house."

Barney went and stood next to Vinny, and they both looked quite formidable, with Barney looking most likely to kick off. Staring Luggy down, who walked slowly to the door.

"You'll regret this you two. Trust me."

"I'm sure you're going to try at some stage you rat, but remember you can't hide behind your badge forever," said Barney.

Luggy walked out the door, and Barney told Vinny to pack a bag for his dad. After he did so, Barney slapped him awake. He then took him by the arm, hauled him to the door with his bag, and kicked him out. Vinny saw him taking off down the road. Probably to the house of one of his drinking cronies.

He sat down and put his arm around his mum, while Barney went and made a cup of tea for them all. They sat for a while, just going through the motions, before his mum said she would like to go to her bed for a lie down. Vinny took her through and let her lie down on the bed and quietly closed the door.

When he went back to the living room, Barney was still there.

"We need to talk Vinny, about the whole situation. Is your mum capable of looking after herself? If not, what are we going to do about it? Will the Health Service put her in a home? If not, we are pretty screwed pal, as you can't look after her yourself. As for your dad, I doubt he will be back in this house again. As for Luggy Burns, then no matter how long it takes he will get his revenge."

"Your right Barney, so I need to get an appointment with Dr. Henderson to see about care for her. Mrs Brunton next door will help me with her until it gets settled. Oh, and I realise we will have to watch our backs with Luggy."

Barney asked Vinny if he would be alright, as he had to get back to make something to eat for his Grandfather. Vinney said he would be fine.

"Oh, and by the way Barney, thanks for having my back."

"Anytime amigo."

As Barney left, Vinny put his head in his hands, and cried. He couldn't believe how quickly his life had gone down the drain. There was a lot of thinking to be done. After a while the front door opened, and in walked Billy carrying a bag.

"Hi Vinny, I heard from Barney about what had happened. I am so sorry. How is your mum, and also just as important, how are you feeling?"

"Mum is just feeling very tired Billy. A good night's sleep and she will feel better. I just don't know what to do about her. I never had many aspirations about my future Billy, but any I did have just went up in smoke. I hope that doesn't sound selfish. No matter, I will manage somehow."

"Everything will work out Vinny, but you just have to be positive, no matter how hard you think things are. Anyway, my mum had already made a pie with corned beef, and she said you and your mum could have it for your tea."

"You're a good friend Billy, and please thank your mum for us. Oh, and I know you weren't here when Luggy started on Barney and me, but please watch yourself."

"No worries pal. I'll pop in tomorrow to see how you both are. See you."

More tears flowed from Vinny after Billy had left, and he knew there would be more to come. After his mum got up, he made her sit down and eat some of the pie, although she seemed to just pick at it. He told her he was going up to Mr. Hamilton at the farm to let him know what the situation was. Just as he got to the door his mum said, "Remember son, no matter how bad I get, and I have taken on board what all the doctors have said, I am not going into a home. Okay?"

Vinny just nodded and walked out the door. Mr. Hamilton was very understanding, and said he could do as much work as he felt fitted in around his homelife. He also said that Vinny was to take home as many eggs as he wanted, and not to even ask. Vinny thanked him and said he would come to work tomorrow, once he got his mum sorted out. As he walked back, he felt there was a great weight on his shoulders. He knew that things couldn't get any worse. They did.

The next morning, Mrs Brunton came in an got his mum bathed and dressed, before making them eggs for breakfast. She said she would like to do more, but she had her own family to think about. Vinny said he appreciated everything she was doing, and to make sure she put her own family first. Thank God for Mrs. Brunton he thought.

Vinny had only worked until early afternoon, so he could get home to his mum. He had left her something to eat for her lunch, and Mrs. Brunton had said she would look in on her. When he arrived home his mum said she was glad to see him. When he asked her what she had been doing, she just shrugged her shoulders. He had to get her a purpose for getting up in the morning. Both Vinny and his mum were in their beds early. The work at the farm wasn't hard, but Vinny was constantly thinking about his mum.

Vinny was up early as hadn't got much sleep. He shouted through to his mum, but had never got a reply. He thought she must be sound asleep. After washing himself, he went into the kitchen and prepared their breakfasts and lunches. His mum had never stirred, so he thought he would go in and waken her. There was immediate panic, as his mum wasn't there. Her bed had been slept in, but she wasn't in the bathroom or kitchen. Where the hell was she he thought?

He ran next door and banged on Mrs. Brunton's door. It didn't take her long to open up.

"So sorry to bother you Mrs. Brunton, but is my mum in with you. I can't find her anywhere. I don't know what to do."

"Don't worry son. I'll just put my coat on, and we'll go looking for her. She can't have gone far."

Two minutes later, they were walking down the main street asking anybody that was going about if they had seen Vinny's mum. There was just a lot of head shaking. They asked the delivery drivers at the Co-op, but nobody had seen her. There was a deep ache in the pit of Vinny's stomach by now. Mrs Brunton suggested they go home, just in case she had wandered home.

When they got home there was no sign of her. After a while, the front door opened, and Billy and Barney came in.

"How are you doing pal?" said Billy.

"Where have you and Mrs. Brunton been looking?" asked Barney.

Vinney told him, while Mrs. Brunton went to make a cup of tea. Vinney thought it was amazing how people thought that a cup of tea would make everything okay. There was a continuous stream of people coming to the door,

As word had gotten out Billy seemed to take over, and asked everyone to look in their gardens and outhouses, and ask their neighbours to do the same.

"I know it's difficult Vinny, but how about you, me and Barney divide the village up and we go searching. Mrs. Brunton can wait here, just in case she appears back. Sound like a plan?"

Everybody nodded their heads, and the lads headed out. Billy had suggested that Vinny head towards the farm in case his mum had wandered up there looking for him. While he and Barney would split up the town and head to the main road.

"Vinny, I know this doesn't sound good, but look behind every tree and wall as you walk up. Please look in the ditch on the north road as well. Oh, and try to get a grip of yourself, as you're no use to anybody the way you are. Be back here in a couple of hours. Let's go."

Every time Vinny looked over a wall or into a ditch, his heart was racing. When he got to the farm, he told Mr. Hamilton what had happened. They both started to search the outbuildings, but to no avail. Mr. Hamilton suggested that Vinny head back to Drumbrig where he would be of more use. He would take the dogs out, and scour the fields on and around the farm. If he found her, he would bring her home straight away. Vinny thanked him and started to walk down the road.

His head was ready to explode. Within a few days, his dad had been kicked out of the house, then the police were trying to charge him with assault and battery. Now his mum was missing. Why was life like this he thought. Billy was right. He had to be positive, but it was hard. When he got down the road, it looked like the whole village was out looking. Barney saw him, and came up to him, and said there was no sign of her. Vinny thanked everyone, and suggested they all go home.

As everyone walked home, they were all speculating as to what had happened to her.

Billy went down to the Co-op, and brought some provisions back for the three of them.

It was Barney who sat them down and told them to listen for a minute.

"I know you won't want to do this, but we have to report this to Luggy Burns, although I doubt he will be keen to help. We can ask him to contact the Tayside and Lothian and Borders police. We have to think of all possibilities. I stopped all the buses going

North and South, and if she had managed to slip onto a bus then she could be anywhere."

"You're right Barney. I will go down, but I suggest you two keep out of it."

"That's not going to happen Vinny. I agree Billy should keep well away from it, but I'm coming with you."

They walked down to the police station, whereby Billy had said he would be up first thing in the morning to continue the search.

As they walked through the door, Luggy was standing with a big grin on his face.

"So you have finally come for my help have you? Give me one good reason why I should help you?"

"My mother is missing, and she is suffering with dementia. She doesn't even know who she is at times. That should be a big enough reason is it not?"

"The only thing I am going to do is make a note that you pair of bastards came to let me know why the village was in a state of confusion this morning. So now you can fuck off."

Vinny was about to go for him, but Barney held him back before walking to Burn's desk and swiped his feet off the desk as Burn's had been sitting back with his feet up on it.

"That could be construed as assault Anderson."

"Listen to me you maggot. Charge me then. Somebody will come for you at some point, and then you won't be long for this earth. It probably won't be us, but you have made enough enemies over the years. Trust me."

As Vinny and Barney walked down the street Barney's Grandad was waiting at the front door. When they got there, Jock asked them to come in and tell him what Burns had said. Barney had told him what had happened.

"The pair of you wait here, as I am going to have words that bastard. Don't argue with me."

Jock walked to the police station, with his anger rising. He slammed the main door open giving Luggy a fright, who had been sitting at his desk.

"Right you arsehole you'd better pay attention to me. If you haven't contacted the Tayside and Lothian and Borders police within the next half an hour I will know, as I will phone them. I see by the smirk on your face that you think I'm no threat to you if you don't contact them. Well, here's what will happen. When I came back from the War, I brought back a nine mm Luger and ammunition with me, and as I am an old man, what have I got to lose by emptying an ammunition clip into you. You're not smirking now you cockroach. Oh, and my apologies to the cockroach species."

Jock walked out slamming the door behind him, and headed home. He told the lads what had happened, and Vinny had thanked him for his help, before heading home.

Most of the villagers were out the next day, but Drumbrig wasn't big, and they found themselves searching the same places as before, and they were becoming a bit disillusioned. Vinny was stopping every bus at the main road, and had found himself walking down the river staring into the deep pools, just in case she had fallen in. However, there was nothing. No trace whatsoever. Over several days, Jock had phoned the two police forces, but they had nothing to report. It was beginning to look grim for Vinny, but even worse for Vinny's mum.

He had carried on the search, even although most of the people had given up. After a few more weeks, Barney and Billy had ended up at his house one night. As they sat in the living room, it was Billy who said, "Vinny, I can't imagine how you feel, especially with not having any closure, but you might have to accept that you will never see your mum again."

"I know Billy, but it's hard to give up looking for her. Knowing she's out there somewhere, all alone."

"As brutal as this may sound my friend, we don't know if she's even alive."

"I must agree with Billy, Vinny. Have you had a look at yourself in the mirror lately pal. You're a pale shadow of yourself. We know you're not eating or sleeping, so you have a big decision to make. Do you carry on like this making yourself ill, or just accept that you might never see your mum again."

Vinny never did see his mum again.

He managed to get the council house transferred into his name on a temporary basis, but as the months went on, nobody from the council had come back to him. Maybe it was because he was managing to pay the rent and rates from his work on the farms round about. Billy and Barney often came up to the house, with Billy bringing up his radio on occasion to show off his dancing skills. They had made a pact a long time ago, that they would never touch alcohol, after seeing how Vinny's dad had turned out. Their lives just plodded along, with not a lot of excitement to them.

After a few months, Vinny's sex drive came back with a passion, and he didn't care who he asked up to the house. As long as they understood that it was just casual sex. He still 'pocketed' his French Letters from the Co-op, as the way he was he was going through them was like there was no tomorrow. There was one girl in particular, Amy, who seemed really keen on Vinny, and he found her very experimental in the bedroom stakes. She was never pushy, which suited him, and on occasion he would ask her to just go a walk with him.

As time rolled on, Vinny and his amigos were just leading a tedious life of working part- time fruit picking throughout Fife. Everybody had now left school with very little qualifications between them. They knew that important decisions had to be made, and soon. They had often sat down the Mot, throwing ideas at each other. No matter what was said, Billy had made up his mind. It was the RAF for him.

Vinny knew that he couldn't go through life working on the farms just to make ends meet, but he didn't have a clue as to what he was going to do. He wasn't going into the army. A desk job didn't appeal. Teaching even less. He was going to be twenty this year, and in a few weeks he had to make up his mind. It was made up for him when a police officer from Dundee came to speak with him. Vinny wondered why it had taken as long for someone to come and interview him, but this was just a courtesy visit.

The officer was a very kind guy, and empathised with him about his situation. After about an hour, the guy said he had to get back to Dundee.

"Oh, and don't worry about Pc Burns. We have known about his underhand methods of policing for a long time. It will only be a matter of time before he trips himself up. I'll tell you though, you could do worse than join the force. Please don't think I was prying, but I spoke to your old headmaster, and he thought very highly of you. Remember, we are not all like the arsehole that is

Luggy Burns. Here is the number at Dundee Police Station, and my name is Brian Lawson. Before I go, let me tell you about a guy that came up to Dundee not so long ago to wipe out the corruption in the force, and rid the town of its drug problem. He did it virtually single handed and his name was Denny Rey Foggerty. Bit of a legend to be honest. Maybe you could strive to be like him. Just a thought Vincent. See you."

Vinny watched him drive away, and sat down on the couch holding his throbbing head. He would have to give this some serious thought. He was lost in thought when Barney walked in the door.

"Who was that pal. I would put money on it, that it was a police car. One of these undercover ones."

"You're right pal. Put the kettle on, and I will tell you what he said. Knowing Billy he will no doubt hear the kettle whistling."

True to form, Billy walked in just as Barney was pouring.

"You must have better hearing than Luggy Burns, Bomber.

Vinny told them everything that the police officer had told him. They were quiet for a minute, before Barney spoke up.

"So do you think Luggy Burns is 'bent' then Vinny? "

"I can't see how he can be 'bent' Barney. I just think they are aware of his corrupt ways of policing. It only takes a few like him to give the Police Force a bad name. They can't have eyes on him all the time. I think we have to be very careful with Luggy, just in case he gets wind of Professional Standards investigating him. Let's watch each others backs."

"Are you going to have a real think about the police force Vinny?" asked Billy.

"It will give me something to focus on rather than my mum's disappearance. I would like to find out more about the young guy that sorted out the corruption up in Dundee, but all that information is probably hush hush. There is nothing else at the moment. What about you Barney?"

"I can't think of a single thing I would like to do. The opportunities for apprenticeships are few and far between round about here. It would mean moving away to a big city, but I would have to make sure my Grandad was okay. As you know, working fulltime on the farms pays peanuts, but it is something I have liked doing in the past. I really don't know what I am going to do. What about you Billy?"

"I have always said that I want to go into the Airforce, and I will be truthful with you both, in that I have sent off my application, and I should hear in a week or so, but I am still not one hundred percent sure if I want to go there."

"Don't worry pal, it's normal when you apply for a career that takes you away from home. Remember, the job can take you all over the world. You'll be fine", said Barney.

Reality had hit them all when Billy had said this. The three amigos would be disbanded, sooner rather than later. They sat there not saying very much, until Vinny spoke.

"Let's not get down about all this lads, as we have a lot of time together before decisions are made. Anyway, I've heard that some of the girls are wanting to hire a bus and go dancing in Dunfermline in a couple of weeks time, so how about we put our names down. Barney, you and I could sit and watch all the girls eyeing up 'twinkle toes Clark' here."

Billy threw a cushion at him, and they all started laughing.

Vinny's life started to get a bit better, but his mum was always on his mind, and at times he would just lie on the couch, dream that his mum had come back, and everything was back to normal, but life never 'panned out' like that.

Vinny's sex life wasn't slowing down. In fact it was increasing, and he knew he would have to get it under control. Okay, he knew he was really just using the girls, but very rarely did they give him a 'knock back'. Although he was always nice to them, and he never abused them in any way. Many of the girls loved the fact that he had his own house where they couldn't be interrupted, and they could be inside when the weather was bad. He was the best-looking young guy in the village. Life was good for Vinny in that respect.

Next morning, he went down to the phone box next to the garage. He put a load of coins on the shelf, and got the card out that the police detective Brian Lawson had given him. Eventually he plucked up enough courage to make the phone call, and was put through to Ds Lawson.

"Good to hear from you Vincent. I take it you've been doing a lot of thinking about your future. What is it that I can do for you?"

"I really need to speak to someone, so that I can get more information before I can make a decision on what I want to do."

"How about you come up and see me in Dundee in a couple of weeks, and we can have an informal chat. I will send you a letter with a date and time, also where I am stationed at. If I'm not being a pain in the arse, I will also send you part of the written entrance examination, the difficult part, just to give both of us an idea of how capable you are."

"Sounds good Ds Lawson. I'll send the written exam back to you post haste."

They both said goodbye, and as Vinny started to walk home he felt more positive than he had in a long time. He knew getting in to the force would be difficult, and wondered how Luggy ever did it. He promised himself, that if his career was to be the police, then he would strive to go far, but never to be another Luggy Burns.

He felt he owed it to his pals to let them know what was happening, so he called in on Barney. Fortunately, Billy was there, so that was a bonus.

"So nothing set in concrete then Vinny", asked Billy.

"Far from it pal, but it does seem a bit promising."

"I'm glad for you Vinny, after all you have been going through, but if I get caught stealing anything from the Co-op, then please make sure it's you that arrests me, and not Luggy," said Barney.

Even Jock was laughing with them.

"Listen to me you three. Please don't under estimate what Luggy might have in store for you. You know he's a devious bastard. Twenty years ago I would have given him a right good beating, but now I would have to load the Luger and put a few holes in him."

The three amigos just looked at each other, wondering if Jock was joking, but by the look on his face he wasn't.

Drumbrig seemed to be getting back to normal, except that everyone was wary about going into their outhouses, just in case Mrs Hunter was lying there. Vinny had made a point of thanking everyone he came in touch with. Billy's dad had asked him if he wanted a service to be held for her, as he would get it set up with the minister. Vinny thanked him, but said that as long as there was no proof she was dead, then he didn't think that was appropriate.

For the next week the rain just 'tipped it' down, making his work on the farm difficult. The only thing that was keeping him going was the thought that they would be off to the dancing in Dunfermline this Saturday. They had been talking about it for a while now, and finally it was going to happen. Billy had been the most vocal about it as he just couldn't wait to get on that dance floor. Barney and Vinny had been winding him up that he should pack his tooth brush in his top pocket as he was a certainty to 'pull' one of the girls.

The big day had arrived. Not just for the three of them, but all the folk that had put their name down to go to the dancing. That night everybody had congregated at the Co-op waiting for the bus to arrive. There was a loud cheer when they saw it coming up the road. Vinny had never seen such excitement coming from everybody. The girls with their frocks and new hairstyles. The lads in their drainpipe trousers and short jackets.

Vinny and Barney were waiting on Billy. He was late. Just when they thought one of them would have to go for him, they saw him walking down the road with his usual swagger. They were positive they had seen him do some little dance steps while he walked. He was dressed all in black, with his tight trousers, short black jacket, a white shirt with a frill on the front. Most impressively, he had a pair of black 'winkle pickers' on his feet. He looked a million dollars.

"Bloody hell Vinny, if that lad doesn't get a lass tonight, then he isn't interested in the opposite sex. Know what I mean?"

"I think we are going to be second best on the dance floor tonight Barney."

The bus had picked up a lot of people from some of the villages round about, so by the time the were on the Dunfermline road, the noise was getting louder and louder with the driver telling everyone to quieten down. The bus was old, and the seats were hard and smelly. Vinny had tried to open the small window, but it was stuck fast. The smell of cheap perfume and pungent aftershave was beginning to make him nauseous.

Vinny looked up and down the bus, and saw a lot of the girls swigging from half bottles of vodka mixed with coke. He wondered how many were going to lose their virginity tonight. The bus seemed to take ages to reach the Kinema Ballroom in Dunfermline.

It had been busy outside, but when they got in, they couldn't believe their eyes. It was absolutely mobbed. Everybody was piled around the dancefloor with the guys at one end and the girls at the other end. Vinny thought that this wasn't going to end well. There was a bar selling soft drinks. Three glitter balls hanging from the ceiling, but that was about all apart from the stench of sweat. Most of the guys had been drinking before they came in.

"I have a bad feeling about this lads, what do you think."

"I agree with you Vinny, but what can we do about it," said Barney.

Billy didn't say a word as he was in his wee world of his own. Without saying a word he ran onto the dance floor and started dancing. It wasn't long before he was surrounded by girls, all wanting a piece of him. Barney and Vinny could only stand and watch him. He was poetry in motion. He hadn't stopped after an hour, yet he didn't appear keen on any one girl.

When he eventually came back to where Vinny and Barney were standing, they thought he was wired to the moon. Billy had said that the music from the sixties would never be beaten.

It was then that Barney had said that there was a bunch of lads on the far side looking like they were spoiling for a fight, and not to look their way. Casually, Vinny had looked across and thought this wasn't good as another group of lads were watching the other gang intently with menace in their eyes. It was then that one of the guys had wandered over to them.

"Keep that fucking 'poofter' off the dance floor, as we are going to kick the shit out of that lot from Dundee."

"You are not keeping me from the dancing, so fuck off, " said Billy, and he was in the middle of the dance floor before the other two could stop him.

"Your loss pal," the guy shouted at Billy.

The noise prevented them for getting Billy's attention. Barney said he would go and get him, but just then the two gangs appeared at either end of the dancefloor. Vinny grabbed Barney's arm and hauled him back. Billy was oblivious to what was going on around him.

The noise level dropped considerably, as everybody knew what was happening. All except Billy, who was on another planet.

"Are you seeing what I am Barney?"

"Yeh, I noticed the glare off their switch blades a moment ago. This is not good pal. What are we going to do?"

"Let's rush on to the dance floor, grab Billy, and then run like hell out of here. It's the only plan I have Barney. Right let's go for it."

They bolted onto the dance floor. This was the wrong move, as each gang thought they were being attacked and started running towards the other. Barney and Vinny just made it to where Billy was dancing. Barney grabbed him and pulled him to the floor, before the three of them were being trampled and kicked by either side. They were being kicked all over their bodies, before a kick to Billy's head knocked him out.

"Barney, we'll grab an arm each and drag him off the dance floor. Watch out for the blades."

They were on their knees pulling Billy, while trying to dodge the kicks and knives. When they were almost clear of the melee, three guys came rushing towards them. Vinny shouted to Barney who stood up and started to punch and kick them, leaving Vinny to keep dragging Billy to safety.

"Barney, we still seem to be caught in the middle of it. Head for the toilets, as I think that's the only way out."

As they were dragging Billy, a young guy came staggering off the floor with blood pumping from a stab wound to the stomach. Barney hesitated for a minute, before Vinny roared at him to keep going. Girls were screaming hysterically everywhere, and one or two had fainted. They were making headway, when Billy came too. He got himself up and was starting to head back to where the fighting was, before Barney got him in a headlock and started dragging him to the toilets.

When they were finally in the toilets, Vinny saw their escape route.

"Barney, kick the emergency door open, and lets get out of here, as it seems other people have the same idea as us."

Barney kicked the door open, with everybody piling out, and scattering into the street. Billy was still a bit groggy, so they held onto him, and got as far away from the dance hall as possible. To make matters worse, they saw the bus they had come in, heading out of the town. The fighting had spilled out into the street, so the driver of the bus had seen this, and wasn't waiting for anybody.

"Get down this side street lads, I can hear police sirens. Let's get into this shop doorway and sit down," said Vinny.

"What just happened in there Vinny. It was World War Three at times. I wonder how many people were stabbed. I saw a few guys with cuts to their faces, but I noticed several with blood-soaked shirts. What the fuck is wrong with people Vinny?"

"If I knew that Barney I wouldn't be sitting in this shit hole of a place, with a long walk home. I reckon that we'll struggle to get back by nine tomorrow morning. Why fucking us?"

"How was my dancing lads?" said Billy.

Barney smacked him over the back of his head, almost knocking him out again. They sat with their heads down, before the cold wind was telling them they had to move. As they got up, Vinny noticed blood running down Barney's hand.

" For God sake pal you've been cut. How bad is it?"

"Don't worry Vinny, I got my upper arm sliced, just when we were pulling 'twinkle toes' here off the dance floor. No big deal."

There was nothing else for it but to start walking home. They were only a few miles on the road when the rain started. They thought it couldn't get any worse, but it did. Much worse. After about seven miles of walking, they saw headlights coming towards them. They stood to the side of the road to let the vehicle past. As it passed, they saw it was a police van with Luggy Burns and two others in the front.

The wind was getting stronger, but it was Billy who had heard the police van stopping. When they turned round, they saw the driver trying a three-point turn. The road wasn't wide, so it took him several turns, but eventually the van was heading towards them.

"No point in scattering lads. I fear this is going to be Luggy's revenge. Whatever you do, don't resist or say anything ," said Vinny.

The van drew to a stop several yards from them. The three officers got out with their batons drawn. It was Luggy and two other burley officers, who the lads had never seen before that were standing before them.

"Right, the three of you get in the van. You're going back to the jail at Drumbrig where you'll be charged with rioting. If you don't get in willingly, we will forcibly throw you in."

"Get a life Burns. You couldn't even throw a 'wobbly' you coward. We know what this is about, I hope these two guys do, or it could be their jobs at risk," shouted Vinny.

The two officers just looked at each other wondering if they were doing the right thing.

"Just get in the back you three," said Luggy.

Vinny just nodded his head to Barney and Billy, as Billy was looking scared, and they got into the back with Luggy shoving Billy before slamming the back door. There was no seats in the junk heap of a van, so they had to sit on the floor, which for the next forty minutes, was extremely uncomfortable. When they finally got to the jail they were frogmarched and put into one cell.

"Hey, can we get some medical attention for my friend here, as he's bleeding ?"

It was then that that Luggy ran through, and started dragging his truncheon over the bars of the cell trying to be the big man. The lads weren't intimidated, they were just sitting on the single bed attached to the wall.

"Would you just fuck off Burns, and leave us alone. You're just making an arse of yourself, as well as making a noise. Get lost," said Barney.

While the other two tried to sleep, Vinny was trying to hear what the officers were saying, as they'd left the door to the front office slightly ajar. He heard one of the officers saying that their debt to Burns had now been repaid, and they had to stick to the story they had concocted. They were taking the van back to the depot in Dundee.

Before they left, one of the officers, who had been doing the talking came through to the cell, and spoke.

"I suggest you all go along with what Pc Burns has put on the charges. If it's your first time, then you will just get a wrap on the knuckles, unless you get a strict judge."

"Maybe I should speak to Ds Brian Lawson from professional standards about all this, what do you think?" said Vinny.

The guy's face went chalk white, and he had to grab onto the bars of the cell to steady himself.

"You were an idiot getting involved with Burns. Anyway, probably the next time I'll see you will be at your disciplinary hearing. Now fuck off," said Vinny.

The officer walked away looking slightly crestfallen. He knew he had screwed up.

Barney and Billy were trying to get some sleep, but Vinny was running all the scenarios through his head. He knew Burns would try and throw the book at them, so he thought that they should just tell the truth, and hope justice would prevail. He decided to try and get an hour's sleep. When he awoke, Billy was still out of it, but Vinny couldn't believe what Barney had done. On the whitewashed wall, he had used his own blood to write, in large letters, 'Luggy is a kiddie fiddler.'

"What do you think Vinny? Quite appropriate is it not. That bastard will be sleeping next door, so why don't we start banging on the walls to wake him up. He's not going to charge us for doing that, surely."

Billy was awake by now, so they started to shout and bang on the wall to the adjoining room. It wasn't long before Luggy came storming in waving his truncheon and making threats.

"Don't think you are going to get away with this. My colleagues and I have witnessed the charge sheets, so you are all going to court, and I'll be there to ask for the harshest sentence."

It was then that he noticed Barney's handiwork, and went ballistic, with the three of them laughing.

"Just the truth Luggy. You can't charge us for that. No matter how much you want to," said Barney.

Luggy knew he was on a hiding to nothing, so he just opened the cell door and told them to get out, while standing well back from them, with Barney trying to spit on him.

The lads started to go to home, but Barney had asked them to come in for a tea. Billy thanked him, but said he would rather go home and face the music. Vinny immediately grabbed him by lapels.

"You have nothing to apologise to your parents about Billy, so get a grip. It was Luggy who was the problem tonight."

"I am still going home, so I'll see you both tomorrow."

Barney and Vinny watched him go up the road before they went into Grandad Jock's house, who was standing at the window watching. When they got in, Jock casually asked them what had happened. When they told him, he became very agitated. He started to clean up his grandson's wound. After that was done, he made the tea and told the lads that he would be back soon, and headed out the door.

"Grandad, please don't get yourself into trouble on our account."

Jock never looked back or said a word. He just walked to the police station, and threw the door open, startling Luggy again, who was sitting at his desk.

"Listen to me you fucker, and let it sink in. I know you have concocted these trumped-up charges. Let me tell you though, that if any of these lads get punished through the courts, then I will seriously put several bullets into your head. I thought I had lost the bullets to my Luger, but I have found them. So you won't be alive after the court case if any of these boys are punished. You have been warned."

Luggy was sitting there like he had seen a ghost, but in his usual arrogant fashion, he told Jock to get out or he would have to arrest him to. Jock walked to the door, turned, and laughed.

On his way home, Vinny knocked on the door of the Clark household. Billy's mum answered the door. She looked like she had been crying.

"Come in son. Billy and his dad are in the living room. Just go in."

When he went in Billy's dad Ian was giving his son a lecture, while standing holding his bible. He looked at Vinny if he was a bad smell. It was then that Vinny lost the plot.

"Don't you dare stand there giving your son a lecture, you sanctimonious old bastard. You think you are some preacher of sorts, when in fact you are just a wannabe minister. Billy did nothing wrong. Wrong place at the wrong time, and the charges against him are purely bogus. Made up by a corrupt policeman, as you will find out when we go to court. Sorry you had to hear all that Mrs Clark."

He walked out, pointing his finger at Billy's dad, but not saying a word. As he passed he whispered in Billy's mum's ear.

"Your son is a fabulous dancer Mrs. Clark. He would love to show you sometime."

A large smile came over her face. When he got to the door, he shouted to Billy that he would see him tomorrow after he had finished his work on the farm. He wandered up to his house and lay on the couch for a few hours, until he woke to find Barney standing over him.

"Barney, don't you ever knock?"

"No, because you never lock the door. I'm here to tell you I'm going to make Luggy's life a misery, until we get to court, and then we can take it from there."

"Are you off your head pal, We've just been charged with rioting and your now organising a vendetta against a policeman?"

"What's your point pal?" said Barney.

Vinny started to make breakfast for the two of them, as Barney never refused a meal. When they were sitting eating, Vinny asked Barney what his plan of attack was for 'pissing' Luggy off. He also told him about visiting Billy on the way home.

"Can't tell you pal, as the less you know the better, but it's just small things that will get under his skin, and make his life a misery. What are we going to do about Billy though?"

"Nothing, absolutely nothing. He's big enough and hairy arsed enough to look after himself," said Vinny.

"Yeh, I suppose, but I worry about him at times. Let me ask you something Vinny. Do you think our friendship will last?"

"My honest opinion Barney, is that it will last, but in the near future, we will go our separate ways, but no matter where we are, we will always be the amigos pal."

Next day, Vinny received a call from Ds Lawson in Dundee.

"Hi Vincent, I have received the exams papers, which you have completed. I am going to ask you something, but please don't be offended by what I am asking you. Please answer me truthfully. Did you at anytime get any help in completing the exam papers?"

"Truthfully, no. I sat down and read the questions several times, before answering them logically. I found several of the questions could be answered in two ways, but on reading them again and again, I came to the same conclusion. Why, have I done something wrong?"

"On the contrary Vincent, we up here in Dundee have never seen such a score in any police examination. Well done. It will put you in good stead if you apply to us."

"It probably won't matter now anyway, after what happened a few nights ago.

"Tell me everything Vincent, and don't leave anything out please."

Vinny gave him the story right down to the last detail.

"Rather traumatic for you and your friends. Can I ask you to do something for me. Please get your two pals to phone me, and tell me exactly what their account of the night was. Oh, and I suggest you tell the one that wrote on the cell wall to omit that from his statement. That wouldn't look good at all. I'll get back to you after their phone calls, but no matter what, don't worry about it. Take care."

It was the following day that the lads had come up to see Vinny. He told them what Ds Lawson had said. Billy was right up for it, but Barney was a bit hesitant.

"Barney, what the hell is wrong with you? This could be the chance to get away with it, or even a slap on the wrist. C'mon, get a grip will you."

"He's just another policeman Vinny. They're all the same pal."

"Please Barney, do me a big favour, and just speak to him. For Billy's sake if nothing else."

"Only if you are okay with me kicking the shit out of Luggy, if it all goes wrong."

Vinny knew he would make the call.

For the next two weeks their lives were in limbo, just waiting for their summons to arrive. Vinny thought Billy was going to make himself sick with worry, so he sat him down a few times, and said he would guarantee him that it would be all right. He knew Billy wasn't strong mentally, so he had to be there for him.

Luggy's window in the house adjoining the cells had been 'put in' a couple of times, but Barney always denied it was him. Vinny said he didn't believe him, and to back off. At the end of the second week their summonses arrived. Billy's dad had went off on a rant at him while holding his precious bible, until Billy had told him where to stick his bible. Much to the shock of his dad.

After that, Billy had spent a lot of time at Vinny's house, only spending time at his own house with his mum, while his dad was at work. Barney was just taking everything in his stride, but Vinny knew that deep down he was a bit scared. It was two days after, while sitting having something to eat at Vinny's, that there was banging on the door.

"Don't answer it. It could be Luggy, and his 'pals' coming to get us," said Billy with a little tremor in his voice.

"Settle down pal, I'll check through the curtains. Give me a minute."

Vinny checked, and then went and opened the front door. In walked Ds Brian Lawson.

"Lads, I would like to introduce you to Ds Brian Lawson from the police professional standards in Dundee."

"Are you here to arrest us," said Billy, but it sounded like a girl shrieking.

"Billy, shut the fuck up will you, I've told you before your going to make yourself really ill," shouted Vinny at him.

"Don't worry lads, I am only here to have a word with you regarding your day in court, at the end of next week. As Vincent will probably have told you, Pc Burns is of special interest to us, along with the other officers, who arrested you that night. However, before I start, let me tell you that what I say to you will be in strict confidence. Nothing will leave this room, and definitely nothing will be repeated in the court room. Got it?"

Everybody just nodded. Especially Billy, who was in danger of his head falling off.

"I suggest the three of you refuse a solicitor, and simply stand up in court and tell the judge what went down that night. Don't deviate from the truth. The crown prosecutor will ask you leading question, but I repeat, don't deviate one bit. I'll be in the courtroom, but I have to let everything play out. My part will only be to speak to the judge, if she lets me. I say 'she' as it'll be the Right Honourable Miss Sheila Reynolds that will be presiding. You mess with her at your peril, although I will say she is fair, and she insists on being called Your Honour. Nothing else. Right any questions before I go?"

Nobody said a word.

"Okay," I will pick you up at nine am next Thursday. Unfortunately I will have to drop you off at the far end of Bell Street where the court is, as I don't want Pc Burns knowing I'm there to help you. I'll bring you back to Drumbrig at the end of the proceedings.

"Ds Lawson, can I ask you why you are doing this for us?" said Vinny.

"It's simple Vincent. This is what I do for a living. It's what professional standards are all about. If any officer is thought to be 'dirty' then we investigate. We're not the most popular department in the police force, but the general public need to know we are policing ourselves. We know that there is a problem with Pc Burns, which is why I am asking for total discretion from yourselves.

"Take care, and no more putting his windows in. Understood? Oh, and Vincent I'll leave this envelope on the table at the front door."

They just looked at each other, wondering how he knew about the windows. As he walked out the door, Barney said that they all appreciated his help. Ds Lawson just nodded his head and shut the door behind him.

"Well lads, what do you think of Ds Lawson?" asked Vinny.

"If he helps us with this charge then I'm okay with that, but remember he is still a policeman," said Barney.

Billy just sat there with a blank look on his face. It was obvious that everything that had been going on had affected him quite badly.

Over the ensuing days, the lads only met up now and again. Billy had stayed in his room most of the time. Mainly dancing, according to his mum who still came up to Vinny's house with extra baking she had made each day. Vinny wasn't the best at cooking, so he was glad of her generosity. He knew she did this when her husband was at work.

Barney was neither up nor down, and Vinny would occasionally wander down to his grandad's house for a chat with the both of them, and also to check to see if Luggy's windows were still intact. Barney had asked him if he still intended to join the police force, and if so, where would he go for his training? Vinny said he would decide for definite once the trial was over.

It seemed that the days up to the trial were dragging, and Vinny just put his head down and worked hard on the farm. He had told Mr. Hamilton about his future plans, and also about the trial. He said he was happy with whatever Vinny wanted to do, and that he was making the right decision in getting away from Drumbrig.

As the day for the trial was looming, Vinny asked Mrs Clark how Billy was? She said he had just shut himself away in his room. Only coming out for meals and to bathe. Vinny decided he had to act, as Billy would be a wreck at court. He went down and spoke to Barney, and told him to get Billy up to the house the next night at about seven, and don't take no for an answer.

When they arrived the next night it looked like Barney was manhandling Billy through the door. Vinny had moved the sofa and armchairs out of the way, leaving just the bare linoleum.

"What's happening here Vinny. You got Barney to drag me up here for what?"

Just then, Maja and Anka walked through the door and Vinny put the radio on and tried to find some music to dance to.

"If you're going to do something Vinny, then do it right. Get out of the way will you."

There was a wry smile on both Barney's and Vinny's faces as Billy found the rock and roll channel, and off he went dancing. 'Twinkle toes' was back, and soon the girls were accompanying Billy on the makeshift dance floor. God, Billy's moves were better than ever. Barney and Vinny asked him to teach them to dance, but Billy was getting exasperated with them, and eventually told them to forget it, and to just watch. The girls were loving it, getting Billy all to themselves. Two hours passed, and Billy was still going strong, but Vinny had to call a halt to it as next day they were due up in court. Vinny thanked the girls as they left.

"Right Billy, get your act together for tomorrow pal. We need you to be on the same side as us. Go home and get some sleep. We'll be all right tomorrow, I promise."

They all hugged, and said they would meet here at the agreed time. It was a restless night for Vinny, and he suspected Barney and Billy were the same.

It was Billy who walked through the door at seven forty-five.

"Not get much sleep pal?"

"Bugger all Vinny. I feel knackered, what about you?"

"The same pal. I suggest that when Barney arrives, we go over what went on that night in Dunfermline, again and again, until we are word perfect. Billy, stick the kettle on and make some toast for us all please."

Barney walked through the door smiling.

" Alright lads. What a great sleep I had last night. My grandad had to wake me up this morning, or I would still be sleeping. Right, I can smell toast, but what are we doing after that until it's time to go?"

"I've just said to Billy that we need to go over everything about that 'shit' of a night."

"Fine by me pal."

It wasn't long before there was rapping on the front door, and in walked Dc Lawson.

"I see you boys are keen for the off. Mind you, a bigger bunch of reprobates I have yet to meet," he said laughing.

"Nice to see you've all got your 'glad rags' on. If anybody needs to go for a 'piss' then go now. With heavy traffic it could take us an hour."

They set off with Vinny in the front, and the other two in the back.

Chapter 3

It seemed like a bit of an outing to the lads, especially when they were going through Dundee. Barney was constantly asking the officer about the landmarks in the city. When they got to Bell Street Dc Lawson parked well away from the entrance to the Sherrif Court, telling them to meet him here after the court case.

They were a bit early, so they decided to wait outside, rather than wait inside in a stuffy waiting room. Eventually, they walked in and sat down on one of the benches. It wasn't long before a man in a black robe came in and asked them to follow him. Barney had to put his arm around Billy's waist for fear of him passing out. The official asked them to step up into the dock and have a seat. It was then that a side door opened and in walked Luggy Burns, along with the crown prosecutor, both laughing at something one of them had said.

Vinny had been told not to lose his temper, but his anger was rising. The clerk of the court stood up and asked everyone in the court to rise for the Right Honourable Miss Sheila Reynolds. She immediately looked over at the lads standing there.

"I see you don't have any legal representation with you gentlemen. Why?"

"We came here to tell the truth, so that's what we'll do," said Vinny.

"Admirable, young man. So lets get the proceedings started, but before I do can I ask which one of you is Vincent Hunter?"

"That will be me your Honour," said Vinny.

"This has nothing to do with the trial Mr. Hunter, but is your mum Eileen, married to Thomas, as I'm sure we went to school together, a very long time ago, how is she?"

"As this has nothing to do with the trial then here goes. Yes that's her, and as to how she is I don't know. I don't know if she is dead or alive. After years of physical violence from my so-called father, she ended up with dementia. Whether the beatings had anything to do with it I don't know, but she slipped out of the house one night, and nobody has seen her since."

" How long ago was this Mr Hunter, and was there a search organised to look for her?"

"It was a few months ago now, and as for a search, well me and my friends here organised the village into looking for her, but that bastard sitting down there refused to help," he said pointing to Burns.

"Mr. Hunter, I won't have that type of language in my court, no matter how angry you feel."

The judge took her glasses off and started to pinch her nose, before putting them back on, with a slight shake of her head.

"Pc Burns have you an explanation for your actions, and if you have, then please share them with the courtroom."

"I can't recall, as I would have to consult my notes, but I do know I was on important police business."

"I am angry Pc Burns, but I will give you four days to send me photocopies of your notes, to this court room. For your sake I hope they arrive. Now lets get on with this trial."

Luggy was sitting looking very pale.

The Crown Prosecutor started to read from his notes, which were a complete fabrication that Luggy Burns had made up. He constantly asked Vinny, who seemed to be speaking for the three of them, if what he was stating was correct.

"Utter rubbish, concocted by that bastard sitting there," while pointing at Burns.

Causing the judge to bang her gavel down again, and told him watch his language in the court, or he would be removed.

"I apologise your Honour, but are we the only ones having to tell the truth, because that statement that was presented by the police was a pack of lies."

It was then that someone stood up at the back of the court, asking to speak to the judge.

"Who are you sir, and why are you interrupting the proceedings, and more importantly, why do you wish to speak to me?"

"Your Honour, I have evidence here that will have a bearing on this case. I am Ds Brian Lawson from Professional Standards here in Dundee."

"Ds Lawson, you may approach the bench, but I hope that what you have is relevant to this case"

Ds Lawson walked forward to the bench, while the Public Prosecutor could only sit and wait.

"Your Honour, this is a statement from Pc John Murdoch, who was one of the other officers on the night in question. You will see that he has withdrawn his original statement, saying that it was Pc Burns who had asked him and his colleague to make a false statement to satisfy a grudge against these lads. The other officer is sticking to his original statement, but under interview he is making mistakes when trying to remember what actually happened."

Vinny looked over at Luggy, who looked decidedly ill. He couldn't even hold his head up, and just kept staring at the desk while scribbling on his note pad.

"Thank you for this new evidence Ds Lawson, it certainly puts a different reflection on this case. Have you got any thing to say Pc Burns?"

"Nothing your Honour."

"I didn't think you would. Mind you, I think you will have enough talking to do before the Professional Standards are finished with you. I am going to end this trial by admonishing the three lads over there. You are free to go. Mr Hunter, I would like to see you in my chambers before you go please."

The lads walked out of the court room, but there was no back slapping or hugging. They sat in silence, until the clerk of the court came, and asked Vinny to follow him to the judge's chambers. Vinny didn't know what to expect when he entered the room. The judge had removed her robe and was sitting behind her desk.

"Please come in and take seat Mr Hunter."

"If you don't mind your Honour, it's Vinny."

"Then please sit down Vinny, and tell me all what had been happening with your mum."

Vinny told her everything, and didn't leave anything out. Especially, the way his dad had treated both him and his mum. After he had finished, he found himself feeling a bit emotional, but managed to hold himself together.

"I am so very sorry to hear all that Vinny. Your mum was lovely, and a good friend. She certainly didn't deserve all that. Have you any plans for the future Vinny?"

Vinny told her he would more than likely apply for entrance into the police force.

"I wish you well, and you never know, our paths may cross again some day. Hopefully, not like Pc Burns' situation, and most importantly I hope you get closure on your mother."

Vinny thanked her, and left to catch up with the lads. They were sitting on the wall outside the building, looking pretty down for just having been acquitted. As they walked along to be picked up by Ds Lawson, Billy asked, "Does that mean we'll not have a police record lads?"

"For fuck sake Billy, were you listening to anything that went on in there," said Barney while clipping him over the back of the head.

"Bloody hell Barney, I was only asking."

It was then that Ds Lawson pulled up and they got in the car. It was a very quiet drive back to Drumbrig, but just before they arrived Brian Lawson asked them if they had any questions before he left. Barney was the only one who had.

"What will happen to Luggy Burns? Will he still have a job."

"Look Barney, it could take up to a year before disciplinary action can be taken against him. He will get his union involved, and possible a solicitor, or he might even plead that he had a breakdown at the time. So it will be likely that he will be in his job for a while yet."

Barney didn't look too happy.

They thanked Ds Lawson for his help, and he said he hoped they would just get on with their lives now, and drove away.

Vinny suggested that they meet up at his house that night, to try and get everything clear in their heads. Barney and Billy agreed.

As the boys sat that night, they knew that their friendship was going to be tested. It was Billy who 'kicked it off' by telling them he was leaving in a couple of weeks as the RAF had accepted an early entrance date.

"Look lads, I'm not trying to get away from you, but I am very fearful that Luggy will try something else to entrap us, as I think he's an evil bastard. I'm not sure the threat of being investigated will bother him. I can't have him fucking up my chances of getting in to the RAF. To be honest I'm not sure I want to go, I've thought about trying to get a job in the dancing industry, but I don't know how I would go about that. I love you both, but I'm sure you both realise we were going our separate ways at some point."

"Good on you Billy, for getting out of this shit hole. Remember you are only on probation at the RAF, so if you want to pursue a career in dance then go for it. There will be loads of people, apart from Barney and I, who could give you a reference 'twinkle toes.' Remember one thing though amigo, please make sure your aim is good when you drop a small bomb on Luggy's house."

"What about you Vinny, are you still keen on the Police Force, or is it just a means to an end to get you out of here. Mind you, I can't see you walking the beat pal. What do think Billy?" said Barney laughing.

"I have a good feeling about the force lads, especially the Professional Standards, but I know it will be hard, and if I can prevent injustices like what happened to us, then great. Okay, it's your turn Barney. What's your plans?"

"I'm going to tell it to you straight lads. I haven't a bloody clue. At my age you would think I would have some idea, but the only thing I think about is that it is a very big world out there. Having been stuck in this dump for all my life, maybe it is time to start exploring the world a bit. I have a small amount of money in the bank, and my Grandad has always said he would see me okay when I left. Maybe pick up work wherever I end up. You know me, I'm not scared of hard work."

"Well lads, it seems we're sorted. A Flyer, a Wanderer and a Policeman. We couldn't be any more different if we tried. Let's try and meet up as often as possible, before Billy goes away."

Billy left first, and Vinny then suggested to Barney that it would be good to give him a leaving party. Maybe a gathering of a few friends in the school hall.

"What do you think Barney? Let's get the right people. I'll provide the refreshments, and we'll ask his mum to supply us with the eats. Barney, you speak to everyone we know and like. Oh, and I'll speak to the school headmaster. C'mon, let's go for it, but see if we can make it a surprise. You up for it amigo?"

"Yeh, he deserves a good send off pal. I'll really miss him Vinny."

"Me too pal."

They organised the party, telling everyone to keep quiet about it. Billy's mum was well up for it, however his 'creeping Jesus' of a dad said he wouldn't attend. They thought that was a bonus. It was going to be a problem how to get Billy to the party in his 'glad rags'. Vinny came up with the idea that one of the Polish girls was having the party, and they definitely wanted Billy there.

They both went down to speak to Billy one night. Hoping that 'Holy Ian' the dad, wasn't there. He was no where to be seen, so Barney spoke to Billy in his room, while Vinny was secretly speaking to his mum about the 'eats'. She asked that if on the day of the party they could come down and take Billy away for a while, so that she could get all the food to the hall. Vinny said that it wouldn't be a problem. After they left Billy's house, Barney said that Billy seemed withdrawn, but Vinny reassured him that it would just be nerves.

The next morning by chance, the post was early. There was a letter asking him to come to Dundee to sit all the exams and to be interviewed. Assuming he was still interested in joining the police force. Now who was nervous thought Vinney.

It was two days until the party, and life was carrying on as normal. Barney and Billy came up to Vinny's house each night, and they would just talk, and talk. Sometimes it was just drivel, but they didn't care as they knew their time together, as the three amigos, was coming to an end. Sadly.

The party was on the Saturday night, and they all sat together in Vinny's house the night before, reminiscing about what their lives had been like living in Drumbrig. They all said they'd been glad of their friendship, and Barney said having pals like Vinny and Billy had kept him sane. Billy was near to tears, until Barney spoke.

"Billy, for fuck sake, it's not as if we won't see each other again is it?"

Billy didn't say a word, then started telling them that he was to be stationed at RAF Lossiemouth, which was a few hours away, and whenever he got leave he would come down and see them.

"Will that be by your private plane pal?" asked Barney.

Billy was about to say something until he realised that Barney was winding him up. He then dived on top of him while trying to hold him down. It was a bit of a mismatch to say the least, as Barney just shoved him off while laughing.

"Okay lads let's make a promise, that no matter where we are on this earth we keep in touch, whichever way we can, and try to meet up on occasion. Are we up for that? Oh, and let's make it the last time down the Mott with our fishing poles at about four o'clock tomorrow afternoon."

"Why four o'clock Vinny?" asked Billy.

"I'm working to just after three o'clock," lied Vinny.

When the other two had left, Vinny lay on the sofa and did a lot of thinking. He knew he couldn't be the keeper of the other two, so he was determined to give his entrance exams his best shot. He felt drained, and his mind again wandered back to his mum's disappearance, wondering if it would ever get any easier. It was five o'clock in the morning when he woke up, still on the sofa.

At three o'clock in the afternoon the next day, he grabbed his fishing pole and headed off to get Barney, and then Billy to take him away from his house.

As they were fishing it was a strange feeling that everybody was experiencing. It seemed that they couldn't keep eye contact with each other, as if this was going to be the last farewell. Barney had brought the juice and a few cakes, promising that he had paid for it all. The glint in his eye said otherwise.

"Are you all packed Billy, and who's taking you tomorrow?" asked Vinny.

"Yeh, all packed lads, and my dad is taking me to Dundee for the train to Lossiemouth. The RAF sent me out a travel voucher, so I am all sorted."

"Do you feel a wee bit more confident about going pal? asked Barney.

The way he answered left Vinny in no doubt that this lad didn't really want to go, but he never said a word, as Billy knew he could get out after the probationary period. Maybe then he would get the chance to fulfil his dream, and that was to just dance.

"I think we should head home and get ready for the party. Let's be fair lads, we are pretty rubbish at fishing, aren't we?" said Vinny.

They were laughing as they walked up the road.

"I hope you're getting dressed up tonight ' twinkle toes' ? said Barney.

"Not sure yet, and stop calling me 'twinkle toes' pal "

"You had better pal as you'll be in a headlock very quickly my ' boogie boy' and to make sure, we are coming to take you to the party. What do you think Vinny?"

"Headlock or not Barney."

The three of them headed back to their respective houses to get something to eat and change for the party. For some reason Vinny wasn't really feeling up for it. After bathing, he lay down on the sofa, and if Barney hadn't walked in then he would probably be still lying there the next morning.

"Oh, for Christ sake pal, buy a robe that covers your 'tackle'. It's enough to make me want to throw up."

"Piss off Anderson. This 'tackle' might be up for it tonight."

"Yeh right pal. It will probably be 'Palm and her five sisters' again for you, my soon to be 'bonnie boy in blue'.

As they walked down the road they didn't say anything until Vinny spoke.

"Barney, do you think it's going to work out in the air force for Billy?

"Nope. Not a snowball's chance in hell."

"Why would you say that?"

"Oh c'mon Vinny, you know as well as I do that he's too soft. Can you see him getting shouted at all the time. He has never been mentally strong, and I don't think his heart's in it."

"Unfortunately, I think you're right, but let's give him a good send off, so no more negative thoughts on our part. Agreed?"

Barney just gave him a thumbs up.

They knocked before walking in to Billy's house, hoping that the 'Holy Willie' was out. He was. Billy was sitting in his 'glad rags', but it was like he was on a different planet, until Barney started to ruffle his hair.

"For fuck sake Barney, I've just spent ages getting my hair right."

"Listen you little prick. I'm not bothered about your hair, it's your legs that better give Drumbrig the best show of dancing they have ever seen."

Billy walked away smiling, to fix his hair.

As they got to the school it was Billy who said, "This looks like a bust lads, there's no noise coming from the hall, and no lights on. We should just go home."

"Let's give it a try anyway pal. What do you say Barney?"

"We're here anyway lads. If there's nobody there, then it would be a shame for the lassie who's party it is. Let's go."

As they walked through the hall door, the lights and music from two radios came on, and all the people started cheering and clapping. Billy got such a shock that he turned and tried to run out, but Barney grabbed him by the arm and virtually threw him on to the dance floor. Maja came running over, and asked him to dance with her. It didn't take Billy long to recover from the shock. He was dazzling everyone on the dance floor.

As Vinny and Barney stood watching in envy, Billy's mum walked over and gave them both a huge hug and said, "Thank you for being Billy's friends. He might have struggled without you, as he didn't get much help from his dad."

It was then that Billy saw his mum, ran and hugged her, before dragging her onto the dance floor to dance with him and Maja. The thing was, Billy didn't really dance with anyone, he danced for himself. Several time during the night, either Vinny or Barney would drag Billy off the dance floor, before he would drop with exhaustion.

It was ten thirty when the janitor came to close up the hall, to much jeering and booing. Everyone wanted to say goodbye to Billy. The girls hugging him, and the boys either shaking his hand or slapping him on the back. Billy's mum walked up the road with the three amigos, before she said she'd leave them to say their goodbyes.

"Well lads, thank you for my party. I never expected anything. Most importantly though, thank you for being my friends."

Billy started to shed floods of tears, before Vinny grabbed him, and held on to him. He then walked over to Barney.

"Billy, for fuck sake stop your blubbering as you'll be staining my jacket, and it's the only one I have."

They stood together in one final hug, and Vinny said they'd be there to see him away at the road end at nine o'clock tomorrow morning.

Vinny and Barney left Billy, and walked up the road.

"It won't be long till we see him again Vinny. What do you think?"

" Not so sure Barney."

"What do you mean by that?"

"Nothing Barney, just forget it."

As they went to their own homes, Barney turned and looked at Vinny wondering what Vinny was on about.

When Vinny got home, he set his alarm for seven thirty the next morning. He then stripped and just lay on the bed. There was a knock on the door, so he got up thinking it was Barney who'd forgotten his keys and didn't want to wake his Grandad up. When he opened the door, there stood Amy from the village. She hadn't come up to the house for a while.

"I thought you might like some company tonight Vinny. What do you say? I'm feeling a bit cool, so if we stand here much longer in the cold, even you might struggle to get it up Vinny," said Amy laughing.

Vinny let her in, and asked her if she wanted a tea or coffee.

"No Vinny, just take me to bed please."

That night, Vinny was never as glad in all his life that he had 'acquired' as many French Letters from the Co-op. Amy was just insatiable. As soon as they had finished in one position, she was trying to get Vinny 'hard' to start again. She even put Big Irma to shame with the positions she had Vinny in. They both fell asleep at about four o'clock, but Vinny didn't need the alarm, as he was wide awake by seven o'clock.

He ran a bath, and was so glad bathrooms had been put into all the council houses a few years back, as the thought of washing in the tin tub made him wince. As he lay back washing himself, the door opened and a naked Amy walked through, stepping into the bath. Vinny thought she was a lovely looking girl with a beautiful body. Her breasts were pert, but surprisingly she had no pubic hair, which Vinny had found to be a big turn-on.

"I know you'll be going away at some stage Vinny, so I don't expect a relationship, but it would be nice if we meet up when you come home on an occasion."

"Amy, I enjoyed last night, but I will be away soon staying up in Dundee, so I don't know when, or even if I will be back, but I promise I will see you if I'm home."

"Sounds good to me Vinny, now maybe I could give you a hand washing that lovely penis of yours."

She laughed which set Vinny off.

After a quick breakfast, they walked down the road to where Barney was waiting. Amy gave Vinny a kiss and said goodbye.

"Had a good night Vinny? Here was you telling me that you thought you had a sex addiction, and was trying to get to grips with it. What a load of rubbish you come out with at times Vinny Hunter."

"Yeh, I think my addiction might be with me for ever Barney, but I'm not complaining to be honest."

They were waiting at the main road for Billy's dads' car to appear.

"Have you heard anything about Luggy lately, Barney?"

"I heard he had been hassling an older couple from up the top of the village about where they were parking their car. Apparently there is a piece of derelict land next to their house where they were parking. Luggy was threatening to have Bert Richardson tow it away. Nobody knows why. Probably just being the bully he is."

It was then that they saw the car coming up the street to where they were standing. They immediately started to wave their arms like an aeroplane. They could see Billy laughing in the passenger seat, but his sour faced dad never cracked his face. It was when the car was drawing up that the two of them stood to attention and saluted Billy, who saluted back. They watched the car disappear down to the main road and head towards Dundee.

They never said much as they walked back up the road.

Life for Barney and Vinny over the next few weeks was a pretty mundane affair after Billy had left. Both working hard on the farm, with not a lot of conversation between them. Vinny was waiting to go to Dundee for his entrance exams. However, he was a bit concerned with Barney, who still hadn't thought about what he was going to do with his life, and Vinny wondered what would happen to him when he moved to the police force in Dundee.

Eventually, a letter arrived asking Vinny to go up to Dundee for the exams. He told Barney who seemed to be really happy for him, but Vinny wasn't too sure. When the day came for Vinny to head off, Barney walked him down to wait for the bus.

"According to my letter, I may be asked to stay for a few of nights pal, but I have told Mr Hamilton that. I presume you will want to stay in my house. If so, I bloody insist that you leave me some toilet paper, just in case I get back late one night, and all you've left me is a cardboard roll, with the Co-op closed"

"Heard and understood Pc Plod."

As the bus was going up the road to Dundee, Vinny looked back and could just manage to see Barney walking up the road. He seemed to be kicking a stone, and didn't seem to have a care in the world. He was going to try his best with the exams, and if his best wasn't good enough then too bad.

When the bus rolled into the Seagate bus station in Dundee, he asked the driver how to get to Liff road where the exams were being held. The driver advised him to get a taxi, as it was a fair walk.

When the taxi pulled up at the police station, he was starting to get a bit nervous. It was then that a young girl came out the doors and asked if he was Vincent Hunter. He said yes, but preferred Vinny.

"Not here Mr. Hunter. Maybe if you are asked to join the force, but until then it will be Vincent. You okay with that?"

"Fine by me. Anyway, what do I call you?"

"Miss Miller will do fine. Let's keep it professional please. Follow me."

They walked past several offices, before entering a large room where desks had been laid out facing the front. Two people stood at a portable blackboard. One was Ds Lawson, the other was a very prim and proper looking lady who was first to speak. There were six people standing waiting, so she asked everyone to take a seat at any desk they wanted.

"Okay everyone. My name is Mrs. Kelly, and I will be overseeing the exams today. I am not going to ask you to tell each other your name, and I already know, so I suggest we just get on with it. The exam will take four hours, and we will stop after two for some lunch. Accommodation has been organised for anybody that needs it, although it won't be for anybody who lives locally. Right, pencils and a glass of water have been provided. If you need to go to the toilet, then go now and be back in ten minutes, no longer. Any questions before we start?"

Nobody said a word.

Chapter 4

Vinny was sailing through the questions, when Mrs Kelly asked them to put their pencils down, as lunch was being brought in. Ds Lawson had disappeared just after the exam had started. After he came back, he started to pour himself a coffee.

"Ladies and gentlemen, can you refrain from talking to each other about the exam please. Plenty time for that after. Thank you," said Ds Lawson.

Vinny had noticed that he had never looked his way.

The second half of the exam had started, and after about another hour Vinny had finished. He put his pencil down, sat back, and closed his eyes. He was going over everything he had written. It was Mrs. Miller who interrupted his thoughts.

"Mr. Hunter, I suggest you carry on with the exam, as the last part is very important."

"Mrs. Kelly, you very kindly gave me the chance to take this examination. I have, but I can assure you I have finished. I have even signed the papers as Vincent Hunter, not Vinny."

She turned round, and looked at a smiling Ds Lawson, who could only shrug his shoulders and give an imperceptible nod. She seemed quite taken aback by this, as it had never happened before, but she just left his exam papers on his desk.

Another hour passed when she told everyone that time was up, and to stop writing. She then collected the papers, and coffee was brought in for everyone. They mingled, started nervously chatting, and introducing themselves to each other. A couple of guys were up their own backsides, and more or less telling everyone else that they had 'aced' the exam.

"What about you Vincent? Did you find it too difficult, as I heard the lady saying that you had finished too early."

"I think you've got your wires crossed a bit pal. I found it very easy. That's why I finished an hour early."

The look on the guy's face was priceless. Just then Mrs Miller came in and said everyone should go home, and to be back here at the same time to get their results tomorrow.

Vinny lifted his bag and headed to the door, but Dc Lawson had shouted on him to hang on a minute. He told Vinny that a reservation had been made for him at the Angus Hotel. Vinny got a taxi to the hotel, and thought the receptionist had looked down his nose a bit at him when he signed in. He had never been in a room as opulent as this. In fact he had never been in a hotel before in his life.

He decided to skip the dining room that night, but instead opted to go for fish and chips, and a wander round the centre of Dundee. He thought it wasn't a bad looking town, but he had nothing to compare it to, as you couldn't mention Drumbrig in the same breath. He sat on a bench in the centre and watched the world go by. People from all walks of life, just going about their business. Some with not a care in the world. After a while he decided to head back to the hotel for an early night.

Next morning after breakfast, he got a taxi to Liff street station, and was greeted by the same girl from yesterday. Vinny wondered if he should ask her out, as she was looking as if she was interested in him.

" Good morning Vincent. I trust you had a good night's sleep?"

"I did indeed Miss Miller, but maybe if I am asked back, we might go out on the town for a night. I must say now though, is that I don't touch alcohol, and my dancing is terrible. So what do you say?"

"My name is Katie, and if you come back up I'll think about it. However, everyone is in the room waiting for you."

As Vinny walked through the door, Mrs Kelly told him he was late and asked him why.

That's easy Mrs Kelly, I was chatting up Miss Miller on the steps up to the station. My apologies."

She couldn't say anything, and Ds Lawson was smirking behind some papers he was holding up as if reading them.

"Okay everyone, I have your results here. Only two of you will be asked to join our Professional Standards team here in Dundee, and the rest of you will be offered places in our normal rank and file police force if you want it. I will read out four names, and we would like you to leave the room, and the other two please stay seated. The four of you who have been asked to leave will be contacted by letter in the next few weeks. Please make your mind up about what you have been offered and get back to us."

She read out the four names who had failed the exam. They got up from their desks and started to walk out. However, the guy who had asked Vinny if he had struggled during the exam, never took his eyes of Vinny while walking out. Vinny just gave him a wink, and a slight smile. Mrs Kelly then asked Ds Lawson to take over.

"Well done to the pair of you. Your marks were extremely high. It is my intention to fast track you through to become an integral part of this department, if you still want to join our team. However, it is also my intention not to keep you away from the day to day work of the rank and file police officers. You will work on different cases, and I can assure you, you will see the brutal side to policing certain aspects of the population. Also, you will work with the other emergency services. Without the fire, and ambulance services we would struggle. Anyway, Vincent Hunter please meet Kim Nicol."

Vinny got up, walked over and gave her a hug, even although she had her handout for a handshake.

"Please to meet you Kim. If we both take this job, then I suspect we will be seeing a lot more of each other."

"We might make a good team Vincent. What do you think?"

"It's Vinny, Kim and you might be right."

"Right folks, I suggest you head home, and digest everything that has gone on in the last two days."

Kim grabbed her backpack and headed out of the building.

"Vincent, may I have a word with you before you go please," said Brian Lawson.

Vinny stood wondering what was going on. Before Mrs. Kelly came into the room.

"Before you go, let me tell you that your exam paper was the best that we have ever seen. To do it in three hours was pretty remarkable. We would love to have you here with us, and I am speaking for Mrs Kelly as well. How do you feel Vincent?"

"I am going to the backwater that is Drumbrig, and I will have a serious think about it, but at the moment I feel good about it.

When I get your offer through post I will phone and tell you my decision. See you sometime."

Vinny shook Ds Lawson's hand and gave Mrs Kelly a hug, which surprised her a bit. He walked out of the station and hailed a taxi. He just caught the bus, which would drop him off at the road end at Drumbrig. As he was getting nearer to home, he wished that he was still in Dundee. It seemed a friendly, vibrant city. He also wished he was lying in the arms of Kim Nichol right now, but he knew he should put such thoughts out of his mind. He got off of the bus, and started to walk up the road to the village. He felt his feet were made of lead, and he was forcing himself to get to the house.

When he tried the door he found it unlocked. Putting his bag down quietly, he slowly walked into the lounge. Expecting to see Barney lounged out on the sofa, but got a shock to see Luggy Burns rifling through the drawers of the unit under the window.

Luggy didn't hear him, until Vinny shouted, "What the fuck are you doing here Burns?"

Luggy got such a shock that he dropped the papers he had in his hand, onto the floor.

"Pick them up Burns, and put them back where you got them. It's a good job that it's me standing here, because if it was Barney, then he would literally kill you."

Luggy started to make some pathetic excuse about looking for some more information on his mum, to pass on to Tayside police.

"You're a fucking liar Burns, but no surprise there then. Get out of my house, before I phone the station at Dunfermline, and report you for breaking into my house. Move."

No sooner had Luggy had started to walk down the road, when Barney walked in.

Vinny told him what had happened, while chastising him about the unlocked door at the same time. Barney sat with his head in his hands. Vinny could see he was very angry. After a while Vinny asked if he wanted anything to eat, but he said no as he was going to see to his Grandad. He got up and started to walk out.

"Vinny, I'll hear all about your couple of days in Dundee tomorrow, but please accept my apologies for leaving the door open. Have you any idea what Luggy was looking for?"

"I've no idea Barney, but remember he still has an agenda against us, so please tell your Grandad to lock his doors when he goes out walking."

"Will do pal. Speak tomorrow."

Vinny sat down and prayed for the day that one of the men from the village would put an end to Burn's evil reign.

The following week Vinny was feeling very low, with not a lot of enthusiasm for working on the farm. Barney had been quiet after Vinny had told him that he would take the job in Dundee if offered. Vinny knew he would have to work and stay in Dundee, and that would affect his pal massively. Barney had still no purpose to get up in the morning, and Vinny had sat down with him on occasion trying to give him a few ideas as to what he might like to do. However, Barney would just put his head down, and refuse to join in the conversation.

At the end of one week, the letter from the police arrived. Vinny, for some reason, didn't want to open it until two days later. The letter was really just an offer to join the Professional Standards team. The renumeration he was offered each month was more than he could earn on the farm in six months. They advised him that he would have to move to Dundee, and a bed and breakfast had been organised for him. Assuming he wanted the job.

The next night he and Barney were sitting talking about Billy, wondering how he was getting on. They told each other that they should be asking his mum. They heard a car draw up outside. There was a knock on the door, and in walked Ds Lawson.

"I see you haven't done anything about security for your house Vincent."

He told him about what happened the other day with Luggy wandering about the house.

"You mean that Pc Burns entered your house when you were out?"

"I just got back from Dundee, and unfortunately Barney forgot to lock the door. As I walked in I saw him rifling through the unit over there. I challenged him and he gave me some lame excuse that he was looking for more information regarding my mum, to give to Tayside police. I told him to get out, otherwise I would phone the station at Dunfermline. Then he left."

"Do you know what he might have been after Vincent?"

" Not a clue Ds Lawson, but it will be for his benefit."

"I will note this incident in his file, which is getting thicker by the minute. The second police officer has changed his story, and he hasn't sent copies of his notebook to the judge from the trial claiming he had lost it, or someone had stolen it from his desk in the station. All bullshit of course, but his Union are digging their heels in, citing he had a small mental breakdown at the time."

"For fuck sake this is a shambles. Let's hope he picks on the wrong man, and they send him to Hell, with all the other arseholes," said Barney.

"Unfortunately, the British Justice System doesn't work like that Barney."

"Well, you can stick the system up your arse Ds Lawson, as it sucks. I'm off. See you Vinny."

"He seems a bit bitter doesn't he."

"Can you blame him. We have to live in a village where the local policeman is a bully. It shouldn't have to happen."

"Vincent, in our job we have to be patient. Anyway, I came down here to see if you had made up your mind about the job. I have been given the task of rebuilding the Professional Standards for the whole of Scotland, and I want the best team I can to help me. I want you in that team as your exam results were actually through the roof, but we didn't want to say it at the time. Well, have you made up your mind?"

"I have, but there will be conditions. I want, sorry need, to be kept busy most of the time. The job will be interesting. I will be called Vinny, and there will be the possibility for promotion."

"All guaranteed Vinny. Now, please sign your acceptance letter and I can take it back with me."

Vinny did as he was asked and handed the letter to him.

"Oh, I meant to say, that you'll be lodging with a Mrs Dunn. She is the widow of a police officer who was killed in the line of duty, but that is another story. Lovely lady though. Right, I must go."

They shook hands, and Vinny stood at the door watching his car disappear down the road, wondering if he was doing the right thing.

The weeks flew in, with Vinny and Barney both working on the farm. Barney always started to argue when Vinny gave him the majority of the wages, as Mr. Hamilton couldn't afford to pay two wages. Vinny kept telling him he would need it for travelling around the world, but always wondered how far he would actually get.

The time came for Vinny to leave. Barney came up to the house to see him off. They walked slowly down to the end of the road, calling in on Billy's mother, who said he was fine, before giving Vinny a hug. Grandad Jock stood at the door and waved him away. He was nearing the road end when he heard a girl's voice shouting to him. It was Amy running down the road. When she got to him, shew threw herself into his arms.

"I know we probably won't see each other again Vinny, as I'm moving on as well. The times I spent with you were very special, and I will never forget them. There's a very lucky girl waiting for you out there somewhere. Take care."

She gave him a big hug, turned, and walked back up the road, feeling very emotional.

As the bus was approaching the road end, Vinny gave Barney a hug, and told him he would see him soon. Little did he know how soon that would be.

When he got into Dundee, he did the usual and hailed a taxi to take him to the boarding accommodation in Aberlady Cres. As he walked up to the door with his holdall over his shoulder, the door opened and a woman with a big beaming smile stood there. This was Mrs Dunn, a short stocky woman, with her flowery apron on and a duster in her hand.

"You'll be Vinny then young man, come away in. The kettle has just boiled, and my fruit cake is due out of the oven in a few minutes."

Vinny immediately felt at home. The house was spotless, and Mrs Dunn told him to sit in the big armchair, and she would bring him something to eat. As he sat there he noticed a large photograph of a uniformed police officer just above the fireplace. He got up for a closer look. She caught him unaware.

"That's my lovely husband Bill, son. Sadly taken away from me by evil people when he was out on the beat. I miss him terribly."

"I'm so sorry Mrs Dunn. Did they catch those evil people?"

"They thought they knew who did it, but unfortunately they couldn't prove it, so may they rot in Hell son."

"Mrs Dunn. I have no doubt it won't be in my remit, but would you mind if I look into your husband's case in my spare time. I would have to get the go ahead from Ds Lawson, but I am keen to learn, and I hate evil people."

"You have my blessing son, and I am sure Brian, who is a lovely lad will be okay with it."

They sat filling themselves up with cake and tea, while chatting. Vinny told her about his mum, and she was genuinely shocked. She said she couldn't get her head round losing someone, when there was no closure.

As Vinny lay in a strange bed that night, he wondered if he had been talking rubbish to Mrs Dunn, about looking into her husband's case. Hell, it was only his first day tomorrow. He knew he had to calm down and just learn his job.

Tomorrow morning came quick enough, and Mrs Dunn insisted he have a hearty breakfast before he left to walk to Liff St. police station. When he arrived there he found he was slightly out of breath as it was further than he thought, so he decided that would have to change. He met Kim Nicol in the reception area, and they sat and exchanged pleasantries, before Ds Lawson came through and asked them to follow him to the same room where they had taken their exam.

"Right Kim and Vinny, here's what's going to happen. We are going to fast track the pair of you, so that you are fully functioning officers in this department as quickly as possible. We won't cut any corners, but we expect you to put the hard work in, so you reach the standard we expect within the allotted time. Over the first few months you will be going out with Sergeant Reynolds to various incidents throughout Dundee, and beyond. It will be difficult at times, even gruesome, but you have to get acclimatised to what the police force is all about. Any questions will be put to Sergeant Reynolds."

As if on cue, in walked this 'brick shit-house' of a man. Vinny thought that when he walked over to greet him and Kim there had been an eclipse. When he spoke, it was like the thrusters of a

Boeing seven four seven, being switched on. He made a mental note never to cross this giant of a man.

"Right folks, get your raincoats, as we're heading to the Tay Bridge. It appears there has been a couple of early morning 'jumpers', so I hope your not squeamish. Let's go."

They drove out to the bridge, and down a side road to where a fire engine and an ambulance were standing. They parked their car and walked over to the ambulance, where the medics were attending to a body on the ground. Sergeant Reynolds just nodded, and asked the two of them over to have a look at the body, while he crossed himself.

"Bloody hell sergeant, his body is absolutely mangled, and his face is just a bloody pulp. Did he hit something on the way down?"

"No son, there was nothing to hit. Let me explain about what happens when you decide to end your life this way. You don't die while falling, it's when you hit the water you die, immediately. The water has the same quality as hitting concrete. When you let go from up there, then you're either going to heaven or Hell. Lots of these poor souls have lost their way, and jumping is the only way out.

Kim was looking a bit white, but she was holding it together. The fire brigade's inflatable boat was bringing in the other body. They brought it to where the first body lay.

"Kim, Vinny this is Craig who is head of the search and rescue in Tayside. In my book, him and his colleagues are the real heroes."

Craig just nodded his head and said, " Looks like another lover's suicide pact Sergeant."

It was Kim, who then spoke.

"Sergeant, she only looks about sixteen. What a waste of life."

Craig replied, "You look like a pair of rookies, so the only advice I can give you is, what you have you have seen today, you will see often in different situations, and the quicker you suck it up the better."

Just then a police patrol car arrived.

"These are the guys that will have to tell their families. So let's go," said Sergeant Reynolds.

The drive back was quiet, until Sergeant Reynold turned the radio up, and started to sing. The loudness of his voice could have been heard from miles away.

"No disrespect sir, but you have a 'crap' singing voice," said Vinny with Kim agreeing with him.

"None taken Vinny."

When they got back to the station, they were met by Mrs Kelly.

"Any reservations about joining us?"

Both just shook their heads.

The rest of the day was just being told of the ins and outs of the police force, which they both found a bit boring, but they knew they had to go through it. It was only three pm when Ds Lawson walked in and told the pair of them to go home, as that was enough for the day.

As Vinny and Kim walked out, he asked if she would like to go for a coffee, and she readily agreed. While sitting in a café in the centre, they got to know each other really well. They both seemed to have had a hard time over the previous couple of years, so they bonded really well.

"I'm enjoying our time together, and having a coffee now and again would be great, but I don't want to get into another relationship at this moment in time. Let me tell you that I was in a horrible relationship, with a person I should have ditched a lot sooner than I did. You are very good-looking guy Vinny, so at the present time, I want to keep our friendship on a professional level. Who knows what might happen in the future. You okay with that?"

"Fine by me Kim, but what you have just said won't stop me asking you out in the future. I can be very persuasive, trust me."

"I hope you do Vinny. I must go now, see you tomorrow, ready for more dead bodies." She was laughing as she left the café.

Vinny knew she was right, and he had to concentrate on getting through his probationary period, and getting fully into the job, as he felt this could be really good for him.

The weeks passed, and Vinny and Kim were involved in about every incident in and around Dundee. There was a murder, assault, arson, money laundering, as well as major theft, and gang fights over drug distribution. You name it, they were involved in it with various detectives. It was pretty hectic.

One day Ds Lawson walked into the room and asked to speak to Vinny outside. By the look on his face Vinny knew that something was wrong.

"Have I done something wrong Ds Lawson?"

"On the contrary Vinny, your work has been exemplary. I have some bad news for you, so please come into my office and have a seat."

"Have you found my mother?" Vinny blurted out.

"I wish I had Vinny, but it's about your friend Billy."

"Don't tell me he's been injured, has he?"

"Vinny, calm yourself down and please listen. Unfortunately, Billy was killed in a training accident when a plane used for practice came down, killing Billy and two others. Several others survived. I'm very sorry, as I know you were close to him. Sit there for a minute, and I'll get you a tea."

Vinny just sat there with his head in his hands, feeling sick. When he tried to move his legs they felt numb. He couldn't believe the news.

In came Kim with a cup of tea and gave him a hug.

"I'm so sorry Vinny. I take it you were close to him?"

"Me, Barney and Billy were like brothers Kim. He was a very gentle guy, with the best dancing feet you could ever imagine. We used to call him 'twinkle toes' and deep down he loved the adulation he got when he was on the dance floor. I bloody loved him so much Kim, now I'll never see him again."

"Keep your memories Vinny. He will always be in your head."

"Thanks Kim."

Ds Lawson walked in and told Vinny to finish his tea, and he would take him to his accommodation, pick up his stuff, and then he would take him back to Drumbrig.

Mrs Dunn gave him a big hug, and an hour and a half later they were driving up the road to Vinny's house. As Vinny got out, Brian Lawson asked him if he would be okay. Vinny said he would be fine, and thanked him for the ride home.

"Take as much time as you need Vinny. No rush to get back to work. I'll see you sometime."

Vinny just gave him the thumbs up, and walked into the house. As he walked through the door he saw Barney sitting on the sofa. It was obvious that he had been crying. Vinny didn't say a word, he just threw his holdall down, and sat beside him. Nothing was said for about ten minutes, before Barney spoke.

"Why him Vinny? He was just a beautiful, lovely lad, with not a bad bone in his body. Yet, there are scum walking amongst us every day. Where is God when you really need him pal."

"I think we can allow ourselves to be a little bit bitter, but let us remember our amigo how he was. We'll go down to see his mum tomorrow morning if that's okay with you."

"That's fine pal, as long as we don't get a sermon from the 'creeping Jesus' Vinny. Do you know who is to blame for all this, Luggy Burns. Billy just took the RAF option as it would get him away from that bastard. I knew Billy was scared of him. At least Billy will be up there, and when it's time for the demise of Burns, he will be going down below. I fucking hate that scab."

After Barney was gone, Vinny sat thinking that for his time back home, he would have to keep an eye on Barney.

It was after ten o'clock the next morning when Barney walked through Vinny's door.

"C'mon Vinny, let's get down and see Billy's mum. Hopefully his dad will be out."

They wandered down, and knocked on Mrs. Clark's door. Nobody was like answering, until she opened the door slightly.

"It's Barney and Vinny, Mrs. Clark. We have just came to pay our respects. May we come in? We won't stay long."

"Come in lads and take a seat will you. Ian is at the minister preparing a bloody speech would you believe. Our Billy isn't cold yet, but that bastard is away speaking about which service to give at his funeral. No doubt he will have persuaded the minister to let him do it. I will bring you through a cup of tea in a minute."

When she had left, Vinny whispered to Barney.

"What do you think pal. She looks awfully calm, don't you think?"

"I think she's still in shock Vinny, and I have no doubt her husband won't have been much comfort to her. I don't remember

Billy talking about any relations, so we'll have to be there for her at the graveside, don't you think?"

"Spot on Barney, as I think 'Holy Ian' will want to be the centre of attention."

Mrs Clark came through with tea and some biscuits, and sat talking about Billy, even smiling a few times. She then dropped a bombshell.

"Vinny, how long will your house be vacant for? I know Barney uses it now and again, but I'm going to say this in confidence. It is my intention to leave Ian, as all he's interested in lately is the bloody church, and reading sermons from his precious bible in this house. I've had enough. My sister lives in Ayr, and is sorting out accommodation for me, but it may take a week or so. Would that be okay?"

Vinny said it would be fine with him, with Barney nodding his head. They said their goodbyes, with Mrs Clark telling them the time of the funeral, and would they do her the honour of being pall bearers for Billy's coffin. They both said they would be honoured, and would see her there. As they walked away, Mrs Clark shouted after them.

"Boys, thank you so much for organising to let me see my precious son dance. It will live in my heart for ever."

Both smiled, and continued to walk up the road, then just before the Co-op, they heard a shout. It was Amy coming from her house.

"Lads, can I ask you for a big favour please. I'm not good at going to funerals, so can I walk down with you on Friday? I can walk back myself if you want."

"Not a problem. Come up to the house at ten thirty, and we'll walk you down. Okay?"

Vinny knew the way she was looking at him, she was wondering if she should come up to the house that night. He gave a slight nod. Barney noticed, and just started to laugh. They walked up to the Co-op, where they left Amy. Barney went in and bought some provisions for their meals over the next couple of days.

Barney worked hard over the next two days, just to try and keep his mind off Billy. He was finding it hard. He had to make a decision about his own future soon. His Grandad was still in good health, so he had no problem finding work elsewhere, and then coming back at weekends to be with him, but he had to do it now.

The days leading up to the funeral were pretty hard for Vinny and Barney. They sat around talking a lot, with Barney asking Vinny all about his new job.

The morning of the funeral came, and Barney was up at the house early. Then it was Amy's time to knock on the door. Vinny made the three of them the obligatory cup of tea. Billy's dad had been putting it around that everybody was to wear black, but everybody was just ignoring him, saying they would attend wearing whatever clothes they found most comfortable. It was just his dad trying to be controlling.

"Right let's go folks. Let's go and wait for Billy arriving from the RAF base. Try and keep your tears to a minimum Amy, as you'll set Barney off."

She didn't know if he was joking or not, so she just stayed quiet. As they walked down the road, most people were coming out of their houses to walk to the graveyard at the far end of the village. It was pretty small, and overgrown in places, with headstones fallen over, and others where the writing on them couldn't be read. Vinny thought it wouldn't be his first choice to be buried here. Yet Billy hadn't had that choice.

They went in through the squeaky iron gate, and stood reasonably near to the grave where Mrs Clark was standing on her own.' Holy Ian' was bending the ear of the minister. The three of them walked down and linked arms with Mrs Clark, who was standing visibly shaking. Tears were streaming down her face, yet that big 'balloon' of a husband of hers was standing with his bible in his hand, no doubt trying to persuade the minster to let him give a sermon.

It was starting to get cold, with some black clouds appearing in the sky. A few people were stamping their feet to warm up their toes. Barney was first to see the two official cars turn off the main road, and head up to the village cemetery. Vinny held Mrs Clark's arm a bit tighter. Amy started to cry when she saw the cars, but Vinny whispered to her to stay strong.

Vinny's ire was starting to rise, seeing 'Holy Ian' still standing with the minister. As the cars grew nearer, Mrs Clark was nearly at the fainting stage. Seeing the cars come up the road had made many people very emotional. When the cars stopped just before the graveside, three young lads in full uniform and two undertakers got out. The lads looked about the same age as Billy, with the same youthfulness. They carried Billy's coffin to the graveside. The coffin was absolutely beautiful, if you could use such a description for a casket to put a body into the ground.

Then it started, with 'Holy Ian' starting his bloody sermon. He just couldn't wait.

Vinny wondered if he got an erection every time he held his bible in his hand or gave a sermon. It went on and on, and everyone was getting agitated. When one of his sermons ended, he started another. When he was virtually shouting, 'the Lord said this, the Lord said that, over and over, Vinny had had enough.

He walked up to the minister.

"I make no apologies for my language minister, but get that fucking idiot to shut the fuck up, or he will be in the grave before Billy. He wasn't a religious person, and religion was rammed down the poor guy's throat, every single day. Now get that idiot to stop preaching now, so that we can bury our friend. Do it now."

The minister walked over and had words with Ian, but 'Holy Ian' wasn't for shifting until Vinny went over and grabbed him by the arm and pulled him back out the way, but Billy's dad was still spouting out the sermon

The undertaker took over the proceedings, and said, "Billy's mum has given me a few names of who she would like to be pall bearers. Myself and my colleague here, as well as the three lads from his squadron will participate, along his two best pals Vinny and Barney, so would we all step forward please.

"Amy, be very strong and keep a firm hold of Mrs Clark for a few minutes please."

Amy nodded her head and gave a thin smile through her tears. Before they lowered the coffin into the grave, one of the RAF cadets covered it with a large Union Jack. When they were lowering it in, Vinny wasn't sure he was going to hold it together. When he looked at Barney he knew he was welling up too. Billy was laid to rest, with the minister saying a few words, and thanking everyone for coming to give Billy a good send off.

The three young officers walked in front of Mrs Clark and saluted. She walked forward and gave them a hug each, while thanking them for bringing Billy home.

It was then that Vinny and Barney heard the squeak of the cemetery gate, and looked round. Here was Luggy Burns coming through the gate.

"Vinny, please don't fucking dare try to stop me."

He marched over to where Luggy had come in.

"What the fuck are you wanting Burns?"

"I'm here to pay my respects Anderson, what is it to you?"

"I'll tell you what it is to me you bastard. Billy didn't particularly want to go to the RAF, but after being falsely arrested by you and your bent cronies, he took the quickest option out of this shithole. Now he is lying in that hole in the ground over there."

"Nothing to do with me Anderson. Now get out of my way."

That was it for Barney. He grabbed Luggy by the tunic, dragged him to the gate, and threw him out. Tearing several buttons of his tunic. Luggy landed on his knees, uttering profanities at Barney, who told him to disappear very quickly, or he would regret it. It seemed that the funeral had come to a standstill, and Vinny thought some people might have even applauded Barney, if it hadn't been such a solemn occasion. Barney watched Luggy trundle up the road to the police station.

Vinny watched Barney walk back, and hold onto Mrs Clark. Vinny walked up to where 'Holy Ian' was and told him he had better get a grip and tend to his wife. He seemed reluctant to leave the ministers side, but Vinny grabbed his arm again and dragged him to his wife's side.

They left Mrs Clark to be with her soon to be ex-husband, and walked up the road with the rest of the other villagers. Barney said he would see Vinny tomorrow, and said goodbye to the two of them.

"Vinny, I would love to come up to your house, but I am too emotional, so maybe tomorrow night."

"No worries Amy. You take care, as its been a pretty full on day. Try and get some sleep tonight."

Vinny never slept a wink that night, and got out of the bed at about six thirty. After showering there was a knock on the door, and in walked Barney, with a holdall over his shoulder. He put it on the floor, and sat on the sofa.

"Going somewhere amigo?"

"Yeh, I have some bad news for you pal. I'm leaving Drumbrig. I'm really sorry pal, but I can't trust myself when that bastard Burns is around. He might try and get me back for yesterday, so I'm off. Billy's death has affected me mentally, so I need a new start somewhere, just anywhere"

"For Christ's sake Barney, I just saw my other best friend buried yesterday, and now you're leaving me today? What's happening?"

"Vinny let's be fair. You'll end up living in Dundee, or possibly further afield, so we won't really see each other will we?"

"I suppose your right Barney, but this is becoming the worst year of my life, with everything that has happened. Why is life like this pal? Will I ever see you again?"

"It's simply life pal. I intend to never come back here again, apart from a quick visit to Jock if I am ever in the area. However, it's my plan to see the world if I can. Grandad Jock has given me quite a bit of cash, and told me to get out of here, before Drumbrig strangles me. He said a phone call now and again would be good. Now I'm going Vinny, and you never know, we might meet again."

Barney came over to Vinny and gave him a hug, and whispered that he loved him, in his ear. He picked up his holdall, and walked to the front door. Vinny said, "Love you big man"

Barney turned, and gave Vinny that lopsided smile and was out the door. Vinny stood watching him for a few minutes, before going back inside. Suddenly, he heard glass being smashed. It took only a few seconds to realise that it was Barney putting Luggy's window in again as he passed. He sat down and laughed, before crying.

That night Amy came up and shared his bed. Vinny's sexual appetite was insatiable, but he felt a bit guilty, as he was invariably thinking about Kim from work, while making love to Amy. Once, while in the throws of climaxing, he had uttered Kim's name, however Amy was too busy enjoying her own climaxes to notice, or she just didn't care. After breakfast, Amy told him she was moving to Edinburgh in a couple of days, as her Aunt Ethel had got her a job in one of the big biscuit factories there. They eventually hugged, and Amy left, crying.

Vinny thought that he had enough of where he had stayed all his life, so he packed two large holdalls with the clothes he wanted to take with him. There was nothing more left here for him. As he walked out the door, he turned and thought about his mum for a few moments, and locked the door, remembering to hand the keys in to Mrs Clark.

Vinny's feet were all over the place, as he trudged down the road to wait for the bus.

Chapter 5

Vinny's brain was in absolute turmoil, as he sat on the Dundee bus. He couldn't come to terms with what had happened over the last week or so. He knew he had to put everything behind him and concentrate on his job. Barney had been right, in as much as they would drift apart when, and not if, he moved to Dundee.

As the bus drove through the streets, Vinny wondered how much work there was in Professional Standards. One young guy came to Dundee, and got rid of the corruption in the town in one easy lesson. He wondered if could live up to what that guy did before him.

He got off the bus and hailed a taxi to Mrs Dunn's house. As he went through the door, she gave him as big a hug as he had in a long time, apart from Barney.

"I was so sorry to hear about your friend son. I hope he got a good send off."

He had no sooner put his holdalls down, when Ds Lawson came through the door.

"How are you Vinny? I didn't expect you back so soon. If you need more time then just say."

"I need to be kept busy Ds Lawson, I just can't be hanging around. The bad news for me is that my other pal packed his bags, and walked away from me and Drumbrig this morning."

"Barney has gone? To where Vinny?"

Vinny just shrugged his shoulders.

"He certainly put on a show with Pc Burns yesterday, didn't he?"

"You were at the funeral Ds Lawson? I had no idea you were there."

"Professional Standards teaches you to try and be in the background, and after watching the villager's reaction to Pc Burns turning up at the funeral, I made a decision there and then. We will suspend him from any duties. We can't make him leave his house just now, as he is pleading that he was unwell at the time of the incident, with you, Billy and Barney. I'm sure the residents of the village will be happy, although there will be no police presence in the village, but they can't have it all roads."

"I have to speak to you at the station tomorrow please. I need to know where I am going in the force, and how long it is going to take me?"

"Slowly wins the races Vinny, we will discuss the structure of your training soon, but not tomorrow. I suggest you try and get a goodnights sleep, as you look knackered. I wonder why?"

He walked out with a sly grin on his face.

Vinny wondered if he knew about Amy, or he was just guessing.

As Vinny walked into the station the next morning, he met Kim, and she asked him how things had went. He told her everything, except about Amy.

Mrs Kelly told them, that for the next two weeks they would have to learn about Employment Law and Scots Law. She said it would be long and tedious, but they were a necessary and vital part of the job.

After four days, Vinny thought that Mrs Kelly hadn't been joking. At one point he thought about going back to work on Mr Hamilton's farm. He was just about to tell Brian Lawson to 'stuff' it, when Sergeant Reynolds came into the room.

"Right you two, get your coats, I'm taking you to a murder scene. I'll get you up to speed when we're in the car. There will be a couple of dead bodies, but you have seen that at the bridge, although it will be slightly different this time. Kim don't throw up at the crime scene, as you won't be very popular with the forensic people. Okay?"

"Don't worry about me Sergeant. I'm pretty sure I will see a lot more in this job."

"Okay folks, here is what we have. There are two bodies lying with their throats cut, and their tongues pulled through the neck, in a lockup in Fintry. This is a method used by the Mafia in the olden days as a warning to others not to inform on them. Rest assured, there is no bloody Mafia in Fintry. It's probably some young punk trying to be the big man, or he's been told to do it. The two guys are in their early twenties. I'll bet my pension that it is a drug deal gone wrong, or they've been skimming off the top. Trust me."

They drove into the scheme, and Vinny thought how Drumbrig seemed like the end of the world, but this took the 'biscuit'. There was a hell of a lot of poverty here, but he was sure there would be a lot of nice people living here as well, or was he just being delusional.

As they got out of the car, the sergeant told them to stick close to him as he didn't want to lose them. Kim just looked at Vinny wondering why the sergeant would say that. The sergeant said that a crowd would soon gather, and abuse would be aimed at them, but to just ignore it.

As they walked into the garage lockup, the smell was terrible as it appeared the bodies had been there for a few days. Kim tried to divert her eyes from the scene, but one look from the sergeant made her change her mind. Stones had started to land on the corrugated roof which startled them now and again, and the crowd were getting a bit vocal.

"Why don't you 'polis' just fuck off and leave us alone. Your not wanted here," came a shout from somebody. Sergeant Reynolds immediately turned to Vinny and said, "Hang on here for a wee minute. I recognise that voice."

"Jakey Jackson, I know your voice by now, so bloody well show yourself 'ya' wee smelly bastard. C'mon show yourself."

Nobody showed, so Sergeant Reynolds ploughed into the crowd knocking down people like they were ninepins. He lunged behind a big guy and grabbed Jakey Jackson. The guy he'd been hiding behind tried to obstruct the sergeant, but a powerful backhander to the guy's right jaw soon sorted that out. Jakey Jackson was being dragged through the crowd with the sergeant's massive hand on the back of his neck. When he got to the front, he booted Jakey in the 'balls', before booting his arse for about twenty yards up the road, much to the amusement of the remaining crowd.

"Anybody else want to have an opinion about the police force? 'Nah' I didn't think so, now the rest of you go home before I really get angry. Go on, fuck off."

Vinny thought that if he was ever in trouble, then he would want the sergeant on his side. Forensics were just finishing up, when an ambulance came down the road for the bodies. Vinny walked around the crime scene, both inside and outside with Kim at his side. It was the sergeant who told them that their time here was over. When they were outside, the sergeant stopped and said, "Well Vinny, what did you observe with your little walkabout?"

"Mainly two things sergeant. The big thing was that there was no real blood in there, so they must have had their throats slit and then bled out elsewhere. Also, even in their decaying state they looked very similar, as if they were related."

"What about you Kim? Did you see anything?

"The only thing I noticed was when the forensics pulled the garage door down for more privacy, there was a new padlock on it. Although, it seemed like a run of the mill lock, but maybe they can get some prints off it. It seems though sergeant that we are being shown some of the worst incidents, and I can't relate them to Professional Standards."

"Let's try and hang tight. Brian Lawson will be speaking to you in a few weeks. I know he will have some mind-blowing news for you both, but we will keep this between ourselves."

Another two days of studying Scots Law, and both Vinny and Kim were just about packing it in. No matter what sergeant Reynolds had said. It was the end of the week, with Vinny wondering what he was going to do for the next day or so.

"Vinny, do you fancy a walk in Clatto Country Park tomorrow? Let's take something to eat with us. We can meet in the town centre and get the bus out there. Let's go for the ten o'clock bus. Sound okay to you?"

"I would love to Kim, but let us make sure we are kitted out with the right clothes, as the weather forecast looks 'crap'."

They were just saying their goodbyes, when Brian Lawson appeared at the front door.

"Either of you pair drive?"

"I'm taking lessons at the moment Ds Lawson, although I can't speak for Vinny."

"I don't have a licence, but I can drive a car, four by four, JCB, tractor, quad bike, and you can even throw in a horse for good measure," said Vinny laughing.

"You should have stopped at not having a licence Vinny, so don't be cocky. Next week, you are going for lessons, the pair of you. Have a good weekend."

Kim thanked him, and Vinny gave him a mock salute.

Brian Lawson watched them walk away, and thought his plan for them was going in the right direction.

As Vinny lay in bed that night he was feeling a bit excited about meeting Kim, but he had to calm down, as this was just a walk with something to eat at the end of it, but to Vinny it was a start. Of what, he had no idea.

Next morning, Mrs Dunn was banging on his bedroom door telling him he had over slept, and she had run a bath for him, but not to be too long. He went down after his bath, and Mrs Dunn had made a mountain of toast with a pot of tea on the kitchen table.

"Mrs Dunn, you will have to cut back on the breakfasts, as I'm going to end up with a big belly, then I would have no chance chasing after the criminals."

"You won't have to son, you will just use your brain to catch them. I wish my husband had done that. I've packed my husband's rucksack with food and soft drinks. Enough for you and the lassie. What is she like son? You seemed a little excited when you were telling me about your plan for going a walk up at Clatto."

"She is lovely Mrs Dunn. She makes going into the station more bearable each morning, but I am under no illusion that anything will come from our friendship. It's far too early."

Vinny thanked Mrs Dunn, and headed off to the bus station. The taxi took ages due to the volume of traffic, and he had to run to where Kim was waiting. Vinny paid the fare for them both, and as soon as they sat down the bus was off on its twenty-minute journey. It felt good sitting so close to Kim. They didn't really speak much on the journey, as this had been the only time they had been together out with work.

When they walked into the park, Kim suggested that they walk the five-mile circular route around the reservoir. Vinny said that would be great. While walking, they chatted, just really getting to know each other. For once the weather was nice, and they both seemed confident in each other's company. They were soon back where they started from, and Kim suggested they go into the woodland where there were picnic benches for something to eat. As soon as they had finished eating the heavens opened. They saw a large tree with plenty of foliage, so they headed for it.

Vinny took his raincoat from the backpack, and put it over the two of them. The rain was torrential, so they just sat close keeping warm and dry. It happened so unexpectedly for Vinny. Kim leaned in close and started to kiss him. Although taken aback, Vinny responded, and their kissing became more intense. Eventually, Vinny put his hand inside her coat and started to caress her breasts. It was then that Kim gently pushed him away.

"I'm sorry Vinny, but I'm not ready for that yet. You see it wasn't that long ago that I was in a horrible relationship, which didn't end very well. Also, I don't want to get too involved with you, as I'm not sure I want to be in the job I'm doing. It's probably not the job for me, and if truth be told, I don't think we've been told the whole truth about what's in store for us, job wise that is. What do you think?"

"I'm not really sorry for what just happened Kim, as it was just a normal reaction, and to be honest, I have wanted to do it for a while. Well, more than that obviously. I am sorry about your last relationship, but why didn't you just walk away from it? Nobody should be stuck in a bad relationship. As for our jobs, I'm going to have a word with Brian Lawson this week, as I agree there are a lot of things he might not be telling us."

"I don't know why I stayed in that relationship Vinny, but it's taken me a while to get past it. Maybe in a while we can get to know each other better. What do you think? I think speaking to Brian Lawson should be a joint thing."

"That's sound by me."

They took the next bus back into the centre, where Kim gave him a peck on the cheek, and said she would see him on Monday. He sat on one of the benches at the shopping centre, wondering about what had just happened earlier.

Bloody hell what is happening here. A few weeks ago I thought I was a sex addict after all the bed sharing with Amy, and now the most I am getting is caressing Kim's breasts through her jersey. No way that is going to stop my erections throughout the night he said to himself. As much as he liked Kim, he wasn't going to live his life like a monk. If he and Kim got together then fine, if not then he would just move on.

Monday came quick enough, and Vinny wandered into the station feeling a bit down. It wasn't just about Kim or his uncertainty about his job, it was everything that had gone on in his life lately. He knew he had to push everything to the back of his mind and get on with his police training. He would make a decision after speaking to Brian Lawson.

The weeks went into months, and Kim had never spoken to him about approaching Brian Lawson about their future. They were taking driving lessons every week and Vinny's instructor advised him to put in for his test sooner rather than later. He had been out with Kim quite a few times, but she was very distant at times when it came to intimacy.

One weekend however Kim said she was going away with her parents, so he had gone to a nightclub in the town centre and met a girl called Heather. She was a great dancer, putting Vinny to shame. He thought that Billy would have loved dancing with her.

He had gone back to her flat, and spent the next five hours making love to her. She had said that she was on the 'pill', so they were relaxed with each other. Heather knew how to use her body. For Vinny it felt good, and his body needed it. About eight o'clock in the morning, she had got up and made them a tea to have in bed, and the love making continued.

"Vinny, the whole of last night was incredible, and you are a beautiful lover in bed, but I'm not looking for a relationship. However, if you are in the Oscars nightclub, and you see me, then please give me a dance. No matter how 'crap' you are at dancing."

They both laughed, and after his tea, Vinny got dressed and kissed Heather goodbye. He doubted he would ever be in her bed again, or possibly see her again, but it had been a lovely night with her. He decided to make a decision about Kim in a few weeks, but he was going to ask her about her reluctance to be intimate with. Maybe her last relationship had been abusive, either physically or verbally. If so, he would try to help her through it, but he was young and didn't want to be laden down with her problems at his age, but he would try.

It was several weeks later that he took the 'bull by the horns', and asked Kim if he could have a serious discussion with her one night. He also asked Brian Lawson if he could speak to him about the job he was training for. Both Brian and Kim wondered what he wanted to speak to them about. He asked Kim one Friday after work, to go for a walk with him. He chose a path along the river Tay which he had noticed previously from the office they worked from. He took her hand, walked for a while, before asking her to sit on one of the benches.

"Kim, please don't think I am being too pushy, but I need to speak to you about the way our relationship is going, because in my opinion it's not going anywhere. I want to be with you, but I am also a young guy in his twenties who has a very healthy sexual appetite. I love making love, but not just to anybody. As it happens, I want that person to be you. Not sex Kim, but making love. However, it is not happening between us. Can you please speak to me about your previous relationships, unless it's too painful for you. I just want to help you, and in turn help our relationship to another level."

She seemed a bit shocked before coming around. Tears had started to fall, but Vinny didn't put his arm around her to comfort her, as he knew she would just think that would be enough for him.

"If you really don't want to speak about it so that we can try and make something of the relationship, then I will understand and move on, and no hard feelings."

"Okay Vinny, I'll try and explain it to you, but if it gets too painful, then I will stop, and then we'll both move on, albeit in different directions. My previous boyfriend was a complete manipulator. He was a Jekyll and Hyde character. At times he would be all sweetness and light, the next time he used to criticise everything about me. From my appearance, my looks and even my performance in bed. I used to wonder what character would turn up when I went out with him. It got to the stage that I thought that whatever he did or said was normal, and I suppose my self esteem got so low, that I couldn't get out of the relationship. Eventually, I had to get my parents involved, and fortunately my dad warned him off, and I've never seen him again. I don't know what more I can say."

"I don't know what to say Kim. Being stuck in a little village, I never really came across a situation like yours. I appreciate how hard it must have been for you, but please believe me I am not that type of guy. It would be lovely to have a relationship where there is no baggage on either side, but that doesn't happen often, I know. I won't ask you again about your past, as long as you don't bring anything up. Our pasts are our own, so lets leave them there, in the past."

"Please just give me a little more time Vinny, as I do want a relationship with you, but let's not kid ourselves, it will be difficult while working with each other, but I'll try hard if you will. What do you say?"

Vinny said he was more than willing to give it a go. They walked to the centre to get a bus to their respective homes. Vinny kissed her, and she got on the bus waving to him when the bus drove away. He only had to wait ten minutes before his bus arrived. While sitting there, he started to think about what had been said from both of them. He wondered if he had been a 'pure bastard' making Kim bring up her last relationship, but he felt he needed to get a reaction from her, to see if it was worth pursuing any type of relationship with her. He got off at his stop, and as he walked to Mrs Dunn's house, he wondered if things had gotten too complicated with Kim. It had never been like this with Amy.

The next day he spent a lot of time making notes to put to Brian Lawson on Monday. He found the weekend a bit boring, so he needed to start doing things on his own, rather than waiting for Kim to be with him.

On Saturday night he decided to go and visit some pubs to get the lay of the land and see how the other half live. He would take Brian Lawson's advice, and just try and blend in.

After getting something to eat, he showered and got a taxi into the town. As he sat in the taxi, he wondered if it might be time to rent his own flat, but with all the doubts in his mind about the job and Kim, maybe he should just leave it at the moment.

The first pub he went into was the Club Bar. It was a lively little bar, and when he went in the karaoke was in full swing. Some of the people were really good singers, but one or two were dire. One singer called Colin was an afront to music, trying to sing an Elton John song, but Vinny did notice a couple of guys continually blocking the guy's view of the lyrics on the screen.

After a couple of soft drinks, he moved on to a place called Sinatras. There wasn't a lot of atmosphere compared to the Club

Bar, so he got his drink, sat at a table and blended in. It was amazing what you noticed when you weren't looking for anything in particular. One guy 'kidney' punched another guy, who was standing at the bar waiting for his drink, then just walked away. He saw another guy slip something small into a guy's hand. Probably drugs.

His next stop was going to be the Globe, but it seemed like it was on the verge of falling down, so he bypassed it, and moved on to an area called the Nethergate, where he saw a small bar called the Pheonix. It looked a bit Victorian, but they probably wanted it to look like that. He decided that this would be the last visit to a pub.

He noticed a big guy looking worse for wear holding on to the end of the bar. For no apparent reason he just 'smashed' the guy next to him in the face, putting him down on the floor. Nobody got up to help pick the guy up from the floor, until two police constables came through the front door. They grabbed the drunk guy, and frog marched him out the door. The barman was propping the victim against the bar. After about twenty minutes the constables came back in minus the drunk guy.

They shook hands with the barman, who poured them each a pint of 'bitter' and a whisky chaser. Vinny wondered what the hell was going on. Was this par for the course, or was it particular to these two officers and this pub. He didn't want to get involved, but as he left the bar he memorised the police number on their shoulders.

It was back to the grindstone on Monday. Kim seemed a bit happier after her weekend away with her parents. Brian Lawson had set up some hypothetical case studies, asking them both to assess each case, and see what verdict they would have come up with. This went on for three days. When they were just coming to their conclusions, Sergeant Reynolds came in, and quietly spoke to Brian Lawson, who just nodded.

"Vinny, you and Kim get yourselves organised to head down to your old stomping ground, Drumbrig. One of our own has been murdered. You will be travelling with Sergeant Reynolds and Ds John Harvey, who you haven't met yet. He will be in charge. Vinny, you know who we're talking about. Please clear your mind, as you can't be prejudiced in any way. Go with an open mind."

"I take it we are talking about Luggy Burns then?"

"No, we are bloody not Vinny, it's Pc Harry Burns, and don't you forget it. Got it?"

"Loud and clear sir. Do we need to take a change of clothes sir?"

"No, you will be coming back each night. As you know too well there is no accommodation in your old village. Officers from Dunfermline are already there protecting the crime scene. Forensics have just arrived. Good luck, and just go with what John Harvey says."

As they headed down in Ds Harvey's car, Kim could see Vinny was a bit nervous, so she just squeezed his hand, without the other two seeing her.

"Right, Vinny please tell John and I all about Drumbrig, and your upbringing there. Don't leave anything out as there could be a clue in what you tell us."

After about half an hour of Vinny telling them about Drumbrig, warts and all, Sergeant Reynolds and Ds Harvey gave each other a look of surprise.

"Vinny, the part of wife and child beating is accurate?"

"Not every parent hit their kids, but they were very, very strict with them. I should know, as I was one of them, remember. If I didn't have my two pals, then you would probably be going down there to arrest me. We kept each other sane."

"With regard to what happened to your pal Billy, do you think it could have been his dad who killed Pc Burns?"

Vinny started to laugh.

"Not unless he beat him to death with his bible. However, he would be more concerned about protecting the bible."

As the car turned up the road to the village, Vinny realised that twice he had been back here, and twice somebody had lost their life. Ds Harvey drove right up to the police station. It was Sergeant Reynolds who turned and told Kim and Vinny to stay where they were until he gave them a shout to come in. The two of them sat for what seemed like an age, until Ds Harvey came to the station door, and motioned for them to come in.

"Okay you pair, it's not a pretty sight in there, so be prepared."

Vinny thought that Ds Harvey hadn't been kidding.

As they walked through the station office, there were two forensic officers trying to look for finger prints. When they moved away from the body, it was such a gruesome sight. Here was Luggy Burns handcuffed half way up the bars of the cell. The strength in his legs had given up, so he had slumped with his lower body spread out. Vinny could just recognise him, as his face was a bloody mess, swollen to the size of a football. Worst of all was that his truncheon had been rammed down his throat, with only a couple of inches protruding. Blood had seeped out from his mouth, and had dried on his cheeks.

Kim had turned and started to walk away, until she walked into the massive frame of Sergeant Reynolds, who held her shoulders and turned her back around.

"You'll not see much if your not looking young lass. You're here to observe so bloody well observe."

Ds Harvey had suggested that they let the forensics finish up, and they would talk outside, plus the air inside was a bit rancid. As they sat in the car, the Ds said they would head to the school, as the headmaster had kindly offered them the school hall to conduct interviews.

"What did either of you pair observe in there, if anything? Remember, any little thing may help," asked the Ds.

"Well let's be fair, there must have been a lot of rage going on in there. However, that doesn't surprise me as there must be loads of people in Drumbrig who had a grudge against him. It was only a matter of time," said Vinny.

"What about you Kim?" asked Sergeant Reynolds.

"Well let's not concentrate on one perpetrator, as it must have taken a lot of strength to do what he or they did to him. Plus, he would have to be overpowered, which wouldn't have been easy."

"Good point Kim. Let's get to the school, and have a discussion on what our way forward is going to be," said the Ds.

They were greeted at the school by the headmaster, who was especially pleased to see Vinny, saying he would it would be better to have met him under nicer circumstances. They got started on setting up an interview area. The Ds had brought all the necessary forms. So, they sat down and talked about how they would proceed. It was Ds Harvey who suggested that they interview as many males as possible from sixteen to sixty five years. They would get a few more officers from Dunfermline for a door to door interview.

They managed to get everything organised before returning to Dundee, ready for returning the next day. During the return journey, it was the Ds who asked Vinny a question.

"Vinny, do you think we have a chance of catching the killer, seeing as it's quite a small community, and you having lived there for a long time?"

"I will give you my honest opinion, but I don't think you are going to like it. We haven't got a snowball's chance in Hell. Pc Burns was a hated man, and it wouldn't surprise me if they were celebrating his demise in the Star pub as we speak. They will close ranks, and remember, Pc Burns tried to force himself on to a lot of the women, so they will be glad he's no longer a threat to them. Unless somebody confesses, or somebody gives another person up, then I'm sorry, but no amount of detective work will catch the killer. When were you last at a crime where you had over a hundred suspects, all with motive?"

They drove back in silence, until arriving at the station. John Harvey said they would leave at seven o'clock tomorrow morning to escape the traffic. Everybody said their goodbyes.

Kim had been quiet on the way back, and had just given Vinny a quick peck on the cheek, when they were well away from the station. Vinny knew that today had taken a lot out of her, but at least she wouldn't have to see the sight of a dead Luggy Burns again tomorrow.

Vinny had headed off to bed soon after eating, as he knew tomorrow would be challenging. He would try his best to find the killer, but as he said in the car, it would be a futile investigation. They were waiting for him the next morning.

"When I say seven o'clock, I mean exactly that Vinny. Don't be late again. Do you hear?"

"My apologies Ds Harvey. It won't happen again, I assure you."

"Okay, but let's start by calling everyone by their first names please."

Drumbrig was quiet when they arrived, with only the women going to the co-op for their groceries. They went into the police station and Bob Reynolds put the kettle on for the 'magic brew ' of tea. The phone rang, it was the head of the forensic team from Dundee.

"Good morning folks. I thought I would catch you before you continued with your work down there. Right, here is my preliminary findings. Pc Burns had been dead for about three days before we arrived. I can't specifically say if the beating killed him or if it was the truncheon blocking his airways, leading to suffocation. Either way, he would have suffered a horrible death, regardless of his reputation. Oh, one other thing. I found that his genitals had been badly swollen, from somebody punching or kicking them. There is nothing else I can really say, apart from the crime scene being spotless. So whoever did it, made a good job of wiping everything down behind them. Good hunting folks."

"Well, that didn't tell us anymore than we already know," said Vinny.

"Okay, let's not be too disappointed. Maybe something will crop up in the interviews. The officers from Dunfermline are already out and about doing door to door interviews, so let's get to the school and see who turns up."

Very few people turned up, with it mainly being women giving their stories about Pc Burns' lecherous advances to them. Kim had said she might be better speaking to the women, as they might open up to her rather than a man. However, there was nothing helpful in what they had said. She knew that this going to be a very long investigation.

Vinny was sitting waiting for the next interviewee, when in walked Billy's dad. John Harvey was about to ask him to sit down, when Vinny had indicated that he would like to do it. The Ds had just given him the nod. Vinny was going to give it to him 'tight'.

"Come and sit down Mr Clark. I see by your face you recognise my face. Yes, it's Vinny Hunter, now working for Her Majesty's Finest in Dundee. I see that you've still got that fucking bible glued to your hand. Your God didn't help you out much when it came to your son did it? Now I hear your wife has 'buggered off,' so please just tell me what you were doing for the last four days and nights."

He told Vinny he had been working days at his job in Dunfermline, and he was up at the minister's house at night reading the Scriptures.

"Anything going on between you and the minister Mr Clark?"

"Don't be disgusting Hunter, and if you want to know, my religion forbids me to inflict harm on anybody, never mind kill them."

"Listen you pompous prick, your religion has been the cause of countless wars, which have killed millions over the ages."

It was then he felt a vice like grip on his shoulder. With Bob Reynolds telling him that if he was finished with Mr Clark, then he should move on to the next person to interview.

"Everybody to their own son. Try and be impartial, and keep an open mind."

The day was long, and when they sat down afterwards John Harvie asked everyone for their thoughts. The consensus was that they were just 'pissing in the wind'. Most of the men they interviewed just smiled when they were asked about Pc Burns' death, and a few had said to let them know if they ever caught the guy, as they would shake his hand and buy him a whisky. Bob Reynolds had said he was concerned about the lack of men coming to be interviewed. Vinny had said that they would be entrenched in the Star.

Just then Bob Reynolds, stood and motioned for Vinny to follow him. Bob marched up the street, right into the Star, almost taking the door off it s hinges.

"Right you lot. Put your drinks down and listen very carefully. I don't care if you hated Pc Burns. However, he was brutally murdered. Do you fucking drunkards understand what I am saying? Somebody will go to prison for life for what they have done, make no mistake, so I want your arses down at the interview centre, either tomorrow or tomorrow night. If I have to come in here looking for you, then God help you. Understand?"

There was a lot of nodding of heads, but as Bob and Vinny turned to walk out, there was a shout of 'No chance of me coming down to the school, to speak to you lot'. Bob turned to Vinny and laughed, saying that they had another Jakey Jackson here in Drumbrig. Bob turned, almost knocking Vinny out of the way. Vinny was cringing as he had recognised his dad's voice. Bob could see the culprit trying to make himself invisible in the bay window seating. He didn't barge people out of the way this time, but instead he just pushed anybody's chair out the way with the palm of his hand, until he reached the person that had spoken. He grabbed him by the front of his jacket, and hauled him along to the door.

"Right you arseholes. If we get anymore back chat, then you will end up like this cretin, who's going to have two nights bed and breakfast at the expense of Her Majesty. Although, breakfast might be at my discretion. Anybody got anything else to say?

He marched Vinny's dad across the road, and into the police station. When he got in he said to the officer there, "Two nights in the cells for this cretin, and don't put any paper- work through. I will decide when he gets out."

Vinny and Bob walked down to the school. It seemed that even in the short time from Bob announcing himself in the Star there were more men waiting to be interviewed. After another few days most of the people in the village had been spoken to, so John Harvey asked everyone to a meeting.

"I think this investigation has run it's course folks, so I am proposing we wrap everything up, and head back to Dundee tomorrow. We will leave this case open, just in case new leads turn up. I will organise with Dunfermline police to have the station manned a couple of days a week. Everybody agree?"

Nobody complained, and it was then that Bob asked Vinny to follow him. He marched down to the Star, and as before, barged through the door. He stood there in the middle of the room and never moved, until he had everybody's attention. Even Vinny, who was standing next to him, was wondering what was happening, as the silence was deafening.

"Right you lot. Here is what's going to happen. I know you are just a bunch of drunkards, who after you get kicked out of here, go back home and kick the 'crap' out of your wives and kids. Well as from this moment, that will stop. If I get to hear of any of you inflicting violence on any of your family, then I will be back. There are plenty of cells in Dundee to house you all. Oh, and my sister is a court judge, and she would be more than happy to send you down for a considerable amount of time. I'll be back every so often, and I will be knocking on doors to see if any of you have been misbehaving. Nobody got anything to say? Well, I will bid you goodnight, until we meet again."

Vinny could see on their faces that they thought their world had come to an end.

Next day they packed up and headed back to Dundee, with everybody not saying very much. Vinny hoped he would never have to set foot in that place again. It was never easy leaving a case unsolved, but there were far too many suspects, and Pc Burns had 'pissed' of so many people, both male and female. When they got back to the station, Brian Lawson had suggested to Vinny and Kim that they just go home, as they would be debriefed in the morning.

As they left the station, Vinny suggested that they go for a coffee, as it was only mid-afternoon. Kim agreed and they walked into the centre. They sat for a bit of the time in silence, before Kim came out with a revelation.

"Vinny, can I tell you I've been having second thoughts about this job. Having seen the gruesome sights we have recently, then I'm not sure it's for me. I was up for it at the start, but it's not what I expected or wanted."

"Kim, please don't make any rash decisions, as I've a feeling that there will be more to this job than professional standards. I don't know what, but I have this gut feeling that it won't just be what we've been told. I fully intend to confront Brian Lawson tomorrow , and ask him to come clean, so just wait until I've met with him. Okay?"

Kim nodded and they drank their coffee in silence until it was time to leave. She gave Vinny a hug and whispered in his ear. "Mum and dad are away for a long weekend, do you fancy keeping me company?" she said with a glint in her eye.

"Would love to, let's speak about it on Friday."

The next day he saw Brian Lawson coming out of his office.

"Ds Lawson, at some point during the day can we have a discussion please. Not just a ten-minute chit chat though."

"Sounds ominous Vinny, but not a problem. I'll give you a shout. Let's go for the debriefing, as I hear the investigation didn't work out as expected."

They all sat in the debriefing room, with John Harvey leading the meeting.

"Right folks. Any thoughts on the Drumbrig investigation? Anything we didn't do, or should have? Before you have your say, can I just start by saying that I felt it was one of the most difficult investigations I have been on. There was not one bit of evidence. The crime scene was one of the cleanest I have ever seen. Nobody we fancied for it."

"I think we made a mistake in concentrating on the men from the village. Delivery lorries arrive at the co-op each day, although that would have been difficult trying to interview the drivers, but what would they have against Pc Burns is anybody's guess. Buses stop at the bottom of the road. Maybe it was a random visitor to the village, but again what would their motive be. Let's be fair about it, we were just pissing in the wind at times," said Vinny.

"Bob, what did you think?"

"I thought it was weird. No matter how many crime scenes I've been at, there has always been one small piece of evidence. Kim was right when she said there was a lot of rage directed at the police officer. Was it to make a statement. If it was, then he or she certainly made their point. I can't give you any rational explanation for what happened."

After about another hour, Brian Lawson said they should file all the necessary paperwork and move on.

Ds Harvey left the station, and Bob Reynolds started working out of another office.

"Vinny, both you and Kim wait here please, as I need an in-depth conversation with you."

"Well Vinny, I take it you have worked it out that all your training hasn't been solely about you joining our professional standards team. Your right. I make no apologies for trying to get you trained up for what I'm about to ask you. Police Scotland has been in decline for a long period of time now. The hierarchy in their ivory towers have come up with a plan to revamp every police force in Scotland. From the top to the bottom. There is still corruption in the force, and it needs to be routed out. The two of you in about a year will be trained up enough to undertake this task. By the look on your faces this has come as a bit of a shock to you. Have you got anything to say?"

"Bloody hell Brian. We're only in our twenties. Do you think we'll be ready in a year?"

"Listen Vinny, we wouldn't have chosen you if we didn't think both of you could do it. Obviously you will have a team behind you, but that is for discussion in the future. Let me tell you though, it's a massive job, but would be immensely rewarding. Your training now would be structured towards this job commencing, but we can't afford to get this wrong."

"Maybe you should rehire that guy Foggerty, who made such a good job of cleaning up Edinburgh and Dundee."

"If only Vinny, but that was some time ago, and the circumstances are different. This time it would be done legally. So I'm going to give you the weekend to think about it, and I will be wanting an answer on Monday morning. Oh, and bye the way, your driving tests have been booked for the end of next week, and I expect you to pass first time. Vinny can I see you in the next room please."

As they sat at a desk Brian Lawson came right out with it.

"Vinny, after speaking to Bob and John Harvey, we are all having doubts about whether Kim has the mental aptitude for this task. What are your thoughts?"

"I know she's been having some doubts, but I think after what you've told us, she'll come round, but if I have any doubts about her then I'll tell you and her as soon as possible."

"Okay, I appreciate your candour Vinny, and before you go I have another thing I would like to bring up. Firstly, you have three times mentioned Denny Foggerty in conversation. I would suggest you try and get him out of your mind, as by all accounts you are no Denny Foggerty, but I'll tell you what I'll do. I'll try and set up a meeting with his good friend, a guy called Stevie, and he might be able to let you know what he's like. However, I don't think he'll tell you much, but after that you get him out of your bloody mind. You do this job your way. Agreed?"

Chapter 6

Both Kim and Vinny walked out of Liff Station with their heads in bits. They knew after the discussion with Brian Lawson that their future had been mapped out for them, and now there was no going back or just resign. It was going to be hard work for quite some time, and the pressure on them would be immense. They just said a quick goodbye as they would see each other tomorrow.

Vinny had decided to walk home, he wanted more time to digest the day's events. He thought everything was happening too quick, and as much as he felt a bit excited about the job, he didn't want it taking over, and ruining his life. There wasn't a lot of sleep that night. His erections during the night reminded him about what Kim had said regarding her mum and dad going away for a long weekend.

As he walked into the station the next morning, Brian Lawson waved him into one of the offices where Kim was sitting.

"Right, I am not messing about today. Are you both up for the challenge we talked about yesterday?"

Kim said she was, but if it was affecting her life, or her well being, then she would have to take stock, and make a decision.

"Fair enough Kim, I respect what your saying. What about you Vinny? I fear I am going to hear a few buts."

"Okay, here are my thoughts. If I am going to do this, then I need to be trained up to the highest level. I don't want to be rushed, and most importantly, I need to do the job my way, without interference. Obviously reporting to someone in Police Scotland. However, like Kim, if it affects my mental health, then I'm off. Agreed?"

"We have every faith in you both, but Kim, the reports I have received back, have said that you must toughen up if you happen to be at a messy incident, although I think this job won't bring you up against many of them. Right, your training starts in earnest now, so be prepared for hard work. Your driving test are next Thursday, so as I've said before, pass them."

As they walked out of the station the next day, Kim asked Vinny to give her a call after ten o'clock the next morning, as hopefully her mum and dad would be away by then.

He called Kim the next morning, and she said to come over as her parents were long gone, and to remember a holdall. Vinny thought he would be more excited, but that might happen when he got there. He was looking forward to just spending time with Kim, and if anything else happened, then it would be a bonus.

She opened the door just as he arrived, and gave him a full-on kiss before he even got through the door. When he went into the living room, he thought what a nice house her parents kept. She told him to sit, and she would bring him a tea through.

"Vinny, we have two days together if you want, so have a think about how we're going to spend the time. Get your mind off the bedroom though, but don't worry, that will come later."

"I thought you might like to show me around Dundee, as I really haven't explored much, and then I'll take you for lunch. I'm sure there must be a few parks in and around where we can go for a stroll. No doubt in the rain, as it was trying to start when I came over."

They spent the day just strolling around the city, before eating in one of the restaurants. Walking in one of the parks was next on their list, where they sat down and chatted away.

"Kim, what are you really thinking about this job opportunity we have been offered? It seems that at times you are non-committal about the whole thing."

"Vinny, I have my doubts at times about my own ability, and yes Brian Lawson was right when he suggested I toughen up. However, I don't want to take the lead on any of the investigations. I know I could be good as back-up, but unlike you Vinny I'm not assertive enough, and I'm not angry enough."

When they got back home, they pretty much just watched TV, which Vinny wasn't enjoying. Kim noticed, and put it off, she asked Vinny if he could tell her everything that had happened in his life, even previous girlfriends should he want to. Vinny thought that all this was a bit strange, and didn't really want to participate in the conversation.

"Kim, my past is my own, and I am not the type of person to share it with anybody. Everyone has a past, and I don't want to know yours. You've told me about a couple of previous relationships you had, but I don't want to know any more. If we are to have a relationship, then lets start afresh. If it works then fine, if not, then we remain work colleagues and nothing more. My life hasn't been great, and I don't want to share it with anybody. Sorry if that upsets you."

Kim looked a bit shocked, but nodded her head in agreement.

"Bloody hell Kim, we might get fed up seeing each other every day. We might not be compatible when making love for God sake, but I would like to find out at some stage," he said laughing.

It was getting late, and Kim went round the house checking that all doors and windows were locked. The house was a mid-terrace two bedroom, but couldn't have been classed big in anyway. When finished, she came into the living room, took Vinny's hand, and asked him to come upstairs with her. As they went into her bedroom, Vinny thought that it was pretty functional. There were no pictures or posters on the wall, and curtains and bedspread were pretty bland. Vinny thought that this was a bit strange.

It didn't take long for them to start undressing each other. They stood there admiring each others naked bodies. Vinny couldn't help admiring her pert breasts, and was a little surprised that she only had a small strip of pubic hair leading down to her vagina. She started to hug Vinny, and hold his penis, which made him immediately hard. They didn't bother going under the bed covers, but just lay next to each with Vinny giving her a lot of foreplay, which made her climax, with Kim giving a little squeal at the crucial moment. Vinny lay on top and then entered her. Her hips were slowly gyrating to the movement of his, and after a while their movements became more energetic, until both climaxed. As Kim's legs wrapped around Vinny's body, he thought she was trying to squeeze the life out of him. It was Kim that instigated making love in every position that night, and Vinny wasn't complaining.

After making love for a few hours, Kim slipped under the covers, and went to sleep, but Vinny just lay back with his eyes open, until he to felt a bit chilly and went under the covers, holding on to Kim, until morning came.

Their lovemaking carried on as soon as they woke up, until eventually Kim had said she was going for a shower, and slipped out of the bed. She had felt a little sore while washing, but didn't really care, as Vinny had been a beautiful lover, and was the only person who had ever made her climax through intercourse. She genuinely felt that this was the first time anyone had truly 'made love' to her. After her last two relationships, she had come to hate the word 'sex'.

Sunday was just a restful day for them, until Kim asked Vinny to take her up to the bedroom in the afternoon. The session was just as energetic as the night before, but neither were complaining. After tea, Vinny had said he should go back to his 'digs' as they were working tomorrow, and with the intensity of the training, neither could afford not to be on top of their 'game'.

Just as Vinny was leaving, she put her arms around his neck and whispered, "Thank you so much Vinny, I really needed these two days."

When Vinny got home, Mrs Dunn told him that there was something on the kitchen table for him. When he went through, there was a large envelope with something inside. It was the file on Sergeant Bill Dunn. A note on the front from Brian Lawson said, that if Vinny would like to look into it, then fine, but in his own time. The note also said his murder had never been solved, so maybe a fresh pair of eyes might be the way to go. As Vinny went up to his room, Mrs Dunn said, "Its been a few years now son, so nobody is expecting much from you, so don't worry."

Vinny lay in bed that night, reading the file from cover to cover. When he finished reading it he started again, until he fell asleep. When he awoke, he sat up in bed, as something was bothering him. What, he couldn't fathom out, so he decided not to read the file every night, but took a couple of notes from it, and put them in his pocket.

That day it was training as usual, and both Kim and Vinny thought it was getting more and more intense, they knew it wouldn't be that long before they would be told to take on the restructuring of each police force.

It was Thursday, and the day of their driving tests.

"Are you still taking lessons, asked Brian Lawson.

"Yeh, every week Brian."

"What about you Vinny?"

"Just let me borrow a car from the pool and I'll be fine."

"Bloody hell Vinny, have had any lessons at all?"

"Nah, it will be fine, trust me, Oh, I have read the Highway Code though. Can you get me the keys for the car, just so that I can sit in it one lunchtime to get to know where the controls are."

"I need you to pass this test Vinny, so what are you playing at?"

"Relax Brian, put your faith in me."

Brian Lawson walked away shaking his head.

On Thursday, the weather was fine for Kim's test in the morning, but the heavens opened in the afternoon for Vinny's test. The windscreen wipers could hardly cope, but the conditions suited Vinny, as it took him back to the times when working on Mr Hamilton's farm on a tractor with no cab. He knew this test wouldn't be a problem for him. Both passed with flying colours.

When Vinny arrived back at the station, he went into Brian Lawson's office and handed him the keys, but Brian told him to keep them.

"Put petrol in for any mileage you do for your own private use, and no long journeys. Oh, and did you get Bill Dunn's file? I was never involved in it, but the consensus of opinion was that the investigation was pretty shoddy work. Most of the officers who investigated were at the end of their time, and even though it was one of our own, it was a pretty half-hearted investigation."

"Well, I've read it several times, and I concur, the investigation was by officers just hanging on for their pensions. Something is in there, and each time I'm left with a niggle in my head that something wasn't right. I'll keep reading it, but how far can I go if I find discrepancies. Can I interview people?"

"You must bring it to me, and we can both deal it with you on lead naturally. Also, I'm taking you and Kim to speak with a guy called Stevie Martin or Steve Marten or whatever he calls himself nowadays. He is the only person that we know of who was friendly with Denny Rey Foggerty at the time he was in the force. I have a feeling that he may not open up to you, but I did say I would try. I'll take you to a café in the centre, where he'll give you a little of his time, but as soon as he says that he's off, then it's over. Okay?"

Vinny left the office feeling quite excited, and went and congratulated Kim on passing her test, also telling her about meeting with one of Denny Rey Foggerty's friends.

"Vinny, I'm with Brian on this. Why are you so fixated with this guy Foggerty? By all accounts he was a bit of an enigma to say the very least. Do we really want to know about him, as by all accounts he was a very dangerous man, police officer or not."

"Kim, that man was the main guy in wiping out police corruption here in Dundee. Single handed, may I remind you. All this training we've been doing is fine, but if we come up against that level of corruption, then any advice we're given will make the job a good bit easier. I know we won't get it from the guy, but maybe this other guy, Steve Martin, may give us an incite. Are you up for it?"

Kim nodded reluctantly, she wasn't sure getting to know all about this guy Foggerty was the right thing to do, but she'd wait and see.

It was the following Monday that Brian told them to grab their coats as Steve Martin had contacted him, and told him where to meet up. Brian drove, but said they would be on their own in the café.

When Vinny and Kim walked through the door of the café, Vinny immediately knew that the guy sitting in the corner was Steve Martin. There was just something about him. He had this air of authority about him. The guy motioned for the two to come over to his table, and then hailed the waitress.

"What can I do for you? Your boss had said this was about Daniel Foggerty, but I'm not sure I can help you. However, I am always willing to help the police out if I can."

"Can I ask if we are speaking about the same guy, as you said Daniel Foggerty", said Kim.

"Yeh we are. He prefers to go by the name Denny, rather than Daniel."

"We've been given the task of restructuring all the police forces in Scotland, which would incorporate getting rid of any corruption within. We know Denny Foggerty was instrumental in doing that in Dundee and partially in Edinburgh, so we were wondering if we could get an idea of what type of man he was, or is."

"I can't tell you anything about him personally, except that when he started his 'mission' here in Dundee he was a very driven guy, unfortunately whisky was involved, but he turned that around. He took no prisoners though, and he just didn't seem to care. If you were in his way then he would step all over you."

"Are you still in touch with him?"

"Yeh, we meet up now and again as he has an estate called the Albach Trust Estate about a couple of hours from here. The estate caters for underprivileged kids, and they are taken in on a residential basis to learn everything about nature in the surrounding area."

"I have heard that he's a millionaire, is that true?" said Kim.

Steve Martin just laughed.

"Listen young lady. Denny Rey Foggerty is a multi, multi, multi billionaire, and let me tell you that money has not changed him one bloody bit, and means very little to him personally."

"Right, I probably have spoken too much, so it's time for me to go, but I would suggest you don't go up to the estate, as the chances are he'll be at his other estate in Bavaria. Plus, he is a very private person, and doesn't like uninvited guests if he is in Scotland. I hope I have been a little help to you both, and good luck with your task."

Steve shook their hands and walked away.

They got a taxi back to the station, and when they walked in, Brian Lawson asked them through to the conference room.

"Well what did you think of Mr Martin? Did you learn anything from him?"

"He wasn't giving much a way, and I feel the way people speak about this guy Foggerty, they're making him into some super human being, when in fact he is or was some ruthless drunk who got lucky in his job. What we learned today, we could have just looked up his police personnel records. What do you think Brian?"

"Well Kim, what I think is pretty irrelevant. What I know is that you couldn't be further from the truth. I've never met the guy, but I have come into contact with several officers who have, and they assure me that he wasn't just some lucky drunk police officer. As for his police records. There aren't any. As far as the police force goes, Denny Foggerty doesn't exist. He's just a ghost."

Kim just sat looking at him in disbelief.

"Are you telling me that there is absolutely no trace of this guy in the system? Surely that can't be right. Can it?"

"What's your thoughts Vinny?" asked Brian.

"To be honest, the guy intrigues me, and you did say I could go about this job the way I want. So I intend motoring up to the Albach estate in the slight chance he might be there. I need to see him, even if it's from afar. I'll go myself, and if I'm asked to leave the estate, then fine. It'll be next weekend, and if you say no then you can stick your job. I'm going."

They all just sat there looking at each other, until Brian Lawson said that they could both do as they wished, but he didn't look too happy.

Each day was more and more of the same thing, but Vinny could see that things were beginning to come together, and soon it would be their turn to put in a presentation to the hierarchy as to how they were going to go about restructuring the force. He talked to Kim about it, and he thought she was just going to go along with what he proposed. He asked about what she thought about their relationship.

She said she was loving their time together outside work, but she wanted their relationship to go slowly, so that hopefully it would last.

The following weekend was approaching, and Vinny said to Kim that he wouldn't see her on the Saturday, as he was driving up to the estate in the off chance of meeting Denny Foggerty. She asked if she could come, but he wasn't really sure she wanted to.

"Listen Kim. I'm going up there for a reason, and I don't want you fucking things up. It's my decision, and mine alone. Please go with an open mind if you want to go, but on no account be 'gobby' about anything."

"So I don't get a say or an opinion about what happens up there."

"No Kim. Lately, you have been contributing very little to the work we've been doing. It's not all about me doing most of the presentation to put to the bosses".

Kim got up and walked out of the room.

"Your first fall-out Vinny?" asked Brian with a grin on his face.

"Probably won't be our last, I'm sure."

For the whole of that week Vinny had been using the police car to come into the town early, and just sit around in the centre. Mainly people watching, and getting a real feel for the place. Kim wanted to have her own space, but on the Thursday she asked him over for tea and to meet her parents.

He wondered what was going on in her head, as one minute she wanted her own space, and the next he was to meet her parents. However, he motored over to her house at six o'clock and was met at the door by Kim. She asked him in, where she introduced him to her folks. Her dad 'Dod' was a stocky little guy with a beaming smile, who tried to shake Vinny's hand off. The mother was the exact opposite of her husband. She was tall and lean, and looked very much like Kim. They were very kind and asked him through to the living room. He had to watch what he was saying, as Kim had never said if they knew he had stayed over.

After tea, Lynn, Kim's mum, offered Vinny a whisky, and both parents were surprised when he said he had never touched the stuff. Even more surprised when he said he had never touched alcohol full stop. Just before nine, he thanked them for their hospitality, and said he must go. As he went out the door, he turned to Kim.

"Kim, how about I pick you up after work tomorrow, and we go for a drive, and then I can take you into the back of the car, undress you, and make love to you. Any chance?"

He turned to walk away, unaware that Kim was about to jump on his back.

"Where and when Hunter, and I wonder if you can keep up with me?" she whispered in his ear.

"About eight o'clock Kim, just when it's getting grey dark. Oh, and don't worry as I'll have the heater on full blast on the way over."

Next day was work as normal, and Vinny thought that Kim was showing a little more vigour, so there was hope for their working relationship he thought.

After work he told her he would pick her up around eight and left her to get the bus home, as it was quicker than by car.

After his meal, Vinny lay back on his bed, and started to read Bill Dunn's file again. He knew he had to find the anomaly in all this. He drifted off, and by chance woke up just in time to have a bath, and head over to Kim's place. When she got in the car, Vinny said, "Kim, I promise not to talk shop tonight, but can I ask you something. Can you spare me half an hour here and there to read Bill Dunn's file, as there's something in it that I can't get my head around. No worries if you say no, I'll just concentrate on getting you to a quiet place, and slowly taking your clothes off."

"Of course I will, and there's a lovely quiet wooded area just on the outskirts of the town, so get moving, and don't be too slow at undressing me."

After half an hour they were parked behind a shed that was obviously used by the council when they were working in the wood. Kim wasted no time in getting out, and into the back of the car. As they sat kissing, Vinny started to take her top off, only to find out that she had no bra on. He caressed her breasts, while kissing her nipples. She was moaning, and slightly opened her legs. Kim had a short skirt on, and when he put his hand under, he was surprised to find she wasn't wearing any knickers either. Nothing like being prepared he thought. After a while of foreplay, he took his own clothes off. His penis was harder than he had ever known, and when he entered her, she was loudly moaning, and thrusting her hips. It didn't take long for both of them to climax.

They made love in every position that the back seat of a Ford Anglia would allow. Sometimes Vinny thought he might take cramp, as at times he was tending to go on forever. They sat there when they were finished, or so Vinny thought, but Kim had other ideas, and she was trying continually trying to get him erect. The cold was starting to get to them, so they put their clothes back on, just as a guy walked past with his dog.

"I hope we never stop doing this Vinny. It was so beautiful, and talk about intense. Remember, I don't go out without knickers all the time, just sometimes, so if we go out, I'll let your imagination run wild."

The next morning Vinny was up sharp, as he'd told Kim he would pick her up at eight fifteen. No later. He was sitting outside when she finally came out. They headed off up North. Vinny had done his homework, and providing the weather was favourable then it would take them about two hours. He put the radio on, but after an hour the static was so bad he turned it off, and asked Kim to just speak to him.

There was a signpost after about an hour and a half which stated the Albach Trust was fifteen miles ahead. When they were getting near, another signpost said 'Stag's Head Inn' off to the left. Vinny thought he might stop off on the way back for something to eat. He turned a corner in the road.

"Bloody hell Kim, do you see what I am seeing. What a truly magnificent building. Look at all the lodges built on stilts around it. The main house, if that's what you can call it is massive. It looks like trees have been planted all around it, as if there had been a bit of a decimation, and they've planted more."

Within a couple of minutes, Vinny drove the car to just inside the big gate. They sat there for just a minute, before Vinny spoke.

"Kim, look out the back window to our right and tell me what you see please."

"I see a guy standing up there with a rifle over his shoulder. He isn't moving , but I can feel his eyes are on us. Do you think he has been shooting rabbits or something."

"No, I don't Kim. I think he has something to do with this estate, and I'm getting a bad feeling about this place. I don't know why, but it feels like something happened here. Something very bad."

They sat there for a minute or two, not saying anything.

"Well, we're definitely in the right place Kim. Look at that plaque on that wall over there. It says this place is dedicated to Petra and Lachlan Foggerty, who I presume were his parents."

Just then about a dozen youngsters came out of a side door, all partnered up, and with their backpacks and kagouls on. They were obviously excited, and just couldn't keep still. A teacher came out and calmed them down. Vinny started the engine, and very slowly drove towards the front entrance. He stopped the car about twenty feet from the door, which was a large arched doorway, and rather dimly lit. Vinny sat there wondering what he was going to do next.

"Vinny, can you see something or someone in the back of the door way? I'm struggling to see what it is."

"Not sure Kim."

It was then that, what Vinny could only describe as a sinister 'presence' walked forward with a fierce looking dog either side of him. A good-looking guy, who was probably in his late thirties, well over six feet, and wearing just a shirt and jeans stood in front of them. Kim grabbed Vinny's arm and squeezed it hard, while giving out a small squeal. The guy just stood there with an evil-like grin on his face, never taking his eyes of them.

"Bloody hell Vinny, they look like the Hounds of Hell ready to protect their master."

"Kim, I think we have found Denny Foggerty. Lets get out, and don't appear rude."

"Vinny I'm afraid, very afraid."

As they got out, Denny Foggerty walked forward until he was close to them.

"Well, well, if it isn't two of Her Majesty's Finest. I assume the same two that Stevie Martin told not to come up here. Anyway, what can I do for you, but make it quick as I've these two beautiful boys, Jiri and Jan, to give instructions to before they escort the children out on their field trip. It's nice to see how excited the kids are is it not."

Kim looked at the dogs and then over to the children.

"You appear a bit sceptical young lady, about me sending the dogs out with such young children, are you not? You see these children over there, well the dogs will make sure that no animal or human will harm them."

Just then, Denny Foggerty gave an imperceptible sign, and the dog Jiri dived up onto the bonnet of the car, and with his legs spread, started snarling and baring his teeth at Kim, with 'slavers' dripping onto the car. She gave a squeal and turned her face away, while holding on to the car. Vinny was about to go to her, but he looked down at the other dog who was looking back at him, and showing just as many teeth, so he stayed where he was.

Just then, Denny Foggerty gave a low whistle, and the two dogs ran over to the children, with some of them putting their arms around the dog's necks, and the dogs licking their faces.

"Jiri does get a bit excited, and just being a youngster he is eager to please. So what can I do for you, and may I say your time is running out."

"I'm sure Mr Martin told you why we wanted to get to know about you. The whole of the police force in Scotland restructuring rests with us, so I was wondering if you could give us any advice?"

"It was a long time ago, and as Stevie probably told you, I was in a bad way with whisky, but what I will say is that you have to be ruthless when needs be. You won't have many friends in the force, but that's no loss. Any personnel you have underneath you, must be totally loyal. Just like the dogs. Oh, and you do it your way, and if you get too much interference, then tell them to stick the job up their arse. I hope you can do it without killing anybody though."

Denny started laughing, but Vinny and Kim didn't.

"Thank you for your time, and sorry if we've bothered you too much."

"Listen son, never apologise as it's a sign of weakness. As you leave, which you're going to do right now, please acknowledge the guy on the hill with the hunting rifle."

" A friend of yours?"

"Yeh, a very loyal one is Tomaz. A brilliant shot, but truly magnificent with a knife."

Denny Foggerty stared at them for a minute, grinned, before walking back into the house.

When they got back in the car, Kim looked at Vinny and said, "Get me the hell away from here as quickly as possible Vinny. I'm shaking."

As they drove towards the main road, Kim told Vinny to watch his speed, as there were plenty of 5 miles per hour signs on the wall. When they got to the road end, they both looked up at the guy on the hill, and gave him a curt wave, with the guy giving them a mock salute back, before he walked away. When they were on the main road it was Kim who spoke again.

"Put the foot down Vinny Hunter, but at the next layby, please stop."

There was too much going through his mind to ask why, but a mile down the road he pulled in. Kim immediately got out, walked to the nearest rubbish bin, lifted her skirt, and then took her knickers off, and deposited them in the bin. Vinny wondered what the hell was going on.

"What was that all about Kim?"

"The truth is Vinny, that when the guy walked out into the light with his fucking Hounds from Hell, he scared me that much, that I 'peed' myself a little, and when that fucking dog jumped on the car. Well, I really did 'pee' myself and my knickers were 'sopping'. I've never felt like that in my life, and I don't want to feel like that again. Please can we stop at that Inn we noticed on the way up so that I can freshen up, or you will be smelling 'pee' all the way home."

Vinny could imagine how she felt, as he too felt a little scared, especially when the other dog was looking at him with its evil eyes.

As they turned off towards the Stag's head, he turned to Kim and said, "Do you know what the scariest thing for me about today was, when he said he hoped that we wouldn't have to kill anybody to get our job done."

They stopped outside the Inn. There were a few cars already parked up.

When they went in they were greeted by a lovely lady who introduced herself as Maggie, and asked if they were they looking for something to eat? When they said they were, she showed them to a table and told them what foods were available. They both chose the steak pie, and Maggie said she would bring it over as soon as. They sat talking casually, before Kim asked him if had got anything out of today.

"I did Kim. Mainly, that we will have to work very hard, and be ruthless to attain the success level that we are expected to achieve. I'm glad I met the guy, and I know now that Denny Rey Foggerty wasn't just a myth. Anyway, I have got all this out of my system, and the one thing he said I am taking on board, and that is loyalty."

Before their meal came, Maggie came up to their table, and asked if she could sit down for a couple of minutes with them. They said of course.

"I couldn't help but overhear you mentioning Denny Foggerty a few minutes ago. If you don't mind me asking, are you here in an official capacity. The giveaway is your bog-standard car, in the same greenish colour like every other police car."

They both just looked at Maggie, before Vinny started to speak.

"We never thought about it being that obvious Maggie, but now when I think about it I understand."

"What did you think about him."

I was very scared of him Maggie, and I'm not scared to admit that I 'peed' myself a little when I saw him, and fully 'peed' myself when one of his bloody devil dogs jumped on to the bonnet of the car snarling at me, so I'm knicker less at the moment."

"Which dog was it, Jiri or Jan? As Jiri can be a bit playful. Did Denny laugh when he did it?"

"Maggie, I was too bloody busy waiting for my throat to be ripped out to notice for God's sake."

"He helps train them for his friend up on the hill, who breeds horses as well, and very successfully by the way. Let me tell you lassie, the Foggerty family are such a lovely, kind, caring family. His wife is a beautiful Scottish girl, and his two sons Col and Fin are two stunning looking boys, who help out on occasion in here. You will meet their daughter soon. One thing though, and that is if you cross Denny Foggerty, then not even God can help you. Excuse me now, as I must go to the kitchen."

It was about twenty minutes later, that this beautiful young girl of about ten or eleven came through with their meals followed by Maggie. The young girl had a smile on her that would light up the sky on a dark night. After she put the plates down, Maggie said, " Folks I would like you to meet Mali Rey Foggerty."

The girl said she was pleased to meet them, and mentioned that Maggie had said that they'd visited the estate and met her dad, along with her little pal Jiri. Kim just looked at Vinny. They said they were pleased to meet her. She left them as she said she had other customers to serve.

When they were finished, both Maggie and Mali came over, and the youngster was just about to go to the kitchen when Vinny handed her a five-pound tip.

"Thank you very much, you're very kind, but can I ask you to put the money in the tin on the bar please. It's to stop cruelty to animals, if you don't mind. It's being lovely to meet you."

They were getting ready to move when Maggie came to their table with a carrier bag.

"No need to return them. At least your bum will be warm on the way home. Take care"

" Maggie, can I ask you about young Mali before we go. Here she is working in the kitchen, yet her dad is supposed to be a multi billionaire."

"Not supposed to be son. For miles and miles either side of the road belongs to the estate. He has property and businesses all over Europe. Can I just say that the boys and Mali work here because they want to, and do you know what I pay them? Absolutely nothing. They don't want anything. Oh, and can I finish off by saying that Denny Foggerty bought this Inn, and then immediately gave it to me. Wasn't that nice?"

They both gave her a quick hug, and said they hoped they would see her again.

For the first hour, very little was said between them, until Kim spoke.

"What just happened up there today Vinny? I've been sitting here trying to get my head around it, but failing miserably."

"I'm not sure Kim. It was as though we were in a different world."

"Listen Vinny, please don't take this the wrong way, but I won't be seeing you tonight, as my head is all over the place. I feel really tired. How about I come over tomorrow, and we can take Mrs Dunn for her lunch. Sound?"

"Fine by me, as long as you've had a shower and put fresh knickers on."

He wished he hadn't said that, as she punched him on the top of the arm. He knew that would hurt in a while.

About eleven o'clock the next morning, Vinny was lying on his bed reading the cold case file of Bill Dunn. He was getting nowhere, and it was frustrating him. He knew that in his new job he would have to be more patient. He got up and slammed the folder onto the bed just as Kim came through the door.

"What's the matter babe? Hope you don't mind, but Mrs Dunn let me in."

"I know the answer is staring me in the face, but I just can't see it. What the hell am I doing wrong."

"What about I take the folder home with me, and I'll read it tonight and we'll compare notes tomorrow and see what we come up with. Sound good?"

" Yeh fine, we'll take it with us and then you can take it after lunch. Let's go."

When they got down stairs, Mrs Dunn was sitting waiting with her best dress on.

"C'mon gorgeous let's hit the town. Well the Queens Hotel anyway. Lunch awaits."

"Oh, that's an awfully posh place son, are you sure now?"

"The Queens Hotel, fit for a Queen. Are you ready?"

When they got there Vinny sensed that Mrs Dunn was a bit nervous, so he asked her to take his arm as they were shown to their table. The women seemed to be chatting about everything and anything, which suited Vinny. After a couple of sherries Mrs Dunn was really opening up when she came out with a bit of a surprise. She said that her husband Bill, had never trusted his partner Jimmy Jardine. He reckoned he was on the take, but Bill couldn't prove it. He looked at Kim, who recognised the significance of what she had said.

The meal was lovely, and after her third sherry, Mrs Dunn seemed a bit 'tiddly', so Vinny decided it was time to take the ladies home. When he dropped Kim off he handed her the file, kissed her goodbye, and headed home with Mrs Dunn.

The next day Brian Lawson gave them a bit of a shock.

"Right you pair, it seems that the top brass want your report within five weeks. Do you think it can be done? If not I have to speak to them."

"I don't know about Kim, but I think if we work very hard over the next few weeks, then we'll be ready. What about you Kim?"

"If we have to work at night then fine, I feel we need to get this restructuring up and running. We need a starting point."

"That's perfect, I'll let them know."

"Brian, just to let you know we're going to try and solve the killing of Bill Dunn before we go, but it won't affect the main aim."

"Bloody hell, you're asking a lot of yourselves, but if there's anything I can help you with, then please ask."

Over a coffee, Vinny and Kim started to work out a plan for the next five weeks.

"Vinny, I read the file, and I think we have to retrace Bill's footsteps that fateful night, but my gut is telling me that Jimmy Jardine is the key."

Chapter 7

Vinny spread it around the police stations that Bill's case would be re-opened, and if anybody could remember anything, no matter how small from back then, they were to contact the Liff street station. Even anonymously.

It only took a couple of days for information to come through. A plain envelope with Vinny's name on it, arrived in the post. When he read it, all it said was 'Ask Jimmy Jardine how he could afford a brand-new car on his so called retirement pension, considering either the pub or 'bookies' had got most of his wages.' There was nothing else. He put the letter in his drawer and locked it. He told Kim, and she suggested they would have to up the ante on this investigation, and why didn't they walk the route which Bill did that night. Vinny agreed, and said he would call on her at eight o'clock. He told Brian Lawson what they were going to do.

"Do you have a lead?"

"Sort off, but it's promising."

He picked up Kim, and they headed into the town, but parked well away from where they were going to investigate. Each had the route memorised, and what any witnesses had said, especially Jimmy Jardine.

As they walked along the route, they passed the pub Sinatras, which had a closing down soon sign on the window, with somebody scrawling the word 'again' on the outside glass.

"Bloody hell Kim, I was in there a few months back, and it seemed a busy pub. It shows how 'fickle' the pub trade can be."

They walked for a while until Vinny suddenly stopped, alarming Kim a bit, before taking her arm, and telling her they were going for a drink. He took her in to Sinatras, and asked her what she wanted. She asked for a soft drink, and asked him what the hell was going on. He ordered, but didn't say anything to Kim, except he started a casual conversation with barmaid, which made Kim feel a bit jealous.

"Excuse me. I'm sure this place was closing down several years ago, am I right.?"

"Listen, this bar has closed down several times over the years. Why?"

"It's just that I am writing a book on Dundee, and was doing a bit about the pubs."

"Well, you'll get all you need from the City licensing department, as any pub closing have to submit their licence to be revoked."

Vinny thanked her for her help.

"Oh, just one more thing, do you sell cigarettes?"

"There have never been cigarettes sold in this pub. The owners have never believed in that."

"What are you thinking Vinny?"

"Well, in Jimmy Jardine's statement he said he left Bill Dunn to walk on, as he went in here for cigarettes, putting his hands up to having a quick half pint, but what if this place was closed at the time, Kim. Did any of the inept officers actually check to see what Jardine had said was fact. Or, did they think that what he said was the truth, just because he was a police officer? I think we should walk to where Bill was found dead, and see what we find there."

They walked for about another fifteen minutes, before standing on the corner where Bill Dunn was fatally stabbed.

"Look all around you, and see if there is anything that stands out. After a while, Kim said, "The only thing that slightly stands out is that grubby looking pub down that road advertising 'music played here' every weekend."

"I've looked all around as well Kim, but like you, that's the only thing that stands out. However, we might be clutching at straws, but I think we should take this to Brian Lawson."

Vinny suggested that they head home. He arrived at her house, and gave her a long lingering kiss. He was of a mind to put his hand under her skirt to see if this was one of these times she was knicker less, however they were sitting right outside her gate, and he was sure he saw the curtains twitch, so he reluctantly reconsidered. He thought he would have to stop thinking about this, as it was just making him frustrated each time. He wondered which police area they would be tasked with restructuring first, because if it was Dundee, then he might think about renting a flat somewhere, just to have privacy for him and Kim. However, he didn't think Dundee needed that much cleaning up, so he would just have to wait a few weeks.

As he entered Liff Station next morning, he got the usual shout from Brian. Kim was already in his office.

"First things first. How did it go the other day at the Albach Trust Estate? I don't suppose you got to meet the supposed myth that is or was Denny Rey Foggerty did you?"

"Yeh, we bloody did Brian, and I am still a bit traumatised by it all. We even met his fucking Hounds from Hell."

"You're getting a bit worked up Kim. Care to tell me exactly what happened."

Kim shook her head, before Vinny started to tell him everything that had went on. Afterwards, he said that they had even met his beautiful little daughter, a nicer angelic little girl you couldn't hope to meet. Brian sat back and listened in awe.

"It would have been nice to meet him at some point. So he is obviously not a myth then. Did you take anything away from your visit?"

"There were a few things Brian, but you were right about one thing, and that was he told me I had to do this job my own way, trust absolutely no one. To hell with what other people say, always go with my gut instinct, but he came out with a strange thing, and that was he said he hoped we could do our job without killing people. Any idea what he was on about."

"Lots of rumours went around during his time in the force. He was supposedly brutal when he came up against people. There is a bit of a mystery as to what happened to the drug king who lived here in Dundee. So many stories about what happened to him, but everybody was in agreement that he didn't escape the clutches of Mr Foggerty. Well I hope you've got him out of your system."

"Brian, you don't meet a guy like that, and just get him out of your system. It was one hell of an experience. If you ever have to go after him for any reason, then I guarantee I will be on extended leave when that happens, or I might just be on his side. Trust me."

"Did you take anything from it Kim?"

"Yeh, I did Brian, and that was to take a spare pair of knickers if I every meet him again."

"What are you on about Kim?"

Kim told him all about it, and at the end, told him that this conversation would never leave the room, and to get the smile of both their faces.

"Okay folks, what about the Bill Dunn file. What progress have you made as time is of the essence."

"Here is where we're at, and before I go on can I say that Kim has played a big part in this. The key to all this is Jimmy Jardine. It was staring us in the face. There are too many anomalies in this investigation, and as you said yourself, the officers who investigated must have been totally inept, or and I don't say this lightly, corrupt. So we will present you with all the evidence we have, and you can give us your opinion, but before we do, do you have any connection to Jimmy Jardine or the officers who investigated? Oh, and don't take this the wrong way, but are you on 'the take' or not?"

"What the fuck are you on about Vinny Hunter? On 'the take? Why would you ask that?"

"Just to see from your face if you're lying on not, but don't worry I couldn't see anything in your face giving you away," said Vinny laughing.

Both of them presented their evidence to Brian who quickly read it, and put his head in his hands.

"I am so bloody angry with the officers, and also myself. It was just staring at us wasn't it. I take it you have no idea who sent you the note?"

"Not a clue Brian, but it makes sense, doesn't it."

"Right you pair, what's your next step?"

"Vinny will try and find out who owns the 'grotty' pub at the bottom of the street where Bill was killed, and how long they've had it. I'm contacting the Council Offices to see if their records can tell us if Sinatras was open at that time. Also we would like to see if Jimmy Jardine still has his car, and how much it would have cost back then? Then we need to sit down together, and work out the best way to proceed. Oh, and our main aim, the presentation of the restructuring, will only be another two or three weeks."

"Okay, I'll leave you to it, but I suggest we keep this to ourselves at present, as you never know if there was anybody else on the take back then who may still be here. I need to go as I'm really 'pissed off' hearing what you've just said. Another 'bent' copper for God's sake."

Kim said she would check with the council offices on Sinatras and to see if they could give any information on the pub at Kirk Lane. Vinny was going to work on the presentation, but would try and check on the cost of a new car back then.

Kim came through to the office that Vinny was working in a while later looking very happy.

"Just as we thought Vinny. Sinatras was closed at the time of the incident. The name of the pub at bottom on Kirk Lane is the Belford Arms, and the owner is a guy called Dave Wilson, but I can't get any info on him, so why don't we bring Bob Reynolds into our confidence, as he might know the pub, and the owner? Surely Brian would be okay with that."

"Great work Kim. There are a few things we need to speak about with regard to the presentation, so maybe we can go over it during the last hour. What do you say?"

"Sounds good to me. I was wondering if you fancy a walk tonight? Just a nice walk pal, as my periods started yesterday, so unfortunately you won't be inside me tonight, but don't worry sunshine I won't leave you frustrated," she said smiling.

Just then Brian walked in, and Kim took the opportunity to ask him about Bob Reynolds. He agreed that it would be a good idea, then proceeded to hand them each a warrant card. When they opened them up, they couldn't believe what they were seeing. They were both given the rank of Detective Sergeant.

"Bloody hell Brian, are you sure about this, as it seems that Kim and I haven't been in the force five minutes."

"You will both need that rank to do the job we've asked you to do."

"Oh, and by the way Brian, Sinatras was closed for renovations during the time that Bill Dunn died."

Brian Lawson looked at them, not saying a word, but Vinny could see he was livid. He just turned, and walked out slamming the door. Vinny looked at Kim. Ten minutes later Bob Reynolds walked in and asked if they wanted to speak to him

"Yeh we do Bob, and we would fully understand if you don't want to help us. We have reopened the cold case on Bill Dunn. We've spent a bit of our own time investigating his murder, and we have come up with several discrepancies in the statement of Jimmy Jardine. Which throws a lot of things in doubt, so we thought you might like to help us in any way possible?"

"Bill was a good friend, so yes I'll help you in anyway I can. If it means meeting up here at night, then so be it. I don't do a lot at nights now since my wife passed away a couple of years ago. Please tell me what you have so far, but I'll have to run my involvement past the boss, but I think he'll be all for it."

Kim read out everything they had jotted down, with Bob concentrating hard with his eyes closed.

"I always knew that snivelling weasel Jardine was no good. He was continually late, due to him struggling to get up in the morning after drinking the night before. His hygiene wasn't good, stinking of stale smoke, and always borrowing money which he never paid back, until everybody got wise to him. The new car makes sense, as I saw him sitting in it a few weeks after he retired, although we did wonder about why he retired early, as he only had twenty years service which wouldn't have given him that much of a pension. What is the plan of attack, and may I say congratulations on becoming detective sergeants, you will need that authority, trust me."

"I'm sorry to hear that about your wife Bob, but can I ask if you have ever thought about moving out of Dundee, but still doing the same job?"

"Not sure what you mean son, but maybe we'll speak about it soon."

That night as they walked through the park Kim asked him what he was speaking to Bob about? He told her that he wanted to have a team behind them when they started their restructuring project. He said Bob would be ideal, as he was a no-nonsense officer, and maybe a change of scenery might be good for him, but we should be looking to add to the team wherever we go, even if it's temporary.

When they got back to the car, Kim had said not to drive away just yet, as she was going to fulfil her promise, and not to let him get too frustrated. Vinny just smiled.

Bob came into Vinny's room the next morning.

"Are you and Ds Nicol up for coming a wee drive tonight, as it would be good to see if Jardine still has his car and to work out the cost of it back then. Possibly try and find out where he drinks, and what money he's spending."

"I would be up for it, but Kim isn't feeling that great, but if she feels okay to come then fine. I'll pick you up about eight. How does that sound Bob?"

"No car Vinny, as it sticks out like a sore thumb, so I suggest it will be bus and taxis for us, and remember to keep your receipt for any transport we take. How about we meet in the centre, and I'll get Jardine's address from the records office. See you then."

When he left, Vinny thought what a great asset he would be to the team.

Kim had to go home as she wasn't feeling well, due to the time of the month, so Vinny just plodded on with the restructuring project. He felt things were beginning to come together, and they had put down some revolutionary good ideas.

When he got home that night, after tea he lay on the bed, but made sure he didn't fall asleep, but instead went over everything he had to find out about Bill Dunn's case. He realised he had no experience of this since he entered the force, so he knew he would have to rely on Brian Lawson's and Bob's experience. He got the seven thirty bus into the town, and when he got off he recognised Bob right away, well that wasn't difficult he thought.

"Are you up for this Vinny? I have Jardine's address which is on an estate not that far from here. Also, I know where he drinks, so a pint might be in order later."

They walked for a while before arriving at the Hilltown estate.

"His address is just past this block of flats, so lets hope he has left his car outside."

There it was, a five-year-old red Ford Escort. This had to be his. Vinny memorised the number plate, but Bob had a better idea. He wandered over to where a bunch of kids were kicking a ball about.

"Any of you lads know whose car that is over there, the red one?"

"Why do you want to know mister, are you the 'polis, cause if you are I'm not saying."

"Ah don't worry son, I'm sure it's Jimmy Jardine's car, however there was going to be fifty pence in it for the first person who confirms it to me."

Bob thought he was going to be overwhelmed by the lot of them. They were giving him a lot of information about Jardine, as they were virtually fighting over who was going to get the money. Bob walked back to where Vinny was standing.

"Well, what happened there Bob."

"They confirmed it is his, but more importantly one of the kids said he was boasting about getting the car from a guy who owns a pub in the town, he had heard his dad speaking about it. Right, let's get to the watering hole and see that bastard Jardine, but please follow my lead Vinny."

As they walked back to the centre, Bob told Vinny they were heading to the Masonic Hall, which was open to the public, but Bob warned Vinny it was a bit grotty. When they got there Bob said to Vinny to be two faced, and if Jardine asked you anything, then lie through your teeth. They entered through swing door into a large hall, with their feet sticking to the carpet, with the bar over to the left.

Bob nodded at several guys sitting at a table over by the window.

"He's the one with the receding hair which is going grey."

They moved to the bar where Bob ordered a pint, and was cheeky enough to ask for a clean glass, and a soft drink for Vinny. As they stood there, they saw Jardine passing a twenty-pound note to one of his cronies, who walked up to the bar and ordered five pints of heavy. They sat down at one of the tables where Bob had hoped Jardine would see him.

After half an hour, Jardine eventually noticed Bob.

"Hey Bob, how are you doing," Jardine shouted over the room.

He came over to their table, and grabbed Bob's hand and started shaking it vigorously, obviously half 'pissed'. Bob played along as if they were long lost cousins.

"Good to see you Jimmy, what've you been up to pal?"

"Oh this and that. I'm doing a bit of security at the Belford Arms on a Friday and Saturday night. What about yourself Bob? And who's this guy ?"

Vinny took the initiative and said, "Billy Clark at your service. I take it you were on the force with Bob then. Were you good pals? I've just started on the force, so it's nice to meet an other officer, even though you've now retired."

"Best of pals son we were. It's been nice seeing the pair, but I need to go and get my pint before it goes flatter than it already is. Don't be a stranger Bob."

Bob finished his pint, and nodded towards the door. When they got outside, Bob leant against the wall and breathed deeply.

"Let's get the fuck out of here before I start to lose it."

"That was quite impressive Bob. Good acting skills," said Vinny laughing.

Just before they headed off home, Bob said he would hear what Vinny was on about regarding leaving Dundee.

When Kim walked in the next morning looking like 'death warmed up', Brian Lawson sent her home right away. Although she was protesting, he told her they would see her tomorrow, if she was okay.

"Okay, but Vinny can you come over when you finish today, and give me an update on everything that's been going on?"

Vinny said he would, and offered to run her home, but she said the bus would be quicker in the rush hour.

Brian surprisingly made Vinny and Bob a coffee, before asking them what happened last night. Bob suggested that Vinny explain everything, as it was going to be his case. When he had finished, Brian sat contemplating for a couple of minutes.

"At this stage, have either of you any doubt that Jardine is mixed up in this?"

"I don't think he killed Bill, but I think he was instrumental in setting him up," said Bob.

"Everything is pointing to him Brian, but let me try and find out how much his car was worth back then. Also, I think we should find out all about the Belford Arms. Obviously, who the owner is and what his background is. Maybe Bob can find out from any of his one hundred percent trusted pals what the word is out on the street about the pub. No disrespect Bob."

"None taken son. I'll see what I can do."

"Okay folks, let get moving with this as we don't know if Vinny or Kim will be here very much longer, but the hierarchy have been known to drag their arses on things like this." Keep me informed, and as we we've agreed before, lets keep the secrecy going, or we'll just have wasted our time."

When Brian left, Bob stayed where he was. Vinny knew that he was waiting to hear what Vinny had to say about the restructuring.

"Well Bob, as you know, Kim and I have been tasked to restructure all the police forces in Scotland. Why they would ask us beats me, however it would appear that we get to pick our own team. It would consist of three people, plus someone from the area we're in at that time. So, here it comes Bob. How would you like to join Kim and I to make up the team? We need an experienced officer, and you certainly fit the bill. We'll need advice as we go along. The only problem is that we're sure we'll be starting the program elsewhere, which means everyone leaving Dundee. What do you think?"

"Leaving Dundee is not a problem son, as my wife died a few years ago, and my only son lives in New Zealand. My wife is not in any cemetery, as she was cremated, so that wouldn't be a tie. I do have a lady friend here in Dundee, but nothing serious, more the company, but on saying that she has no ties here either, and might like a change. However I am getting ahead of myself. Give me few days to think about it, but Brian might not be up for it."

"If he isn't up for it, then how about Kim and I telling him to stick his job up his arse? As told to me by Denny Rey Foggerty."

"Foggerty? Are you bloody serious? Well that's a story I would like to hear, and do you think the three of us telling Brian to stick his job might have a bearing on his decision?"

"Okay, let's concentrate on Jardine, but what I'll do Bob, is give you a copy of our report to read, so that will help you make up your mind. Sound?"

"Good for me lad, but can I ask you something? "What happens if all the restructuring plan goes belly up."

"Then I'm off. Where? I don't know, but I couldn't do the job you do everyday. Maybe try and find my mother, maybe go back to Drumbrig, and beat the shit out of all the wife beating scum, or just pack a holdall, and walk the roads looking for work. I'm not proud."

"Do you know what son; I believe you and admire you for that."

"I'm heading into town now Bob, as I want to wander past the Belford Arms. Might even have a Coca Cola, and just try to make sense of the place."

"Bloody hell son, that could be dangerous. Do you want me to come with you?"

"No disrespect again Bob, but you would stick out like a sore thumb. How about you trying to contact the garage that sold the Escort to Jardine, and find out who actually paid for it. I'm sure you'll persuade them to hand over the information."

Vinny walked out without telling Brian Lawson. He felt it was time to make decisions, and he would sink or swim on his own. He walked into the centre, and headed for the Belford Arms.

As he walked down the road to the pub, he just knew this place would be connected to Bill's killing. Bells were going off in his head. As he walked through the door, he thought it might have been a mistake not taking up Bob's offer. He sat down at the bar, and waited for the barman to finish pouring a guy's pint.

"Just a coke please pal. Normally, I would have a pint and whisky chaser, but I'm driving."

"Are you waiting for somebody?" asked the barman.

"Yeh, I'm up from Fife with the girl, and unfortunately she loves shopping, so I just bailed. Anywhere other than clothes shops."

"You got a name pal?" asked the barman.

"Barney Anderson at your service my friend," said Vinny holding out his hand for the barman to shake, which he did reluctantly.

He engaged the man in conversation, mainly about the type of music that was played in the place. Eventually, Vinny said cheerio and walked out.

Just as soon as the door closed behind him, a guy walked through from the back.

"Who the fuck was that Gordon?"

"Just some yokel up from Fife, who thought I was his best pal. A right prick."

"I'll get Jamie to tail him to see where he ends up."

Vinny was expecting this, and at the top of the street he went into his pocket, and casually took some coins out before spilling a few on the ground. As he bent down to retrieve them, he didn't lift his head up, but instead just lifted his eyes to see who was tailing him. He walked on, and at one point sat on a bench just watching the people going about their business. The guy that was following him was terrible at it, and so obvious, but Vinny knew he had to get rid of him soon.

He walked over to a busy clothes store and wandered in, while looking at his watch. Shaking his head, as if he was getting fed up with the time his girlfriend was taking. He wandered through the store for about half an hour, continually looking out the big glass windows on the front of the store. The 'tail' was getting a bit antsy, and wasn't really keeping an eye on the front door. Vinny thought it was time to lose him.

He walked down the stairs, and by chance there was a young lady walking to the front door, while struggling to carry several large bags packed with clothes.

"I'm just going to my car, but can I help you with your bags as you seem to have your hands full?"

"Thank you, that would be wonderful. My car is just along the road."

He escorted her out while chatting about shopping mainly, which made her laugh. They were about fifty yards from the shop, when he looked in a car wing mirror and saw the young lad heading off back to the pub.

"Well this is my car, and once again thank you for your help," the young lady said.

Vinny said his goodbyes and walked for five minutes, before stopping in the doorway of a pub. He waited for about another ten minutes, but by then he was convinced that nobody was following him. He headed straight back to the police station and was met by a rather stern looking Brian Lawson.

"Where the hell have you been Vinny? Bob said you were away following up a lead. You can't just go off on your own like that without some sort of back up for God's sake."

"Point taken Brian. I did run it past Bob, and to be fair to him he did offer to come with me, but I convinced him I would be fine. However, I think we should shout Bob through so that I can tell you both what happened."

As the three of them sat chatting over a 'cuppa' it was Brian who said, "Well, I think the Belford Arms has something to hide don't you think. What's your thoughts on putting 'eyes' on the place?"

"My inexperienced opinion is that we should focus on Jardine, and get as much evidence as we can, then bring him in and really 'squeeze' him, until he gives us something, and I think the dominoes will start to fall."

"Bob, what do you think?"

"Brian, I agree with Vinny, but please make sure that if we get any evidence against Jardine, then it's enough and watertight. Oh, and by the way Jardine's car was bought for £800 by a guy just walking in off the street, and driving it away. So, we have to be very careful, as he could say one of his pals had bought it for him, which would be hard to disprove."

They all agreed that they would up the ante on Jardine, and speak in a couple of days, as to how they would do it.

Vinny headed home via Kim's house. When he rang the bell, her mother answered the door, but warned him she wasn't very well. When he entered the living room she was lying on the couch with a cover over her, and a pillow under her head. She had been sleeping, but managed a smile for him.

"Vinny I'm sorry, but can you sit away from me, as I must have caught a bug or something, and I have been vomiting all last night. You can then tell me everything that's been going on."

Vinny brought her up to speed, and she seemed quite surprised at the progress they had made in such a short time. After a while he could see she was getting tired, so he said he was off, and would give her a ring tomorrow.

"I would like to give you a kiss, but best not to."

"Listen Vinny Hunter, I haven't had a bath for about thirty-six hours, so I don't think you will want to come near me."

"A right Dundee 'minger' young Nicol," he said laughing as he walked out the door.

He heard her laughing before he closed the door. He headed home, and before his tea, he started jotting notes down for the restructuring and the Bill Dunn case.

When he had finished his breakfast the next morning, he phoned Kim's house, and got her mother who said she'd had a really good night, and was up walking about, but still weak. She was in the bath, so he left a message saying he would call in after work.

When he got to the station, Brian shouted him in, where Bob was sitting.

"Right Vinny, Bob has something to say to us. Okay Bob, off you go."

"Well, here we go. Brian, a couple of days ago Vinny asked me if I would like to join his team when he starts the restructuring of the police forces. I said I needed a couple of days to think about it. I have, and I would like to join the team, if that is sanctioned by yourself."

"Well Vinny, you've rather blindsided me with this. However Bob, I feel it might be a good move for you."

"Brian, have you any idea where this project would start?" asked Vinny.

"The consensus from the big bosses is that it would be in the Borders. Lovely area, but a 'shit' police force with 'crap' personnel, but please don't quote me on that. Vinny how far are you away from finishing the report?"

"Kim being off has put us back a bit, but probably about another three or four weeks."

"Okay, here's what I am going to do. Bob will now be seconded to work with you and Kim on the project as well as the Bill Dunn case. However, I fear we may have taken on too much, so I'll get involved in trying to nail Jardine. We all in agreement?"

They nodded, while grinning.

Vinny thought it prudent to let Bob read the report he and Kim had written up. He wanted to make sure he agreed with everything. Bob came back after a few hours, and pointed out a few things that needed adjusting. Vinny would never have thought about what Bob had suggested.

"I've just opened my mail, and this letter was in it," said Brian.

It read, "Belford Arms, cigarettes and now drugs. Si Kramer."

"This is somebody who knows a lot more than we do. The Belford comes into the equation again. Maybe Bill had got a tip-off regarding cigarette smuggling? It might be that they have progressed to drugs, I'm not sure. As to the name Si Kramer, I haven't a clue."

"I have," said Bob with an air of menace in his voice.

"He is or was back then a thug for hire. He would do anything for money. Wouldn't say he was the hardest of men, but he could be very handy with a knife. Bill was stabbed wasn't he. He would have to have been ambushed, as he could handle himself. Another name we have to look into, but that means more secrecy, as we don't want anybody doing a runner, plus once we interview Jardine we have to make out that we have enough evidence to charge him, so we can remand him until we can go after anybody else."

"Good thinking Bob. This has to be done with speed and precision, and I would like to throw in the word, ruthlessness, " said Vinny.

"I'm going to speak to one of my colleagues who I can trust, from Edinburgh, and ask him about any information on cigarette smuggling. However, I don't want them involved, as they'll just come in and stomp all over this case. I'm pleased at the speed this case is going, and at the sound of blowing my own trumpet, I think we make a good team. However, please think about this. We need a real breakthrough. Right, let's get to work."

"Okay Brian. Kim should be back tomorrow, so I'll get her to work with me, while you and Bob get on with Bill's case. Personally, I don't think we will get much more evidence on Jardine, but I think we should look into the owner of the Belford Arms, Dave Wilson. Let's see if he comes up in any of our old investigations."

With Kim back, the report would just about be ready after another couple of weeks. Although Kim was working hard, again she didn't seem to be happy in her work. Vinny was starting to get worried about her, but he couldn't take his eye off the ball. This report had been very hard on both of them, but he hoped it would be completed soon.

One night, when every one had left, he sat her down and asked her what was wrong with her. She burst out crying, and Vinny thought that this was going to be the end of their relationship. She said that she had been receiving anonymous calls from a person trying to hide his voice from her, although she knew it was her old boyfriend. Her mum had been the victim of these prank calls as well.

"Kim, why didn't you tell me for God's sake. You can't bottle something like this up."

"I don't want you doing anything that will jeopardise your job. Some of the things he is inferring is making me scared. Not just for me, but mum and dad. I'll deal with it."

"Not on your own Kim. I'm going to sort this out, but I need you to show me what he looks like, and where he likes to drink or where he works. He's not going to do that to you never mind anybody else."

He phoned for a taxi to take her home, telling the driver to wait outside until she was inside, and when she had left, he went to see Brian Lawson who was working late. When he told him what was happening he was very angry.

"Vinny, this shouldn't be happening to anybody at anytime, but this is bad timing for the team. Leave it with me, and I'll let you know tomorrow what we can do, but please don't try and take this into your own hands. Understood?"

Vinny went home that night via Kim's house, and had a word with her parents, telling them that the police would sort this out, and not to worry about it.

"Kim, I need you to point out this scumbag to me. I won't interfere in this as Brian Lawson has said he would deal with it. However, if he can't then I will. Do you know where he'll be tonight?"

"He'll be in the Globe pub, as he is most nights.

"Okay, let's get your coat. Don't worry, he won't see you. If you can see him through the window then fine, if not, then quickly look through the door with me shielding you, and let me know where he's sitting."

They parked well away from the pub. When they were there, he asked her to look through the window, and see if he was there. She pointed him out, and he told her to go back to the car, and lock all the doors.

"Vinny, please don't get into any trouble over me."

Vinny walked in, and went to the bar and ordered an orange juice. When he looked around he could see the bar was like any other city centre pub. It definitely needed a bit of work done on the interior. He strolled over to the guy's table, and sat down virtually tight up against him. The guy hadn't been paying attention, and got a shock when Vinny sat down.

"Who the fuck are you 'ya balloon', get away from me, before I punch your lights out."

"Now we both know that's not going to happen, don't we? Unless I was a girl, because it seems you can only pick on girls, doesn't it 'dick brain'. You see the young lady I am going out with is Kim Nicol. I'm sure you will remember her, as you made her life a misery in the past. I'm not going to smash your head in today, but what I will say is that as from today all the malicious phone calls will stop. If not, then you will regret it. I bid you farewell."

"You can't tell me what to do. It's not as if your the fucking 'polis' are you?"

Vinny just stopped, turned around, and smiled, while walking out the door. Kim was standing along the road when he came out, instead of being in the car.

"Right Kim let's walk slowly to the car, and if I turn round, then on no account do you. Just keep looking at me."

They were near the car when Vinny pretended to look over the street, only to see Kim's ex-boyfriend looking at them from the pub doorway. He told her to keep walking when they got to the car. They walked another ten minutes, until they couldn't be seen from the pub before doubling back. Eventually, Vinny thought it clear to drive back home.

"Kim, I'll speak to your mum and dad when we get back, as it's important that we all know what's going to happen. Okay?"

Kim just sat and nodded her head. When they got back they went into the house where her mum and dad were waiting.

"Mr and Mrs Nicol, I've something to explain to you. I met with Kim's scum of an ex-boyfriend, and I made it plain I would sort him out if the phone calls didn't stop. However, that was just a ruse on my part. I hope I have provoked him into sending you more calls. That might seem strange, but steps are already being put into place to catch him. Remember, your daughter is a serving police officer, and any harassment to her will be dealt with very severely. I have no doubt the calls will escalate, but I assure you, you will be in no danger. This is just a coward thinking that he can do what he wants. Oh, and please don't mention to anybody anything I've said today, as my boss has warned me about getting involved. He will be the one to sort this guy out, and I promise he will. Is that fine by all of you?"

The Nicols thanked him, and Kim gave him a big kiss before he said he was off home. He felt just as angry as Brian Lawson. He wondered if it would be possible to 'fit' the guy up with another crime. Now he thought he was just being absurd, and put all thoughts from his mind, but he would think about it if Brian couldn't do very much.

Next morning came and he was sitting up in bed, just as he had been for half the night. He found life hard not being able to speak to Barney and Billy. He wondered where he would be now if that fateful night in Dunfermline hadn't happened. Would he be working on the farm, and continually hoping one of the Polish girls would creep into his bed at night. Maybe going to visit Billy, wherever he would have been stationed. He realised he was becoming silly now, so he tried to clear his mind, just as Mrs Dunn shouted that his bath was ready.

He met Kim on the steps of the station, and he asked her how she was, she replied she was fine. When they got in Brian motioned his head for them to come into his room. When they got in, there was a guy standing in front of a machine on the table.

"This is Arthur folks. What he doesn't know about technology isn't worth knowing. I'll let him tell you about the machine he has in front of him."

"It would have been nicer to meet you under better circumstances, but please let me explain about this machine here. We'll put it in Miss Nicol's house, connected to the house phone. You and your folks will use the phone as normal, but when the crank phone calls are received then try and explain to your folks to try and engage with whoever it is on the end of the phone for as long as they can. Tell them not to hang up, and if need be ask the person who it is, and why he is doing this. Talk about anything. The call will be recorded, and we should be able to eventually find out which telephone exchange they're coming from, and even the number. It might take a few weeks, but if you play your part, then I can guarantee you we will find him and arrest him. Offences like this against police officers can carry a mandatory sentence of up to five years."

Vinny could see that Kim was a bit shaken, and he knew he would have to have another talk to her about toughening up. He was getting fed up doing this, so this talk had to be the mother of all talks.

Vinny and Kim worked hard over the next few weeks to finish the report, but Vinny thought they were neglecting each other due to their workload. One night he was feeling a bit sexually frustrated, so he asked Kim to come into the office where he was working. By the look on his face, she had an inkling as to what he was thinking. When she was in, he locked the door, and lifted her onto the table, lifted her skirt up and removed her knickers. She opened his trousers, and grabbed his penis. It took only a moment for him to get hard, and enter her. She put her legs around his hips and her arms around his chest. They were both loving it while thrusting their hips together, but Vinny knew there was an officer on the front desk, and couldn't fully concentrate just in case he was doing the rounds checking the offices. Kim seemed like she didn't care one bit, and when she climaxed she let out a squeal. Vinny was taking forever, but he eventually climaxed, with Kim giving a little groan.

They quickly got off the table while laughing, and got dressed. Kim took out a paper hankie and wiped the table, so that they wouldn't leave a stain on it.

"Bloody hell Kim I needed that. I don't know about you, but I hope if we end up in the Borders, we might have at least a police house that we can share together. If you feel that's good for you too."

"A house together would be great, but what are you talking about, the Borders?"

"I should have mentioned it Kim, but Brian reckons if the restructuring gets the go ahead, then it will start in the Borders."

"Vinny, I never thought about having to leave home. Mum and dad have always been a part of my life, and the thought of leaving them fills me with dread."

Vinny knew the time had come for that talk with her.

"Listen Kim, and listen well. You're being a pain in the arse about lots of things. Maybe you should have left the house a long time ago, especially at your age. What did you think was going to happen when the restructuring was going to take place for God sake. We have spent the best part of a year on this, and now I'm not so sure you are going to be up for it. What are you playing at?"

By this time Kim was in tears, and Vinny lost it again.

"You need to stop shedding tears when things don't go right for you. I really don't know what you've been thinking about over the last year. Hell Kim, the Borders are only just over a couple of hours away, not the other side of the world . You can come up or they can come down. I suggest you head home, and have a right think about where you want to be. Speak to your folks, but when you come back tomorrow, you had better be honest, and tell me what you want to do. I need to know if you're onside, otherwise I will look for another officer to be part of this team. Got it?"

Kim picked up her bag not looking at Vinny, and went home.

Chapter 8

Kim didn't appear until later the next morning, and Brian Lawson commented on it, but she just looked right through him, and walked into the office she was working out of. Brian looked at Vinny who just said, "It was crunch talks last night Brian, and the fact she turned up is a plus point."

Vinny wandered into her office.

"You okay Kim?"

"I'm fine Vinny, but we'll speak after work, so now get lost, and let me get on with my work."

Vinny knew that it was going to be a long day, until Brian shouted for Kim and him as well as Bob to come into his office. He appeared to be quite excited, and motioned for them to sit down.

"Good news folks. A guy who worked in the garage that sold the car that Jardine was given, has just walked in with information as to who bought it. It was a guy who worked for Davie Wilson, the owner of the Belford Arms. He said he no longer worked at the garage, but he was the one that handled the transaction for the garage owner. He said he even counted the cash, and would testify to that. He had heard that we'd been asking about it, and didn't want to be implicated in any police matter. Where does that leave us now?"

"I'll tell you where it leaves us folks. We should be bringing that little weasel Jardine in, and promise him the earth if he gives us all the people involved in Bill's murder. Naturally we will be lying through our teeth," said Bob.

"Is everybody agreeing?"

Both Vinny and Kim agreed immediately, with Brian being slightly hesitant.

"We'll have to watch this everybody. Jardine could turn round, and say Davie Wilson is a mate, and that's why he got the car."

"We know that Brian, but if we can convince him that we have a lot more evidence on him, then his alcoholic brain won't be able to comprehend what's happening. Tell him whoever gives a statement first will get an easy time of it, but like Bob says, we lie, lie and lie. Making sure the tape recorder is off at the right time."

"Isn't that illegal what we're doing?"

The three of them turned round and just stared at Kim. She realised what she had just said, and put her hands up in a sort of apology.

"Vinny you and Bob, as soon as I have the warrant for his arrest, go and pick Jardine up at his favourite watering hole, and I suggest you don't be too gentle in bringing him in. I know it will be difficult, but try and get him alone in the pub, as we don't want any of his cronies contacting Davie Wilson. Good hunting."

They waited for three hours before the warrant arrived. They then took off with Vinny driving. Bob making sure Vinny was going in the right direction. Both of them seemed uplifted with what they were going to do. Afterall this was Vinny's first arrest. Traffic was slow, and they reached the Masonic Hall at about two o'clock. They parked the car slightly away from the front door. Bob looked through one of the windows, and said, "He's sitting with two of his so-called mates. You just stand inside the front door, and I'll put my head through the internal glass door and shout him over."

Vinny was waiting inside the front door when Bob just stuck his head through the glass door, and shouted on Jimmy Jardine, while waving his hand for him to come over. He saw Jardine speaking to his pals, who it seemed couldn't care less. Jardine walked over to the door, and just before he got there said, "Glad to see you pal."

"Well I'm not glad to see you, you little fucker."

Bob grabbed Jardine and pulled him through the door, not caring that his head smacked off the side of the door. Vinny put him against the wall, brought his arms around his back, and cuffed him.

"Jimmy Jardine, you have been arrested for being complicit in the death of police constable Bill Dunn."

Vinny went on to read him his rights. He thought how good that felt.

Bob grabbed him by the scruff of the neck, marched him to the car, and threw him in the back.

"What the fuck is going on here. I never had anything to do with Bill's death. What are you playing at?"

"We have you bang to rights Jardine," said Vinny who was sitting next to him.

"Who are you to say that to me?"

Vinny took out his warrant card and showed it to him and said, "Ds Hunter, Mr Jardine. I'm sure we will be having some interesting conversations over the next few days."

Half an hour later they were marching him through the station doors. All the officers came from inside their rooms, and stood staring at Jardine; which made him start shaking. Lots of them started swearing at him, until Brian came out and told them to go about their duties.

"Put him in interview room number three lads, and get the recorder set up please. Then come in and see me."

When they went to Brian's room, he told them to go and get a coffee, and something to eat, as he wanted Jardine to sweat it out.

"How are we going to play this out Brian? Good cop, bad cop? I think we should do what we talked about. Promise him an easy time, but we should emphasis that he has to give us who ordered the killing of Bill, and who actually did the deed. However I want to be the one who interrogates him with Bob at my side."

"Vinny, you are relatively inexperienced in this, but if Bob agrees then I'll go along with it. Although, I will be watching, and listening at the side window."

Bob just nodded and sipped his tea.

Vinny went through to Kim's office, and asked her to get all the paperwork for him. She had anticipated this, and had them all in a file ready. He thanked her, and looked around to see if anybody was looking before trying for a kiss. She quickly turned her head away, before getting on with work in front of her. Vinny thought the talk between them later would be very interesting indeed.

He walked into the Brian's office and handed the file to Bob, and asked him to give it a once over to make sure they have everything. Bob read the first half a dozen papers.

"Vinny, what are all these papers at the back of the file. It's just a lot of blank pages?"

"Not quite Bob. That is all the evidence we have accrued on Jardine, but he won't know that" said Vinny grinning.

"That will do for me son. Let's go and get us a conviction."

As they went into the interview room, Jardine was shouting that they had nothing on him with regard to the killing. When they sat down they saw that beads of sweat had formed on Jardine's forehead. It hadn't helped him that Brian had cranked the central heating up in the room, while Jardine sat it out. He looked very uncomfortable sitting on his hard chair, while Bob and Vinny had brought through two soft cushions to sit on.

"Well Mr Jardine, you know why you're here, don't you?"

"I'm here on a trumped up charge you bastards. You couldn't find Bill Dunn's killer, so now you want to pin it on me. Well, you can go and fuck yourselves."

"Mr Jardine, I am Ds Hunter, and I am sure you know Dc Reynolds. If its okay with you, I will call you by your first name."

Vinny made a show of slamming down the folder in front of him.

"Jimmy, this thick folder, holds every bit of evidence we have on you. Do you think we would be charging you with such a serious charge if we hadn't done our homework? Very soon I will make you an offer, and if you turn it down, then I pity you. So let's get started. Where were you on the night of the fifth of April nineteen seventy-two? "

"How am I suppose to know that you plonkers? It was years ago. I can't even remember where I was last week."

Bob slammed his fist on the desk giving Jardine a fright.

"Listen you cretin. That was the night you were supposed to be on duty with Bill Dunn. Supposedly having each other's backs, but no, you let Bill be killed. Didn't you? Ds Hunter, I think we should charge him with Bill's murder, and get this 'crap' over with."

"Ds Reynolds, I think we should give Mr Jardine the chance to comment after we've presented him with the evidence we have, after all he was one of us," said Vinny while nudging Bob with his knee.

This was just an act between the pair, but Jardine didn't pick up on it. Bob just slowly nodded.

"Okay Mr Jardine, I am going to show you a copy of your statement back then, that stated you 'nipped' into the Sinatras bar for cigarettes, and you quickly had a half pint, while Bill walked on. Is that correct?"

"That's exactly what happened. It's the truth, and I don't have to read it."

"You see Mr Jardine, that can't be the truth, as during that period of time, Sinatras bar was closed for renovations, so there is no way that what you told the investigating officers is true. What do you say to that."

Jimmy Jardine went pale before saying, "Well, it must have been another pub on that road then."

"Sorry Mr Jardine. There are no pubs on that route. Trust me, as I have walked the route with another officer, so what are we supposed to think. We also have the matter of a new car being given to you by a man called Davie Wilson of the Belford Arms. A lot of money's worth back then. The Belford Arms is only a stone's throw from where Bill Dunn was killed. Do you see where this is going Mr Jardine?"

"I'll tell you Ds Hunter. He is a snivelling little weasel, and he is going to jail for life," Bob shouted at him.

"I think we'll give you a bit of time to think about this Jimmy, but don't be too long as my boss is at the moment speaking to the Procurator Fiscal, and by their last phone call, he thinks we have a good case. See you in a while. I'll get an officer to bring you in some water."

They both smiled when they were out the door. Kim walked out of her office, and asked how it had went. Vinny asked her to take a glass of water into Jardine, and assess his well being.

When she came out she grinned, and said the sweat was lashing from him, and reckoned he had been crying. Bob and Vinny just grinned. They went through to Brian Lawson's office, and told him what had been going on.

"That's good lads, but I have spoken to the Fiscal, and he reckons we need a confession, as we don't have enough evidence. Do you think you can get one?"

"He's beginning to feel very uncomfortable, and Kim thought he had been crying," said Bob.

"Look, if we have to set him free we may have to close this case for good, as he'll go running to whoever was involved in the killings. Try for that confession."

They waited another twenty minutes while they got a coffee, before going back in.

"Okay Jimmy, here is what we've just heard. The Fiscal thinks that with a sympathetic judge we have a good case for a guilty verdict, and you know what that means Jimmy. Life in jail with no hope of parole, and somehow a 'cop' in jail isn't going to fair very well. What do you think Bob?"

"I think there'll be a lot of boiling water being mixed with sugar. God, I would hate that to be poured over my face. What do you think Jimmy. Although, what I'm going to say may be a life saver for you. You see, neither my colleague or I think you actually killed Bill, but you need to tell us who did, and who ordered the killing. We will then look at a very short prison sentence in a soft prison, which will be just like a holiday camp. Anything less, then you can go and fuck yourself, as we will recommend life. At this stage I am getting 'pissed' off speaking to you, so I'm all for just going with the fiscal on this. Life for you Jardine. Let's go Ds Hunter."

They had no sooner closed the door on their way out, when they heard Jardine shouting.

When they went back in, he was sitting crying.

"Okay, I'll tell you my involvement in Bill Dunn's killing, but I don't want to do hard time, with the minimum time to serve, do you hear? I was supposed to make sure I wasn't around when Bill got to the top of the road where the Belford Arms is. He had been watching the pub for a while, as he thought that the owner Davie Wilson was smuggling cigarettes into Scotland, and distributing them through his pub. Bill was obsessed, and we would stand for ages at the top of the street, just watching which 'pissed' me off no end. He was only supposed to be 'roughed' up, and warned to stay away from the pub, but Davie had chosen the wrong guy who instead knifed Bill. When I came on the scene, Bill was dead. There was nothing I could do for him, I swear."

"Okay Jimmy, if you want to salvage anything for yourself, then who killed him?"

They could see he was starting to shake now, but they needed a name. Vinny phoned through to Kim, and asked her for more water for Jardine. She came in, and handed Jardine a glass of water. When he had finished Vinny and Bob knew it was time to go for the jugular.

"If you're the one to get the best deal Jimmy, then I need you to tell me who killed Bill Dunn?"

It was apparent that he was nervous, but eventually he just blurted it out.

"Si Kramer."

As they left the room, Vinny asked Bob if it was the same guy that he had mentioned before with Bob just nodding. Brian suggested they go to his office, and work out their next move. He shouted on Kim to come through.

"Here's my thoughts on this. Jardine has never asked for a lawyer, so I can only assume he is rattled, and has not been thinking straight. We need to get him to sign his statement, we'll get you Kim to type it, and ask for him to sign the typed copy as well. This is a crucial time for us, and Kim please make sure there are absolutely no mistakes in the typed copy. Get Bob to go over it, and then Vinny you read it. After he's signed it, go home quickly for a change of clothes, as we're going on a raid about four o'clock in the morning. Before you go Bob, please find out where this Si Kramer lives."

After the statement was signed, Vinny sat with Kim going over every word, while Bob was phoning some of his contacts for Kramer's address. It wasn't long before he found the address in the Hilltown Estate. Brian went and told several officers to get a change of clothes as well, but he didn't tell them why, just that they wouldn't be going home to their beds tonight.

"Oh, and Pc Graham, please take money out of the petty cash, and go to the 'chippy' to get that bastard Jardine a pie supper."

"On one condition boss, and that is I can spit on it before I give it to him."

"Fine by me Pc Graham, as long as you're not seen."

"Right folks let's take it in turn to go home and get ourselves ready. Chop, chop."

Vinny ran Kim home, and he could have cut the silence with a knife, while they were in the car. He was quite glad when he had changed his clothes at Mrs Dunn's house, and got back to the station, after picking Kim up. The wait was long, and there was only so much coffee and tea they could take. At about two in the morning, Brian had gathered everybody together. There were seven officers, plus Vinny and Bob. Kim was to be the radio operator, with both Bob and Vinny supplied with a two-way radio each. All they could do was sit about the offices. Some were reading, some doing crosswords, but Vinny had found a comfy seat, and was sitting sleeping, which surprised Brian Lawson.

"Right everybody let's go, Brian Lawson shouted at three o'clock. We're off to Hilltown. Bob will tell you where you'll be positioned at the tenement. Don't bloody dare come back and say you lost him, by all accounts he was seen going into the flats earlier, and hasn't come out."

"You coming Brian?" asked Vinny.

" Not me Ds Reynolds is, as I couldn't trust myself. I'll leave it to you and Ds Hunter."

"Boss, I think you got my rank wrong there," said Bob.

" A bit premature on my part Bob, but you will be before or if, you head to the Borders, now head out, and bring me Kramer, or you might be writing parking tickets until you retire."

Bob rounded everybody up with a smile on his face. The seven officers were to go in the police van, and Vinny and Bob in the car. Nothing was said between them during the journey. The police van driver had been told to stop about one hundred yards from the tenement main doors. When they were all gathered, it was Bob who started giving the instructions, as Vinny had never been involved in this type of operation before.

"Right, I need you Pc Graham at the bottom of the stairwell next to the front covering both the stairs and lift, I'll bet my last pound that the lift will be out of order, but take no chances. You two officers head around the back, if Kramer does a runner then he'll head down the back stairs. Remember everybody, you all have shields and truncheons, so don't be loath to use them as this bastard could be carrying a knife. Okay, let's go Dundee's finest. Let's be heroes."

With the front and back covered, Bob led everybody else up the stairs as quietly as possible. Vinny's heart was thumping, so he thought the other officers would be the same. Bob took the 'big red key' from one of the officer. He 'mouthed' one, two, three, before virtually smashing the door of its hinges. Vinny was first in and went through the door of the bedroom. As he ran for the bed, a female was screaming her head off. Kramer was still lying there confused as to what was happening. Vinny was virtually shoved out of the way by Bob, who went to the bed, turned Kramer over, knelt on his back, with him screaming, and handcuffed him.

"Ds Hunter, please read this scum his rights. After which, you lot take him downstairs. If he doesn't want to walk then drag the bastard, even if it's feet first. Vinny, you and I will search this place, but let's make sure we get a statement from the girl in the next room, although I think it will be useless."

They were nearly finished searching the place, and about to call it quits, when Vinny noticed a lose skirting board under the window. When he looked inside he shouted on Bob. He had found 'pay dirt'. Here were several knives. All different.

"Bloody hell Vinny, its like we have struck gold here. Maybe one of these killed Bill Dunn. We have plenty of leverage against that bastard now. Let's finish up now."

When they walked out of the tenement, one of the locals who was obviously a 'jakey' started to walk towards them asking in a slurred voice what was going on.

"No matter what time you're out and about, there's always a bloody drunk trying to tell you how to do your job. Give me your shield please Vinny."

The guy got within two feet of Bob when he smashed the shield into the face of the drunk, who went flying backwards, and landed on his back, out for the count.

"He'll wake up in a while thinking he's been in a fight. Probably telling his pals how he beat his opponent."

When they were driving back to the station Vinny said, "That was some smell in Kramer's flat was it not Bob? The covers on the bed were absolutely filthy. The 'lassie' wasn't bad looking, so it beggars belief what she was doing with him."

"Vinny, nothing about society surprises me nowadays. I try not to judge, as you never know people's circumstances. That 'lassie' might have come from a broken home, and even Kramer might have been a better option for her."

Nothing more was said, and when they got back they saw Kramer being dragged into the cells wearing just a pair of 'y' fronts shouting how cold he was. However, nobody was paying him any heed.

"Right officers, get back home for a quick 'kip', and be back for mid-day. Oh, and very well done. I'll buy you a pint when this is all over."

"Just one?" came a remark from one of the officers, but Brian just smiled. "Right folks, that was a brilliant result, so if you want to go home for a sleep as well then fine as I want to let Kramer sweat for a wee while yet before we interview him. "I think I'll just have a 'nap' in my chair if it's okay with you?"

Bob and Kim said they would do the same.

Chapter 9

When everyone seemed to be compos mentis again, Kramer was taken into the interview room. Brian could see he was almost blue with cold, so he asked Kim to get him a blanket from the stores, and get him a cup of tea. He apologised to Kim for her being the 'gofer', but she said it was fine.

When she went into the room, Kramer asked how long he was going to be here.

"That will be entirely up to you Mr Kramer. Just tell the truth, and it will be over very quickly. You might even get bail," she lied.

"Well Kim, what was he looking like," asked Brian.

"Like 'crap', and I think he even believed me when I told him he might get bail."

"Nice one, and welcome to the team. Okay, who is taking the lead on the interview? "

"Can I suggest Bob, and I'll be his sidekick this time" Vinny said.

"Fine by me. Kim and I will be watching, and listening at the side window. If I need to interject in anyway, then Kim will come in saying that more information has come in, and one of you should come out. Got that".

When they entered the room, it felt Baltic, and Kramer wasn't doing well with just his underwear on, and a blanket around him.

"Mr Kramer, has it struck you yet, as to why you're here, and what you're being charged with?

"You haven't any evidence 'pig', so you can go and fuck yourself, as I know my rights."

"Your rights? Well let me tell you that you forfeited them when you stuck your knife into Bill Dunn. I wonder what forensics will find when they examine the knives we found behind the skirting board?"

"I was only looking after them for a pal."

It was Vinny who laughed first, then Bob.

"Oh, c'mon Mr Kramer. What's the chances they will find your, and only your fingerprints on them. Also, they will match one of the knives to the entry wound on Pc Bill Dunn. All evidence is still on file Mr Kramer. However, we really don't need too much evidence, as Jimmy Jardine has already advised us it was you, and it looks like Davie Wilson is about to throw you under the bus, both saying it was all your plan."

As they both looked at Si Kramer, they felt he had aged twenty years after what Bob had said. He was slumped over the table, and tears were in the corner of his eyes."

"Now, my colleague is a bit of a soft touch, and he has suggested that you tell us everything, and we put it to the judge that as you've helped us, we are only asking for ten years in prison. Listen Mr Kramer, you could be out in seven, still a young man. Me however, I'm going for life in prison with no parole, as I think you will be a pain in the arse in here today, but remember whoever gets in first between you, Jardine or Davie Wilson, will get the best deal. What are you going for?"

Kramer must have sat silent for about fifteen minutes, before Bob had enough and slammed his palm down on the table startling Kramer.

"Right Ds Hunter, I've had enough of your 'goodie two shoes' bullshit. I am the senior officer here, and I say we go for life, and that's the end of it, okay?

Vinny just meekly nodded his head, hoping the deception wasn't being picked up by Kramer.

Vinny was going to continue the argument, but Kramer let out a roar and started punching the table. He was going to cuff him, but Bob's face said no. They waited until he had calmed down.

"Okay, I will give you Davie Wilson, and Jardine's involvement, but I want the shortest jail term possible. I'm not going down for a life sentence, do you hear me."

It was Bob who said he would agree to it, against his better judgement.

Kramer went on to give them more information than they had expected, which would put all three of them behind bars for a very, very long time. Vinny was writing his confession, and was struggling to keep up with him. Both Vinny and Bob were glad when he was finished, as the room was becoming rancid with the smell from Kramer.

"Thank you Mr Kramer, you are doing the right thing, and we will go out of our way to keep our end of the bargain. Trust us. Now if you would just sign your confession, and we'll get you something to eat and drink, as well as some clothes."

Kramer signed, and sat back in his chair with a smugness on his face that suggested he felt he had achieved something. When they walked out of the office, Brian was standing there with a massive grin on his face.

"Well done lads. What a result. I will say this though, and that is the Davie Wilson situation is going to be too big for us, so as soon as I heard what he said about him I contacted Edinburgh CID, and they have despatched several officers up here. I have to get the warrant for Wilson's arrest before they arrive, so please excuse me. Bob, get Pc Graham to obtain some food for that scum in there, as he'll have no qualms about spitting on it."

There was such relief on Vinny and Bob's face as they sat in the office, with Kim making them a cup of tea.

"God, the pair of you don't half stink," she said.

Vinny went through to the changing rooms, stripped to the waist and gave himself a good wash. He always kept a clean shirt in his locker, and when he went back, Kim had neatly typed up Kramer's confession, which Bob took off her, read it, and went in to get Kramer to sign. Brian sent out for food for the whole station, as he had asked them to go the extra mile, and wait for the CID arriving. There were a few grumbles, but generally they were happy to be in on the biggest arrest in Dundee in a long time.

Two hours later, the 'cavalry' from Edinburgh arrived, and by the look of them they were hand picked. The guy in charge introduced himself as DI Ben Raft. His second in command was Ds Willie Niven.

"Ds Lawson, as time is off the essence, can we head over to see this Belford Arms. Oh, and how do you know they are involved in smuggling counterfeit cigarettes and alcohol."

Brian was a bit angry at this, as it seems not all the information had been passed on to the CID.

"I'll tell you how we know. One of my officers was stabbed to death on the orders of the guy you are about to arrest. He was constantly surveying the place until that fateful night. We only found that out two days ago, and now we have the killer and one of his accomplices in the cells."

"Pretty impressive Ds Lawson. Can we take a couple of your men with us to show us where this place is. If they want, they can make the arrest on Mr Davie Wilson, while we search the place."

"No problem. Please take Ds Reynolds and Ds Hunter with you. They will be under your orders."

Bob and Vinny took Ds Niven and Di Raft with them, while the 'gorillas' followed them in their van. Vinny thought that he didn't fancy anybody's chances against them. They parked about fifty yards from the door of the pub, and as the door was open, the 'big red key' wasn't needed. They stormed in, and grabbed the barman who was lifting the telephone. The young man, who was standing just behind the bar was also cuffed. Some of the men ran upstairs, and brought down Davie Wilson, who was protesting his innocence.

"Found this idiot trying to hide under the bed, but with the size of his belly, it must have been a struggle."

Vinny and Bob had taken a bit of a back seat up till now, just leaning against the bar, watching how the professionals did it. When everyone was cuffed and taken to the police van the CID started to search the place, but after half an hour they came back empty handed.

"Nothing here folks, they maybe got word that we were coming."

"Absolute bollocks. There is no way any of our officers let anything slip. Can Bob and I have a look?"

"Carry on Ds Hunter, but your wasting your time."

Vinny gave a slight nod of the head, and they started to search the whole building. They were coming up with nothing, until Bob walked over an area of the floor in the back room. Next to several empty kegs and boxes of crisps.

"Bob, please retrace your steps, but slowly, until I tell you to stop."

Bob did as he was asked several times.

"Bob, every time you walk over that area with that old carpet covering it, the floor boards creak, unless it's your legs pal."

Bob smiled, stepped back and lifted the carpet up to reveal a trap door of sorts. They both lifted it, and Vinny got down on his knees and looked in before saying, "Bloody hell Bob, get yourself down here and see what I'm seeing."

They didn't have to go down the ladder to see hundreds of boxes of cigarettes, and the same amount of boxes of alcohol. Davie Wilson must have commandeered cellars either side of the pub, and had knocked archways in the walls. The stacking of boxes went on and on.

It was Bob who suggested that they tell the CID boys, and let them go down into that dusty cellar.

"DI Raft, can you come here please," shouted Vinny.

When Raft came through, Bob just pointed to the trap door. When Raft looked in he said, " Oh my God," and shouted his team through.

"My apologies to you two for inferring you would be wasting your time searching, and this was a bit of a school boy error on our part. However, bloody well done."

Vinny and Bob said they would see them back at station, and headed off in the car, both with large grins on their faces.

They told Kim and Brian all about it when they got back, and they had never seen Ds Lawson looking so happy. He shook both their hands, as well as all the officers who had been involved in arresting both Kramer and Jardine. He sent them home in shifts to get some sleep.

There was a tete a tete between DI Raft and Brian Lawson in one of the offices. It sounded heated at time, but when they came out, both were smiling.

"Right, everybody please listen. We will be charging Wilson, Kramer and Jardine for the murder of Pc Bill Dunn."

A cheer went up.

"CID Edinburgh will be charging Wilson with smuggling cigarettes and alcohol, but their main aim is to find the people who are supplying them, and it's their aim to involve Interpol. So basically, Wilson will get life for ordering the hit on Bill, and probably another twenty years for the smuggling operation. Let's just say he is not going to be a happy 'chappy,' and will die in prison."

Another cheer went up.

Vinny looked over at a smiling Kim, and motioned for her to follow him through to the office where she had been working. He asked her to sit down.

"Okay Kim. This your chance to say your piece, and get it off your chest, I can't have this dragging on. If you're not happy with me then just say, but I can't handle your mood swings. C'mon 'spit' it out."

"Vinny, I don't like it when you're too hard on me, for no apparent reason. I'm not, and never will be as hard as you emotionally, basically you're a hard-hearted bastard at times, and when you complain about me in tears, then I'm sorry, but I can't help it. You've known me for long enough now, so why can't you accept me for what I am. You know what I've been through emotionally, but you can't give me any slack. I have thought about us being posted to another area, but there is no way I'm going with you if there is no come and go with you. End of story."

Vinny looked a bit crestfallen, and just sat back in his chair looking at the ceiling unable to say anything. After he looked at Kim he said, "Look Bonnie Girl, I didn't realise how you felt about the way I work. I suggest we go home later, and I'll have a long think about what you've said, and we can speak about it tomorrow night, as I don't want this conversation to be in here. You okay with that?"

He squeezed her hand, and said they needed to go and interview Davie Wilson. Brian and Bob were waiting for them, and they wasted no time in entering the interview room. There was a constable standing behind Wilson.

"Right Mr Wilson. I am Ds Lawson, and I am here to interview you along with my colleagues, Ds Hunter and Reynolds. It is not my intention to drag this out today. My CID colleagues from Edinburgh are waiting to speak to you about the illegal importation of counterfeit tobacco and illicit alcohol. I won't be asking you about the contraband. What I am asking you is about the death of Pc Bill Dunn."

"Fuck all to do with me."

"Mr Wilson, did I forget to say that we have both Si Kramer and Jimmy Jardine in the cells. Both have given a statement saying it was you who ordered the hit on Pc Dunn, and how long do you think the young lad we have in the cells would last under interrogation from my two colleagues here."

" Leave that 'laddie' alone you bastards, he's my son."

"How long do you think he would last in prison Ds Reynolds?"

"A pretty boy like him, maybe a few months, unless he befriends one of the hardened criminals who would turn him into his bitch. To be honest though, not very long."

Brian nodded to the pair who left the room with him.

"Let's leave him to stew for a while, and get a coffee. I take it you have it all down on paper Vinny?"

Vinny just nodded when DI Raft came along, and Brian suggested they all take a break, and discuss the next tactics. As they sat having a drink, it was Vinny who said they should advise Wilson that they would charge the young lad with being an accomplice to murder. Tell him we will not go for anything less, if he doesn't admit to Bill Dunn's murder. Even if we have to get up, and walk out of the interview room, saying we have had enough, and the lad goes down for murder. Everybody was in agreement.

Half an hour later, they were sat in the room with Davie Wilson.

"We have a once only offer for you Mr Wilson. If you admit to all the charges relating to the death of Bill Dunn, then your son walks free. We won't ask him about your involvement in the killing, or your operation regarding the cigarettes and the booze. However, we are all tired, and need to get home, so we refuse to be 'pissed' about," said Ds Hunter.

"Okay you lot. Give it to me in writing that my son will be admonished, and I'll sign anything you want, but what I will say is that idiot Kramer was only supposed to rough up the 'polis' man. Now, fucking hurry up with what I have to sign, as I want a sleep as well."

When they were all standing outside the interview room, Brian Lawson thanked everybody for a magnificent result, and shook their hands, before motioning to DI Raft that it was his turn to interview Wilson. Brian organised a shift pattern for all the men. Vinny and Kim were told to go home, and Bob would be relieved at mid-night by a constable. When Vinny dropped Kim off, she held his hand for a moment, but went into her house without looking back at him. He knew he should be thankful for small mercies. Suddenly, he thought about whether he should mention anything to Mrs Dunn, but thought better of it.

When he went into the station the next morning, he wished he had brought an aerosol of fresh air spray as the rooms were smelling a bit of unwashed policemen. Brian met him as he came in, and told him he was in charge, as he was about out on his feet and needed to go home for a sleep. Bob would be in shortly. Before he left, he said the Procurator's office would be working as fast as they could, and hoped to wrap it up that day.

"Before you go Brian, what about Mrs Dunn?"

"Shit, I forgot about her. Why don't the four of us go when I get back in? I'll be about six hours. You all okay with that?"

Everyone just nodded. When Brian came back in he suggested that they leave Mrs Dunn until everything was finalised.

Vinny got on with the restructuring report with Kim, and left Bob to run the station. When he had Kim alone he asked her how long did she think for the completion of the report.

"If we work hard at it day and night, without you trying to pull my panties down at every opportunity, then about ten days maximum if we still have Bob with us. Oh, mum and dad have asked me to see if you would like to come over for tea tomorrow night?"

"What about you Kim? Do you want me over?"

She just gave a little shrug of the shoulders.

Vinny left it at that, wondering if there were any lovely, and capable police women in the Borders who could replace Kim. He was just getting fed up with her moods. Probably best just to leave her to get on with it. He went through to another room, sat, and put his feet on the desk when Bob came in.

"You still tired Vinny, or what's going on with you? Has the adrenalin worn off son? It can happen like that."

"It's not that Bob. While sitting here, I have been contemplating my future in the force. Yeh, the last few days have been intense, and I suppose you could say exciting, but I never joined up to catch criminals, and incarcerate them for life, even if they deserve it. I came into Professional Standards to catch crooked cops, and improve the systems of policing. I know it was my fault by asking Brian for Bill Dunn's file, and at the start it probably did seem exciting, but now I'm not so sure, plus Kim is being a total pain in the arse, and I am not sure if she has been the right choice on a personal or work level. I feel a bit lost Bob."

"Look son. Throughout my time in the force, I've been told to do jobs that I disliked. I was always questioning my reasoning for coming into the force, but for me, the last few days have been what it's all about. Putting the dregs of society behind bars gives me a great feeling. Hopefully, wherever we are sent, we can make a big difference, so that the officers with boots on the ground are more protected against the scum that they have to engage with. As for Kim, well it's a massive change for the 'lass', so try and be more understanding. She will come good. Trust me."

"Thanks Bob. You've been more help to me in the short time I've been here than that bastard of a father I have. Correction, used to have. Yeh, I must try and look forward to what could be a great career, and if it goes belly up, I can be a 'gentleman of the road' or maybe run away with the circus," said Vinny laughing.

They were both laughing when Brian Lawson came in spraying the room with an aerosol. Complaining about the hygiene of policemen's feet. That day was all about getting the three in the cells to prison. Wilson and Kramer were sent to Peterhead prison in Aberdeen, while Jardine was sent to Saughton prison in Edinburgh. Everyone at the station was glad to see the back of them.

Just as Vinny was about to leave, Kim reminded him about the invitation to tea at her house tonight. He said he would be there, but it was a good job she had reminded him, as he'd forgotten. He told himself to get a grip, or their relationship would definitely be 'down the pan'. When he left the station the rain was 'teaming' down, making Dundee look a very murky town, but wondered what Drumbrig would be looking like if the rain was coming down as hard.

"Where the hell are you mum," he said while looking up to the sky, on the walk to his car.

It was just a quick bath, before heading over to Kim's. He was just leaving when he went and gave Mrs Dunn a huge hug and whispered, "You'll know soon." into her ear, leaving her a bit bewildered. He headed over to Kim's house, but stopping off at the petrol station to get some flowers. He wasn't good at this sort of thing. He parked down the street from the Nicol house, and went and knocked on the door. Kim opened it and asked him to come in. When he gave Mrs Nicol the flowers, he gave her a quick hug as well.

"What did you bring me Vinny Hunter?"

"Me, Kim Nicol."

They sat down to a lovely meal, and talked about anything that came up.

"Are you planning to stay in Dundee? " said Kim's mum.

There was an exchange of looks between Vinny and Kim.

"I really don't know Mrs Nicol, as I may be seconded to work in the Scottish Borders, but I won't know for a few weeks yet."

"Will you be taking our daughter with you son?"

"If she wants me to, but at the moment I'm not so sure," he said looking over at Kim.

She got up, walked over to him, and kissed him full on the lips.

"Thank God for that, as I thought we would never get rid of her," said Kim's dad.

Kim looked at him to see if he was joking, but the expression on his face said otherwise. They sat for a while, with the Nicols asking Vinny more questions about where he thought he might end up with the job. He told them that there was a distinct possibility that they would end up in the Borders to start with, and he had heard good things about it from some of his colleagues. Kim's dad said he had worked as a salesman in the Borders for a wee while, and he absolutely loved it. Kim's face lit up on hearing that. Soon it was time to go, so he said his thanks, and gave Kim's mum a hug, which delighted her. Kim saw him to the door, threw her arms around him, whispering she was so sorry in his ear, before giving him a big kiss.

When Vinny walked to the car, he couldn't believe what he was seeing, There were scratches and gouches all over it. The tyres had been punctured, and on the windscreen had been scratched ' back off ya fucking PIG'. Vinny knew exactly who had done this. Kim's ex-boyfriend. He had to think quickly, and walked back to Kim's house, and told them what had happened. Both her mum and dad were quite upset, but it appeared Kim was just angry. He asked to use the phone, but before he could, it rang. When he lifted the receiver all he heard was somebody laughing.

"That's his laugh Vinny."

He disconnected, and rang Brian Lawson.

"Okay Vinny, don't worry, we will get a truck over to pick it up, and bring it back for forensics to go over it tomorrow. Just make your own way into the station, but may I suggest that you call in for Kim on your way here. I'm going to phone Arthur the tech guy, as I want this dealt with. Stay safe, and we'll speak tomorrow."

Vinny told everybody what was happening.

"Can I impose on you to sleep on your couch tonight please, just in case?"

"Look son. You and Kim have been going out for long enough now that if your not sleeping together, then there's something bloody wrong with the pair of you," said Kim's dad.

Vinny took a taxi to Mrs Dunn's house, and after briefly telling her what was going on, he got a change of clothes and headed back in another taxi. He was angry while sitting in the back of the taxi, and started to thump the seats.

"Hey pal, watch the bloody seats," said the driver.

"So sorry pal. Just in a filthy mood."

When he got back to Kim's house, her mum made tea, and it wasn't long before he said he would have an early night if nobody minded. Kim said she would be up later, and by the time she got into bed, Vinny was out like a light.

Next morning after breakfast, they left for the station with Vinny not being in the best of moods. He was a bit pissed off that a naked Kim had been lying next to him all night, and he had been too tired, and he had slept right through. When they arrived, Brian was waiting for them.

"Not a very nice night for all of you. The car was picked up late last night, and although it's not part of forensics remit, they are doing me a favour, seeing if they can get any finger prints off it. I have also just phoned the electrical wholesalers at the industrial state, just over from your road, to see if they caught the person on their newly installed security cameras. Also, Arthur the tech guy, has been told to get the bloody phone number that the calls are coming from."

Vinny and Bob, as well as Kim set about trying to finish the restructuring report, before they had to give it to Brian Lawson to read. They all gave the impression that this report had taken far too long to complete, and of course there was no guarantee the 'big wigs' would accept it. Vinny wondered how Kim would react to him being a 'gentleman of the road' if they shelved the report.

At about eleven thirty, Brian walked in with Arthur who was holding a file in his hand.

"Good news lady and gentlemen, we have located the numbers where the malicious calls have been coming from. One a residential house, and another from the Tyre manufacturers on Winston road. Do you recognise the numbers and addresses Miss Nicol?"

As soon as she looked at the numbers, she seemed a bit unsteady on her feet, but held herself together.

"Yeh, that's my ex-boyfriend's house and works number. Snivelling coward that he is."

"Okay Vinny and Kim, you are off this case as from now. Bob and I will handle it. Vinny, I can see by your face that you're going to argue, but that's an order, as you're both too close. Oh, and by the way, I am still your boss, so an order is an order. Concentrate on the report as head office are wanting it in seven days now, or is that too soon?"

"No that's fine," said Vinny looking over at Kim, who just nodded.

Brian and Bob organised to bring in Joe Burnett, who was Kim's ex-boyfriend, the malicious phone caller. Forensics had found a few finger prints on the area of the car where the graffiti had been, so Brian was hopeful they could get him for that as well. The electrical company had sent over a video security tape, and although it wasn't the best quality, the guy was still decipherable scratching the car. Even more so, puncturing the tyres. They decided to keep him in the cells overnight, so Brian asked the three of them to come to Mrs Dunn's house at six o'clock with him.

She was rather surprised to see them all turn up on her doorstep, so she promptly put the kettle on, and put out what looked like a feast on the coffee table.

"I take it that this is not a social call folks, although it's a nice surprise."

"It is in a way Bella. Due to hard work, and due diligence from Vinny and Kim here, as well as Bob, the men that killed Bill are now behind bars, and will be for a very long time, probably for the whole of their lives."

It was a good job that Bob was on hand to catch the tea cup that Bella dropped. She sat back in the chair looking very flustered.

"Really? You have actually caught the man that killed Bill? This is incredible. How did you do it?"

"One small anomaly in a statement Mrs Dunn. Unfortunately, it was his partner who set him up. Jimmy Jardine."

"Bill never trusted that bastard, please excuse my language, but he said that he was convinced he was on the 'take'. I know I won't sleep tonight, as I'll be too emotional. However, please accept my heartfelt thanks."

She went round, and gave everybody a hug, although she couldn't quite get her arms around Bob. They only spent another ten minutes talking, before Vinny said he and Kim would stay with Bella, until she went off to bed. Just before she headed upstairs, she sat down with Kim and Vinny.

"Right please listen, I am going to my niece's place in Anstruther for a week or two, as she's always asking, and I need to get out of Dundee for a while to clear my head. So Vinny, the house is yours to look after, and Kim you are more than welcome to stay with him here, but don't be badgered into making his meals all the time. Okay, I must go to my bed now, as the news tonight has taken it out of me. Goodnight."

Chapter 10

Vinny took Kim home in a taxi later that night. When he got back, he sat drinking a tea, wondering if he had come to the end of his time in Dundee. It had been an eventful few years, but maybe it was time to move soon, job or not. Kim or not.

He got in early to the station the next morning. He wandered through to the cells, but telling the custody officer not to mention anything to Brian Lawson. When he got to the cell of Joe Burnett, he sat on the bench opposite.

"Wake up you prick," he shouted, with the prisoner sitting up looking startled.

"Oh, it's you, the guy that will get his head kicked in when I get out of here."

"You have a couple of real problems there arsehole. One, is that you couldn't fight your way out of a paper bag, and two, you wont be seeing the light of day for several years."

"What do you mean? I'm getting locked up for a few phone calls? Piss off."

"Listen you moron. You have been intimidating a serving police officer, by sending her malicious phone calls. It's all documented. Plus, we have you on video vandalising a police car. What've you got to say moron. You're not so brave now are you. Anyway, I'll see you in about seven years if you survive inside, especially when the inmates get to know you're a police informer."

"I'm no fucking police informer," he shouted.

"You want to bet?"

Brian came in, and walked into the office where the three were working.

"Okay folks. I have been advised that I have to present our report to the big wigs in Edinburgh by the end of this week. Can we do it?"

Kim said that would be easy, and he could read the report now if he wanted. She said she was just needing to get photo copies done.

"Great. Bob can you process that scum in the cells, and organise to get the paperwork faxed over to the Crown Prosecutor's office? Remember, we don't need a confession, but if he wants to give us one, then fine. Bob, you do it with one of the constables, as I don't want Vinny and Kim anywhere near him."

Later that morning, Kim presented the report to Brian Lawson. She said that they had read it, and were happy with the work they had done, which had pleased Brian no end. An hour passed when Bob came out of the interview room.

"Well, what did you promise him Bob," asked Vinny.

"Just the earth Vinny. Somehow, I don't think he will get it, do you? Although, he kindly gave us a confession."

Vinny was wanting to laugh, but he noticed Kim with her head down. Brian came out just before everybody was heading home, and said, "That is a terrific report you lot have produced, unfortunately the hard part will be implementing it, but I can't see the bosses turning it down. Well done."

For the next few weeks, it was just a case of waiting for the go ahead from head office. The three of them were getting a bit antsy, Brian was trying to find more and more jobs for them, which Vinny had found totally boring.

Mrs Dunn had left to go to visit her niece, so Kim had spent most nights staying with Vinny. There was a couple of nights that she just wouldn't leave him alone in bed. Not long after they had finished making love, she was trying to get him hard again. She seemed to be always wanting to be on top of Vinny. He wondered if this was because she felt more confident, and less inhibited after her scum of an ex-boyfriend had been locked up. A few times he had asked her to try and let him get some sleep.

In anticipation that the report would be accepted, he asked Kim if she could borrow her dad's car, and they could make a trip to the Borders. She readily agreed, and one Saturday, they headed down the road, with Kim a little excited, but apprehensive as well.

As soon as they were near the town of Peebles, they marvelled at the beauty of the countryside. They couldn't believe the pace of life down here. There was naturally traffic, but not near the volume there was in Dundee and surrounding areas. They had decided to drive right down to where the Borders Police force's jurisdiction ended. In all directions. Some towns and villages they liked better than others, but by the time they reached the sleepy one-horse town of Langholm, they decided that if they were seconded down to the Borders to start their project, they would be more than happy.

"Kim, have you noticed that nearly every small village or town has a police station. That's one thing we didn't factor into the restructuring. I know it's the geography of the Borders, but at the moment, I can't see how we are going to integrate our ideas into such a large area. Let's talk about it with Bob when we get back. What do you think?"

"I think we were dazzled by the beauty of the area as we drove through, and not really thinking about the practicality of implementing our restructuring. It does seem that some of the villages are still stuck in the dark ages, but I think you're right that we should go over it with Bob, but with the three of us looking at a map of the Borders while we discuss it."

On Monday morning, Kim and Vinny told Bob about their impromptu little trip to the Borders, and suggested he might want to do the same with his lady friend.

"Sounds like a plan folks. I'm sure Sharon would love it. I'll speak to her tonight."

They stood pondering over a large map of the Borders on a table. With Bob suggesting they look at crime statistics over each part of the Borders, and then prioritise where the restructuring should happen. He said that it shouldn't be a problem, and not to worry.

Each day was a drag for them, but that all changed when Brian came into their room one lunchtime.

"Right you lot. Get your bags packed, as your off to the Borders within a few days. Kim, sit down with parents, tell them that you're going, and that you're only a couple of hours down the road if they want to visit. You okay with that Bob? Vinny, I know you're desperate for a new challenge so here you are. You will be stationed in a very small town called Innerleithen. There are two houses, and a police station set back off the road just as you come into the village. I haven't seen the place, but I have been told by one of my colleagues that it is ideal. It hasn't been manned for about a year since the sergeant retired, but it should be a good base for you. Remember, you can drive through the Borders in about an hour and a half. Oh, and if you don't have waterproof boots, then I suggest you get some. Your official papers will be faxed through today, and Bob, your warrant card as a Ds will arrive tomorrow. Any questions?"

There was real excitement in the room, with even Bob looking excited. Brian told them that all the information they would need would be here tomorrow to start the preparations for the restructuring to begin, and the two houses were being kitted out as they spoke. Vinny's thoughts went back to what Denny Rey Foggerty had said to him and Kim, about the part of completing his task without killing anyone, but one thing he knew, was that the three of them had to be as ruthless as each other. Vinny asked Kim if she wanted him to go and speak to her parents with her, but she said she was fine.

When Vinny got home, Mrs Dunn was sitting in the living room.

"Mrs Dunn, I thought you would be away for a while yet, did anything happen?"

"No son, it's only when you are away you realise how much you miss your own creature comforts. How have you been, and I hope you have been treating that 'lassie' well?"

Vinny sat down and explained everything that was about to happen. When he was finished, there was a wee tear in her eye. She then smiled, and hugged him.

"Mrs Dunn, I really hope we won't be strangers, as it's only a couple of hours away, and I am sure Brian will be asking you to board my replacement. I'll also be coming back with Kim to see her parents, and what about you jumping on a bus to Edinburgh, and then on to Peebles. You'll love the area Mrs Dunn."

"It's a date young man."

The next couple of days was all about getting everything in order, both professional and personal. Brian had given them a police car to use, and Bob had wanted to take his own car with him. He said Sharon wouldn't be joining him right away, as she wanted to have a few trips down from Dundee, before making a commitment.

It was Saturday morning when they packed their cars, and headed South towards the Borders.

When they were near the village of Innerleithen, Dagon was looking at the signpost on the East coastal path, leading into the Borders. This area was new to him, but it looked promising. He had walked from the North coast over the last few years, obtaining work wherever he could. Life hadn't been good for him at times, but he had just got on with it. His mental health had been poorly for a while, mainly due to the fact that he never had any purpose in his life each morning he woke up. Just survival. He didn't want to think about the past, and he didn't think about the future, as he had no idea if he had one.

The signpost had said Eyemouth ten miles. So that was where he was going to go, but before that he was going to sit down, and have a sandwich, with a bottle of water, and try and think about what his plans would be in Eyemouth. As he sat eating, he wondered how long he could carry on like this. Sometimes, he would find a menial job with some sort of accommodation no matter how spartan it would be, but sure as hell he would be cold most nights. The pay was never great, but it fed and clothed him.

Dagon wasn't his real name. He had chosen it from a book he had stolen from a library in a town up North, always telling himself he would return it if he ever passed that way again. He liked the name immediately after reading it. Dagon was the Prince of Hell, and he thought it was his purpose in life to send people there, if he thought they were evil and deserved it. He couldn't care less about the Sanctity of Life. Using the name Dagon suited him, as he didn't want the police to know who he was. After all, he had killed a few people, but his thinking was that they fucking deserved it. He had made his killings look like accidents whenever he could, but other times he just couldn't care less. He considered himself a Fallen Angel. Never a serial killer.

He wasn't sure if he could stop the killing, as apart from feeling it was justified, deep down he rather enjoyed killing evil people. Now he was heading towards Eyemouth, not knowing what was going to happen.

The three officers arrived at the Innerleithen police station late morning. When they went into their separate accommodation, they were pleasantly surprised as to how well each one had been kept. They took their belongings in, and Kim suggested they sit down with a 'brew', and work out what they were going to do next. Vinny and Bob were in agreement"

"Look folks. Why don't we take a couple of days to settle in, and get our bearings. Chat to the locals, and find out their opinions of the force, and what they think is needed in their town. Let's see if we are falling down in places. I've been thinking a lot about how we go about this restructuring, and I think we should start with the two biggest towns, Galashiels and Hawick."

There were nods all round.

Next morning Vinny was up early, as there was too much going through his head. He stood at the door, and could see right down towards the river, which he presumed was the Tweed. He saw a lone figure walking along the bank, and was sure it was Bob by the size of the person, although he couldn't be certain. After a while he made Kim a tea, and took it up to her. She was standing there naked, towelling herself down.

"Thanks darling, but by the look on your face, I know what you are after, but you can beat it Hunter, as I am all clean from my bath. You have no chance pal, although tonight might be different," she said with a glint in her eye.

"When you've dried your pert little bum, I'll make breakfast, and we can go for a walk through the village. Okay with you?"

"Sound Vinny, but by the look of the village it won't take long."

After breakfast, Bob knocked on the door, and came in when Kim shouted.

"Bob, we're going for a walk through the village. Are you up for it? What was your walk like?"

"Stunning countryside here folks. Really beautiful, but we will have to make the citizens feel safe, as there will always be some 'nutters' wherever you go."

They were apprehensive when they started down the High Street. The people were pleasant when they stopped to speak to them. All but one old dear who gave them a bollocking for the length of time the police station had been closed. They reassured her they would address the situation, and when they walked on, she was still remonstrating with them, by waving her stick in their direction. They returned to the station via the walk along the river.

"I know all the villages won't be like this, but its hard to imagine anything major happening down here, so we'll be able to implement our restructuring without a problem." said Vinny.

"Well, that could be the kiss of death pal," said Bob, with Kim nodding.

It had started to rain, and Dagon thought how typical that was. Just as he was sitting enjoying the view over the sea on the cliffs overlooking this town of Eyemouth. The view was being obscured by the murky rain. He enjoyed looking out over the sea, as it gave him a calming feeling, and at times he felt he really needed it. Getting wet never bothered him, as the coat he was wearing was a full length waterproof, as waterproof as you could get. He had stolen it from a cottage a few months ago. It had been lying over a stone wall at the front of the cottage, so he thought as he was needing to replace his own one, then why not. He never liked stealing other people's possessions, but this was self preservation. His cough had come back, and he wondered what was happening. When he could afford it, he purchased medication from a shop or chemist, but he wasn't sure any medication was working.

As he sat waiting to see if the rain would subside, he looked up the path he had just walked down, and saw a tall gentleman walking down with a small brown dog on a lead. It was only when the guy got closer, he could see him hitting and shouting at the dog for no apparent reason.

The dog was yelping each time it was hit with the man's cane. It was only a small wire haired terrier.

He told himself to keep calm and ignore the situation, but he started to feel his body trembling, especially his hands. The man and his dog were getting closer, so Dagon reluctantly stood up, and when he was within earshot Dagon spoke.

"Sir, would you please not hit your dog with your cane. I have been watching you walking down the path, and I don't think you need to beat the dog like that. Now I am asking you nicely. Please don't do it."

"Who are you to tell me what to do you scruffy, vagrant. Now be on your way, or I will beat you with my cane, and it will be a good hiding. Be off."

"Look sir, I have tried to be polite, asking you not to be cruel to your dog. There is no need. Also, I am not a vagrant, as I work for a living. Now again, I'm asking you not to hit the dog, as I'm going to end up on the side of the dog, and I know you are going to regret that. What do you say?"

"Go away you filthy animal, I'll beat my dog if I want. My dog, okay?"

" Well, that's the wrong answer you pompous prick. Now say goodbye to this earth, as you have only a very short time standing there."

For the first time Dagon recognised fear in his eyes, as he walked over and grabbed the dog off him. He took the man by the throat and started pushing him back towards the edge of the cliff. Eventually the man's legs gave way, so Dagon dragged him by the back of his coat, with the man screaming when he realised what was going to happen. When he killed, Dagon always recited a short poem about death in his head. Now was no different. At the edge of the cliff he stopped, and looked down at the man.

"Yes you cretin, you didn't have the nerve did you?" said the man.

Dagon just smiled, and threw him over the edge of the cliff. The man screamed, but his cries were lost in the wind. The dog tried to run after his master, but Dagon just stood on the lead, with the little dog flipping over, and then looking bewildered as to what had just happened. He grabbed the dog, and held him inside his coat as it felt cold to touch. Dagon was sitting with his legs over the edge, just swinging them from side to side. Still reciting his little poem about death. He looked down, and saw the man lying with his neck at an unnatural angle, and blood oozing out from his caved in head. The blood was seeping into one of the rockpools, making it quite colourful he thought, along with the green seaweed. He had heard a saying once about red and green, but couldn't remember it. He thought he might like to keep the dog, but at times it was hard enough feeding himself, never mind the two of them.

Before tying the dog to the fence, he had a quick look around to see if anybody was watching him. There was only a few sheep in the field, who were only mildly interested in what he was doing. Taking out his knife, he carved out the letter 'D' on one of the fence posts. He wrapped a large handkerchief around the wee dog, and then headed off down the path, while whistling, towards the town of Eyemouth, thinking that it hadn't been a good start. He really was getting fed up with killing, but he didn't think he was going to stop anytime soon.

When he got to the outskirts of the town, he saw a telephone box, and dialled the police.

"I've seen a man throwing himself off the cliff, about a mile up the cliff-top path. He had tied his dog to the fence."

That was all Dogon said.

The three of them had been up early, as they wanted an early start to be in Galashiels by eight thirty earliest. The station sergeant had been advised of their arrival by the headquarters in Edinburgh. The sergeant had been told that they would have total authority over all matters, while the restructuring was going on. When they got to Galashiels station, the sergeant met them and showed them their offices. Bob said he would take the smaller of the two if Vinny and Kim would share the other one.

There was a meeting called for all the staff in a conference room, which had a raised stage at one end. Vinny led the other two up onto the stage, and they sat down. Vinny then stood up.

"Good morning folks. My name is Ds Hunter, and this is Ds Nicol and Ds Reynolds. You will probably have been told as to why we are here. However, I will go over it again, but please leave any questions until after I've finished, if you don't mind."

"You're just here to try, and I mean try, and tell us how to do our jobs aren't you? You can't fool us."

This retort had made a few people laugh. Vinny hadn't picked up who had said it, until he spied a young guy sitting back in his chair, with his feet up on a table. He had obviously bought his clothes out of Burton's window. A right 'gobby flash Harry.'

"Excuse me, but what's your name?"

"Ian Soutar, and by the way it's Dc Soutar."

"Well Dc Soutar. Get your fucking feet of that table, and any time you address me it's 'sir'. It sounds like you have a chip on your shoulder with authority, so if you're not happy with your lot, then I suggest you get the fuck out of the force, okay?"

Most of the people in the room were now laughing at Ian Souter, who by now had a very red face.

"Okay folks, please accept my apologies for the interruption. It appears they promote anybody nowadays."

More laughter.

"What we are doing is we aim to restructure the whole of the Borders police force. Not just the Borders, but the whole of Scotland. Including Edinburgh and Glasgow. We will not make wholesale changes just for the sake of it, and we don't envisage anybody losing their jobs. It's our aim, along with yourselves, to improve efficiency where possible, as well as your own working conditions etc. Please don't think of us as the enemy, and if you have any suggestions, then please come in and see us, and if you're that way inclined to bring a cake or two in from that nice looking bakery we passed this morning, then we would appreciate it. Especially Bob."

With the laughter, Vinny now thought they were warming to the three of them, but there was a hell of a long way to go. Kim stood up to give a small talk, and a low wolf whistle went up. Vinny just gave a thumbs up to the crowd, incurring a stern look from Kim. She talked for about twenty minutes, before Bob took over.

"Can I just say to you all, that I will not put up with any bloody nonsense from anybody. I have seen a lot of sights in Dundee, Edinburgh and Glasow. You might say that I've seen it all, and it is up to us to improve our own performances so we can serve the public better. Oh, and can I just say that if you turn up with shoes like that again Dc Soutar, then I will stick them up your arse. 'Winkle pickers' are for the dancefloor son."

This time Ian Soutar seemed broken, but Vinny thought it might be good to build him back up in their mould. However, he might not even turn up for shift tomorrow.

"I will finish off by saying that I have seen a lot of police corruption in my short time on the force, but one legend of the police force once told me to be as brutal as I need to be, and I will. Thank you for putting up with us, and I will leave my office door open, and for those of you who don't want to speak, then please put any suggestions in the box outside my door. Right, let's get to your shifts."

When everyone had left, Vinny asked Kim and Bob what their thoughts were on the meeting. Both said it had gone well, and felt it won't take much to get them around to their way of thinking. Bob then suggested that they head to the bakery, as it was getting closer to lunch time. After lunch they tried to walk the length and breadth of Gala, as the sergeant had suggested they call it. They had to give up by four in the afternoon, as they had totally underestimated the size of the place.

Dagon had walked down to the harbour, when he heard police sirens going. He was glad that they had taken his message seriously, as at least the wee dog would get looked after. On walking into the town, he first came to the harbour which seemed to be the hub of the town. There wasn't a massive amount of boats moored up, and they had obviously dropped their catch off this morning, as they were just washing down the large shed which was used for the fish sales. Lorries were being loaded with boxes of fish packed in ice. He decided to ask anybody he could, if there were any jobs to be had.

After about half an hour of asking around, he thought it was futile. Nobody seemed to want to hire him, until he walked into the last ice house.

"Excuse me," he asked the guy who was mopping up the floor.

"Is there any chance you would be hiring someone. I'm a hard, and reliable worker. I would do anything."

"This might be your lucky day son. The little 'prick' who worked for me has just walked out, so how about giving me a hand to clean up, and we can talk."

Dagon went over and took the mop off him and started to clean the floor. After a while, the guy, whose name was Rick came out from the back with cups of tea. No milk, no sugar, but Dagon was glad of it.

"Where are you from son, and what brings you down here to the end of the bloody earth, i.e. Eyemouth ?"

"I'm from the Aberdeen area," he lied to Rick.

"Fell out with my parents a long time ago, and have just been walking the countryside looking for work ever since. Can't say its been easy."

"Can you not go back son?"

"Nah, its been too long now Rick. It's best that I'm on my own now."

"Well son, you've got a job here for the next week, and if we both agree, then we can make it permanent. There is a room at the back which has a bed, and washing facilities, along with a cooker which can give you a bit of heat. Sorry it isn't much, and I'll pay you as much as I can, but as you will know the fishing can trade can be up and down."

Dagon shook his hand, and thanked him. Just as they were finishing up, there was a knock on the side door. It was two constables, and Rick let them in. The taller of the two spoke first.

"There was an incident this morning, where we got a report of a man committing suicide, by throwing himself off the cliff, about a mile up the coastal path. We've been asking if anybody knew anything."

As quick as a flash, Dagon said, "I came that way earlier this morning, but to be honest I never saw anybody. Maybe it was the rain and wind that was keeping everybody indoors. Why would anybody do such a thing officer?"

"Beats me son, but there is 'nowt' funnier than folk as they say. Okay, we'll leave you to it, but if you hear anything, them please call us. Goodbye"

After the officers left, and everything had been cleaned up, Rick said he was leaving and as he stood at the side door, he turned and said, "See you tomorrow son. I never did get your name though?"

"No you didn't Rick, take care."

Dagon felt the day had been long, so he decided to walk to the nearest fish and chip shop for his supper. As he walked into the centre, the town was very quiet, although the pubs seemed busy. He took his supper back to the harbour, and sat eating while looking at the reflections from the boats on the water. After finishing eating, and downing a bottle of juice, he put his head back, closed his eyes, and fell asleep. He was woken up much later, by an altercation outside one of the pubs in the harbour. Time for bed he thought.

As he lay in the makeshift cot, he was reflecting on the events of the day. Did he have to throw the guy off the cliff, or did he just enjoy doing it. He probably just enjoyed it. The main thing he thought about was that the wee dog would be safe and warm with someone. More than he would be. That night Dagon was struggling for sleep, with too many bouts of coughing, but mainly because he couldn't keep the ghosts away. He saw them floating towards him, and then disappearing. Their faces were obscured, except for their snarling teeth. Their swirling black robes in tatters. Several times he had to get up and get a drink of water, which made him cough even more. He realised that working, and sleeping in this damp atmosphere was going to exacerbate his health problems, but what options did he have.

He was up early the next morning, and got the ice making machine working, before he opened the main doors. When he had got up, he had filled a large tub with cold water, and stood in it, while washing himself. He knew he would only be here at this job for a few weeks as the weather would turn, and the fishing boats would be out less frequently. However, before he moved on he was going to give Eyemouth a big shock. Wake them up.

Before Vinny, Bob and Kim left the station at Gala, Vinny asked Bob if he would like to get a few hours 'kip', and they could head down later to see what transpired in the nightshift.

"Better than watching 'crap' on TV son. I suggest being down there for about two am. How does that sound?"

"Okay for me Bob."

"Count me out boys, I'm knackered," said Kim.

It was just a matter of killing time until they left at about one thirty. Vinny had suggested to Kim that she might like to go to bed for a while.

The only thing I am going to bed for Vinny Hunter, is sleep, and don't think about touching me up when you get back. Okay?

Vinny was a bit disappointed, but understood as today had been long. However, she didn't say anything about just before her shower in the morning. God loves a tryer thought Vinny. He must have fallen into a deep sleep, as he felt Kim kicking him awake when there was a knock on the door. Vinny opened the window, and told Bob he would be five minutes.

On the way down the road, he asked Bob about what had happened today, and his thoughts on the way forward. Bob had said they would find every town, and the people in it, different.

When they got into Gala, it was quiet apart from a few stragglers, who seemed mostly drunk.

"Bob, please park up the road. Away from the station, as I don't want to announce ourselves."

They walked straight into the station, and showed their badges to the officer on the front desk, as the night shift personnel wouldn't know who they were.

"Please don't be phoning through to any of the rooms," Bob said to the officer.

They strolled through, and into the staff room, which doubled up as a canteen, quietly closing the door. Two guys were sleeping with their feet up on a chair, another was looking at the horses in the newspaper, no doubt for placing a bet tomorrow. Bob walked forward and booted the first guys legs so that he fell off his seat, landing on the floor. The second guy was sitting there like he was comatose, so Bob did the same to him. When they came around they both wanted a piece of Bob, until Vinny shouted at them to stand down. They didn't know how to take all this, until Vinny showed them his warrant card.

"What time are you three supposed to be out there on your respective beats? asked Bob.

"We are supposed to be out by eleven pm sir."

"So why the bloody hell aren't you, you sorry excuses for police officers?"

"Right, the lot of you. Get the bloody hell out of here, and report to my office at nine thirty tomorrow morning, and I don't care if you are supposed to be getting sleep by then. You had better not be late. Now get lost."

The officers walked out with their faces 'tripping' them. Vinny went through to the reception, and' bollocked' out the duty officer, telling him the same as the others, to be in his office at nine thirty.

"What a shambles Bob."

"Yeh, I think this restructuring will be a long haul son, but may I suggest we start being brutal. We knew from the start that we would never win any friends, so lets concentrate on the officers we think might come round to our way of thinking, and fuck the rest. Was that what Denny Foggerty said to you?"

"Remind me to tell you the story of our encounter. It still goes through my head now and again."

On the drive home Vinny said, "Bob, do you think we have bitten off more than we can chew?"

"Not really Vinny. It's just easier doing it on paper than in real life, but it's early days, so let's stick to the plan."

As Vinny got into the house, he was so tired, but when he got upstairs and pulled the covers back, revealing a pert, white bum, suddenly the tiredness left him.

"You can forget it Vinny, and please keep your cold hands to yourself."

He was disappointed, but just got under the covers, and was asleep as quick as his head hit the pillow. He was woken at six thirty by Kim, bringing him a cup of tea. Sitting up in bed, he told her what had happened last night.

"Are you and Bob in agreement, as to how you go about disciplining these officers."

He told her they would take it as it comes.

"Kim, I will be brutal with anybody who makes a mockery of being a police officer, but I won't crucify anyone for their first mistake, if that's what it was. Now you had better get out of here, as there is something stirring under the covers that would love to meet you. Go."

Over the next two weeks, they made it clear to all officers, and civilian personnel, that anything short of professionalism, wouldn't be tolerated. The three officers caught sleeping on the job, were verbally warned, and it was suggested to them that they might start looking for another profession. They knew that larger towns like Gala would take a lot longer, so they had to be patient.

Chapter 11

Dagon had worked for three weeks for Rich, but he knew his time was coming to an end in Eyemouth. The boats were out less often, and he knew Rich was taking money out of his own pocket to subsidise his wages, so he waited one morning for him coming in to tell him.

"Rich, I have appreciated the work you've given me, but I know that there is less and less for me to do, so I'll be leaving at the end of the week. I'm sure you'll understand."

"Thank you for being honest son. Yeh, work always slows down around this time. If you can help me until Friday, then great."

"Fine by me."

Over the next few days, Dagon was thinking about where he would go after Eyemouth. It wasn't a new problem, but one he wished he didn't have to continually think about. When Friday arrived, Dagon had made an extra effort to have the ice house as spotless as it could be. His boss had disappeared for a while, and when he came back, he had a bundle of clothes over his arm.

"Listen son, please don't be offended, but I have a few bits and pieces of clothing from my wardrobe here. Choose whatever you want, and it won't bother me if there are any bits you don't want to take, if any."

Dagon took the clothes through the back, and started to look through them. There was a tweed jacket, several checked shirts as well as a couple of pair of trousers, and a pair of good quality boots. He packed his holdall with all the clothes and boots, and walked out to speak to Rich.

"Thank you so much for the clothes, I really appreciate your generosity, and for giving me work, and a place to stay."

Rich walked over and gave him some money, and shook his hand.

"This is far too much cash Rich, you don't have to do this."

"I hope it helps you son, and if you're ever in Eyemouth again, then please look me up."

"I definitely will, thank you."

With his holdall over his shoulder Dagon walked away. Never looking back. He saw the offices of the Border Bulletin along the main street, and posted his letter through the post box. It read:

' I want to let everyone in Eyemouth, and surrounding area to know that the guy who supposedly threw himself off the cliff recently, didn't. It was me Dagon, who threw him over. You see he repeatedly refused my requests to stop beating his small dog. So I had no alternative but to kill him, by throwing him off the cliff. It was so easy. It is not the first time that I have killed, and it probably won't be the last. As truth be told, I kind of like killing evil people, or those who deserve it.

'If you don't take this letter seriously, then you can see I have left my mark on a fence post, at the incident. My initial, D.'

'Please don't think of me as a serial killer, just a Fallen Angel.'

' Dagon'

The signpost said Duns, so he thought why not. It was probably as good a place as any. He knew he wouldn't be able to make it before nightfall, as it said thirteen miles on the signpost, so he would have to find a barn or outhouse to sleep in tonight. Something he wasn't looking forward to, but the rain was starting, and the wind getting stronger.

He had walked about six miles, when he across a run down barn in a field, literally at the side of the road. After quickly looking around to see if anybody was watching, he jumped the fence and went in. Closing the dilapidated barn door behind him. It was dark, but empty except for several bales of hay lying in one corner. It was obvious that it hadn't been used in a long time. As he looked through one of the broken slats, he could see a light in one of the windows of a large farmhouse about five hundred yards away. Perfect.

He proceeded to cut the twine on the discarded bales, before spreading out the hay and making a make-shift bed. Rich's wife had given him a plastic box, full of chicken and pieces of fruit for him, so he sat down on his bed and ate, saving some for the next few days. Not long after, he put his head down on his holdall, and fell asleep.

Next morning he rose, and ate what was left in the plastic box. There wasn't really anywhere to wash, but the rain was still running off a broken gutter just outside, so he washed as best as he could. The weather was cold, but dry now, so he didn't put off any time heading for Duns. When he got there, he thought it was a rather uninspiring town. Maybe that's what all the towns are like in the Borders. He needed a hot drink to warm him up, so he trudged off looking for a café that would be open at this time in the morning.

As luck would have it, he saw the lights on in a pretty rundown café just as he entered the town square. A large hot tea and a bacon roll were very welcome. When the lady came to serve him, he asked her if there was any seasonal jobs around here. She told him the potato growers at Dodwell Farm were always hiring. She explained how to get there, but warned him that the main road to the farm was narrow, and could be dangerous due to people speeding.

Twice he was almost run down with young idiots thinking the road was a race track, before he came to a farm track that said Dodwell farm.

Back in Eyemouth in the office of the Border Bulletin, there was quite a buzz going around. They had faxed Dagon's letter through to the editor who was based in Gala, and he was going to run the story in tomorrow's edition, with the headlines, 'Serial killer strikes in the Borders.' The staff at Eyemouth weren't sure that was the best idea, as they wanted to hand over the letter to the police to see if they thought it could be a hoax. However, the editor, who was such an arrogant bastard, had said no, as he was the boss. He wanted the circulation of the paper to increase dramatically, and this was his chance.

The editor had been right, as sales of the newspaper went through the roof. The printing presses couldn't keep up with demand, so he had them running day and night. A lot of the actual facts had been fabricated, but it was the headlines that were selling the papers. The whole of the Borders was talking about the supposed serial killer.

Dagon was oblivious to all the hysteria, as he knocked on the door of the farm office, and entered. An elderly gent, who was sitting behind a desk, asked him what he wanted, and Dagon asked if there were any jobs going.

"Plenty jobs on offer son, but I only tend to employ people who I think I can trust to work, and work hard. People who will turn up, and work in all weathers, and can take a telling."

"That's sound by me sir. When can I start?"

"You're a bit cocky son, but I like that. Tomorrow at seven. Where are you staying about?"

"I don't have anywhere to stay at the moment."

"Well, Mrs Herbert takes in lodgers. She is number thirteen on the main street, just across from the town clock. She is a lovely lady, who doesn't charge too much, so make sure you behave yourself if you go there. Meanwhile, if you have time, I'll take you into where the potatoes are sorted and packed, as you'll probably be on the production line. It's just a case of redding out all the defective potatoes, and boxing the good ones. Right, are you up for it?"

Dagon nodded his head, and they walked to the large sorting shed.

At the same time Vinny was sitting at his desk working on their restructuring plan when Bob walked in.

"Looks like we have a problem pal."

He threw a newspaper on Vinny's desk.

"Bob, I am in the middle of something. Why have you thrown a fucking newspaper on my desk?"

"Just bloody read the headlines Vinny, while I go and make us some coffee, as we'll need it."

Vinny couldn't believe what he was reading. How irresponsible had this newspaper been. There was nothing like scaring people. This was going to be a disaster for their restructuring, as all their shift changes would probably have to change again, to take care of all the phone calls that would be coming in.

The three of them sat drinking coffee without saying very much, until Vinny interrupted the near silence.

"Right, let's get the fucking editor of this newspaper in for a talk, and Kim tell him we need the original letter brought in. Let's all have a think about how this really will affect the job we're trying to do, and how far it will put our schedule behind. Oh and Kim, tell him we want him in pronto."

"Vinny, I have spoken to him, and he says he's busy at the moment, and will come in when he has time. In anticipation of your anger I have the address of the newspaper's head office here in Gala."

Bob thought that Vinny was going to explode.

"Okay Bob, you're with me. Kim please hold the fort. We'll be back in an hour, no later."

The office was on the main Innerleithen road, but in a small industrial estate. As they arrived at the office door, they wasted no time and marched straight in, showing their warrant cards to the protesting receptionist. They found his office, and walked in.

"Who the hell are you, and what are you doing here. In fact, just get out, I'm busy."

Bob slapped his warrant card down on his desk so hard, that all the pencils lying on his desk flew up in the air. They didn't put off any time, and told the guy that he was to come with them this very minute. With or without handcuffs. This had the desired effect, as the guy quickly stood up wondering what the hell was going on, and followed them out the door.

Back at the station, they told him to sit down, and asked him for the letter that had been posted to him by the so called serial killer. The guy started to protest that he had to protect his sources, until Bob told Kim to get the keys for one of the cells as the guy was going to spend the night there.

"Now hold on a minute. You have got to understand the position I'm in here. If there is no confidentiality, then I won't get any news handed in, will I ?"

"Kim, put him in the holding cell please," said Bob.

As quick as a flash, the guy went into his inside pocket, and brought out the letter in question, and laid it on the desk. Vinny read it, before passing it to Bob and Kim. He was really angry, but knew he had to compose himself.

"On the strength of this letter, you have made out that there is a serial killer in the Borders. Sensationalising a piece of news, just to sell newspapers. I have no doubt, that some people in Eyemouth will be scared to go out of their doors now. Do you understand how much pressure you've put on the police force now. Could there be a killer on the loose? Of course there could, but that can happen at any time. What I should do, is to charge you with obstructing justice by withholding this letter from us. However, the damage is done. Now get out of this station, and in future, if any of these letters are delivered to you, then we want to see them first. Got that? Oh, and I will be holding on to this letter for a while."

As the guy walked out of the room, Vinny had to wonder if all the 'dicks' in Gala bought their clothes from Burtons, although Vinny thought the guy should maybe buy a size up by the look of his bulging arse. While there was still a few hours of daylight left, he told Kim that they were going to Eyemouth, to see if the so called serial killer's boast of leaving his initial was in fact true. Bob said he was off home, as he fancied a pint in one of the establishments in Innerleithen.

Vinny wasn't putting off any time until he got to the station house at Eyemouth. He spoke to the duty constable, asking him what his thoughts were on serial killer theory. The constable said there had been no evidence at the scene, but as he was about to go off duty, he would take them up the cliff path to see for themselves.

When they got up the path, Vinny asked Kim to look for any sign of the initial 'D' on several posts, and he would look at several along the path. Kim had finished looking, and walked up to where Vinny was looking at the last post.

"Fuck," said Vinny as she approached.

"What is it Vinny?"

"Have a look at this post Kim, will you?"

As clear as day, there was the letter 'D' cut into the post. Why didn't they look at all the posts here, he asked the officer, who said that he hadn't been involved, so he couldn't hazard a guess. Vinny thanked him, and told Kim they were heading home. During their car journey, Kim asked him what his thoughts were.

"If we hadn't found that carving, then I would be leaning towards it being a hoax, but now there are doubts in my mind. However, how do you go about catching a serial killer, when it's not in our remit, plus I don't think Bob has even been involved in anything like this, but we'll ask him tomorrow morning."

Meanwhile Bob was sitting in one of the pubs, enjoying a nice pint of beer. He found the surroundings similar to some of the pubs in Dundee. He only ever limited himself to a couple, although as a young man fifteen pints a night wasn't a bother. The pub had a juke box, a pool table in the small room off the bar, and the usual dart board in the corner. It wasn't overly busy, but it had a good feeling to it or so he thought until a guy stood there swaying in front of him.

"So you're the fucking new 'polis' man are you? Well my name is Jock, and I'm the hardest man around here. So, I'll guarantee you that you won't be arresting me, if you know what's good for you. Get my meaning?"

"Well Jock, it seems that I have nothing to arrest you for, as bragging that you're a hard man isn't an offence, but I'll tell you what is a crime. If you disturb me again, and my pint goes flat, well that is. So, please leave me alone."

Jock wasn't for leaving, and kept on niggling, until Bob had enough. He put Jock's arm up his back, and marched him towards the door, before running with him for the last five yards, and smashing his head through the swing doors. He left him lying against the wall of the pub, went back in and spoke to the barman, a guy called Bill.

"Sorry about that sir, but I don't like to be bothered while enjoying my pint."

"No apologies needed pal, he's a pain in the arse anyway. Here's a fresh pint on the house, and your welcome in here anytime."

When Bob finished, and walked outside, Jock was coming to. He bent down and whispered into his ear, "You're only the second hardest man in the village now pal. Remember there's always somebody harder than you. Goodnight."

When Bob got in, there was knock at the door, and when he opened it Vinny walked in.

"Bob I think you were right. My gut feeling is that we might have a serial killer starting in the Borders. The Eyemouth officers who initially investigated the incident, were pretty 'shit', and probably couldn't catch a cold. The three of us need to talk about this, before we go down on Monday."

"Don't let it bother you over the weekend Vinny. On Monday, I'm going to suggest that we'll do nothing, but I'll explain then. Now 'bugger' off. As I need sleep."

Vinny walked away thinking about what Bob had just said. Unfortunately, it went through his head all night, and sleep only came in fits and starts. This was Saturday, and they all agreed that they should be taking the weekends off.

Vinny and Kim decided that they would explore their surroundings. They were going to start by walking in the hills, which were all around them. There were hills behind the police houses, and when they got to the top of one, the views were spectacular, looking both east and west.

"I wasn't sure about coming here a few months ago Vinny, but I'm glad we did, even although I know at some point we'll have to move on. The thought of being a nomad all my life doesn't appeal to me. Maybe at some point I would like to settle down, and have a family, whether it be with you, or someone else, I really don't know."

"Bloody hell Kim. Thanks for the heads up about the marriage and 'bairns.' You certainly know how to surprise me. Anything else hidden away in that overactive brain of yours?"

"You never know Hunter, it might have nothing for you to bother yourself with. Probably fed up with you before then."

Vinny didn't know how to take that.

"Kim, speaking off 'bairns', don't you think we should be practicing just in case. Look, we're at the top of this hill, and we can see for miles, with nobody in sight. So why don't we indulge in a bit of open air love making?"

Kim started to take her shoes off, then her trousers, and finally her panties.

"Let's go for it, but I'm not taking my top off. I'm not getting my nipples freezing for anybody."

They were soon enjoying each other's bodies, with Kim feeling the cool grass on the back of her legs. It took Vinny back to his first time with Big Irma down by the river. Kim was experiencing climax after climax, more intense each time, but the last one, when Vinny came inside her, was absolutely mind blowing. When her climaxes stopped, she felt a bit disappointed, but held Vinny inside her for as long as she could. She wondered why this had happened, but she wasn't complaining. They were both satisfied, so they quickly dressed, which was just as well as two hikers were just walking over the brow of the hill. That weekend was taken up with more walks, and a trip to the next town, which was Peebles. Bigger than Innerleithen, and it appeared more opulent, and really quite lovely.

Monday morning came quickly, and Bob said he wanted to speak to them both before they left for Gala. As they sat in the station, Bob started to give his opinion on the serial killer scenario.

"Right, here is my opinion on this situation. Firstly, we don't know if he's real or not, with the possibility of him being a crackpot. Secondly, has any of us been involved in hunting down a serial killer? We haven't a clue how a serial killer picks his victims. Christ, it might be the guy that delivered my paper this morning. What I am suggesting is to just leave it alone, get on with the job in hand, and let the rank and file deal with it. I'm sure the bosses will tell us if we are to be involved at any time. What do you say?"

"I think we're both in agreement Bob, as I see Kim nodding her head. Let's stay out of it."

Vinny's brain fog seemed to clear in an instant. When they got to the station at Gala, Dc Soutar was waiting in reception, and when they walked in he asked if he could speak to them. They all thought that he would be handing in his resignation, but were surprised when he said, "Look, I realise I was a proper 'dickhead' previously, but I want to speak to you about helping you out with the restructuring here in Gala. I have an extensive knowledge of Gala, and of what problems we have here. I'm ready to make it up to you for my 'gobby' mouth. What do you say?"

"Well son I don't know about this pair, but I'm all for giving people another chance," said Bob.

Kim went into a drawer, and brought out a folder, which she placed in front of Dc Souter.

"When you're on a day off, please read through our restructuring plans for Gala, and come back to us. If you don't want to be involved, then fine."

Dc Soutar picked up the file, shook hands with the three of them, then walked out.

"Well, that was a bit of a surprise to me. What do you say Kim? and you Bob?"

"Listen Vinny. After we've done our job here, we have to have someone we can rely on to keep the changes going, or it'll just slip back to what it was. We did say that he might be the prime candidate to mould into the type of person we want to run the Gala station".

"We should wait until he comes back to us."

It was five am when Dagon woke. He never needed an alarm. Last night he couldn't get used to be lying in a bed, so he had tried lying on the floor with just a blanket over him, but found himself still too warm. Yet he could see by the windows it was cold outside. When he lay on top of the bed the nightmares found him. He was scared. The sweat was lashing from him. His body ached all over, probably from holding himself so tightly in case the ghosts grabbed him, and the coughing racking his limbs, while never giving him any peace.

After washing, he headed out to the potato farm. He reckoned it would take him about forty minutes walking. One young girl left the accommodation at the same time, and he casually asked her where she was going. As it happens, she was starting a job at the farm as well. He asked if he could walk with her, and she readily agreed. They stopped at the café he had visited the day before, and Dagon bought two meat pies, plus he paid for the food that the girl wanted. Her name was Beth, and by the time they reached Dodswell Farm, he thought he knew her quite well. Just another lost soul like him.

When they went into the large shed, there were a lot of people standing around waiting to be told where they would be working. There was one guy, with a face Dagon reckoned he would never tire of punching, ordering people around. Being rude and arrogant, just because somebody had given him a bit of authority. He told himself to take it easy, as it was only his first day, bloody hell. It didn't help when the guy shouted and pointed at Dagon.

"Hey you. The guy with the hat on. What's your name?"

"Why do you need my name. I thought I was here to sort out potatoes?"

"Funny guy are you? I want your name, so that I can tell you where you are going to work."

"My name is George, and that is as much as your going to get."

The so called foreman tried to stare Dagon out, but he was never going to win that one. He told Dagon to work at the station where the potatoes were brought in from the fields. It was the draughtiest, and coldest place in the whole operation, as the doors had to be left open to let the tractors in and out. When Dagon looked out the double doors, all he could see was field after field, with people picking potatoes, before loading them onto trailers, with a large harvester going up and down the fields. A pretty depressing sight he thought. It gave him a different perspective on a bag of chips.

His day really dragged. Just standing at the conveyor belt sorting out the bashed or diseased potatoes. Twice the foreman had come up to him, and told him he wasn't working fast enough.

"Listen you prick. I don't see you doing any work at all."

Several people standing around agreed with him.

"You can't speak to me like that. I can have you fired you know."

"How about you and I go and speak to the boss in the office, and see just what you're supposed to be doing around here."

The guy just turned, and walked away, fuming.

Dagon knew he had to keep his anger in check, as he couldn't afford to send someone else to Hell, it was too soon after the guy on the cliff, but that prick was a promising candidate. He would just have to see how things played out.

Beth was the only person that was keeping him sane day after day. He knew that nothing would come from their friendship, as he was certain that he wasn't going to be on this earth for any length of time if his cough had anything to do with it, or if he was caught killing evil bastards. Then again, he wouldn't let himself be arrested. He knew what to do.

He was sitting at the tables and chairs that were provided for the workers, when he picked up a newspaper that someone had left. There it was on the front page, 'Serial killer in the Borders.' He smiled thinking that they had jumped the gun by publishing that, as he knew the police would have probably put it down to it being a hoax. Soon he might give them something to waken them up.

Each night he would walk home with Beth, but he would have to make things up about himself when she asked. He had realised a long time ago, that you had to have a good memory to be a good liar. He enjoyed her company, and on a couple of occasions she asked him if he wanted to go for a walk at night, but he couldn't exactly tell her he was scared of the dark, and it's hoards of Demons continually coming after him. He knew that at some point he would just walk away from Duns, and it's millions and millions of fucking potatoes.

Dc Soutar came back to them within a couple of days. He said that he had agreed with the report, but there were some areas in Gala that it wouldn't work. He explained what he meant, which was all about work shifts and several beats not being compatible.

They were quite impressed with his honesty, and when they sat down and looked at the plan for Gala, they saw what he was meaning. It was decided that Dc Soutar could be a good asset for them. The team felt that that they were making good progress, but they knew that sorting out the Borders would take longer than they envisaged.

A memo had come through saying that every station had to be on alert, just in case the news of a so called serial killer could be true. They left anything like that to all the other officers, to concentrate on their real purpose. Rumours had been rife in the Gala station, but the fact that the reported incident was about fifty miles away, didn't seem to bother them much.

Work for the three of them was pretty repetitive, and one day Vinny asked Bob when his lady friend was coming down to visit. Bob said he was picking her up on Friday night, and bringing her down for a couple of nights.

"Right, how about the four of us going out for a meal on Saturday night. There looks a nice hotel just down the road from us. I don't know how to pronounce the name, but it's spelt Traquair Arms Hotel. Are you up for it?"

Bob said he was, and Kim said she would look forward to it. The week was long, and Vinny had several talks with Dc Soutar, who he thought was trying his best to fit in the team. Kim had also been trying, but she was thinking about the multiple orgasms she had experienced up the hill, and really not getting there. She had confided to Vinny about what happened up the hill, but he said he wished she hadn't told him, as that put a bit of pressure on him. She told him not to be silly, as she was still climaxing during love making, and it was still so enjoyable. At the moment, it was still at the back of his mind though.

Bob left early on the Friday to go back to Dundee to pick up Sharon. Vinny and Kim picked up fish and chips on their way home, to save anybody cooking. Vinny thought that a 'fish supper' was the best meal ever. After their meal, Kim asked Vinny if he was up for a walk, but keeping their clothes firmly on. She wished she hadn't mentioned her orgasms, as it seemed that Vinny was trying a bit too hard in bed. They just got back from their walk when Bob drew into the car park at the station.

When Sharon got out they couldn't believe their eyes. She was such a diminutive figure, with Bob towering over her. Kim had asked them in for a cuppa, so that they could meet. Vinny and Kim found Sharon to be both delightful, and funny. The meal that they had at the local hotel the next night was excellent, and Bob certainly made up for Vinny's sobriety, the way he was knocking back the pints. He said the roaring, open fire was making him thirsty. Not that the other three believed a word of what he was saying.

Next morning, Vinny looked out the window to see Bob and Sharon out for a walk. Kitted out for the eventuality of all weathers. Bob didn't look quite right with his wellington boots on. It made Vinny laugh. Everyone was sorry to see Sharon go on Sunday night. She told Bob to drop her off in the bus station in Edinburgh, and she would get a bus home to Dundee. Bob knew better than to argue with her.

Each day was becoming harder for Dagon. It was just a daily grind. After a few hours in the morning, he was starting to feel nauseous, was it just looking at bloody potatoes, or his health. The animosity with the foreman was coming to a head. He had told Dagon to drive one of the cab-less tractors in the pouring rain several times. There was no waterproofs supplied, so he was soaked through time and time again, with the foreman just laughing at him.

As the foreman sat at a table having a tea on his own, Dagon walked up to him and whispered in his ear.

"I feed on human souls pal. It's a pity you can't come back from Hell, and tell me what it's like down there. Oh, and you will be seeing it soon."

Dagon walked away, while still facing him with a sinister smile on his face. There was a nervous sneer on the foreman's' face. It was obvious that he didn't know if Dagon was for real or not. Dagon had given the guy a chance, so he should have taken it. Dagon had a bit of thinking to do, and he knew it would take a bit of planning. One thing for sure though, it would happen, and soon.

He knew that he had to keep this job for a little while, to try and build up a pot of money to last him in between jobs. Although it didn't cost much to live in people's sheds or outhouses, or even under a bridge. At least they were dry. A couple of times, while working next to Beth, he thought that she had deliberately touched his hand, before saying sorry, but with a slight smile on her face. He had to keep his distance as he was going to head off soon, after he had dispatched the evil bastard to the ground.

He watched the foreman's movements over a period of days. Always first in and last away. Obviously trying to impress the boss. A total 'arse-licker' he thought. He was going to wait for a few weeks, but the bully of a foreman had turned on Beth. Giving her row after row for no apparent reason. Dagon thought it was because of her friendship with him.

Dagon made the excuse to Beth that he couldn't walk home with her as he wanted to speak to the boss, although he wasn't sure she believed him. The first night he stayed back and watched the foreman going through his pathetic ritual of making out he was somebody important. The guy never changed his routine, which was going to make it easier for Dagon. The second night there was a power cut, and everyone was sent home as the electricity company was going to take all night fixing it. Dagon hung back, and fortunately so did the foreman.

He knew how he was going to kill the bastard. Dagon hid behind the potato boxes and when the guy came into range, Dagon took one of the spades, and swung at him, nearly decapitating the guy. He knew he was dead, so he dragged him out the back door by the legs, while still holding onto the spade. Dagon knew he had to be quick, because the floodlights could come on at any time. It wasn't easy, so he decided to drag him over to an area of potatoes that he thought wouldn't be harvested for a while. He knelt down every time a car passed on the main road. He quickly dug a shallow grave, pushed the guy in, and covered him over.

After every kill he asked himself the same question. 'Why am I doing this?' This time, standing over an almost headless corpse, just singing his little song about death, but then he just shrugged his shoulders. It was important to cover his tracks, by levelling off the drag marks with his feet, and the spade. When he got back inside the shed, he saw blood on the concrete floor. He got two buckets of water, and threw it on the blood stains. The letter 'D' was then carved into one of the potato boxes. Although it wasn't very prominent, it was job done.

He was tormented later, while trying to get some sleep. His ghosts were back. Floating around his room. 'I have no fear of death and darkness, as it brings me no sorrow,' he told himself loudly, but he knew he wasn't convinced of what he was saying. Suddenly, he sat bolt upright. How many people had he killed without even knowing their names. Surely that wasn't right. He wondered if he had been touched by madness.

Although he hadn't had any sleep, he was up and ready to go as normal. Beth met him in the corridor, and they did their usual, stopping off at the café to get their food. When they were walking along the road Beth said," were you having some bad dreams last night, as it seems you were shouting in your sleep? I could hear you over the corridor."

"Yeh, I was Beth. To tell you the truth, I am not a very well person, and my condition is getting worse, and it's bad when I lie down. However, please don't ask me anymore about it."

Dagon knew that he had to act as normal for a few days, before heading away from Dodswell Farm. The first day was work as normal, and the workers seemed to be a lot happier without the bully of a foreman looking over their shoulders. It was damp, and cold outside, which didn't help his coughing, and when he was having one coughing fit, he noticed a few people watching him. He had to make a plan to get away from there, as he didn't want to leave without having a plausible excuse.

The boss had come round in the morning asking if anyone knew of the foreman's whereabouts. Nobody had a clue, well apart from Dagon. Later in the day, the boss had said to the guy driving the potato harvester to move to another area, as the yield wasn't good enough where he was.

Dagon knew that his time was up when he heard that, as he stood at the big doors, watching the harvester at the bottom of the field coming towards where he had buried the corpse. He stood transfixed when the machine made the first pass over the area, but no body came up. This was his chance. He pretended to have a massive coughing fit, and three people, including Beth, guided him to the boss's office. The boss made him sit down, and gave him some water.

As he sat chatting to the boss, there was a barrage of screams coming from the big shed. The driver of the harvester came running in.

"Boss you have to see this. Quickly please."

The boss ran out, with Dagon strolling after him. It wasn't as if he didn't know what was happening. When Dagon went through he grabbed Beth, and led her away from the grizzly scene. Lying on the conveyor belt was a mangled, headless torso. Not a lot of blood, but that must have been from it seeping out from the top of the neck. Lots of women were crying, with some of the men just standing staring, unable to move.

"Somebody get to my office, and get an ambulance," said the boss.

"Boss, isn't a bit late for an ambulance? We'll have to get the police," said Dagon.

The boss just stood there nodding, with his mouth open. Dagon told everyone to go away from the area, and wait for the police to arrive.

"Nobody touch the body," said one guy who had regained his composure.

Dagon was beginning to feel elated by this time, and he couldn't wait for the conveyor belt to start again, and bring the guy's head through. People were being ushered away from the scene, but Dagon hung back.

It took the local 'Pc Plod' thirty minutes to arrive, and he was still eating part of his lunch by the look of it. However, he couldn't keep that down when he saw the body. Dagon thought what a 'plank' he was for vomiting in a possible crime scene. It was obvious that the officer was out of his depth. He managed to keep the 'bile' down while he tried to examine the body. He was uttering a lot of nonsense, about the guy having fallen into the harvester by mistake which was in fact impossible. It was Dagon who spoke up.

"Excuse me officer, but shouldn't you be starting the harvester to see if his head is in there? "

"Yes, I was just getting to that son. I know what I am doing. This is complicated you know."

Complicated? Dagon was trying hard not to laugh.

The harvester driver was given the nod to start the machine, and one of the guys fired up the conveyor belt. It only took a few minutes for the guy's head to come through. 'Pc Plod' deposited what was left of his lunch on the floor, with a loud retching noise.

What a useless officer he was, thought Dagon. Twice he had contaminated the crime scene now. Mind you, the guy's head was lying on the belt, with his eyes wide open. It was like he was just staring at everyone. It was time for Dagon to start the completion of the plan he had concocted in his head. He played out a coughing fit, whereby one of the guys came over to him, and asked if he was all right. Although, a lot of the coughing fit was for real.

"Yeh, I'll be fine pal. It was just the shock of seeing the torso, and then the head, which set the coughing off. Thanks for asking. I will probably have to give up this job, as I no doubt will have bad nightmares about all this, and working in here may trigger some of my coughing fits."

An ambulance had been called to pick up the body. Dagon knew this was the wrong thing to do, as the crime scene had still to be processed, but there had been too much talk of this being an accident, which suited Dagon. Everyone had been sent home, but told to report tomorrow morning, in case the police needed to speak to them.

That night, while lying on his bed trying, and failing miserably, to fight his demons, there was a knock on his door. It was faint, but he had heard it. He didn't know if he should open it or not. When he did, there stood Beth. Wrapped in an old dressing gown, which was a few sizes too big.

"I'm sorry to bother you, but I am cold, and a bit frightened after what just happened at the farm. I can't stop shaking. Can I please come in? I'm not looking for anything, just a bit of company if you don't mind."

Dagon ushered her in, and lay down on the bed, with Beth lying beside him. She was shaking uncontrollably. He held her tight for a few hours, but before she fell asleep he thought she had said that she knew it was him, and then she nodded off. It was four in the morning when she stirred from her sleep, and got off the bed. She turned to Dagon and spoke.

"I don't know who you really are, but what I do know, is that your name is not George. I said while you held me last night, that I thought you had something to do with the incident regarding that bully of a foreman. If it was, then all the workers should thank you. Don't worry, I'll keep my thoughts to myself."

"Beth, I'll walk you to work tomorrow, but I'll be leaving the job, and the area from there. I would love to have known you better, but I am not a very well person, and I don't know how much time I have left. Please don't judge me though."

She ran forward, held him tight, and kissed him on the cheek before walking out the door, in tears.

The next morning he walked Beth to the job, and walked into the boss's office.

"Sorry boss, but I'm in here to tell you I'm leaving. Being in the cold and damp hasn't been good for my health, and that incident yesterday has put me over the top. So I'll pick up my wages and be off."

"I fully understand son."

He went into his drawer and brought a cash box out with a small ledger.

"I see you are down here as just George, is that right?"

"That's right boss. I appreciate you giving me a job, and I'm sorry it didn't work out."

The boss gave him the envelope, and he walked to the door.

"Hey George. I didn't get your second name."

"No you didn't."

As he walked out the main entrance, Beth was standing near by. He just gave her a nod, and she gave a slight wave of the hand, and then he was gone. As he started walking towards Duns, he felt a bit emotional about Beth, but knew he had to quickly put her out of his mind. It was then that the rain came down 'heavens hard' with Dagon thinking that God was punishing him again.

Chapter 12

Vinny was sitting at his desk when the phone rang. It was Brian Lawson.

"Good morning Vinny, I trust the restructuring is going well? However, that is only partly why I'm phoning you. Head office have had a report of another suspicious death, not far from the first incident in Eyemouth. Did you check out the first incident, and what were your thoughts? Head office know that you're not far from the second incident, and they were wondering if you can go and check it out?"

"For fucks sake Brian. There are plenty of officers stationed all over the Borders. Can a couple of them not go and investigate. What the hell are we paying them for?"

"Calm down Vinny. I appreciate it's eating into your time that should be spent on the restructuring, but if by chance we do have a serial killer running amok, then all hell will break loose. It will only take you half a day, so just go for it."

"Okay Brian. I'll head down there today with Bob, so we can get an idea as to what's happening. Please fax me through the details. Speak soon."

"Yeh, but only to me Vinny. Nobody else at present. Okay?"

Vinny went through to the next office, and the fax machine was spewing out the details they needed. Kim was busy typing. So he said to Bob, "You're with me Bob. We're going to Duns. Can't promise any excitement down there. I'll explain on the way."

As they were walking out the door, Dc Soutar was walking in.

"You're with us today Dc Soutar. Let the front desk know please. Oh, by the way. What's your first name again? Apologies for not remembering."

"It's Ian."

They headed out the Earlston road, and then thirty minutes later they were standing in the two man police station. Bob had read out all the details, while Vinny drove, with Ian in the back. Vinny had said they should wrap this up very quickly, and if there was no sign of a serial killer, then they should return to Gala post haste.

The officer that had been involved was named Neil Critchley. Bob thought immediately that he was a 'dinosaur' who was just waiting for his pension. After reading a copy of his report, they all thought that they would have to start this investigation all over again. Vinny sat with his head in his hands.

"What a 'shit storm' this is lads. A total fuck up. I suppose that's why we're restructuring the force. Get rid of the old guard who are too set in their ways."

Bob was just nodding, with Dc Soutar a bit out of his depth.

"It's the potato farm we go to lads. Hope you haven't got your winkle pickers on today Ian. Buy yourself a pair of waterproof boots, for the future. If by chance you are size seven, then you're in luck, as Kim has a pair in the back."

It was raining heavily when they got to the farm. On entering through the doors at the front of the farm, they could see maybe forty or fifty people, just sitting around. Vinny sought out the boss, who asked them into his office. He explained what had happened, and trying to emphasize what the Duns officer had said, that it had been an accident. Both Vinny and Bob were sick of hearing the word accident. They asked the boss to take them to where the body was discovered on the conveyor belt.

When they got to area, Bob couldn't believe what a screw up this was. The officer hadn't cordoned off the area around where the body was found. He could see umpteen sets of footprints from the area to outside. There were two patches of what Bob thought might have been vomit, which had water thrown over them, and brushed out the back door. He thought this was getting worse, and he genuinely hoped it was an accident, so that they could do a quick report, and get the hell out of here. The body had been taken away by ambulance on the night of the incident.

"Where's the harvester driver?" shouted Vinny.

An older guy stood up, and shouted he was the driver. He walked over, and asked how he could help. Vinny asked if they could go to the machine, and go over the workings of it.

"Now, please think about this very carefully. How do you think the body could have been in the machine?"

"That's easy sir. The only way would have been if the body was in the ground, and the harvester has picked him up as it went over the ground, and the machine has spewed him out at the conveyor belt."

"There couldn't be any way that he was lying on top of the ground, and you've ran over him by mistake?"

"Listen sir. I've been doing this job for thirty years, and my eyesight is still good, plus the foreman had a yellow rain coat on. So there was no chance that I could have run anybody over. He must, and I repeat must, have been in the ground."

Vinny and Bob just looked at each other. Both were then resigned to the fact that this was no accident. They started to interview all the workers, but it was pretty futile, as nobody had a clue as to how this had happened. The one common factor was that they all said the same thing, and that was he was a bully, with nobody liking him. When Bob was interviewing a girl called Beth, he thought that she might know more than she was saying.

"Beth, do you know of anybody that might have had a grudge against the foreman?"

Beth just started laughing, and said it could be anybody, as he was a hated man. Bob thought she knew much more, but wasn't going to give anything up. He thanked her for her time, and went on to the next person.

Vinny asked the boss if everybody had turned up today, and when he said yes, except for one guy whose health was bad, and he had quit. This made Vinny think that there might be a connection.

"Have you got his details please?"

The guy went into his drawer and brought out his ledger.

"Yeh, that's him there," showing the page to Vinny.

"Sir, no disrespect, but all that says is that his name is George, for the love of God. Do you have any other information on him?"

The boss just stood shaking his head to Vinny's disbelief. He asked the guy if they could make themselves some tea or coffee, which he agreed to. He shouted to Bob and Ian to come for a break, and as they sat discussing the progress they had made, Bob quietly said to them.

"Don't look over to where the workers are sitting, but there is one young girl continually staring at us. I interviewed her earlier and thought she knew more than she was saying."

"I see her Bob, but are you sure it's not my good looks that have captivated her?"

"Got a feeling you got that one wrong pal," Bob laughed.

"I'll speak to her after my coffee."

After their break, Vinny walked over to where the girl was sitting, and asked her to go for a stroll through the factory with him. As they walked, Vinny asked her about herself, but she wasn't very forthcoming, so he decided to get right to the point.

"Beth, have you any thoughts about who could have done this to the foreman, as my colleague thinks you're holding information back."

"Listen, I will tell you everything I know, just as I told King Kong over there."

Vinny couldn't help it, but he burst out laughing, drawing looks from Ian and Bob. He asked her about George, and all she could say was that he was a really nice guy. When he asked her about what he looked like, she gave a completely different description of him. She told him that he suffered from terrible coughing fits, and the guy knew he was an ill man. When there was nothing else to ask, he thanked her for her time, and wished her all the best.

When he got back to where Bob and Ian were sitting, he asked for their opinions on whether they thought this was an accident or a crime scene. It was Ian who came out with the most pertinent facts. The fact that the harvester driver had told them that it was near impossible for anyone to accidentally fall into the machine, plus the guy hadn't been liked. They both agreed, and decided that this was no accident, but it was too early to connect it to the incident in Eyemouth, even although it was very close mileage wise.

"If you both agree, then I am reporting to Brian Lawson that we feel the guy was unlawfully killed, put into a shallow grave, only for the harvester to pick him up. That's about the only thing we can do here. The body will be in the morgue at the hospital in Berwick -upon- Tweed I believe, but let's leave it to the powers that be as to how they are going to move any investigation forward. Do we all agree?”

They packed up, and told the boss he could have the harvester cleaned out, so they can get production going again. The boss was so grateful, and thanked them for their understanding, plus their help. They were just heading towards the main road when Vinny slammed the brakes on and reversed up the track to the main door.

“C’mon you pair. With me please.”

Vinny walked quickly to the back door where the large wooden crates were stacked.

“Right, I want us to look at these crates, and see if there is a letter ‘D’ carved into any of them. If either of you find it, then give me a shout.”

As they looked, Ian was obviously trying to impress by climbing up the crates. However, after twenty minutes it was Bob who gave a shout to Vinny.

“I’ve found it Vinny. Come over here.”

As they all stood there just looking at the letter, Vinny shouted a loud obscenity, to nobody in particular. Although, it seemed that all of the workers had heard it.

“What does this mean,” asked Ian.

“It means we have a fucking serial killer on our hands, and now any death, suspicious or not, has to have particular attention paid to it. Bloody time consuming.”

They just drove past the police station in Duns without a second look.

“We’ll have to write up a report after I’ve spoken to Brian. Ian, you probably don’t have a lot of experience in these matters, so get Kim to help you format it. When we’ve completed each report, then Kim will look through them all, and collate them into one, to be sent off.

For what was supposed to be half a day away from the station, turned out to be nearly a full day. Kim said that she should take money out of the petty cash, to get fish and chips from the place around the corner. They all agreed.

By the time seven o’clock came, they were tired, but were all happy with the report that would be sent to Brian Lawson. Vinny phoned Brian Lawson, who was still at the station in Dundee.

"Good evening Brian. Are you ready to know what we found today?"

"I hope it's good news Vinny."

"Sir, it's more than likely that we have a serial killer on our hands down here."

He told Brian what they had found.

"Sounds like it Vinny. I trust there was no trace of who the killer could be?"

"None at all sir. Except we got a name. George. He was a guy who left the farm the next day due to ill health. The description we got of him, made him out to be the devil himself, but to be honest the witness wasn't reliable, and she could have been just making it up, for whatever reason. However, I just have a feeling about this one, and the one at Eyemouth, although I can't explain it. Probably nothing. You do realise that this situation could put the restructuring back months, and months, if we're to be involved."

"Vinny, through no fault of your own, my night has been ruined. For fuck sake, George? Is that the best you have. There must be thousands and thousands of guys with that name in Scotland. Vinny, I'm going to hang up now, as I'm getting a fucking headache. Speak tomorrow."

Brian knew that he would have some difficult conversations with the top brass tomorrow. He thought he wasn't getting paid enough for this 'shit'.

Dagon thought he had to stay under the radar. He didn't know if the incident at the farm would be picked up as a killing, or just an accident, but he didn't think it would be the latter. There was no doubt in his mind that Beth would protect him, and nobody else at the farm could give a description of him to any policeman. There was a stone post at the side of the road which said, 'Greenlaw eight miles.' He was in no hurry to get back into the general population. It was just a case of walking off road to Greenlaw, and finding an out of the way place to hole up, as long as he could walk into the village for food.

The village came into sight after about three hours. It certainly didn't inspire him. It was much smaller than Duns, so he had to spend as little a time there as possible. The weather wasn't great for open air sleeping, but it wouldn't be the first time, and probably not the last. He saw a small hill that overlooked the village, with a heavily wooded area on top. That's where he would head for.

After an hour, he was wandering through the wood looking for a suitable area to set up camp. He came across a small stream, and a flat area where he could lie down. It was important now to build a shelter, so he set about making a bivouac. There were plenty of fallen branches, and within a couple of hours he had a substantial shelter, which felt quite wind-proof when he sat inside. Being waterproof was another thing. The next step was to gather branches and strip their leaves off, and put them down for sleeping on. Not great, but not the worst place he had slept in.

He had enough money to keep him in his meagre existence for a while, but he had no food for tonight, so he knew a walk into the village was needed. Before he went, he needed to concoct a story about himself, just in case somebody tried to engage him in conversation. Probably just play it by ear he thought.

The path to the village was just a track made by sheep. It was muddy and slippery, so he had to careful not to turn his ankle. The boots that the guy at Eyemouth gave him, were a God send. Warm and comfy, with a good sole on them. It took him about thirty minutes to arrive in the heart of the village. As he was walking through, he saw a telephone box, and gave a little smile, thinking he would give the people of Berwickshire another wake up call. He still had the number of the Border Bulletin, which was a Galashiels number.

"Good afternoon, may I speak to the editor please?"

"I'm sorry sir, but he's busy. Can you please leave a message and your number."

"Listen young lady, he will want to speak to Dagon, trust me. Now make it quick."

When the editor came on the phone, even after a few words, Dagon thought him to be an arrogant 'prick'.

"Who the hell are you. How do I know you are who you say you are? I'm a busy man so just get on with it."

"Listen you arrogant arsehole. I am Dagon. I have killed many times, and my latest was at the potato farm in Duns. The guy that met his demise, was a bit of an arsehole just like you. So, if you don't believe me then I suggest you contact the police, or go and look for my mark, the letter 'D' on one of the potato crates. If you don't want to do either, then you can go and fuck yourself."

The editor immediately phoned the Galashiels station, and asked for Vinny. He asked Kim to take the call, as he was waiting for Brian Lawson calling him.

The editor started to tell Kim of the phone call he had just received, and asked her if the information he had just received had been true. Kim did her usual, by telling him it was an ongoing investigation, and to watch what he put into print.

"It sounds like the police are trying to hide something doesn't it? Well, if I don't get an answer by Wednesday, then I will be putting something into print. I'm here to sell newspapers, and that's just what I'll do, regardless of what somebody's 'lackey' tells me to do."

"Well sir. I will let my superior listen to what has just been taped. I'm sure he will be giving you a visit soon."

Kim put the phone down, just as Vinny and Bob walked into her office. She asked them to listen to the tape. When they did, it was Bob that lost his temper first.

"This guy is a moron. Kim told him it was an ongoing investigation, yet it seems like he only hears the parts that suit him. Do you think there's anything that we can charge him with?"

Vinny sat there shaking his head.

"Don't think so Bob. Not until he messes up any investigation we're in involved in. However, I will have a word with him soon."

That would be sooner than he thought, as the boss from the potato farm phoned him the next day to ask if the police had given permission to a guy from the Border Bulletin to come and take pictures of the incident area, as well as interview some of the workers. Vinny asked him if he'd gone under any of the police tape that had been used to seal the areas off. The boss said he had, and several people had witnessed it.

Vinny told him, that if he was still there, then get two burley workers to throw him out, and put a guard on both entrances. I'll make sure he doesn't come back. He told everyone about the phone call, and then said, "Now we have a reason to charge him. We'll pick him up tomorrow. I'm going home to go for a walk down the river Tweed to clear my head, as I feel it's ready to burst."

When they did manage to get home, he asked Kim if she wanted to come with him, and she readily agreed. As they walked down the road, Kim asked him if they should have an early night, as they'd been neglecting each other for a few days. Vinny agreed, as long as she wasn't expecting multiple orgasms, because he couldn't guarantee that. Kim put her arm around his waist and laughed.

They stood on the bridge and looked both east and west, and thought what stunning scenery it was. There were a couple of guys fishing, so they walked down the path so that Vinny could speak to them. He asked them what they were fishing for, and did they need a permit. They told him, and they asked who he was. Vinny introduced himself and Kim to them, and they seemed really nice guys.

"I would like to get back into fishing, but I don't have any equipment, and I'm reluctant to buy any, just in case I don't have the time, or I get moved to an area where there are no rivers."

"Don't worry about any gear pal, you just have to go along the High St, and knock on number sixty nine. That's where 'auld' Charlie lives. He'll give you a loan of a rod and reel."

Vinny thanked them, and they walked down the small road to a place called Walkerburn. It was a one man and his dog town. They strolled through it, and back up onto the main road without seeing anybody. About forty five minutes later they were back at their house. Although, Vinny did check out number sixty nine High St on his way past.

Dagon went into one of the small village stores to buy provisions. It was just a young girl serving, and she didn't want to strike up a conversation, which suited Dagon. He left the shop carrying enough food for just a couple of days, as he didn't know what his plans were. When he got back to his 'hide', he opened his bag and took out a tin of corned beef, and started to eat. He had never been so tired, and the tiredness and lethargy were getting worse. As he ate, he wondered how long a life he had left, and when he was gone, would somebody find his body in one of these bivouacs. Maybe in a month, a year, or possibly never.

Because of the tiredness, he thought that he might never wake up after falling asleep tonight. Probably best.

When he had walked back up the path to his shelter he had found several animal feed bags, carelessly discarded. The clouds were looking angry, and he knew he was in for rain. He no sooner finished cutting up the bags and spreading them over the bivouac, when the rain started heavily. He put his collar up, lay down on the leaves, and went to sleep.

When he did manage any sleep, the rain kept waking him up, as well as all the noisy animals, especially the barking fox, and he would gladly have rung it's neck, but when he did look out, he felt that at times the darkness never looked so good. Decisions had to be made in the morning. He knew that he couldn't stay there that much longer, in case somebody stumbled upon his shelter. Maybe a 'gentleman of the road' might be glad of it, but it was a bit out of the way. However, after today it wouldn't be his problem. He decided to rest up for a few hours, as his stomach wasn't feeling good. He blamed it on the corned beef, but he knew he was grasping at straws regarding his health.

He had picked up a map of Berwickshire when he was in the shop, so when he felt able, he started to study it. It seemed that it was just a load of smaller villages, with one or two towns dotted about. After he packed up, he went down to the stream, stripped and gave himself a good wash. As much as it was freezing, he felt exhilarated after it. He was just about to move on, when another coughing fit stopped him in his tracks. This one was bad, and when it subsided, he looked down to see old blood on the ground where he had been bent over.

'Well Dagon. That just confirms your fears pal. You are well and truly fucked,' he said to himself.

He decided to walk over the hills to a place called Lauder, but before he could get anywhere near it, there was a sign at the end of a farm track. It said, 'Help wanted for a reliable worker. Accommodation provided.' Dagon thought he had nothing to lose as he didn't fancy sleeping rough for a while. He slowly walked up the track, wondering if he was doing the right thing, as he had a bad feeling about this, but needed to keep his pot of money up, as jobs would get scarce over the winter.

As he walked into the farm yard, a small guy with a shotgun, came out the house. He was wearing thick moleskin trousers, thick grey shirt, and braces. A torn flat cap finished off his attire.

"Who are you, and what do you want?"

"I came looking for work, as per your sign at the start of the track. Yet, here you are aiming a shotgun at me. What's your game?"

"I have to be careful, as we're isolated here, and we've had a few break-ins."

"Not a problem. I'll leave immediately. Thanks anyway."

"Now wait a minute. Have you worked on a farm before, and what about working with sheep and cattle?"

"I've done the lot, and may I ask your name please?"

"My name is Alan Kinghorn. I farm here with my brother Walter. Here he is now."

Walter walked from behind one of the buildings. Dagon could tell right away that he was challenged both physically and mentally. He walked with a bad limp, and it looked like he had a withered leg. Every so often he would give out a weird laugh, which Dagon found a bit unnerving.

"Well Mr Kinghorn, do you need help or not?"

"Okay, I'll give you a chance, but remember I'm the boss, and you do exactly as I say. Got it?"

Dagon said yes, but he knew at some point that this guy was going to have lodgings with the Devil. He told Dagon how much he was prepared to pay him, and said he could bunk down in the barn. Dagon wondered why he got himself into these situations. There was a small storage area inside, with an outside tap for washing and getting drinking water. Dagon thought it could have been worse, but not much. The farmer walked to the barn door, and shouted, " By the way, what's your name?"

"Tam."

"Tam who?"

" Just fucking Tam."

Dagon walked forward and stared at the guy. The staring competition was interrupted by Walter, with his weird laughing. Kinghorn grabbed Walter by the scruff of the neck, and hauled him out of the barn. Dagon hadn't liked that, but it was too early to say anything. He started the next morning working with

Walter, who surprisingly was a real grafter. The conversations between them were limited. It was a case of Dagon saying something, and Walter either nodding, or shaking his head. When he started laughing it put the fear of death into Dagon. No noise like that should come out of a human being.

The work was hard, and to start with, the food was terrible, until Walter started bringing him better food on the sly. He just kept putting the money he earned into an inside pocket of his working coat, as he didn't trust Alan 'bloody' Kinghorn. Several times over the following weeks, he fell out with the boss. Often down to the way he treated Walter and the animals. The bed he had was just an old mattress that had seen better days, but at least the storeroom was dry. He was just going to wait and see how this job 'panned' out.

Brian Lawson had phoned Vinny, and asked him to bring in Kim and Bob to the office. Vinny did, as well as Ian.

"Right Vinny, turn the volume up on the phone as high as you can, and everybody please listen. The powers that be have told me that if there are any more deaths connected to a possible serial killer, then they want your team to investigate, full time. Before you start complaining, I tried to fight your corner, but I was told to get on with it. Sorry."

"Brian, I told you when I started this job, that I wasn't interested in normal police work. I was in it for the Professional Standards part. Now here we are making real progress in the restructuring program, and these 'pricks' want us to chase a fucking serial killer, who appears to be bloody elusive. A bloody ghost Brian. How do you start looking for a serial killer. He might not even be in the Borders by now."

"Are you finished ranting Vinny? Just remember, I'm still your boss. You have to look at this calmer. There might be no further incidents, so you can just get on with the job in hand. We will monitor this closely if it comes up again and make decisions. I did get your report on the restructuring, and it's looking good, so keep it going."

Everyone in the room wasn't saying much, as they seemed a bit deflated. Nobody had any idea about catching a serial killer.

"Bob, have you had any experience in being involved with a serial killer?"

"None what so ever, although there are probably a few future serial killers running around Dundee that we don't know of. I appreciate what you said to Brian, but we don't really have much of a say in this. Afterall, there is a guy killing people indiscriminately here in the Borders."

"I suppose you're right Bob, but it still 'pisses' me off. Kim, what do you and Ian think?"

"The hierarchy probably know that we're down here anyway, so we're on hand to respond quickly. If they send officers down here, then they could be sitting around for a length of time just twiddling their thumbs. Like Brian said, lets just wait and see," said Kim.

"I'm just being led by the hand on this folks. I've read a few books where serial killers are mentioned, but I don't think that counts," said Ian, laughing.

They got back to their work without much enthusiasm. Vinny thought casting a line tomorrow into the Tweed might be the medicine he needed. Afterall it worked in the Mot, with his pals. He didn't dwell on thinking about them. It had been a lifetime ago.

When he drove back that night. He told Kim that he was stopping off on the High St as he wanted to do something. She just nodded. When they had finished work, Vinny did as he had said, and stopped off at sixty nine High St. He knocked on the door several times. as it seemed nobody was answering. Then a shout came.

"I can bloody hear you. What's your hurry?"

This old guy opened the door. Bald and wearing a gilet, with a flat cap covered in fishing flies.

"What are you wanting son?"

"I got your name from a couple of guys fishing at the Tweed Bridge, Charlie."

He introduced himself, and asked if he could help him out with the loan of a rod and reel for a few weeks, and he would gladly pay for his help.

"No need for any payment son. Go round the back, and I'll meet you at the back door." 'Auld' Charlie met him at the garage at the back. When he went in, it was wall to wall fishing rods, reels, and fishing baskets.

Charlie lifted a rod and reel down from a rack that seemed like it was ready to fall off the wall.

"Here you are son. The strength of the line will be sufficient to catch what you're after. Take a basket, as there's plenty of lines and flies in each one."

Vinny thanked him for his help, before asking Charlie one last question.

"Charlie, can I ask you what your garage is made from?"

"It's called asbestos son. The best of stuff. My youngest son and I built it in two weekends. Can't tell you where I got the panels from though, as you'd have to arrest me," he said laughing.

Vinny thanked him and walked back to the car. Kim just shook her head, and said he should walk up to the station as the rod wouldn't go in the car. She drove away, still shaking her head.

That night Vinny was quite excited over his acquisitions. Though Kim couldn't care less. He couldn't wait to try his rod out, but if that serial killer struck again he would be as well handing it back to Charlie.

Over the next week Dagon, just bit his tongue every time Kinghorn got on to him and Walter about how they were working. Considering he was the laziest bastard he had ever come across. Every time he had 'yoked' on either of them, Dagon would just laugh and walk away, with Kinghorn shouting at him to remember who was the boss around here. Just wait he thought, just wait.

Over the following days, he told Kinghorn that one of the dogs was lame, yet he still worked him on the sheep. He told him that the dog needed a vet. Eventually, Kinghorn took the dog into a shed, and shot him. Walter was beside himself with grief, as he loved every animal. Dagon wondered if he knew where the animals were going to, when a cattle truck was loaded and went off down the track. Surely he knew, but there was always a doubt in Dagon's mind.

After the shooting, Dagon had decided that Kinghorn had to go, but he worried about what would happen to Walter. He would worry about that when the time came, and that time was going to be soon. One day, when Kinghorn was away in his pickup somewhere, Dagon took the opportunity to try and look in the house. The doors were locked, but when he looked in the window, he couldn't believe his eyes. The guy was a hoarder, with piles of everything and anything stacked high, with only a small passage way to get past the piles. How can anybody live like that.

Dagon wondered if he should just walk away, but that was not his way. He had to keep reminding himself that he was the Fallen Angel, and when it was his time to depart this earth, then he would end up sitting at the right hand side of his master, Satan. He was happy when he thought about that. He was in a bit of a quandary though. Did he try and make his death look like an accident or not. To heck with it he thought. Any killings from now on wouldn't be hidden as an accident. He was going to have fun with the authorities. Especially if any of them came after him. He needed a bit of amusement in his life, and rejoiced each killing.

He felt his spirits were lifted a bit, knowing that the joy of killing would come soon. It wasn't going to take much planning. He was going to make Kinghorn so very scared when he knew what was going to happen to him. Walter and Dagon kept working on the farm, and it really needed it. Walter was continually checking the legs and feet of the animals. Anytime he found a problem, then he would rub a lotion on the area, and within days the problem would disappear. The lotion was Walter's own concoction, and it really smelled. Dagon kept well clear when he was applying it.

Life for Dagon was boring, and normal as usual. He knew how he was going to kill Kinghorn, but didn't know when. However, that time came early when he witnessed Kinghorn knocking the 'living daylights' out of Walter behind the barn, accusing him of leaving the gate to the cattle field open. Dagon had been alerted to what was happening by some 'Banshee like' screams, and when he heard they were coming out of Walter, then he knew the time had come, which put a smile on his face. He walked over and smashed Kinghorn on the jaw, dropping him like a stone.

He waited until he came round.

"You'll never do that to Walter again you bastard. Go and get the wages that I'm due, and don't try and swindle me, if you know what's good for you."

By this time was Walter was cowering behind Dagon.

"Your fired. I will give you your fucking wages, and then you can get off my land, do you hear?"

"When I get my wages, I will decide when I go."

A few hours later, Kinghorn came into the storeroom, and threw Dagon's wages on his straw bed.

"There you are, now get lost."

"All in good time you arse hole. Unfortunately, you won't be around to see me walking off your land."

Kinghorn just chose to ignore that last remark. Dagon knew he could take his time to despatch him to Hell. He wondered if his master was okay with the number of people he was sending down to him. He knew that Kinghorn would never phone the police due to the state of the place, and Walter. His plan had been in his head for the last few days, so there was nothing to work out. The only thing he did have to work out was where he was going to next. It was more and more apparent that he was never going to get any better health wise, but he was finally getting fed up with the life style he had. Eating 'crap' food. Working for pennies, and often sleeping rough.

Dagon had been sitting in the storeroom for a while, when Walter came in. He had obviously been crying. Whether it was from his beating, or the fact that, his only ally Dagon was leaving he didn't know. Dagon sat him down.

"Listen wee man. None of this is your fault. Your brother is evil, and can't look after you. You need specialised help, and I hope that will happen after what I'm going to do. I know you probably don't understand, but I'm going to change your life. Hopefully for the best, but I can't guarantee. Are you okay with that?"

For the first time since he had known Walter, it looked like a light had gone on in his head. By his facial expression, it appeared that he knew what Dagon was going to do. He started to laugh, which pierced through Dagon's brain.

"For fuck sake Walter, please stop laughing. My head can't cope with that noise. At six o'clock tonight, I'm going to shout to your brother that I want to see him, but whatever you do, don't come with him. Got it."

Walter just nodded his head, as if to say he understood, but Dagon wondered if he did.

He went over to where several ropes hung on the side of the barn. He chose one carefully, walked over to the middle of the barn, and made a noose on one end. It took him a couple of throws to loop it over one of the big beams in the centre. It was then tied off to another beam at the side of the barn. He looked around and found an old box, which he put standing up just under the noose. Excitement was running through his veins by now, and he was loving it. It felt the same this time as it did the first time, and all the other the times. He shouted towards the big house. He knew Kinghorn would come running.

"Kinghorn, you're short on the money, do you hear me?"

He stood just inside the barn door, and heard Kinghorn's footsteps coming across the gravel. He waited. Just as he stepped through the door, Dagon stepped forward and put his arm around his neck and squeezed. Not enough to kill him, just to make him pass out. Too early to kill him. Dagon lifted him up onto the box, put the noose over his head, and held him while slapping him awake. When he came too, there was utter panic on his face on seeing his predicament. He could only stand on the balls of his feet. He tried to loosen the noose, but Dagon had it tight on his neck, plus he was wobbling about on the box.

"You see Kinghorn, my name isn't Tam. It's Dagon, the Fallen Angel, and I'm here to send you to Hell. I will make sure Walter will be taken care of, probably for the first time in his life. I just can't make up my mind when I'm going to kill you, but by the look of your wobbling legs, you might just do that yourself.

"I can give you money, if that is what you are after. Just let me go, please, please."

"What makes you think I am interested in money you 'prick'. 'Ah' fuck, I can't stand looking at your face any longer."

He walked forward and kicked the box from under him. Kinghorn started kicking, and squirming, but within a couple of minutes he was gone. A wet patch appeared on the front of his trousers. The final humiliation.

As if on cue, Walter walked in with two mugs of tea to the storeroom. Why? Dagon didn't have a clue, but he was grateful for it. He wondered what his reaction would be to the body, but as soon as he drank his tea, he ran out and pushed the body back and forth, while laughing.

"Walter, will you just stop that fucking laughing. I'll go to my grave hearing it. Don't worry son, there will be someone here tomorrow morning to look after you."

After a while, Dagon told Walter to go and get something to eat, and then try to get some sleep.

Dagon thought he might do the same, but the dream, if that was what it was, that came to him that night really scared him. He dreamt that Heaven had sent down a heavenly body to persuade Dagon to change his ways. He had become angry, and confronted the entity. It had told him it wasn't too late to repent. However, Dagon had lost his temper, and killed whatever it was in his dream. He didn't know if that was what woke him up, or it might have been the bugs biting him, from the hay he was sleeping on.

The crows had come in to feed on Kinghorn's body all night. They squabbled and fought over every scrap of flesh they tore off the body. A wind had got up in the early hours, and the body kept gently swaying back and forth. Unfortunately, the beam that it swung on, creaked every time it moved.

He heard the laugh, before he saw Walter. He came into the barn, and started pushing the corpse of his dead brother, back and forward. The crows had made a mess of Kinghorn's face. The eyeballs must have been the first to go, then they had been tearing strips of his cheeks. Dagon looked up at the corpse.

"I couldn't give a fuck about you. You should have tried to be a better brother to Walter, so go and rot in Hell. I hope your body putrefies before I get there."

He shouted on Walter who had gone to see to the animals. When he came running back, Dagon asked him to take him into the house. Walter was only too pleased to take him in. Dagon wished he hadn't. The place smelled so bad, that he held his sleeve over his mouth and nose. You could hardly move in between all the rubbish that had been piled from floor to ceiling, a veritable death trap.

"Walter, can you please show me your room."

Dagon was sure that Walter thought that this was a game, and kept giggling. Dagon was glad it wasn't a full blown laugh, or Walter would be in danger of following his brother. When they walked into his bedroom, Dagon couldn't quite believe what he was seeing. All that was there was a single bed, bare floorboards, a window covered up with an old feed bag. Absolutely nothing else. It was pure and simply, squalor.

"Walter, have you any other clothes in here?"

He went and lifted up the decaying mattress, and pulled out a shirt and jeans. Both had seen better days.

"Please go, and find where your bother hid his money, and fill a bag full of food as well."

Walter knew exactly where to find his brothers money. It was hidden in an old leather satchel behind a chair. When Dagon looked inside, he was surprised to see that the bag was full to the brim with bank notes. He thought that Kinghorn hadn't trusted the Bank of Scotland. The money could only have come from the sale of the sheep and cows, at the yearly market.

"Right Walter, come with me please, and bring the food and clothes."

Dagon led him into the barn, with Walter unable to resist the temptation to push his brother's corpse back and forward again, while sniggering. Even just overnight hanging there, Dagon was starting to smell it, and he would be glad to be away from here.

"Walter please sit down, and try and understand what I am saying. Put this money I have here in your pocket. It's for you. The rest of the money is in the satchel, and please give it to the police when they come. There is going to be a big fire outside, so you can either stay in here, or go into the fields, keeping the animals quiet. It's whatever you want to do. I won't see you again, but don't worry, you'll be okay."

Walter had intimated he would go out beside the animals in the fields, so Dagon knew it was time to go. Before walking out, he carved his usual signature on the partition at the side of his bed. This time he made it about a foot high, and hung a blanket over the partition. He thought to himself that he wasn't going to make it too easy for the police. He was ready to go, and as he walked past the crows feeding on the corpse he said, "Enjoy yourself lads. Have your fill."

He went into the house, and used the telephone dialling the emergency services.

"Emergency services, how may I help you?"

"There's a large fire at Netherburn Farm near Lauder. There's also a vulnerable young man in the fields, tending to livestock. You might want to send an ambulance as well. Oh, and the police might be an idea."

"Okay sir, help is on the way, and can I ask you what your name is please?"

"Dagon."

As he started to leave the house, he picked up a box of matches from the kitchen, walked to all the rubbish in the living room, and set it on fire. He quickly went through the door, and up a side path on the hill, and hid in a small wooded area. He wanted to make sure that Walter was safe, plus he was interested to see how the circus was going to play out.

It was about half an hour before he could hear the sirens in the distance. Eventually, the fire engine came flying up the farm track, and stopped near to the house. Walter was clapping and laughing, while standing in the nearest field. This was the nearest thing to excitement he had experienced in his life. The ambulance was next up the track, with the police car following close by. Dagon watched as three police officers got out of their car. They appraised the situation, before coaxing Walter to come down from the field. Three officers, just because he mentioned the name Dagon. Oh, the fun starts from now he thought.

Walter ran to them, and it was obvious he couldn't wait to show them the barn. He kept gesticulating to them that they should follow him. It wasn't long after they went in that a young officer came out and threw up. Dagon was loving this. Half an hour later, the young guy who seemed to be in charge, came out with the blanket that Dagon had draped over the partition to hide his signature. The officer didn't look in a good mood, and walked to the burning house, throwing the blanket into the flames. Dagon reckoned that there wasn't going to be anything else to see. He was just about to head off, when he heard the officer shout.

"Everybody, and I mean everybody, stand still, and look around in every direction to see if you see any movement. Please stay perfectly still, look and listen."

After ten minutes of everybody just looking, the officer roared at the top of his voice.

"I know you are fucking watching us. I can feel it in my gut. I will find you, and lock you up. Be seeing you soon."

Dagon laughed, and thought how right the officer was. They would lock horns at some point, but not today. He was now off to Galashiels, to see what excitement he could have there.

Bob was trying to calm Vinny down by now.

"Vinny, standing shouting isn't going to help the situation here. Let's contain the crime scene, and see if there have been any clues left. I doubt it though, as this guy is very clever."

Vinny sat down on the edge of a water trough, and just looked down at the ground. After a while he stood up, and walked into the barn where Bob and Ian were going over everything. After about thirty minutes it was Bob who spoke.

"Right, let's wrap this up, as we are just 'pissing' in the wind. I tried to speak to the young guy earlier, but as he has limited mental capacity, I couldn't get anything out of him. I know what's going to happen now though. Head office will be on to us to catch this killer, and sooner rather than later."

They decided to head back to Gala, but not before speaking to the Watch Commander who was standing giving instructions to his crew.

"Mr Robertson, did you find any evidence of more bodies in the house?"

"Impossible to say, as it seems that the guy was a hoarder. If anybody was trapped inside, then there was no chance of them getting out. We have radioed to the Hawick station to come over and relieve us, as this could take a couple of days. With the amount of rubbish inside, there is always a chance of it reigniting. If we find anything, we will call the police station at Gala."

There wasn't a lot said as they drove back to Gala. Ian had his head to the side against the window, and his eyes closed.

"Don't think you're going to get that image out of your brain for a long time Ian. Remember, you can always speak to us anytime you want."

When they got into the station, they updated Kim on what had happened. There was genuine shock, and worry on her face.

"Do you think he'll come after any of us."

"I don't think so Kim. It is obvious that he likes to do his work on vulnerable individuals. If he tried coming after a police officer, then he knows he would have the full might of the force on top of him. Don't worry," said Bob.

"I know what's going to happen after I phone Brian in a while. So I suggest we have everybody in here tomorrow morning. Apologise to anybody that will have just come off night shift."

"I'll leave it up to you Kim to organise this please. I'm going into the other office to phone Brian. Wish me luck."

It wasn't just the folk in the next office that heard the shouting, and arguing. Bob reckoned the whole of Gala would have heard them. When Vinny finally came out, they gave him time to calm down. It was Bob who then asked what had happened.

"There is only one thing stopping me from being a gentleman of the road, and that is that I reckon the killer is toying with us. I fucking knew he was either sitting, or standing watching us today. Probably laughing at us if truth be told. Brian Lawson has told me that the bosses will want us to track this guy down. I wonder if there is a part in the police manual that tells you how to catch a serial killer. What a total fuck up. It's times like this I could go home, and drown myself in alcohol. I suppose you could do it for me Bob. What do you say?"

Bob had a very large smile on his face.

Chapter 13

When they had got back, Vinny had phoned the forensic department in Edinburgh, and asked them to go over the crime scene. It was standard procedure, but he reckoned that they would struggle to find anything, so it was just a matter of waiting for their phone call. They headed back to Innerleithen, so that they could sit down and work out where they would go from here. As they sat looking at each other, it was Vinny who spoke first.

"I know you are looking at me for inspiration, but I'm telling you how it is. I have fuck all. We know the guy has no problem killing people, and the only hint of a clue is that in his eyes, he is killing evil people. For God sake, that covers a lot of people. It appears that he doesn't go looking for his next victim, but if he comes across them, then he has no compunction about killing."

"Vinny, I think we have to get Kim to log every single clue, or bit of knowledge we have. Think about this. He said in the letter at Eyemouth, that he had been coming down the path along the cliffs. So does that mean he had been in Midlothian, or further afield, so maybe Kim should be making enquiries to other forces about any suspicious deaths. We don't know about his motives as to why he wants to kill anybody. There are loads of reasons in somebody's mind. Vinny, you can't get angry about this, or mistakes will be made."

"Yeh, your right Bob. We know we have zero chance of catching this guy, unless he screws up."

The first phone call was from the front desk at the Gala station, to say that the Watch Commander from the Gala fire brigade had caught a guy from the Border Bulletin taking photos inside the barn, and around the yard. He claimed he had permission from yourself, but Mr Robertson didn't believe him, and threw him off the site. This left all three of them absolutely fuming.

"After the meeting tomorrow, we have to find this bastard from the Bulletin, and charge him, with whatever we can. Everybody agree with that?"

"I'll look through the rule book to see what we can or can't charge him with. Leave it with me," said Kim.

The second call was more disturbing.

"Are you the police officers who attended the incident at the farm? If not then please find them, and put them on the phone."

A massive feeling came over Vinny. He knew who this was, so he turned the phone up as high as it would go, and gestured to Bob, Ian and Kim to stop what they were doing, and gather around the phone. The guy was disguising his voice.

"Why do you want to speak to us?"

"That's simple. I would just like to know who will be after me. I've left you enough clues, as to who I am. Yet, I don't know who you are, so I was interested to know your names."

"May I ask what your name is, and why you are doing what your doing?" asked Vinny.

"Oh, come on now. You know by now, that my name Dagon. I am a Fallen Angel. Soon to serve my Master in Hell, but before I leave this earth, I will kill any evil people I come up against, and I will rejoice over every death. Now it's your turn to furnish me with your names."

"Well the guy sitting next to me is Bob."

"Is that the guy that is built like a Sherman tank?"

"That's the one Dagon."

"What about you."

"My name is Ds Vinny Hunter."

There was a long pause on the end of the line. Vinny thought he might just have left the phone hanging, and walked out of the phone box.

"Well Mr Hunter, I think this will be a battle of wills and I'm looking forward to it, but may I say that you will never win, but please do try and make it quick, as I'm not a well man. I have nothing against any of you, as you're just doing your job, and I promise you that we will never be in a situation whereby I would have to kill any of you."

"Dagon, can I ask you two things please? What is your real name, and if I end up putting you in the ground, will your master be displeased?"

"Mr Hunter. These two things will never happen. Now I must go, but it's been an interesting chat. Regards to the Sherman tank. Happy hunting folks."

Before the line went dead, he heard Dagon having a coughing fit.

"You will have to excuse me, as I'm feeling sick," said Kim as she headed to the toilets. "Looks like we have a challenge in front of us," said Bob."

"The thing is Bob, I haven't got a clue what to do next. Do you?"

"Lets talk about this in the morning. I suggest you go and see how Kim is."

Kim was just walking out the toilets, and he asked her how she was.

"I feel the same way as you Vinny. I didn't sign up to go chasing after a serial killer."

"Let's get something to eat and have a quiet night, and as Bob says, we'll talk about it in the morning."

Kim held on to Vinny all night in bed. He had went out like a light as soon as his head hit the pillow. It was obvious that last night's phone call had frightened her, and Vinny thought he would have to keep an eye on her.

Next morning, Bob was knocking on their door, and telling them to hurry up, as they had a busy day in front of them. All the officers were present at nine am. Firstly, Vinny thanked everyone for being here, especially those that had just come off night duty.

"Right everybody, the reason we're standing here probably comes as no surprise to any of you. You will all know by now that we have a serial killer operating in the Borders. I see one or two of you raising your eyebrows, but I can assure its true. Last night the three of us here received a phone call at the Innerleithen station from him. I won't go into details, but I need you all to be aware when you are out and about. I have no doubt that officers from other divisions will be drafted in to help, but here is the deal. We have no idea when, or where he will strike next, but I can assure you he is a very clever adversary, and cannot be underestimated. Please do everything by the book, as he's only interested in what he describes as evil people. Right, any questions so far?"

"I have one sir.

"If he is only killing evil people, then why are we looking to arrest him?"

"I was wondering if someone would come up with that. Simple answer to it really. By the letter of the law, you can't go about killing people, just because in your mind you think they're evil. Sometimes I know it's hard to accept, but even killers have human rights."

There were a few mutterings about that.

After everybody dispersed, the phone rang, and Kim took the call.

"Vinny, I would suggest you take this call, it's from forensics in Edinburgh."

" Good morning Ds Hunter. As you know we went down to the farm to look for any clues that may have been left by your serial killer. Well to be honest, we didn't find anything, except in the sleeping area of the barn. What we found were traces of blood on the floor. It looks like the person tried to erase any evidence of it by covering it over with the soil on the floor. In my opinion, he or she must have been coughing it up, and then spitting it onto the floor. We analysed the blood, and found that your serial killer has a very aggressive cancer of the lungs."

"That comes as a bit of surprise to me in one way, but it makes sense in another. We received a phone call from him last night. He did say he wasn't a well man, and he was asking us to get a move on in trying to find and arrest him. To be honest, we thought he might be toying with us. How long do you think he has?"

"Well, being an aggressive form of cancer, I estimate he has six months, possibly a year. As his illness gets worse, then there will be the possibility that his mood swings will get worse as well, so he might be capable of anything at some point. I hope this helps you Ds Hunter."

Vinny thanked him for their help, and asked Bob, Ian and Kim to grab a coffee and come and sit at his desk.

"Okay folks. I need to tell you about the conversation I've just had with the forensic department in Edinburgh. It appears that Dagon, our killer, had been coughing up blood in the area where we thought he had been sleeping at the farm. He has an aggressive form of lung cancer, which will kill him within a year.

Forensics have warned me that his whole demeaner may change, which could make him unpredictable. So he wasn't toying with us. So Kim, get on to every hospital, and see if anybody has come in for help. It's a whole different ball game now."

"Not necessarily Vinny, as it could work to our advantage at some stage. Being as ill as he is, might make him slip up at some point, but let's not rely on that. We need to go and visit the moron at the Bulletin."

They left Kim and Ian in charge. Bob said they should walk, because if they needed to bring the guy back to the station, then they should handcuff him to let the public see what they were doing. Bob didn't knock on the door. He just marched in past the girl sitting at the reception. He went into the editors office, but it was empty, so he went to the reception, and said," Okay, where the hell is he, and don't try and tell me any lies."

"I'm sorry, I don't have a clue where he is. It looks like he was in all night, as the printing presses are in need of cleaning. If he has printed the newspaper off, then I presume he is out distributing it. That's all I know. Again, I'm so sorry."

"I want his address, and if I find out you have tipped him off in any way, I will be back here to arrest you. Understand?"

Vinny couldn't be bothered with her crying, so he headed out to wait for Bob, who came out with a piece of paper in his hand.

"Right, let's get back to the station, and get Ian to take us to this address."

As they walked back, Vinny said to Bob," What do you think this bastard has written in his bloody newspaper this time. I have no doubt the killer will contact the paper any time there's a killing."

"Whatever it is, the editor will have sensationalised it. Scare people, just to sell newspapers no doubt. Maybe tell lies."

"Bob, maybe we could use this guy to our advantage if we put enough pressure on him."

"Run your plan past me before I agree to anything. For a minute it sounded like you want to use him as bait."

He looked at Vinny and said," You're not are you?"

They arrived back at the station, and shouted to Ian to accompany them to the address they were given. The house was in Wood St. which was on the way out of the town. They climbed the back stairs and knocked loudly on the door. There was no answer.

"Maybe if I just happen to lean on the door, it might miraculously open. What do you think lads?"

Vinny just smiled, but there was a look of disbelief on Ian's face.

"Don't worry son. You were never here," said Bob.

Bob just put his shoulder onto the door, and the lock gave way easily. The house was empty. It wasn't that clean, and there was a smell, as if windows hadn't been opened in a while.

"It was worth a try lads. Ian, I have a job for you. Do you own a car? If so I want you to stake out the newspaper's office. If you see the guy going in, don't try and apprehend him. Give the station a call. I don't want you getting all the fun."

Dagon walked into Galashiels, and sat on a bench in what was Bank St. gardens, which ran adjacent to one of the main streets. He watched all the people walking up and down the street. It seemed that there wasn't a lot of happiness in this town by the looks on their faces. He was going to find a small bed and breakfast, and stay in it until his money ran out. After that, who knows. Although he reckoned that he would have more than enough, before his body gave out. When he walked from near the place called Lauder, his chest was causing him problems. Sharp pains were stopping him enough that he had to sit down at the side of the road. Twice a couple of cars had slowed down, but he had just waved them on, while raising his hand to say thanks. He thought he was bringing up more blood, but he wasn't going to worry about it.

He noticed a couple of charity shops on the street across road, so he thought it might be an idea to change his appearance every so often. His beard had grown quite a bit, so his idea was to grow it, then shave it off, and so on. He headed off to find a bed for the night, and as he walked, he would make up a story about who he was. Another one. More and more lies. As he walked, he thought that this town needed a bit of a face lift, but a lot of the towns he had travelled through had been the same. He spotted a sign saying Bed and Breakfast pointing to one of the side streets which would be perfect. When he got there, he couldn't believe his luck. About fifty yards up the road was the police station. He managed to get a room at the Bed and Breakfast, which was being run by an elderly couple. They said he could have a room at the back, so he wouldn't get much noise from the traffic, however he asked for one of the upstairs rooms which looked directly along the road to the police station. They weren't fussy either way.

The only people who knew what he looked like were now dead, so he felt confident he could walk around the town without any suspicion being raised. He walked up the road, and straight in to the police station. His heart was racing a bit, but he was up for a bit of fun. Something that had been sadly lacking in his miserable life lately. There was a young girl on reception, obviously not a police officer, so he asked her if there was bus station, and as he was on holiday, he wanted to visit Edinburgh. She explained that it wasn't a very big station. Really just an area where the buses drew into, with a small shelter to keep out of the wind and rain.

Dagon wasn't really listening to her, as he could see right through to the back of the station where lots of officers were milling around. It was then that Ds Hunter had walked through, asking the receptionist to mail a file to somebody. Dagon turned his head away, pretending to look at a notice board. He smiled, as Ds Hunter walked through to the back of the building. Meanwhile, the girl was doing a small sketch for Dagon, as to where the station was. He thanked her, and just before he left, he looked through to the back just in time to see the Sherman tank casting an eclipse over the back office. Another smile came over him.

The nights were bad for Dagon. Each time he lay down, his coughing would start, and he would have to bring up the blood into toilet paper. Every morning he would just flush the paper away. He found that being in a sitting position helped him, so he lay each night propped up by pillows. It wasn't ideal, but at least he managed some sleep. However, the nightmares were relentless. More and more entities seemed to want to kill, and devour him. He wondered if every Fallen Angel had to go through this, before it was time to be with their Master. Maybe I have wings of shadows, and a heart of fire, if I have one he thought.

Over the next few days Vinny felt that someone was watching him. Even asking the girl on the reception who the guy was that he had seen standing there the other day. She explained who he was. Vinny went about each day thinking that someone's eyes were on him all the time. He tried to explain it to Kim and Bob, about the feeling, but that was all it was, a feeling. It was even stronger when he stepped out of the station to go home. He always stopped, and looked up and down the street, but there was nobody he could relate to being the killer. However, the killer was looking at him from the bedroom window. Just smiling at his bit of discomfort. Dagon knew he couldn't get too close, but a little bit of toying with the police would be fine.

As Vinny drove up the road, he said he wanted to speak to the pair of them when they got to the Innerleithen station. As they sat round the table he told them about the feelings he was getting.

"I know it may seem a bit weird, but I genuinely feel that someone is watching me. Just like the time at the farm near Lauder. I feel he is toying with me. I haven't a clue why. There was a guy in reception the other day when I went through, and throughout the afternoon I had the same feeling in my stomach, that he might have been the killer. However, I might just be 'pissing in the wind,' and being a bit paranoid, what do you think?"

"Vinny, there is every possibility that the guy is now in Gala, as it's not far from Lauder. However, can I ask you this? Have you ever felt threatened by this guy?"

"No never Bob, especially after his phone call to us. I think he feels we're not evil people, and only doing our jobs. However, do I think he will surrender himself to us, even if he's trapped, then no, not a hope in hell. He probably knows how ill he is, although he won't know how long he's got to live, but people know their own bodies."

"Kim?"

"The thing is Vinny, both Bob and I don't have this feeling, but maybe we're not in the same zone as you. Maybe you should find time to relax. Go fishing, even if it's just to get that bloody fishing rod out of the kitchen."

They all laughed, which was the first time in a long time. Vinny knew they were just playing the waiting game, so he told

Bob he should head up to Dundee and see Sharon, which he gladly agreed to. Kim said she was going up to Edinburgh to do some clothes shopping, and there was not a hope in hell that Vinny would go with her. It was fishing for Vinny tomorrow.

Bob was away early in the morning, and Kim wasn't far behind. Vinny had been woken up a few times with really hard erections throughout the night. Occasionally, he had hugged Kim, hoping she would get the hint. However, she was either not interested, or she was in deep sleep. When she was showering, and starting to get ready to go, then it was shopping 'one' and Vinny's love life 'nil'.

He felt quite invigorated while walking down to the river with his fishing rod and basket. When he got to the road bridge over the river Tweed, he looked up and down, and couldn't see any other fishermen, which was a bonus. He walked down to the river bank, and got his rod already to start fishing. After a short time, he put his rod down, and started to look all around him. He couldn't shake this feeling of being watched. He admitted to himself that it was getting to him, but if he didn't get a grip then paranoia would overtake him.

He had no sooner started to fish when he heard this voice.

"Who the bloody hell showed you how to fish like that?"

Vinny looked up to see 'auld' Charlie peering over the rails of the bridge. He had been warned by the other fishermen he had met, to expect a visit from Charlie.

"Right, give me the rod, and I'll show you the proper way to cast. You have to cast your fly up the river and let it slowly float down. You're just casting your line in any old how. The bloody fish will be laughing at you son."

After an hour of tuition from Charlie, Vinny thought that if the biggest salmon came up the river just now, he would catch it. Unfortunately, after another half an hour, he hadn't got one single bite.

"Charlie, are you sure there are fish in this river? An hour and a half and no bloody bite. What am I doing wrong?"

"Nothing son, welcome to fishing," said Charlie while he walked away laughing.

Vinny gave it another hour, but had only one nibble on his line, so he called it a day and started to walk home. He actually felt exhilarated, even although Charlie had said the fish had been laughing at him. He didn't know what had made him do it, but he walked into the cemetery through the big black gates, and found a bench which looked over all the headstones. For some reason, after sitting for a while, it made him think about the way his life was going. He was happy with Kim, and his job had been okay, but he felt there was something missing in his life. As for the serial killer, he knew it was just a temporary blip. He knew the guy would be dead, sooner rather than later, and he would be so glad. Little did he know how these thoughts would come back to haunt him.

As relaxing as it was just sitting in the cemetery, he knew he would have to get back to the house, in case there were any developments with regards to the killer. He just walked into the station when the phone rang. It was Brian Lawson.

"Hi Vinny. I'm just wondering if there's an update on the serial killer. Head office have been asking what's happening."

"Nothing since the last time Brian, although he did phone us here at the station."

Vinny went on to tell him what the guy had said, and how he was having this feeling of being watched a lot of the time.

"Do you think he is actually watching you Vinny? That's a bit scary is it not?"

"I don't feel scared Brian, but I know he is definitely watching me. Why me I don't know. I presume you got the report from forensics, so we know he hasn't got that long left to live, so maybe we just have to ride out the storm, until his demise. The thing is Brian, we have talked and talked about how we can catch him, and we still can't come up with anything."

"I wouldn't have a clue either Vinny, so it might be a case of him slipping up, or as you say him dying. Just when the restructuring is going well. Do you think the press he is getting is hindering you, if so, we can try and shut that fucking newspaper down."

"Unfortunately, it is only telling the truth, but if the editor starts to print lies, then yes we can. Kim has looked into it. There is another issue out in a few days, so we'll see. I meant to say that we have brought another guy onto our team. His name is Ian

Soutar, and he's showing good promise for being in charge when we leave the Borders."

"Sounds good Vinny, but remember you can't trust any killer, never mind a serial one. Take care."

Kim arrived back early afternoon, with more bags that you could shake a stick at. Vinny knew then it would be a bloody fashion parade for about an hour. What should she keep, or what should she return. Vinny's head was just buzzing.

"Right Kim, go and get all your bits washed, and I'll take you for a drink in one of the pubs, but remember you're a police officer, so no fighting, cussing or spitting, although dancing on the tables half pissed is acceptable."

"Good plan, but how about you come upstairs first, and give me a good reason to wash my bits."

Vinny sprinted up the stairs in record time, and had all his clothes off before she was half way to the bedroom. It was like they had never made love before. They were making love in every position. Kim was enjoying her orgasms, but at times she kept them from Vinny, in case he became obsessed about it again. She never understood why the last one was always so intense, but she would never complain. As they lay spent, it was Vinny who whispered," Do you really want to go for a drink Kim?"

"Of course I do Hunter. You get in the shower, and wash everything thoroughly, as you never know what the morning might bring, but don't be poking me all night with your erections in anticipation, as it might not happen."

They walked down the road, and the first establishment they came to was the Union Club. After looking through the window, neither of them fancied going in for a drink. Next stop was the Tweedside Hotel, which apparently the locals referred to as the Middle Pub. They heard the juke box, and decided that it was worth a try. A certain song from the 'jukie' had gotten everybody up on their feet dancing. One or two were dancing on the seats against the wall.

"Lively enough for you Kim?"

" Yeh. I'll be back in a minute."

Kim took off into the crowd that were dancing, while Vinny ordered a couple of drinks at the bar. He sat down at a spare table watching Kim enjoying her dancing. He looked at the drink he had in his hand, and wondered if he would be better with an alcoholic one. Then his thoughts went back to the low-life, drunken father he had, thinking if it wasn't for him he might still have a mother. Kim came back and sat down.

"Vinny Hunter, get a grip of yourself, and start enjoying life. Believe me, there is nobody watching you in here. C'mon let's dance, and if I end up on the tables, then tough."

When Kim wasn't dancing with him, she was enjoying herself in amongst everybody else who was dancing. Vinny had noticed that she hadn't taken a sip out of her drink. She didn't need alcohol to enjoy herself. Something the three Amigos had pledged many 'moons' ago. After a couple of hours, people were drifting away, so Kim had suggested they head home. When they walked out the door of the pub, they noticed the fish and chip shop across the road was still open, so they decided to share a bag of chips on the way back to the station.

On walking along the road, the ten - thirty bus from Edinburgh drove by. Vinny was stopped in his tracks when he saw a bearded guy looking out the window at him.

"What the hell is wrong Vinny, it's like you've seen a ghost?"

"I'm sure that the guy looking out the window of the bus just now, was the same guy that was in the station the other day. I have that massive feeling in my gut. Bloody hell Kim this isn't right."

"For God sake Vinny, it might not have been him, or maybe just a coincidence."

"Why the gut feeling then Kim?"

She was beginning to worry about him, as this serial killer was taking over his life. She knew he was conscientious about his job, but she wondered why this case, although massive, was affecting him that much. Kim hoped that the killer's illness would get him as soon as possible.

All night, Vinny tossed and turned, forcing Kim to sleep in the spare bedroom. When she went through in the morning he wasn't there, but she heard him downstairs. She showered, before heading down. He was sitting at the breakfast table, 'nursing' a cup of coffee."

"You make a hell of a racket for just making a cup of coffee Vinny Hunter."

"Sorry Kim, I was struggling last night. To many bad dreams I'm afraid. I can't help it."

"Don't worry my gorgeous lover, I forgive you. What are we up for today?"

"Can I be a wee bit selfish, and say that I would like to do another bit of fishing. Get some practice, but as the sun is out, I thought you might like to bring our lunch down to the river. What do you say?"

"As long as you don't ask me to try fishing."

Vinny headed down to the Tweed later in the morning, with Kim following around mid-day. Vinny was trying to impress Kim with his fishing prowess, but failing badly.

"Vinny? How many fish have you caught today, plus the other day? I've been here for half an hour, and I've never seen you get a bite. Is it you, or as you said before, the fish are just 'thumbing' their noses at you," said Kim laughing.

They were startled by somebody roaring, as he walked up the water side. It was 'auld' Charlie with his dog. He seemed a bit animated, and when he got up to them, said, "What the hell are you doing. Don't you know you can't fish the Tweed on the Sabbath? You'll end up getting my gear confiscated."

"My apologies Charlie, I had no idea of the rules. I'll just stop now. By the way that's a 'cracking' looking dog."

"'Aye' I look after him for my son. His name is Breck. Any other rules you're not sure about, then you know where I live. Right, I'm off."

"Well that was you firmly put in your place Vinny Hunter was it not."

Vinny just shook his head, and sat on the bench, where Kim joined him.

"Vinny, you have to stop letting this serial killer situation get to you. It could destroy you."

As he sat eating his lunch, a guy popped his head over the railings and said," Had any luck today pal?"

Vinny never lifted his head, but just said that the fish weren't biting. He was too busy eating his lunch, and thinking about what Kim had said. It was about ten minutes later that he dropped his sandwich, and put his head in his hands.

"Kim, can you see where the guy that spoke to me, went? I've got that feeling in my gut again, and it's so intense. I fucking know that was him. I really know."

"He is just turning left onto the road leading to Walkerburn, but the trees are beginning to obscure him. Why?"

Vinny took off as fast as he could, with Kim shouting after him. He was going full 'pelt' down the road, until he turned left onto the Walkerburn road. After about a couple of hundred yards, Vinny stopped in the middle of the road, and looked all around him. Nothing was moving. He looked over the wooden barrier down toward the river through the trees. Then he saw movement. He ran another thirty or forty yards, where he could get a better look. Bloody hell, it was only cows grazing in the field next to the Tweed. Was he really beginning to lose it? He was beginning to breath heavily, until Kim came running down the road, and grabbed him. Vinny started to shout.

"Why don't you fucking come out, and meet me face to face, instead of all this intimidation. Then running away hiding. C'mon you fucker, I'm waiting, I know you're there."

His breathing had slowed, but the feeling was still in his stomach. He knew the guy was in the forest, just watching. Eventually, he walked slowly back to the bridge with Kim, occasionally turning round to see if anyone moved in the forest, but he was wasting his time.

Dagon sat watching him with smile on his face. If Ds Vinny Hunter carried on like that, it would be a toss up who would 'kick the bucket' first. With Ds Hunter far enough away, he started to cough, and it was no surprise the amount of blood that came up.

Chapter 14

Dagon had decided to walk most of the way back to Gala, through the fields and forests, as he couldn't be sure Ds Hunter hadn't phoned the Galashiels station for someone to meet the buses, just in case he was on any of them. Halfway, during his journey back, he had to sit for a while. He knew he couldn't carry on like this, as apart from bringing up blood, he was struggling with his breathing.

It was early evening when he got back to his room. He decided it was time to shave, and cut his hair. When he shaved, he was a bit shocked at his ravaged face when he looked in the mirror. His illness had been hard on him. There were the start of small scars on his sunken cheeks, and he had to be careful not to 'nick' any of them with his razor. It wasn't a nice look, but he couldn't do anything about it now. He knew it would hit him hard when his illness was going to take him. Still, there was time yet for him to have a little bit of fun with the police, or if anybody needed to be dispatched to see the main man.

Bob had come back late that evening, and Kim had gone out to greet him, telling him about what had happened in the morning. Kim could see he looked a bit fed up by it all.

"Bob, I've told him how worried I am about this serial killer, and how it's affecting him."

"While driving back Kim, something came to me about this case. As much as I am 'pissed off' with it, I really do think that the serial killer has latched onto him, and probably just wants a bit of toying with him, until he departs this earth. It might be personal, but I'm at a loss as to what the reason would be. I'll have a word with him in the morning, now get off to bed."

Before they left for Gala the next morning, Bob asked Vinny into the station office, and asked him to sit down, and don't say a word.

"Vinny, both Kim and I are worried about you. How you're handling this case. I do believe you are having these feelings, but I think you're handling it all the wrong way. She told me about your episode yesterday. Shouting at somebody who might not have been there, and getting yourself in a state is not the answer pal. If he was there, and it's a big if, then he was probably sitting there laughing at you. If it starts to affect your health, then all I can say is that he's won. Do you hear?"

As Bob walked away he said laughing," Oh, by the way, I hope my fridge is stocked with trout, or maybe a salmon or two."

Vinny knew Bob and Kim were right, but something like this had never happened to him before. Maybe, he just had to get on with the restructuring, and if, or when, anything relating to the killer reared it's ugly head, then he would try and deal with it. He knew however, that the feeling inside him would never go away if the guy was near him, unless he caught him, or the guy died. How would he ever know if the guy was dead, unless a body turned up, if the guy was still living rough, then a body might never be found. That for Vinny, would not be a fitting end.

For the following week, Dagon did nothing more than walk around Galashiels. He wore a scarf around his face to protect him from the harsh, bitter wind. As he walked, he saw everyone getting ready for the Festive period. It had been a long time since he had spent time at Christmas with any loved ones. He knew that there would be a lot of joy and happiness for the children soon. This would probably be the last Christmas he would ever see. He had spoken to the owners of the Bed and Breakfast about just staying on indefinitely, and they'd agreed.

He would walk on occasion past the police station. Just slowing the pace enough so that he could have a glance in to see who was about. There was one thing he thought, and that was if that 'lass' was the partner of Ds Hunter, then he was one lucky guy. He tried to remember some of the young ladies he had been with, but there hadn't been many, so he tried to forget that memory. If he was honest with himself, he was getting a bit bored with his life again, and as he didn't have that long left, he hoped something would come up.

That opportunity did arise for him, when he had walked past one of the corner shops with a newspaper stand outside. The headlines in the Border Bulletin read.

'BORDERS SERIAL KILLER STRIKESAGAIN'

Underneath, on the same page, was how the incompetent Galashiels police were incapable of catching him, with photos of the crime scene at Lauder, and the aftermath of the fire which had burned the house down. Dagon sat on one of the benches, and read the paper. Some of the comments that came from the editor, had been nothing but lies. Especially towards the police force. Dagon had lied all his life. Basically for self preservation, but the more times he read it, the more angry he was becoming, so he had to make a decision. Did he dispatch this moron to Hell, or just leave him be. A few years ago there would be no decision to make. He would have been in Hell in a heartbeat. Dagon felt his spirits lifted slightly. A plan had to be made, but it had to be quick, as he didn't know how long he had left. He pocketed the newspaper, and headed back to his 'digs'.

Ian came in, and placed the newspaper on Vinny's desk, before heading out of the office as he knew all hell would break loose when the boss appeared. Ian had just started to make coffee when the three of them arrived. They seemed in a good mood, but that was about to change. When he opened the door and walked in with three mugs of coffee, he had to duck very quickly, as Vinny had just tossed the paper in Ian's direction. All the pages separated and went flying in all directions.

"Apologies Ian. I never meant to throw it in your direction. It's just that I am so fucking angry. We need to find this bastard, and charge him. Kim, please find out what we think we can charge him with, and speak to the procurator fiscal. Ian, can you bring your car in, and we can have you sitting watching the newspaper's office. Bob, what do you say?"

"It certainly doesn't put us in a good light with the public, but let's find him first, and wait until the procurator gets back to us. It's a plan to have Ian watch his work place though, but we have had Ian do this before with no luck."

He wandered through to one of the back offices, and sat contemplating the whole mess that was appearing around him. Vinny, and Kim, had been right, in as much as this wasn't the job they were supposed to be doing. Although, Vinny's idea of just walking the roads was a bit extreme. He wasn't sure he wanted to carry on in the police force. He had thirty years in his police pension now, so it would be more than enough just to walk away from all this, and take up another job elsewhere. Then again, he would be letting the team down, plus letting the public down by not trying to catch this guy. However, he still wasn't sure why the killer had made this personal with Vinny. Only time would tell.

The procurator fiscal's office got back to Kim.

"Okay everybody, are you listening? What the procurator fiscal has said, is that we can charge him with entering a crime scene without authorisation, and hindering an ongoing investigation, However, they said that a good lawyer might get the guy off."

"So we're no further forward," said Vinny before he completely lost it, picked up his letter opener, and stuck it into a page of the Bulletin which was still lying on his desk.

"I think you may not like my plan, but you know the saying, killing two birds with one stone. Well it might have to be that you trust me."

His phone rang, but he lifted the receiver and quickly said, "Not now." The phone rang again, and before he could say anything, the girl said," You will want to take this call, trust me."

"Hello again Ds Hunter. No guessing who this is."

Vinny turned the phone up to maximum, and told everyone to listen to see if they could recognise any noises in the background, with his hand over the mouth piece of the phone.

"I presume the short lull was you getting your team to gather around the phone. Good practice my friend. Anyway, I would firstly like to apologise for all that drivel that the idiot from the newspaper printed about your policing. It was not what I told him. Only about the death, and fire at the farm near Lauder. If your forensics paid a visit to the barn, then you'll know by now that I am a very sick man, so at some point the killing will stop, but not by you catching me. Oh no."

Strangely it was Kim who started to speak.

"Dagon, my name is Kim. I am also a Detective Sergeant in Gala. Can I ask you something please. Were you watching Ds Hunter over the Tweed bridge on Sunday? If so, why the taunting? We know you're dying, and no doubt there will be a body or two for us to deal with before you leave this earth. I can feel for you with the terrible illness you have, but not the killing. We never wanted this job of trying to hunt you down. Just orders."

"It's so nice to speak to a lovely young lady. The last time was at Duns, but don't try and get anything out of Beth, as she won't say a word. Yes, it was me taunting your boyfriend Kim, but I knew you would look after him. As you're listening Ds Hunter, you will really need to calm down, or your health will suffer. It won't be long until we meet at the end, and you will find out why I was taunting you, but remember, you are trying to catch a ghost. An evil one at that. Please leave the editor to me, do you hear? I must go now as I've a lot to plan. Oh, and a very Merry Christmas to you all."

Nobody said a word. Ian just sat drinking his coffee looking bewildered, while Vinny was rubbing his face with the palms of his hands. Bob just lay back in his chair, and closed his eyes. Ten minutes later Kim shouted.

"Fucking wake up the lot of you. Are you just going to bury your heads in the sand for God sake? I'm going to make a bold statement here. We do nothing. It's impossible to catch this guy, and there will be more bodies whether we search for him or not. Let's get on with our jobs, and especially our lives. Report to Brian Lawson that we are in communication with the killer. Although we wont tell him how, or when, but at least he will think that's progress. As for the editor, let him take his chances with Dagon. What does everybody think?"

"No matter who it is, we have to try and protect them Kim," said Vinny.

"Oh, fuck off Vinny. You're the one that's making themself ill, yet you still want to carry on this charade, which to be perfectly honest is 'pissing' me off. Let's take a vote. I know you're in charge, but hands up for letting this go."

Bob, Kim, and Ian voted to let the situation just play out, with Vinny disagreeing with them.

"Right, motion carried. Let's get on with things."

Dagon sat at the window of his room, behind the net curtain, watching people going in and out of the police station. Ds Hunter always stood at the door and looked around him before going in. He thought he would never let go. His mind went to two things. Firstly the editor. He had to make a plan as to how he was going to deal with him, but it would have to be a fitting demise. The other thing was a story he had cut out of the latest edition of the

227

Bulletin, about a lady who had left several dogs to die by starvation at a place near Innerleithen. No animal should have to endure that, so he decided that he would go up there, and check the woman out. He didn't know if he was going to do anything, but it was worth a visit, although he had made a visit to the village a few times.

A few days later Vinny walked in and asked Bob if he fancied a trip to Hawick, which was further down the Borders. When he had asked him why, Vinny said it was just to suss out if some towns needed more attention than others. Bob agreed to it. Anything to get him away from Gala. When they were driving, it was Bob who dropped the bombshell.

"Vinny, can I tell you that it's my intention to quit the force after we've finished in the Borders. I've been a bit disillusioned for a while now. Not just here, but with everything that has been going on, and the force in general."

"What will you do Bob? I can't think of you doing anything other than this."

"Probably nothing for a while pal. Sharon and I have been talking about seeing more of Scotland for a while. So you never know, you might get a postcard from some obscure place up North now and again, he said laughing."

"Let's see how you feel after we have finished in the Borders, and this maniac is in the ground."

As they drove down to Hawick, Bob commented that it was a bigger town than he had thought. He pointed out to Vinny the two large housing estates either side of the main road. By chance, the police station was just at the bottom of the road on the right. They drove into the carpark, and sat for a while.

"We need to have an excuse for just walking in Bob, as we need to see the station at it's worst. What's your thoughts?"

"No fucking excuses Vinny. Let's just go in, and ask for whoever's in charge of the station. It should be interesting."

They got out of the car, and walked through the large double doors. There was a reception area with a large bench against the wall as a sitting area. In the centre of the main wall was a large glass hatch. They could see right through to the officers, supposedly working. Vinny pressed the button, and waited. He could see a constable sitting with his feet up on a desk with a large cigarette in his mouth. They waited and waited, until Vinny pressed the button again, but this time he kept his finger down on it.

Just then, the main doors flew open, and two officers came in dragging a guy by the scruff of the neck. They were knocking lumps out of him with their truncheons, and taking turns at kicking him. Screams were coming out of the guy. They took him through a side door, but Bob and Vinny could still hear him screaming.

"What's your game pal? Pressing the bell like you're some sort of idiot. What do you want?" asked the constable with the cigarette still hanging out of his mouth.

"I want to speak to the officer in charge of this station, and make it quick please."

"Who the hell are you to tell me what to do. I'm in charge here, so state your business, or fuck off."

Vinny pointed to his police number on his shoulder.

"Look you dick head. You are only a Pc, and no constable can be left in charge of a police station."

Vinny had enough, and walked through the door to the side of the window. He walked forward, picking up a can of lager, and threw it through the television where the big match had been playing. The guy sitting watching it got such a fright that he couldn't utter a word. Bob walked through after Vinny, but continued through to the cells, where the guy was getting a real kicking.

"Right lads, you can stop now. If you need to charge him, then do so, and keep him in a cell if need be."

"Who the fuck are you arsehole?"

"Your superior, but if you call me an arsehole again, I will take your truncheon and stick it as far up your arse that is humanly possible."

Bob took his warrant card out, and showed them. There was actual fear on their faces, as they knew their time as serving officers might be coming to an end. He pointed to the front office, and followed them through. As they sat down, he walked over to them and ripped their police identity number off their sleeves. It was Vinny's turn now.

"Your name please?" he asked the smoker whose cigarette was trying to stay alight, but failing.

"Pc Colin Webb."

"Well Pc Webb, I take it you now know that you're in deep shit. Ds Bob Reynolds will rip your number off, when I have finished talking. Right, who is supposed to be in charge of the station today. Your silence will only make it worse for yourselves."

"It's Dc Gordon Shields. He said he would be in after the football match, which should be around now."

"Okay, we'll just wait patiently here, and you may answer the phones, but no outgoing calls. Do you hear?"

Twenty minutes passed before Dc Shields decided to grace them with his presence. He stormed through the door.

"What did you think of the match lads?" he asked the men before realising he had company.

"Who the fuck are you?"

"My name is Ds Vinny Hunter, and this is Ds Bob Reynolds."

"Oh fuck me. I've heard about you from my colleagues at Gala. What're you doing here. We were supposed to get notification when you were going to arrive."

"That's obvious by the state of this place," said Bob.

"You'd better sit down and listen to what we have to say Dc Shields. As from this minute, you are all suspended indefinitely, until a disciplinary hearing can be held," said Vinny.

"Alternatively Ds Hunter, we can suspend everyone here for a short time, until they can reflect on their actions here today. It might make them sit up, and decide if they really want to be in the police force. What do you think? I would like to head into the town, and see if we can find a decent bakers, as I could 'murder' a pie. No pun intended. If we come back, and find you're feeling contrite about what we have just witnessed, then maybe we can work something out."

They were just about to leave when one of the officers said, "I will be phoning my Union Rep about this, as I was only doing my job arresting that guy. I know the rep personally, and he'll see me all right, so I'm not worried about what you are saying."

"Okay son, if you're not taking this seriously then I am going to ask Dc Hunter to dismiss you here and now, not just suspend you."

"Stuff you, I know my rights. I'm off."

Bob walked over and stood in front of him, before asking him to hand over his badge and warrant card. It looked like he was about to protest, until Bob grabbed his tunic and ripped his badge off. He quickly handed over his warrant card, and left the building.

"We'll be back in an hour, and I sincerely hope you'll have good news for us, as it's been in short supply lately."

Bob and Vinny left the station and headed into town. They found a bakers with a sit-in area. Bob fairly 'wolfed' down a couple of pies, with a big mug of tea, and grease from the pies running off his chin. He had just finished when Vinny asked him a question.

"Bob, do you think we'll come up against this type of resistance in every station we have to visit?"

"Before I answer that, can I ask you a question? Are you going to finish that pie, or not. If the answer is no, then 'sling' it over here. As to your question about resistance, then yes. I feel people in the Borders don't want change, as 'it's always been like this.' Strange folk Vinny, but we just have to get their trust, and see how it develops."

They decided to walk along the main street to get a feel of the place. However, they weren't overly impressed. It felt like it needed investment, as there were a lot of empty shops. Plenty of people going along either pavement, but they could see that not a lot of them were frequenting the shops. It was time to go back to the police station.

"What do you think Bob, are we going to find they have capitulated or not?"

"I think you might be surprised pal. If not, then the only success we have had today was finding that pie shop. I think it was called Houston's was it not?"

" I don't have a clue Bob, as my mind works differently from yours."

As they drew up in front of the main door, Bob told Vinny to wait five minutes before going in. Eventually, Vinny said they should go and see what was happening. They were pleasantly surprised as to the state of the place, as they had made an effort to tidy it up. There were no full ashtrays, no television, and no empty tea cups lying about.

"Right everybody. What have you got to say to Ds Reynolds and I ? "

"I am going to speak for all of us in the station," said Dc Shields.

"We have talked, and realise we have let the standards expected of us drop below an acceptable level. Sheer complacency on my part. Hopefully, if you give me another chance, I can bring this station back to what it should be. If not then you can get rid of me. I can't say any more than that."

Vinny looked at Bob, and he could tell by his face that this was exactly what he had expected.

"We'll be back in one month for an unexpected visit. If you're making progress, then fine. If not you will all be out on your arses. That okay with you?"

There were nods all around, but before they left, Bob told them that they could sew their badges back onto their tunics whenever they wanted.

As they drove back to Gala, it was Vinny who said that he had never realised how bad the Borders police force was in, and how hard a job it was going to be. Bob said that he had expected it, and it was one of the main reasons he didn't want to carry on in the force. He said he was disillusioned with the standard of the job he was trying to do. His standards were far higher than most personnel in the job. Present company excepted. His words made Vinny think about his own future. Maybe he would take up Denny Rey Foggerty's offer of taking kids out on trips up on his estate. Probably better than walking the roads. Still, he wasn't keen to work with the Hounds from Hell that Foggerty trained. Maybe he would be a fulltime fisherman, with that thought making him laugh.

Dagon was doing a lot of planning in his head, but he was getting a bit bored, just sitting behind the net curtain, watching the road towards the police station. Tomorrow he was going on the bus to Innerleithen.

He knew going on the bus was a bit risky, but he didn't sit on the inside seat next to the window, and slumped down when he got into Innerleithen. He knew the police force would be down at the Gala station, so he reckoned nobody would disturb him on his mission.

He got off the bus at the last stop, and wandered down the road to the place where the dogs had been starved to death. The place was roughly between Innerleithen and the small village of Traquair, but he didn't know exactly where. He knew the area roughly, as this was where he'd been winding up Ds Hunter. As he walked he was struggling to see the place in question due to the amount of trees on either side of the road. Eventually, he saw a house in amongst the trees on the right hand side.

As he stood 'peering' through the trees, he saw a woman sitting outside with a drink of sorts in her hand. He needed to see the house for himself so he thought he would take a chance and walk in. As he got near the house, two dogs started barking. He could see that they were on chains, but were straining to get off. They looked a bit emaciated, but that didn't come as any surprise to Dagon, considering their owner's history.

"Who the bloody hell are you, and what's your business, If you're a reporter, then you can get lost," said the old woman.

Dagon could tell she was slurring her words, so it was likely that the drink in her hand was alcoholic. The gin bottle on the small table confirmed it. Her house was large, but looked pretty run down. She was dressed in old clothes, and looked like she was in need of a good feed herself.

"I'm sorry to bother you, but I was walking to a place called Peebles, keeping away from the busy main roads, but it seems I have lost my way. Can you point me in the right direction please?"

She just sat there staring into space, with glazed eyes. Dagon had a good look around. The place was like a building site. Burst bags of rubble lay all around, with lots of wooden pallets strewn over what was once a garden. He wondered what she had been building, until a brick building at the back of the house caught his eye, but it was the large metal storage container that caught most of his attention This must have been where several young dogs had been starved to death. He felt the anger rising in him.

"You must be bloody stupid if you can't work out which way to go. Up to the village and turn right. Now fuck off, and leave me in peace will you."

Dagon just gave her a curt nod, turned, and walked away, while keeping his temper in check. When he had walked into the grounds, he hadn't noticed the smell of rot and decay all around, but he did now. Soon it would be the stench of death. He walked back to the Tweed bridge, and sat on one of the benches, contemplating how he was going to kill this evil witch. It had never taken him long to work out a plan to kill somebody, and this one was going to be no exception. The only decision he had to make was which one would go first, the editor or the old hag. However, he knew it was going to be quick due to his illness, but there was one thing and that was it would be brutal, as well as gruesome. He smiled at the thought.

When he walked into Innerleithen, the bus from Edinburgh was just coming along the road, so he decided to get to the first bus stop to return to Galashiels. After getting on, he quickly wrapped his scarf around his face, and sat back. The pains in his stomach were really getting worse, so he thought that when he got back home he would just try a sandwich with some water. It seemed like there was somebody standing at every bus stop, and it was taking forever to get down the road. When he got into Galashiels, he couldn't wait to get off at his usual stop. Instead he got off at a stop not far into the thirty mile an hour limits.

He walked down into a small industrial estate by the river, where he had the mother of all coughing fits. The blood was running out of him from both ends, and he had just managed to get his trousers down before it happened. He supposed it would have happened at some stage, but didn't expect it to be that severe. It made him think that he shouldn't put himself in a position where it could end up being embarrassing for himself, but he couldn't care less he thought. When he got into his room he forced himself to eat the sandwich he had thought about earlier, as well as lying in a warm bath. Both eased his stomach cramps slightly.

Over the next few days, he made a point of watching the offices of the newspaper. It was obvious that the editor got into the room with the printing presses, but how? He still had to work out. It was a couple of days later that he saw him coming out of a small building attached to the main newspaper offices. So that was how he was doing it. From the small building, there must be a staircase up to the main offices. Also, he could easily load up a van, and present the newspapers to all his distributors throughout the Borders from the smaller building. Sneaky, but that could be his downfall.

One night he was sitting observing both buildings, when out came the editor. Dagon followed him to the Privateer bar, which was large, noisy, and to Dagon a rather soulless place. When the editor went in, he waved over to a couple of men sitting at a table. He bought a whisky, and went to sit with his pals. Dagon bought a soft drink, and made his way over to sit as near to the three guys as possible, but he had no intention of taking a sip out of his drink. As he sat, he had to listen to the editor boasting about how sales of his newspaper had gone through the roof. He was even saying how it wouldn't be long before a top newspaper would snap him up. His two sycophants at the table were praising him to the hilt. He had such a smug smile on his face that Dagon just wanted to smash it with a bottle, and keep stabbing him until he had no face left.

"Excuse me folks, but I couldn't help but overhear you talking about the serial killer that's prowling about the Borders. I also happened to hear you talking about newspapers, and I was wondering if any of you had anything to do with writing the great articles in the paper."

"I'm the guy that writes these articles," said the pompous prick that was the editor.

"My name is Alexander Brock, and you will be hearing my name more often. I'm destined for better things."

His pals looked at each other, seemingly a bit embarrassed.

Dagon asked the editor about his thoughts on the killer.

"To be honest he is nothing more than an animal. He has told me he lives rough, and just kills at will. I could trap him in a heartbeat with my writing, but I want to sell more papers. He seems of low intelligence, and if he is living rough, then probably a smelly bastard."

The three of them laughed before the editor turned to Dagon, and said," Probably a bit like you, so if you don't mind, can you disappear, as this is a private conversation. Beat it." Dagon was trying hard not to lose his temper. He was thinking about how brutal he was going to make this guy's death. It did make him smile though. He turned round, and caught the editors attention. Dagon stood looking at him. Was there a slight look of recognition on his face? Maybe a little bit of fear as well? The editor continued his conversation with his soon to be ex-pals.

Not knowing how long he had left to live, he was glad that he would at least put two evil people into the ground. He wasn't sure that the editor was evil, but it was just personal now, and nobody was going to call him an animal. No matter what he had done.

He saw a lot of people gathering across the road from the pub, before realising it was carol singers, getting ready to entertain the public. There was room on the end of a bench, so he sat down next to a couple of old ladies, and put his scarf over his face to keep the bitter wind off. There were little kids with several types of instruments, some which were nearly as big as them. Maybe if things had been different it could have been him standing there watching his kid. There was a big turn out from the public for them.

As Dagon sat, he was becoming emotional listening to the songs. Probably the only thing he liked best about Christmas were the songs. A tear started slide down his cheek, but was hidden behind his scarf. Was this going to be his last Christmas on this earth, he thought. Why did his life end up like this? Where exactly did he go wrong?

Just before the end of the singing, he walked back to his room, but not before thanking the old ladies for their company. He heard one of them saying to the other, what a nice man that was. If only they knew.

Vinny had gathered Kim, Bob and Ian in his room and told them about the state of the force in Hawick. Telling them that if they came up against that type of resistance throughout the Borders then they would be here for the long haul. He had no sooner finished, when Brian Lawson walked through the door.

"What brings you down to Gala? Rather unexpected is it not?" said Vinny.

"I came down for an update on the serial killer folks, and of course the restructuring."

All eyes were on Vinny, as he sat back in his chair, while running his hand through his hair. It was a few minutes before he replied.

"The restructuring is going well, but we are coming up against a bit of resistance to change. We will however get there, but you could have asked me that on the phone Brian. What you really want to know is what we're doing about the bloody elusive serial killer. Well let me tell you, fuck all. Sorry, fuck all sir. The guy is a ghost, a dying ghost at that, who won't be on this earth very long. That's about it Brian."

Everyone could see that Brian was trying to compose himself, but the steam started to come out of his ears, and he started shouting at that point.

"Are you trying to tell me that you are actively doing nothing to catch this killer, What the fuck are you all playing at? Everyday, I have the bosses on at me asking if you are any further forward in catching him. What's going on?"

"Brian, with all your experience in the force, how many times have you come up against a ghost serial killer. C'mon Brian, where do we actually start. Do we put an advert in the local paper asking him to surrender himself to us, or what? You know fucking fine, that if he doesn't want to be caught then he won't, so I suggest you go back to your cohorts in headquarters, and tell them what I've just said. In fact, how about you go and tell them you can stick this job up your arse. I'm out of here. The rest of you make up your own mind."

Vinny started to walk out the door before Bob said," I'm out of here as well Brian, and as Ds Hunter just said, you can stick your job."

"Brian, you are being very unreasonable, as are your bosses, and you bloody know it, so I'll high tail it out of here as well. See you," said Kim.

As she headed for the door, Ian Soutar just shrugged his shoulders, and said he may as well go back to patrolling the beat, and walked out after Kim.

Brian Lawson heard Vinny's car heading off, so he sat at the desk, wondering what had just happened. What a clusterfuck this meeting had been.

As they drove towards Innerleithen, it was Bob who spoke first.

"Vinny have you had anymore thoughts about what you're going to do?"

" I've already told you Bob, a professional angler."

Bob couldn't hold it in. He just burst out laughing, which set Kim off. Vinny was a bit 'miffed' at their laughing, but he too couldn't hold back, and started laughing with them. The laughing certainly eased the tension.

When they got back to Innerleithen, Kim said they should go to the Christmas carol singing tonight at the Town Hall. A couple of hours later they stood listening to carols being sung, accompanied by the town's silver band, with just the fluttering of snow now and again. Many of the town's folk had come over, thanking them for attending, while shaking their hands. Kim had found the whole experience very emotional. This was when she missed her mum and dad. Bob had stood there stoically, but Kim knew he wished Sharon was with him. After a quick couple of drinks in the St Ronans Hotel, they headed for bed, not knowing what tomorrow would bring.

When they were getting ready for bed, Kim had whispered to Vinny.

"Ds Hunter, I would like you inside me a fast as you can, and I don't want us to stop making love for as long as it's possible. Got me?"

At three in the morning, they both lay back totally spent. He didn't know why he said it, but Vinny asked Kim if she was still not wearing knickers on an occasion.

"You must be blind at times Hunter. Try being a bit more attentive will you."

They both turned over and fell asleep.

Five hours later the doorbell went, and Kim got up, looking out the window to see who it was.

"It's Brian Lawson, Vinny."

"Tell him to fuck off Kim, we no longer work for him. I'm tired anyway."

"We can't do that Vinny. Get your arse in gear. I'll go down and let him in. Don't bloody dare go back to sleep."

Kim put her dressing gown on and went downstairs to let Brian in, who was looking a bit sheepish standing on the doorstep.

"Come in Brian. Vinny will be down just now, but beware he is not in the best of moods. Have you eaten yet? As soon as his lordship comes down, I'll make us something to eat, but to be honest I feel a bit like Old Mother Hubbard, as I haven't been shopping yet."

"Coffee would be fine Kim. I stayed in a room only guest house last night. Cold and miserable it was. I should have said that I also rang the bell next door, which I presume is Bob's house, so he might be in for something to eat."

Vinny came down the stairs, sat at the kitchen table, and the first thing he said was, "What the hell are you wanting. I told you last night to stick your job where the sun doesn't shine Brian, yet here you are sitting at the kitchen table. I've told you before that I can easily walk away from this job, and be a gentleman of the road anytime."

"A bloody gentleman of the road Hunter? What about me?" asked Kim.

"I've never heard of a gentleman and lady of the road, have you Kim?"

Kim swiped him with the tea towel, much to the amusement of Brian Lawson. Just then Bob walked through the door and sat at the table.

"Right folks, apologies I have only bread for toast and jam."

"Well Kim, I hope you have a whole loaf then," said Bob.

"Listen guys, I think we got off on the wrong footing yesterday."

"Fucking stop right there Brian. It was you who got it wrong yesterday, not us."

"Point taken Vinny, but can we try and work things out please."

Kim placed a large plate of toast on the table, with Bob wondering when more was coming for everybody else.

Everybody had their say while eating breakfast. Eventually, it was Brian who asked everyone if they would reconsider, and come back to work.

"Only if you come for a drive down the Borders with me today, so that I can explain things to you. I don't know about Bob and Kim though."

They both nodded, as if to say they would follow Vinny's lead. After breakfast, Vinny and Brian headed down the Borders calling in to see Dc Soutar to tell him what was going on, and ask what his thoughts were on the matter. He said he would be glad to stay with the team, and Vinny told him they would be glad to keep him, which put a big smile on Ian's face.

Their first stop was Eyemouth. Vinny parked near the harbour, and told Brian there was a coat for him in the back, as he would need it. He had found Eyemouth to be one of the coldest 'holes' he had ever been in. They walked up the path to the where the incident of the man being thrown of the cliff had happened. Vinny showed Brian the mark that Dagon had left.

" Right Brian. A guy walks down that path, or so he says, and throws the victim off the cliff for beating a defenceless animal. Remember the defenceless part please. Now tell me. Where does he go from here? He could go back the way he came, or walk into Eyemouth, and then go anywhere he wants. Okay, I want to take you to the next place where he struck. Let's go."

It didn't take them long to get to Dodwell Farm at Duns. As they walked in the boss was looking out of his office, whereby Vinny flashed him his warrant card, and shouted that they were just there for a follow up. The boss just waved.

"This was where one of the workers was decapitated, and buried in the field over there. We wouldn't be here now if they hadn't decided to change where they were digging up the potatoes. The guy had obviously been put in a shallow grave, and his body had been picked up by the harvester, and eventually it spewed him out in front of the workers."

Vinny showed him the potato crate that still had Dagon's mark on it, with police tape on it. As they were walking out, he asked Brian to stop, but not to blatantly look over to the workers.

"If you casually look over there you will see a girl looking at us. Her name is Beth, and we believe she knows the killer, and could give us a description of him, but the one she gave us, described the Devil himself."

"Was there a reason for the killing?"

"Yeh, he was the foreman, and was making everyone's life a misery . One described him as an evil bastard. Remember that one Brian. Evil. Oh, and by the way the local police officer was as much good as a chocolate fireguard."

He waved to the boss on the way out. They stopped in Duns for a coffee and bacon roll. During their break, Vinny told Brian about Bob and his experience in Hawick. Brian stopped eating, and said," As bad as that Vinny?"

"Yeh, and we don't have a clue as to what we'll find when we go back in a month, but more importantly, the killer could have walked anywhere in the Borders from here. Maybe even jumped on a bus. Right, when your finished, we'll head over to a place near a village called Lauder. This was his worst killing, that we know of."

It took them about half an hour to get to Netherburn Farm, just south of Lauder. They passed the burnt out house, and Vinny parked up next to the barn, leading Brian inside.

"This is where the guy was swinging on a rope, with the crows having a good feed. No way it could have been suicide. The guy had a brother of limited mental capacity, but according to his nearest neighbours, he treated him appallingly. It was obvious that the killer torched the house on his way out of the farm. We found the brother in that field trying to pacify the animals, who were scared of the flames. The older brother was another evil bastard by the look of things Brian. Evil."

Again, he showed Brian the mark of Dagon. When they were outside, Vinny pointed to the trees up on the small hill, and said he knew the killer was hiding up there, just taunting the police.

"It was bloody frustrating Brian. Just like it is with you and the hierarchy bleating on about why we haven't caught the guy. A killer has to make a mistake, but rest assured, this is a clever guy, who won't make one unless his illness dictates."

"I'm beginning to see all this in a different light Vinny. Let's head back and I can speak with Kim and Bob."

When they arrived back, Brian said he wanted to speak to the three of them.

"Okay folks, I want to ask you a few things before I head off. What progress can I tell the big bosses about this killer then?"

"Absolutely none Brian, as we're not looking for him," said Bob.

" What do you mean, you're not doing anything to try and catch him?"

"Just exactly that Brian. I told you. We're going to wait until he makes a big mistake, or he dies, and then the problem dies with him. Let me tell you what one of our officers asked during a meeting we had. He said, if this guy was only killing evil people, then why are we trying to catch him. I made some lame excuse about it being our duty, but you know what Brian, I felt embarrassed saying that to him, because he was bloody right."

"Okay I need to go soon, take all this in, and sleep on it."

"Brian, you need to go now. Look out the window," said Kim.

The snow was coming down, and the skies were heavy looking. Brian turned to them just before he got in the car, and said that he would phone them tomorrow. As they watched him drive away, it was Bob who said," Do you think we'll still have a job tomorrow?"

"Who cares, as I'm to be a lady of the road soon anyway. You didn't think you were going to leave me behind Hunter, did you?"

"God forbid young Nichol. However, I suggest we have a real think about what we're going to do if the shit hits the fan, we have to protect your pension Bob."

Vinny suggested that Kim get her mum and dad down for Christmas day, as well as Sharon to be here for Bob. Kim said she would organise the meal, and a small present for everyone. Her parents, as well as Sharon, would love to see what a small village could do to brighten up the streets with their Christmas lights.

Chapter 15

Dagon had been twice to Innerleithen to run the rule over the old witch's place near Traquair. It wasn't that he didn't know how he was going to kill her, it was how he was going to get back home, without being caught. He couldn't let that happen, as it wasn't in the end plan. All the buses would be checked, both going to Gala or Edinburgh. If he was able he would have just walked, but he didn't fancy a ten or twelve hour walk. He didn't want to 'peg it' over the killing of an evil old woman. There was what looked like a one man taxi service in the village, but he reckoned they would have been told to be on the lookout for him.

There was nothing else for it. He would have to make the walk back in stages. It wouldn't be the first time he had slept rough, but he would have to find cover in case the snow came down. He would have to make it soon.

Back at the guest house, his coughing was bad, so he ran a piping hot bath, and just lay in it hoping the steam would help his lungs. He wondered about when he had gone, would they just cremate him erasing all trace of him. It didn't bother him, as by then he would be with his master, at least that was what he wanted to believe. Within a few days he was going to kill the old witch, and he would enjoy it. He wasn't sure if he was going to stay for the circus that followed these incidents, but he would see how things worked out.

He still had enough energy to walk up to the police station, and look through the windows every other day, hopefully annoying Ds Hunter. He would let the boys in the police force as well as the fire service have their Christmas day to themselves. This time he was going to see how close he could get to Ds Hunter, if he turned up to investigate. Two days after Christmas day it was going to be then. He felt a bit excited.

Christmas day came, and they were all sitting around with a drink of sherry, although Kim was sure Bob would have preferred a pint of some sort. They just sat and enjoyed each other's company, with the occasional drink.

"Well, it's been lovely so far folks. How long do you think the peace will last," said Vinny.

"Don't bloody jinx it son," said Bob

Kim's parents, and Sharon stayed the night, but unfortunately had to leave next day, which was fine as all three officers had decided to head to Gala, just in case there were any developments on the killer. Ian said it had been very quiet, with just the usual drunken brawls.

"We can only hope has hasn't made it through the month, but I wouldn't bank on that."

"My sentiments entirely Vinny. What do you say Kim?"

"Out of sight, out of mind for me boys."

"Kim, what do think our Christmas dinner will be like next year, when we're on the road?"

"Probably looking in somebody's bin for anything we can find, but can I put something out there to the three of you. Don't think about this guy as a killer, but can you envisage what kind of life he's living? I don't have sympathy for him, but it must be hard living a life like that. I think we are very privileged. Don't you think?"

"Kim your getting a bit philosophical are you not. I believe we choose how to live our lives, and if it's not going the right way, then we have to change it, or at least try. Bob what do you think?"

"I have no thoughts either way folks, other than I am thinking of going for a pint tonight. Anybody up for it?"

"Would love to Bob, but need to be here fresh tomorrow morning" said Ian.

"Count me in Bob. I noticed there was a sign on the 'Middle' pub window advertising music tonight. What about you grumpy Hunter. Are you up for it?"

"I suppose there is every chance you'll be dancing on the seats then?"

"Yip."

"Well, I hope you'll have knickers on this time then."

Bob and Ian just looked at each other.

As Dagon sat in his room, he felt a bit excited knowing that tomorrow, the old hag would cease to exit. Another evil person he would rid the world of. He was a little bit worried that at the end stages of his life, he was beginning to question if these people should die, but these thoughts didn't last long.

He looked through his clothing and picked out the warmest he could find. He was very glad of his sleeping bag, which had served him well. There was no way he was going to lie sleeping for any length of time, just walk for a few miles, then wrap himself in the sleeping bag, and rest his body for an hour or so.

He decided that after he did the deed, he would walk down the river, as he knew it ran down to Gala. The plan in his head for the old hag's demise was gruesome, but beautiful. His Master would be pleased. The one thing he had done over the years, was to write down everything about his kills in detail. Why? He didn't know. What he would do before he died, would be to mail this journal to the Gala police station for Ds Hunter to read, to try to understand what he was about. If he wanted to throw it on the fire, then fine.

Now it was just about resting up, and trying to get some food inside him. How long he could keep it down would be a different matter. He knew that lying out in the frost wouldn't help his cough. As long as he wasn't found lying next to the water by a fisherman a few days later. He still had work to do.

They had enjoyed themselves in the pub, although Bob hadn't been too keen on the disco. Even Vinny had got up and danced with Kim, but sat out when she and some of the locals were going a bit wild. Vinny had deduced one thing though, and that was she wasn't wearing any knickers that night. The three of them decided to rest up the next day, and wait for Brian Lawson calling, but Brian was never that good at getting back to you. Vinny and Kim had went for a long walk up in the hills behind the station, which helped Kim clear her head, with Vinny teasing her, by asking if she was wearing any knickers.

"It's five degrees below zero you bloody idiot. What do you think?"

"Just trying to be more attentive Kim, just like you asked," replied Vinny with a big grin on his face.

"Try not to annoy me today Hunter, as they might find your body lying up here in a few weeks. Frozen stiff. On a more serious note Vinny, when you look all around us at these views, it will be hard to leave this place when the restructuring is finished. Don't you think?"

"Not sure I would want to leave Kim."

Vinny turned away from Kim, and walked on.

Although they had said they were resting, neither Bob, or Vinny were happy just hanging around. Tomorrow would be different, as they would be hard at work in Gala.

Dagon had got the six pm bus to Innerleithen. After walking to the Tweed bridge, he crossed, and walked down the river until he found a fallen tree. He scooped the snow away from under part of it, placing the sleeping bag as far as he could at the back. He reckoned if it snowed or rained, then his sleeping bag would be fine. A bad bout of coughing made him lean over the tree, and bring blood up. This time it was thick and dark red. He told himself, that it wouldn't be long Dagon.

He walked slowly to where the evil hag lived. The two dogs were still out, although he doubted that they were ever afforded shelter. He crept through the trees, trying not to get the dogs barking, but he was at the stage he didn't really care. When he was about thirty yards from the house the dogs started barking furiously. The evil hag opened the window, and shouted at them to be quiet, but they didn't. The hag then walked out the front door, and started to shout at them, while holding what looked like a bottle of an alcohol drink.

Dagon kept in the shadows, and walked around the side of the house, keeping up against the wall. She never saw him until it was too late for her. Dagon grabbed her around the throat and squeezed, until she was unconscious. He let her fall to the ground, before walking over to the metal container and opened the door. There were still traces of dogs having been kept in here. The young dogs that starved to death no doubt. He told himself to keep calm.

He picked her up, walked to the open door, and threw her in, before locking the door. The next part would be the most difficult. Very slowly, he walked towards the two dogs, who were straining on their chains. He wasn't scared, and stood in front of them. They were both snarling. Dagon knelt down in front of them, just far enough away so that they couldn't get to him. He stayed there for a while, until the dogs calmed down, with one actually lying down. He kept talking softly to them until they were totally submissive. Dagon then knew that one wrong move, and he was a goner.

He walked in between them, and untied the chains, but holding on to them as tight as he could. Although they were badly emaciated, they still had strength about them. They were hounds of some sort, but due to their condition, he couldn't tell what breed they were. Now was the time that the evil hag was going to hell. He opened the container door, shouted at the dogs to get them excited, and then threw them in, before locking the door. The screams that came out of the hag were blood curdling, while she was being ripped apart. After a while there was no noise coming from her, but the dogs were snarling and barking at each other. Probably over a certain part of her body.

He took his knife out, and scraped his usual trademark 'D' on the side of the container. Right he thought, it was time to get some heat into his body. On walking into the house it reminded him of the farm near Lauder, but she hadn't been a hoarder. It stank to the high heavens. It was covered in dust, with no obvious sign of any heating in the place. Dagon was about to remedy that. He took a box of matches from his pocket, and lit anything he thought would burn. It didn't take long for a blaze to start.

He took one of the chairs that he had seen the hag sitting on previously, and sat it opposite the front door. The flames were now lapping at the front windows, and he knew they would explode at any time. He thought he would be fine. As he sat, he wondered how long it would be before somebody came running from the village along the road. It didn't take long, as the flames were starting to get to the second floor, which meant the fire would be visible from a fair distance away. There was a lot of shouting from people running along the road, so he decided to move into the forest behind the container, and just watch the spectacle as it played out.

Someone had obviously called the fire brigade, as he heard the siren coming down the road towards the bridge. The people from the village were making a lot of noise, but that was all they were doing. He wondered when the police would arrive.

It didn't need a phone call to the Innerleithen station to let them know what was happening. They could see right over the river to where the house was burning. Bob and Vinny, jumped into a car, and headed towards the flames.

"What do you think we'll find down here Vinny?"

"My stomach is already starting to churn Bob, and you know what that means, I'll need to stay calm, but I'm starting to find this tiresome my friend. I don't know about you?"

"Vinny, all this serial killer 'crap' has just made me make my mind up about leaving the force, a lot earlier than I thought. Maybe if I ever have grandkids, it'll be story to tell them. Then again maybe not."

They parked on the roadside, and walked down the track where the firemen were hard at it, trying to contain the flames, but it looked like they were losing the battle. Vinny got his book out, and started to take notes, until he saw the sign on the container. The usual 'D'.

"Has anybody had a look in that container yet?"

One young fireman walked towards it, but suddenly stopped, and shouted toward Vinny.

"I'm sure I can hear a dog or dogs in there sir. I'll just check."

"No don't go in whatever you do," Vinny roared at him, but it was too late. The guy opened it slightly, and looked in, but quickly slammed the door shut, turned round, and vomited.

"Nobody go near that container," shouted Bob.

Bob and Vinny walked over to where the fireman was being helped to where he could sit down, and continue his vomiting.

"What did you see son," asked Bob.

Although he had started to shake, he told them what he had seen.

"There are two dogs in there eating a person. It looks like a woman, but I can't say for certain, as they started snarling at me, so I quickly shut the door. Apologies if I have contaminated the crime scene, if it is one."

"Don't worry son, just take your time."

"Well Bob, its either me or you having a look in there, but by the look on your face it's going to be me."

He walked over to the door of the container, lifted the lever, and opened the door slightly. What he saw horrified him. Two dogs ripping an old lady apart, and feasting on the flesh. Vinny was a bit traumatised, and took his eye of the ball for a second.

One of the dogs saw the movement at the door, and made a lunge for it. It hit the door with some force, with Vinny struggling to stop it getting out. Bob realised what was happening, and rushed over to put his weight on the door for Vinny to lock it.

Vinny sank to the ground, and it was a few minutes before he could clear his head, before telling Bob what he saw. Bob had been glad it wasn't him that had seen it.

"Bob, can you please contact Kim on the car radio, and ask her to phone forensics, and get them down within the hour. Please don't tell her what's going on though."

Bob gave Vinny a hand up, and he walked over to a bunch of locals who had been standing on the track.

"Has anybody here got a powerful gun, and has no problem using it?"

They all stood looking at each other, until an elderly guy said he had a high powered one, and had no problem using it. Vinny took him aside, and told him what he wanted from him, which was basically to shoot the dogs.

"Are you trying to tell me there are two dogs in there who've savagely attacked the woman that lives here?"

"That's what I am saying, and unless you want to try and recapture the dogs, then shooting them is the only other way."

"Bloody hell, I've seen these two 'dugs' tied up and they scared the life out of me. Okay, I just live along the road. I'll be back in five minutes, but you'd better have a good plan for keeping me safe."

True to his word, he was back soon with his impressive rifle.

"You got a license for that?" asked Vinny.

"You want these two 'dugs' shot or not son? Right what's your plan?"

"My colleague and I will 'crack' the door open slightly, you aim the rifle through, and take a shot at either dog. As soon as you've done it, pull your rifle out, and get ready to take the next shot. We'll make sure you're safe, by securing the door. You up for it?"

"Listen son, if I was up for the War, then I'm up for this. Let's get moving, and don't worry about me, as I saw some gruesome sights in the trenches."

Bob and Vinny took him to the container, and when the time was right, Bob gave Vinny the nod and opened the door slightly. As quick as a flash the guy stuck his gun through the opening. One of the dogs had been slightly distracted, but that was the last thing that it did, before a bullet went through its skull. The guy quickly withdrew the gun, and Vinny and Bob put their shoulders up against the door and locked it. There was an almighty thud against the door. Although it was locked, they kept their shoulders pushed against it, feeling very anxious.

"Well lads. What's your plan for the next one, as I'm beginning to shake."

"We should get one of the firemen to start banging and kicking the back of the container to distract it, giving us enough time to do the same again. You okay with that?"

"Vinny commandeered the help of a lad from the brigade, and told him what they wanted him to do."

When the lad went round the back, and started kicking the container, Vinny opened the door just enough for the guy to get a good aim through. The remaining dog couldn't make up his mind what it wanted to do, either go and see what was happening at the back, or attack the rifle coming through the door. It didn't really matter, as the guy put a bullet into the centre of its forehead. To be on the safe side, they slammed the door shut, locked it, and leaned against the door, and waited. No sounds had come out after about twenty minutes, so they thanked the guy for his help, and he left to walk along the road to where he lived. Several onlookers were edging forward to try and get a look inside the container, but Bob told them to get back.

This was the first time that Bob had seen what had been happening inside, and he was looking a bit pale. They could see the dogs were stone dead, but the woman's body had been ripped to bits, with body parts strewn all over.

"Bob, let's leave it to forensics now."

"Vinny that was horrific was it not? What would possess anybody to do that to a person?"

"I came across her case in the files a few months ago. She had been convicted of gross neglect towards several young dogs who died of starvation. She got off with it due to diminished responsibility, but that hasn't gone down well with the guy who scrawled his name on the container. You saw how emaciated these dogs were in there, so you have to ask yourself if there had been any follow up visits about her animal welfare. Oh, fuck me here comes the bloody snow now."

Just then there came a roar from the fire marshal for everybody to get back quickly as the roof was collapsing. There was a mighty scramble to get back out of the way.

Dagon pushed into the back of Vinny, making him drop his pad he had been writing notes in.

"Watch what your doing you idiot," shouted Vinny, without knowing who it had been. It took a few minutes for Vinny to shout to Bob.

"Bob, the killer is here. I have that feeling again. It was probably him that bumped into me. Can you see anybody that you think shouldn't be here?"

"For God sake Vinny calm down. It could be anybody. There are dozens of people on the track just watching."

"I know it was him Bob, I've never felt this feeling as strong."

Bob just shook his head and walked away. By that time, Dagon was starting to walk away down the road. Just then, a car drew up, and the driver got out while shouting at Dagon to get out of the way. He recognised him immediately, as the editor of the Bulletin. The guy that had called him an animal. He had a camera around his neck. Dagon walked forward, and without breaking his stride smashed his nose all over his face. Dagon jumped out of the way of the spurting blood. As the guy lay on the banking next to his car, Dagon whispered into his ear that he was next. Smiling, he walked down the road until he got to the road barrier, jumped over, and started strolling down the riverside singing, to where his sleeping bag was stashed.

Vinny and Bob spoke to the fire master who said they were just going to let the fire burn, as it was too intense for them to make any difference. Vinny agreed with them, and Bob started to put police tape around the container. Vinny found a large tree branch still with a lot of foliage on it, and put it against the container covering the mark of the killer. An hour later the forensics arrived from Edinburgh. They spoke to the forensic pathologist, explaining about what was in the container, with her asking if it was definitely safe to go in.

She got Vinny's reassurance, so she opened the door and took her team in. Forty minutes later, the team came out, with all of them looking a bit pale.

"Well Ds Hunter. What we can say is that there was only one lady in there. She was elderly, and we can assume that she was alive when the dogs attacked her, due to the defence wounds on her arms. It was a pretty brutal attack by the looks of it.

I'll get the ambulance to take what's left of her to the morgue at Galashiels hospital. Your report will be sent to you just as soon as I've typed it up. Good evening."

Before she started towards her car, he shouted to her," What are we to do with the dogs?"

"Throw them on the fire Ds Hunter, unless you have any other suggestions?"

Vinny and Bob did as she had suggested with the permission of the fire master, who suggested that Bob and him should head home, as the fire would still be burning tomorrow morning. He would radio over to the station when they were due to pack up. With the snow coming down heavily, they were glad to get away from this hell hole.

Dagon had been happy with his night's work, but the thought of his walk home took the shine off it a bit. The walking was tough, as the snow by the river was deep in places. Thank God for his waterproof boots. He was about a couple of miles past the place called Walkerburn, when he knew he needed to rest up. He spied an old shed at the bottom of a field, which looked like it was an animal shelter of sorts. There was what looked like a farm up near the road, so he knew he had to be careful not to be seen, but he reckoned nobody would be out in this weather, except serial killers.

Within fifteen minutes he was wrapped up in the sleeping bag, resting up against a couple of bales of old straw. As he lay there he was thinking that maybe it was just as well he was going to die, as he didn't want to live anymore, especially like this. He spent the next half an hour bringing the blood up, and feeling so down. His body was racked with pain, and he was shaking. What cheered him up a bit, was the fact that he was remembering all the evil people he had killed. He smiled every time he thought about those times. Surely when he was gone, someone would say what a good job he had done, then again maybe not. After a while he got out of his bag, and started walking, again with not a lot of enthusiasm, as the snow was blowing into his face

As Bob and Vinny drove back, it was Bob who said, " Vinny, why did you put that branch over the killer's mark?"

"Bob, if this gets out that it's the serial killer, then Brian will contact head office, and then we'll have a squad of officers down here trying to catch him. All up their own arses. When they can't, we'll be the scapegoats. I don't know if I'll report this as being a tragic accident, but if I do and I am found out, then I may as well start walking the roads there and then."

Bob couldn't argue with him, so he just stayed quiet. When they got to the station, Kim met them with a cup of tea, and Vinny suggested they go into the office so that Kim could be brought up to date. By the time they had finished, Kim looked absolutely shocked.

"Are you positive it was this guy Dagon, and there is no possibility that the lever could have fallen down when she was inside with the dogs?"

"Kim, I would love that it was a tragic accident, only from a selfish perspective, but I am one hundred per cent sure that it was Dagon. C'mon let's be fair about this, his fucking mark was on the container. I spoke to Bob on the way over, and said if I report this as an accident, and get found out, then my feet won't touch the ground. As I have said before, I'm not worried for myself, but Bob is a different matter."

"You'll have to stop worrying about me son. My full pension entitlement came through last week, and nobody can touch it. I'm covered."

"What a terrible situation we find ourself in, but if you want my 'tuppence worth' then we just say it was an accident. If anybody finds out then we just made a mistake, so what, we're human," said Kim.

They sat for a while, before Vinny said that he agreed, and he would put in his report that it was a tragic accident. He suggested that they shouldn't give any details to Ian, as it didn't seem fair. As far as he was concerned it was nothing really, just carelessness on the woman's part.

Dagon could only go another three or four miles, as his legs were starting to ache. There was no shelter this time, so he had to settle for bedding down behind a large oak tree, which at least gave him some shelter from the driving snow. He wasn't as comfortable this time, and certainly not as warm. He knew he couldn't afford to fall asleep as his legs needed to be kept moving, as it would be the start of hypothermia if they weren't. He tried to sing a few songs he had learned at school, but at times his eyelids felt heavy, and it was a struggle. Dagon versus sleep.

He left the riverside at a sign post which said Caddon Foot. It was a risk if there were any police patrol cars going around. He looked up to his left, and saw a small church, which might have offered some shelter. He started to laugh at the thought of him being in a church. How would have to explain that to his Master. He knew he was only a few miles to Gala, so he was going to push on.

About two hours later he was running a bath in his room. There was no way he could sit down in the water, as there was a possibility that he wouldn't be able get out. So he sat on the edge of the bath, and poured hot water onto his legs to ease the pains. When he got out, and dried himself, he caught sight of himself in the mirror, and was pretty shocked at what he saw. All through his life he had a good, strong body on him. Now the illness had ravaged it. He needed sleep, but wasn't sure any would come this morning. However, his bed never felt so good.

Vinny and Bob got a call on the radio in the morning saying that the fire brigade were standing down, as they were confident the fire would not re-ignite, due to the continuous snow falling. They had agreed that they would do everything as normal, so they went about trying to get to the last part of the restructuring of the Gala police force finished. Then it was on to Hawick. Vinny got a call from Brian Lawson.

"What can I do for you Brian, as if I didn't know."

"Just wondering if the incident last night had anything to do with our serial killer."

"Brian, firstly the serial killer has nothing to do with you. Secondly it was purely an unfortunate accident. I take it that you have contacts in forensics in Edinburgh?"

"Vinny, I've read the forensics report, and it throws a few doubts on the accident theory."

"Brian, you know perfectly well that the report should have been sent directly to me, so why the fuck are you reading it? I will be contacting forensics myself asking for an explanation. So they'd better have a very good reason for sending it to you."

"Maybe it's because I am your boss Vinny."

"Yeh, but not for too long Brian."

Vinny hung up, and went to tell the team what the phone call was about. They were all in agreement that they should stick together. Ian wasn't there, but if he had been, then the conversation would have been different. He then announced it was business as usual. He was agitated that morning, so he decided to phone forensics in Edinburgh. It was the woman he had spoken to at the incident who answered.

"The reason I'm phoning is to ask what the bloody hell you were playing at, sending the report of the death at Innerleithen to Brian Lawson in Dundee. You know fine what the protocol is."

"To be honest, Brian phoned and asked us to fax the report through to him. So I didn't think there would be any harm in it."

Vinny was angry by now, and was trying to keep his anger in check.

"If Brian Lawson asked you to jump off the Forth Road bridge would you do it? What I should do is make a formal complaint against you, but you know what? I really can't be 'arsed' with your incompetence. If we're in need of help from forensics again, then please excuse yourself from the team."

Vinny could hear her starting to argue, but he put the phone down. It was two days later when the receptionist rang through to Vinny, to say Dagon was on the phone. Vinny did his usual, and gathered everybody around the phone.

"Good morning Vincent. I hope you don't mind me calling you Vincent, as it seems that we've got to know each other well over the months. You will notice that I haven't disguised my voice this time. You see, there is no point, as I will never be caught. Plus, the fact is, I will be going to see my Master soon. Maybe in a few weeks, or a couple of months, but I don't want it to be months. I'm fed up with the way I'm feeling, and I just want it to be over."

"Dagon, did you have to make it such a gruesome death for that woman?"

"Vinny, we all have to die some way, and maybe if she hadn't been an evil old hag, then there would be several young pups running around in people's lives now. Please don't get on your high horse. Lots of people would agree with me. What I would really like to speak about is the editor of the Bulletin. I happened to casually speak to him, and his sycophants a few days ago in the Privateer bar. That guy called me, or rather Dagon, an unwashed animal, telling me that he could easily trap me with his writing. Really, me? However, I expect you will have seen him at the side of the road at the fire, with his nose rearranged."

"Was that you that bumped into me knocking my note book to the ground?"

"Just a bit of fun, but I must admit you didn't look too happy. Just chill out, as this will all be over soon. Anyway let's get back to the editor. Please, don't put anybody's life in danger by trying to stop me killing that pompous prick Vinny. Just hold out for a couple of weeks, and it will all be over. Hopefully, I'll have enough time left for you and I to meet up. My regards to your team. See you."

" Dagon, will I ever find out who you really are? You're not going to die on me before that happens are you?"

"Yes you will Vincent. I was going to say God willing, but you know that wouldn't be appropriate. Looking forward to our face to face. Speak soon."

Everyone sat around not saying anything until Ian said, "He was so bloody casual, wasn't he? To be like that when talking about killing. Just down right scary folks."

Vinny was sitting back in his chair with his eyes shut.

"What is it, did you recognise his voice?"

"I don't know Bob, but Kim, can you please request a copy of every case we worked on in Dundee, as well as Fife. I know we didn't work on a lot of cases, but it was something that Dagon said that's gnawing at the back of my mind. Maybe it's nothing, and to be honest, I have no doubt I'll find out soon enough whoever he is. Although, I've probably never even encountered him before, or heard of him, I owe it to myself to have a look."

Vinny waited until Ian had left his office, before he spoke. "Okay folks, what are we to do?"

"Absolutely nothing Vinny, what do you say Bob?"

"I agree, it's just work as normal, and we'll keep it away from Ian, as at the moment I feel he's a bit 'soft', hopefully that will change."

Everyone went back to work, with Kim phoning one of the secretaries at Dundee. The girl said all copies would be there tomorrow. As they were home that night, Bob asked, "Vinny, did you get the impression that the guy wants a one to one with you, when the time comes?"

"Yeh, I thought that Bob. I feel he's made this personal between us. He may have chosen you, but I was just the one he focused on. What will happen in a one to one I haven't got a clue, but what I do think is that he bears me no ill will. Although I won't take any chances."

Dagon gave himself a few days to recover, before getting his legs moving by walking around the town. When all the Christmas decorations had been taken down, Gala was back to its drab self. Before Christmas there were lots of people smiling, but that was diminishing now. He was going to spend a lot of time watching the Bulletin offices, to see what the editor's movements were. A couple of times he had went for a soft drink in the Privateer, but sat well away if the editor was in. He had certainly done a job on his nose. It was still bandaged, and he had two black eyes. Dagon smiled, as it would be soon.

The editor's injury hadn't stopped him writing, and then publishing his newspaper. He had written about the fire near Innerleithen, but what he wrote was just sheer fantasy, and he had blasted Dagon for causing the fire, and the 'accident' to the old hag. He had no proof, as the police had made sure of that, but that didn't stop him berating Dagon.

Dagon had read the newspaper, and just laughed. He told himself that people would be hearing the guy's name soon. Well that's what he wanted wasn't it. It suddenly came to him how he was going to kill him. Oh, how wonderful this was going to be. Obviously he couldn't wait too long. Last night had been particularly bad. This morning he had to soak his sheets in the bath, as they were covered in blood. The lady of the guest house let him keep himself to himself which helped. He would just sleep without a bottom cover tonight. Before he finally went, he would leave her some money to replace any sheets that she thought weren't fit for purpose now.

Each day he would 'stake- out' the Bulletin's offices. Sometimes the editor would appear, but other times he could hang around for the whole of the day, or night without seeing him. He also had a think about his office secretary. After all that he had done to hide his identity, there was no point in screwing it up now. He committed everything to memory, and after a week, he knew where and when he was going to kill him. Finally, his purpose in life would be fulfilled. What a great feeling that was.

Afterwards, he would have to get his journal up to date. A journal of his killings.

Chapter 16

Denny asked Bob if he was up for a surprise visit to Hawick to see if progress had been made.

"Only if we can go for a couple of pies, and a cuppa before it, and remind me to bring a few home with me."

"Bob, don't you think your belt is straining enough pal. All credit to the guy who made it though," said Vinny laughing.

They were soon in the car, on the road to Hawick. On the journey, Bob asked Vinny if he had any thoughts on how he was going to go about his face to face with the killer, and had he any idea who it could be.

"I've read all the reports from Dundee, over and over, but all I'm getting is that I may have met this guy somewhere, but remember how many men we interviewed in Drumbrig. Could it be one of them? I haven't a clue really, but from my time in Fife and Dundee, something is niggling me, but you know what Bob, I could just be messing with my own head, and it might just be some random guy that decided to choose me for his entertainment. Who fucking cares."

"You're not going to meet this guy face to face without back up are you?"

"I don't feel threatened by him. In fact I'm looking forward to meeting him, but don't worry, I will have the pie master as my back up."

"Vinny Hunter, don't even think that's funny."

They were both surprised to find that the Hawick station was immaculate, with everyone seemingly working hard. They spoke to the officer in charge, and were impressed with his attitude. Bob asked about the constable who had walked out while threatening them with the Union. The officer said he had returned a few days later, had given him an abject apology, and his work had been exemplary since then. It didn't take them long to be happy with what had been going on, so they said they would be back soon for the official visit.

"That was a nice result Bob."

"Yeh, can't wait to get back."

"I wonder why?"

Dagon had been watching, while waiting for his chance to end the life of the Bulletin editor, but he was being thwarted at every opportunity. The more times he lost out meant the less time he had to kill him. He had to make his death relevant, so he had an idea. The guy would head off to the chip shop before he started work, but had never failed to lock the door. One night as he left, he had failed to catch the latch properly, so Dagon smiled, knowing that tonight was the night. He crept up the stairs just in case the secretary had stayed back. His instincts had been right, as he looked through the crack in the door to see her putting her clothes on. He wondered if the guy had threatened her with her job if she didn't have sex with him. It wouldn't have surprised him.

After looking around, he hid in what looked like the stores cupboard. He heard the girl leaving, with the front door being slammed. Maybe she hadn't been happy with the way he was treating her. He would love to have told her that it wouldn't be like that again. It seemed like an age before the guy came back. Maybe he had gone to the pub for a quick one. It didn't matter. He had just sat down to start his fish and chips, when Dagon walked out and put his forearm around his neck from behind, and choked him just enough for him to pass out.

When he came too, he was tied to a chair by string that was used to bundle the papers up with. Parcel tape was around his mouth. The fish supper looked good to Dagon, but probably not with his stomach. He felt a sense of relief that this time had come, and he couldn't stop smiling. What a glorious killing this would be to end his spree. He took the gag off the editor, warning him not to shout out.

He got a chair and sat down in front of him, with the guy straining at his restraints.

"I wouldn't bother trying to get out of the chair you scumbag. Do you know who I am?"

"Yeh, the smelly bastard from the Privateer. Let me out of here right now, and I might not press charges."

"That was the wrong answer you prick. You see my name is Dagon. Not a smelly bastard, not evil, not an animal, just a guy ridding the world of evil people like you. Oh, and may I say, I think I've done a very good job up to now. However, I hope you know I am going to kill you, and your death will be special."

The guy started to wet himself which Dagon thought was amusing. He knew what was about to happen, with the guy shouting for help, so Dagon quickly punched him on the jaw knocking him out. He then stuffed old newspapers into his mouth. Ones that were about the serial killer. He cut his restraints, lifted him up, and forced him down into the printing press, before switching it on. It had been set up ready for another publication, but after a while it jammed due to the body. If the paper hadn't choked him to death, then having his throat stuck underneath the press would have. The motor of the press was now struggling, and eventually it started to spark, with flames starting. Time to go he thought, but as he walked out, he phoned the fire service.

The call from the fire service came through to Vinny's house at about nine pm. As soon as the fire master mentioned the Border Bulletin, his heart sank. He knocked on Bob's door, and told him they were off to Gala.

"Bob, it's our old nemesis Dagon, I'm sure of it. Hopefully this will be the last of it, and we can get on with our lives. Although, he still wants to meet up with me."

They put the siren on, and were in Gala in fifteen minutes, sitting outside in the carpark of the Bulletin offices. Vinny was given the nod to go upstairs, and met the fire master who showed him the crime scene. Bob looked a Vinny, and they knew right away who had done this.

"We have to call forensics in. Even if the report does go to Brian Lawson. Have you any idea who the fuck Dagon is Vinny. It's now or never to spill it out."

Vinny stood looking at the corpse, but not saying anything. He looked at Bob, and it was then that Bob knew Vinny recognised who Dagon was. He left it at that.

"Right Bob let's phone Kim to get forensics down here as quick as possible. Meantime, let's tape everything off, go for pie and chips, and eat them in the car. I know it's not protocol, but you know what pal, I couldn't care less anymore. Stuff it."

Bob didn't take much persuading when the words pie and chips came into the equation. When they had finished, it was Bob who spoke.

"Have you had any thoughts on how you're going to approach the meeting with the killer?"

" After what I just saw, I'm not sure what kind of danger I would be in Bob, but I will take precautions, trust me. The guy did say a while back that he wasn't interested in harming us."

Forensics arrived, and Vinny was glad to see that the woman who he had the run in with wasn't there. Both, Bob and Vinny waited in one of the downstairs rooms, awaiting the verdict. Eventually a man came down asking to speak to whoever was in charge. Vinny said is him.

"What I can tell you is that the victim was suffocated. Apparently several pages of a newspaper were stuffed down his throat making breathing impossible. On the front of pages there was a headline about a serial killer. It looks like sticking him in the printing press was just for show. Ring any bells?"

"Yeh, we know exactly who did it, but catching him is the problem, isn't it Bob."

Bob just nodded his head looking a bit disinterested. Vinny asked if the body would be taken to the Gala hospital as normal, and he said it would. Bob checked with the fire master to see if they could head off. The fire master said everything was fine, so no problem.

As they drove back up the road, Bob was very quiet, and Vinny left him alone. He knew that with the forensics involved, Brian Lawson would be phoning him in the morning. They went back and told Kim what had happened.

"Do you think you're wise going to see this guy Vinny. Maybe we should just try and trap him."

"Kim, please just give it a rest, as you don't know what your talking about, no disrespect, but I need to know who this guy is, and what his agenda against me is. There is no way I'm leaving this unsolved. It's eaten me up for a long time now. Too long."

The next morning, Kim wasn't saying very much to Vinny, but he just got on with it. The atmosphere on the drive down to Gala was like there had been a death in the family, and Vinny was glad when they were at the station. True to form, Brian Lawson phoned not long after they got in.

"Brian, what a lovely surprise. Have you been reading the forensic report again. As if I didn't know. C'mon, spit out what you want to say, as it should be interesting."

"I take it, that it was the serial killer again. The serial killer that you have refused to pursue Vinny."

"Yip, it looks like it Brian, but we didn't find any mark of Dagon to be honest, but you see there is a reason for it. Within a couple of weeks the guy will be dead, so we can get on with our lives, and possibly, and I say possibly, our jobs."

"How do you come to that conclusion Vinny?"

"Just call it intuition Brian, but you'll have to trust me on that. If by chance he walks into the station here and surrenders, then I'll let you know, and you can hare it down here, and take the credit for the capture. How does that sound pal."

"Don't' be a fucking smart guy Vinny. I really should be organising a search down there. However, you have two weeks for this to come to a conclusion. Do you hear?"

All four of them started to clap, before Brian put the phone down. Vinny said he wondered how long it would be before Dagon called. Bob said they should have a sweep stake, and see if they could make a few quid out of it. It took Dagon two days.

The call was put through to Vinny.

"Good morning Dagon. I see you've been up to it again. That wasn't a very nice way for anybody to leave this world. I see you didn't leave your mark at the scene. What happened?"

"Well I thought it a very fitting way for a bastard like him to go. I was very happy that he 'pissed' his pants when he realised his time had come. I admit I slipped up in not leaving my signature mark, but it wasn't that you didn't know who did it. How about we meet up in the old woollen mill over the railway bridge on Friday night. I could ask you not to bring your back up, but to be honest you won't really need anyone. If you feel the need for it though, only the big guy and the newbie will be acceptable. On no account do I want that 'bonnie lassie' anywhere near the place. Got me?"

Vinny smiled, before saying, "What time should I be there?"

"Just before ten please, but if you have to bring your pals then they must wait outside, as I don't want to hurt anybody. Okay?

"Understood Dagon, and I will finally get to know who you are. Can't wait. See you Friday. Oh, and Dagon. Will this really be the end of all this?"

"It sure will."

Everyone was just sitting looking around, until Vinny spoke.

"What does everybody think?"

"This is a very unique situation Vinny. None of us have ever come across this before. My own opinion would be to have the place surrounded as soon as you are inside, but if we spook him then you could end up in danger. If you don't think you'll be in danger, then we go with what he's said."

"I appreciate your concern Bob, and although I am not one hundred percent sure that he won't turn on me, I think I'll be okay. Ian?"

"Bloody hell Vinny, it wasn't that long ago that I was rounding up a brawling drunkard, or issuing an occasional parking ticket. There's no point in us saying anything, as let's be fair about this, you've made up your mind that your going, with only us as back up. Have you not?"

"Kim, what do you think?"

"It doesn't matter what I think Hunter. I'm with Ian. You're going to do what you want, aren't you?"

"Thanks for your input folks. We'll carry on as normal until Friday, but I am going to ask you one important thing, and that is we keep this under wraps. I'll deal with any fallout, and you were all just following orders. Got it?"

Dagon lay on his bed. Just about every part of his body was hurting. He would be glad when Friday came, and this would come to an end. He would be in the mill well before ten pm, just to make sure that Ds Hunter wouldn't go back on his word, and surround the place, but he was confident it would just be the two of them. As he lay there, he started to reminisce about his life, and wondered where it had all gone wrong. Maybe it hadn't, and this was what his purpose on this earth had been. The nearer it was to Friday, the more content he was becoming. He had written his journal up to date, but obviously he couldn't write about Friday night. He couldn't wait for it to come around. The charity shops would benefit from any spare clothes he had left.

During Wednesday and Thursday, Kim had hardly spoken a word to Vinny, but he didn't say anything. She hadn't been receptive in bed either, he knew there was a lot of talking to be done after Friday, but that could wait.

On Thursday night Kim slid over in bed, and held Vinny tight until morning.

He was up and showered next morning, with Kim still in bed.

"C'mon Kim get your arse up."

"I'm not going in today. You're on your own. If you come back, then great, but just leave me out of all this."

"Don't worry Kim, I promise I'll be back. Just keep the bed warmed up. Please trust me."

She just put her head under the pillow.

Bob drove, while Vinny went over everything that was to happen that night.

"Here's the story Bob. I would like us to be there about nine thirty, waiting outside. At nine forty five I'm going in alone. On no account are you or Ian to come in. No matter what. If I think I know what's going to happen, then I want you to urgently radio for an ambulance."

"For you Vinny?"

"Not for me pal. I can't tell you much more, and I'm sorry for that, but I have to play this out myself. By tomorrow we can start to wrap this up. It has taken a lot out of us, especially me Bob. I'm tired of it all."

"You and me Vinny."

When they got to Gala station, Vinny took Ian aside and told him exactly what he had told Bob.

"What happens if he's armed boss? "

"I know he will be Ian, but regardless, for your own safety, don't come in through the doors. Got it?"

Ian just nodded his head, not looking too happy. He walked through to where he and Kim shared an office. He couldn't face doing any work, so he shouted through to Vinny that he was going out for a walk to clear his head. Vinny didn't reply.

"Bob you might have to keep an eye on Ian tonight. I'm not sure he can handle it."

"He'll be fine Vinny, have faith in him."

The day dragged out, and nearer six o'clock Vinny asked one of the receptionists to go out for fish and chips for everyone. The usual pie and chips for Bob.

Dagon put on the clothes he thought he would look best in. The rest were put into his holdall, with a note asking for it to be sent to a charity shop left on top. He had bathed earlier, as he didn't want to meet his Master not having washed. He had come to terms with the inevitability of what was going to happen. Happy how it was going to end. He lay back and waited for the time to head up to the mill. He was going to be early, to make sure Ds Hunter's team were going to stick to the plan.

Vinny was beginning to get a bit nervous now. He was planning on him knowing what the killer would do, but if he messed up, then God knows what would happen. At nine fifteen, the three of them took the car over the bridge, and parked at the roadside, next to the old mill. They sat for ten minutes without anybody saying a word. Vinny could sense Bob glancing at him now and again, but he just sat focused, while staring ahead. He glanced at his watch, and saw it was nine thirty five, so he thought to hell with it, he was going in.

When he got out of the car, Ian turned to Bob and said, "Are you sure we're doing the right thing Bob?"

"It's madness Ian, but remember, if things go belly up, then you weren't here, just like we've told you before. Deny everything."

Vinny was walking down the steps to the old derelict building. They were slippery, due to the frost, so he held on tight. No point in breaking an ankle now. He had to sit down on the last few steps, as that feeling had come over him, and he felt a bit out of focus.

Dagon stood watching him from one of the upstairs window. He had never wanted him to be feeling like this, but needs must. He would wait until Vinny Hunter was in the big empty building before he came down the stairs.

Vinny walked through the dusty floor of the mill. His torch picking out shadows, with him continually wondering if that was Dagon. He stood for about twenty minutes looking out one of the large windows which overlooked Gala. Maybe Dagon was dead, and all this drama had been a waste of time. Apart from his torch, the only other illumination was the moonlight coming through the windows. Just when he thought he might just head off there was a slight noise behind him. He didn't move.

"Hello Barney."

"Hi Vinny, glad you could make it. When did you know it was me pal? Please don't turn around, as my illness hasn't been good for my features, especially my face."

"Well to be honest my friend you've led me a merry dance for quite a while now. When I was getting the feelings in my stomach, I knew somebody was around, just taunting me. At one point, I naively thought it might be Billy's ghost toying with me. How stupid that sounds now."

"I must admit Vinny, you did make me laugh with your antics, when I was watching you.

"However, when I saw the newspapers stuck down that editor's throat, it reminded me of the demise of Luggy Burns. It was you Barney, wasn't it?"

"Yeh, it was me pal. To be honest when I left that shithole of a place we were brought up in, I had no purpose in life. Each morning I woke up would be the same as the day before. I was so angry over Billy's death, that I vowed to go back and kill Luggy, and Vinny, trust me when I say it was a beautiful killing. From there, I vowed that I would at least try and kill any evil bastard I came up against, and here I am."

"Where do we go from here Barney? Why don't you come in with me, and we will see what treatment we can get for you."

"Don't be bloody silly Vinny. You know I only have a few days until I'm dead, so I won't be coming in with you."

"Barney can I ask you if you are standing there with your grandad's Luger pointed at my back?"

"Sure am Vinny, but you mustn't worry my good friend. There is only one bullet in the chamber. My heart bids you farewell Vinny, but before I go what time is it?

"Why the fuck does it matter what time it is Barney?"

"Humour me pal."

"It's 10:22pm Barney."

"Well, you'll remember that time forever pal."

That was when the gun went off. Vinny hit the floor. He was in shock, and wondering if he had been hit. He lay there before realising that he hadn't been shot. His torch was still on, lying not far from him, so he stretched and grabbed it. When he tried to get up his legs were weak, but he managed to stagger over to where Barney lay. He got down on the ground, and pulled his head and shoulders onto his lap. The blood was still oozing from the bullet hole in his head, but Vinny didn't care.

"Why oh why did this have to be the end pal? We were once such special friends."

Vinny removed Barney's scarf, and was shocked to see his ravaged face, but still with the lopsided smile. As he just hugged him, he heard Bob shouting, and eventually, both he and Ian came running up.

"You okay Vinny?" Can we help?"

"No, just give me a minute please, but what you can do Bob, is to pick up that gun and put it in your pocket, as I might want to get rid of it. Ian, radio for an ambulance, and tell Kim I'm fine will you. After that head off. Walk back to the station, and remember you were never here."

He was about to argue when Bob just nodded to the door, and he went to the car to use the radio.

Twenty minutes later the ambulance men came into the building with their stretcher and carrying their torches. Only then did Vinny let go of Barney's body.

"Did you know the deceased sir," asked one of the men.

"Never seen him before, we were alerted to a shot being fired, and we came up in the car. Please look after him, will you?"

When they had left, Bob sat down beside Vinny, and said, "What now pal?

" I've got to get the body away from the morgue as quickly as possible. There will have to be a post mortem, but all I'm going to say is exactly what I said to the ambulance men. I want to make out that we came across the body, with the gun lying beside him. A tragic suicide pal."

"Was he a good friend of yours Vinny, and how long have you known?"

"Yeh, he was Bob, and only the last couple of days did I know for sure. Let's get out of here please, as I'm struggling."

When they were back at the station, Vinny phoned Kim. He knew immediately that she had been crying.

"Kim, can you bring me a change of clothes tomorrow morning, when you come down please."

"Why are you not coming home tonight Vinny? You need to get home."

Kim, what pisses me off about you, is that you always think you know what's best for me. So please do as I've asked, and I'll see you tomorrow. It's my intention to sleep in the cells tonight, as I need to be on my own."

He knew she wouldn't be happy, but tonight he couldn't care less. He got another couple of blankets, and an old pillow. His clothes were soaked with Barney's blood, so he just left them in a heap on the floor of the cell. Bob had gone home earlier, so Kim would feel safe.

He tossed and turned all night. The nightmares that came were terrible. Lots of things were floating around inside his head, and he couldn't get Barney's ravaged face out of his mind.

It was Kim's voice he heard first. When he looked at his watch he realised it was eight o'clock. He must have gotten some sleep after all. She came running through and jumped on him.

"Don't you ever put me through that again, do you here?

Vinny just held her tight, until Bob came in with a cup of tea. Vinny said he would change, and after his tea he would speak to everyone in his office. When they were all assembled Vinny started to talk.

"Right folks, firstly let me say that that I have no right to ask you to go along with what I'm going to do. I propose to take Barney's body out of the morgue, as soon after the autopsy as possible. I would like to ask you to accept my reasoning behind the suicide. He was just a tragic individual who took his own life. We were on a call out, after there was a report of a gun shot at the old mill. We just happened to be passing, and decided to investigate. Hence we came over the body. We don't have a clue who he is, just another John Doe."

"However there was no way he was the serial killer we had been looking for. I don't want anybody knowing his real name. I know I can at least tell you that. His name was Barney Anderson, and he was my childhood friend. A very dear friend. I am not asking you to cover anything up, just go along with the pretence that we haven't a clue who he is, or should I say, was. I alone will make up the reports."

Ian went and made coffee, and as they sat around the desk he said, "Vinny, you do know you can be in deep trouble for this. If we all take the blame, then the bosses wouldn't want the scandal surely."

"Thanks for your concern Ian, but I'm not sure I want to be in the force anymore. Bob is retiring, and the way Kim dances in the Middle pub, then I think she might have a career as a 'go-go dancer', so that only leaves you Ian, and to be truthful, we have high hopes for you. Although you don't know it yet."

"Hunter, you are in grave danger of having two black eyes," said Kim.

"Okay folks, can we get back to some normality here please, and most importantly, Barney Anderson was not the serial killer."

"Kim, I need you to do something for me."

"Sorry Vinny, I have knickers on today," she said laughing trying to lighten the mood.

Vinny asked her to contact Fife County council, and speak to the people in charge of burial plots, and put them through to him. A while later he was speaking to a women who didn't really know what she was doing.

"Mrs Weatherstone, this is a matter of extreme urgency, and important police business, so it has to be kept secret. So can you help us please?"

The words secret, urgency, and police business galvanised the woman into action.

"Mrs Weatherstone, I'm making enquiries as to whether a certain plot in the Drumbrig cemetery is still free. If you check your charts, you will see that a lad called Billy Clark was buried there a while ago, and what the police would like to do would be to buy the plot next to him. I'll let you look into it, and get back to me. I presume the girl told you my name, and left my phone number?"

"Yes Ds Hunter, I'll phone you back within the hour."

Vinny's next job was to phone the morgue to see when the autopsy would be on Barney. They said there was a backlog, so he asked if they could make this a priority. After a bit of huffing and puffing, the coroner agreed. Vinny thanked him, before requesting that as soon as the autopsy was done they phone him, and no one else.

Several times Vinny left his desk, walked through to the cells, and just sat in silence. Nobody bothered him. He tried to remember everything that the Three Amigos had done during their young lives. Barney had been right when he left Drumbrig, saying that even if Billy hadn't been killed, they would eventually have gone their own ways. Vinny thought that life sitting down the Mot river with their homemade fishing rods, was a more simple life.

Eventually the woman from Fife County Council phoned back.

"Detective, I have found out the information you requested. The plots either side of Mr Clark are vacant. Do you wish me to reserve one for you? The cost would be one thousand three hundred pounds, which includes the cost of digging the grave."

"That would be fine, and a cheque will be sent to you with my name on it if you are okay with it, but I need it done very soon, and I can't stress the secrecy enough Mrs Weatherstone."

"Don't worry Ds Hunter, the police's secret is safe with me."

Vinny thought that he'd made her day. She thought she might be the new Mata Hari. The next part was going to be more problematic.

"Kim, can you come with me please. We're going to see the local undertakers."

She didn't query it, but just picked up her coat, and followed him out the door.

"I'm positive that there is an undertakers business in one of the streets just around the corner. In different circumstances I would say show a bit of cleavage, but I don't think its appropriate where we're going."

"You think Hunter?"

They walked into the undertakers, and were met by the owner who seemed a very amiable guy. Vinny started to explain what he wanted, and the man started taking notes.

"Now let me get this right. We would pick up a body at the Gala morgue, take it up to Fife for internment, then just for us to return home. You don't need any cars apart from the hearse. The coffin has to be simple, and no service at the grave side. A bit spartan is it not sir. Friend of yours?"

"That's exactly what I want, and I don't need any questions, okay?"

Vinny showed him his warrant card, as did Kim.

"Just give me the details, and we'll be only too happy to help."

Vinny said it would be a few days yet, but before he left he asked the undertaker Davie if he knew a place where he could get a head stone made quickly.

"Just give me the details, and I'll get it made, and it'll be in place for when you get up there.

Next day Vinny phoned them and gave details of the stone he wanted, as well as the epitaph. Everything was falling into place except for one thing, Brian Lawson. They all went home that night, and Vinny was glad to have Kim snuggling into him in bed, but he still couldn't get the images of Barney out of his head. He was up early, which was just as well, as the phone rang at seven o'clock.

"Bloody hell, who would have guessed. What do you want at this ungodly hour Brian?"

"I need to know what happened with this apparent suicide. Do you think it was the serial killer? The bloody same serial killer that you have been doing sod all to find."

Vinny put the phone down on him. Ten minutes later Brian Lawson phoned again.

"It appears we were cut off."

"No we weren't Brian. I didn't want to listen to you being a 'dick' again. What the fucking hell are you so worked up about the serial killer for. Is it because you've been promised a promotion if you go back and tell the bigwigs that the serial killer will no longer be a problem. Well, I'm telling you, the reign of the serial killer is over."

"How the hell do you know. What are you not telling me Ds Hunter?"

"Oh, I see we're being official now. I'll tell you what Brian. The restructuring is going well, but if you want it finished, then I suggest you back off, and let us do the job you asked us to do."

The atmosphere at the station was pretty tense that day, with everybody giving Vinny a wide berth. At the end of the day he called in all of the staff for a meeting.

"Okay everybody please listen. As from Friday, we do not have a serial killer problem. The guy is now dead, so you don't have to worry about him roaming about out there. Let's just go about our jobs, as if he never existed. If anyone, and I mean anyone, asks you then you have absolutely nothing to say."

There seemed to be a sense of relief over the station in the next few days. People seemed happier being police officers. Vinny hadn't realised how much this had been hanging over the station. Three days later, he received a phone call from the autopsy department asking him if he wanted to come over to go over their findings. He said he would be over within the hour. He asked Bob if he wanted to accompany him, but he declined saying that this was for him, and him alone. Both Kim and Ian agreed with Bob.

When he arrived at the morgue, he was met by a lovely lady called Dr Thomson, who asked him to follow him into her office. The morgue had a pretty run down feel about it. She asked him if he wanted see the body, but Vinny declined.

"Ds Hunter, do you have a personal interest in this case? Well, what I can tell you is this chap had been suffering from SCLC. It's a very aggressive form of cancer. It grows very quickly, and causes lots of tumours throughout the lungs. The symptoms include bloody sputum, chest pain, cough, and shortness of breath, amongst other symptoms. It's a miracle he has lasted this long."

Vinny thanked her for her help, before asking how quickly she could authorize for the body to be released.

"Ds Hunter that is highly unusual as it's protocol for the body to be held here in case it is claimed by any relative. After all, the body is marked here as being a John Doe."

"Dr Thomson, I can assure you he doesn't have any relatives, and I would like the body released as quickly as possible. "

"Ds Hunter, as I said this is highly unusual, but I need both a verbal and written request, before I release the body."

"Dr Thomson, you seem like a nice lady, but to be honest, I couldn't care less what you think. I have already given you the verbal request, and the written one will be with you within the hour. Good day to you."

As Vinny walked out, the doctor looked towards him, and thought what a strange man he was. She knew she would release the body. When Vinny got back to the station, he immediately asked Kim to type up the request for the release of Barney's body, and take it over to the hospital.

"Is this legal Vinny?" she asked. Vinny laughing gave her the answer. He contacted the undertakers, and told them he hoped to have the grave dug within the next few days, and asked about the headstone.

"All done, and we are waiting for the go ahead to collect the body ready for transporting it to Drumbrig. Just let us know."

Life had to go on for the four of them, but Vinny was struggling. He knew it, and wondered if after he had buried Barney things would improve. Although, he wasn't convinced. He sat Kim down, and explained about the cost of burying Barney, and did she mind. She said of course not, and fully understood.

Three days later, Fife County council, phoned to say they had received Vinny's cheque, and the grave had been dug. That same day he had a call from Dr Thomson to say that the undertakers could collect the body anytime. When he had walked round to the undertaker's offices they advised him that they could do the burial this Friday. Vinny said the quicker the better.

"Oh, can I just say that please don't drive up there at thirty miles per hour, or we'll never get there," said Vinny.

"I've never known somebody who was in such a hurry to bury a body before," said the undertaker.

Vinny just gave him the thumbs up, and walked out.

On the Friday, they left Ian in charge of the station. Bob was going up to spend time with Sharon after the burial. Vinny thought it would be a good time for Kim to spend time with her parents. Davie from the undertakers had suggested they leave at nine o'clock to let the congestion at the Edinburgh by-pass go down. Bob said he would drive, and soon they were following the hearse. Vinny had phoned the council to let them know what was happening before he left.

True to their word, the hearse wasn't putting off any time, and in just over two hours they were approaching Drumbrig. The hearse pulled into the bus stop just before the road into Drumbrig.

Davie came to their car, and asked where they should drive in about, and who were going to be the pall bearers. Vinny asked if he and his assistant Leck would be two, and he and Bob the other two. The hearse drove along the track, and parked as near to the grave as they could. Vinny was glad to see the headstone was up. He asked Davie who had put it up, and he said that one of his friends had owed him a favour, so he had done it. Two council workers had laid out the cords and timber supports, and were standing at the side of the grave.

"Right Bob and Vinny, can you please help us with the coffin."

As they carried the coffin to the grave, Bob thought how light it was, but for a man who had died, 'riddled' with cancer, then he should have known. They walked either side of the grave, and gently lowered the coffin down onto the wooden supports. One of the council workers asked that the coffin be lifted. When the supports were taken away, they all lowered the coffin into the grave, and threw the cords in. Kim was crying, but she didn't know why, as she'd never known Barney. Maybe she was feeling Vinny's grief.

Nobody had heard the squeaky gate at the entrance opening. Brian Lawson walked up to the graveside.

"When did you know it was Barney who was doing all the killing Vinny, and was that why you knew the serial killer wouldn't bother us again."

"Really don't know what you are on about Brian, and if you pursue this, you will be in the grave with Barney, and I would hate to do that to him. I really would, so drop it."

Just then everybody heard the gate, and someone shouting.

"Wait, you have to have a sermon. You can't let this poor soul go to the Lord without a few words being spoken."

"Ah for fuck sake. It's Holy Ian, Billy's dad. This is turning into a fucking circus, not a quiet burial. Get out you sanctimonious bastard."

Holy Ian wasn't for moving until Vinny picked up a couple of stones from the soil at the side of the grave, and threw them at him. Bob grabbed a hold of Vinny, who by this time was threatening to put Holy Ian in the ground. Holy Ian got the message.

Davie and Leck were standing at the hearse, before Leck turned and said,” It's been a while since we have had such a lively burial pal. Maybe they should all be like this. It would make our job a little more pleasant.”

Everyone left Vinny standing at the grave to give him some privacy. Vinny was happy with the headstone. All the epitaph said was BARNEY 10: 22pm. He hoped he would like it. It was time to go, but before he did, he said a few words.

“Well Barney, I would rather be anywhere else than standing here today. I just wish you'd come to me for help, but I suppose I can understand why you didn't. Love you big man.”

He threw Barney's journal into the grave.

Vinny walked over to Davie and Leck, shook their hands, and thanked them for their help. Brian was already walking away, so Vinny didn't bother saying anything to him. He put his arm around Kim, and walked to the car where Bob was waiting.

“Bob let's head for bonnie Dundee, my friend. Please drop us off at Kim's parent's house, and pick us up at eight o'clock on Monday morning, and please give our regards to Sharon.”

Kim and Vinny spent most of the time resting, and Kim catching up with her friends who through her own admission she had been neglecting to keep up with. A few times she had borrowed her dad's car, and they had headed up to Arbroath to walk on the beach. Vinny reckoned she didn't want to go any further North in case they got near to the estate owned by Denny Rey Foggerty. Vinny wondered how he would have handled the serial killer. Would he have gone at it at one hundred miles an hour, stopping for nobody in his way? Anyway, he would never find out now.

When they got back to Gala, Vinny called a meeting between the four of them just as soon as he got through the station door.

“Okay folks, here's the plan for the foreseeable future. I think this restructuring will take us another five months at the latest, and then we can get the hell out of here, and start afresh. Ian, what would you say if we asked you if you thought you were ready enough to run the Borders police. Obviously it would have to be a recommendation from us, and we would have to ask for a promotion for you. However, you will have to put a lot of work in over the next few months.”

"I'm honoured that you all feel that I'm capable of doing the job, and the answer would be, yes."

"Right that's all folks. Let's get to it, however there is one more thing I need to do. Fancy a trip to see millions of potatoes Kim?"

As they got in the car she asked where they were going, and why? He said just to wait.

When they turned into Dodwell Farm, Kim was looking a bit perplexed.

"What the hell are we doing here Hunter?"

Vinny parked the car next to the office and went in.

"Good morning, I take it you remember me?"

The guy said he did and what could he help them with. Vinny asked if a girl called Beth still worked for him, and if so could he have a word with her in private. The guy was only to happy to help, and went into the factory to get her. When she entered the office, Vinny could see she was a bit nervous.

"Don't worry Beth, you haven't done anything wrong. We're here to tell you something. I knew when you were interviewed that you knew more than you were telling us about Dagon. Don't worry, you're not in trouble for it. What I would like to tell you is the guy you knew as Dagon, is now dead."

Beth looked down, and after a few seconds, she lifted her head and said," How?"

"He had terminal lung cancer Beth, unfortunately he didn't have a long life."

"Dagon wasn't his real name was it? He used to tell me about where he came from, and about his two pals, but he never mentioned them by name. The cancer makes sense, as I could hear him coughing in the room next to me at the lodgings we were in. He really was a nice soul. He bought my breakfast for me every morning until he left, because of that bastard of a foreman. Was he the serial killer in the Borders?"

"His name was Barney, and as for the serial killer, we can't really comment."

Beth just smiled.

"Here's my card, and any time you feel like talking, I'm at the end of the phone."

She turned to Kim, and asked," Is he your boyfriend? "
Nodding at Vinny.

"Yes he is, why?"

"Well, can I just say you're one very lucky lady."

Kim just laughed and said "thank you I guess I am."

Beth left, and Vinny took Kim into see the spectacle of millions of potatoes getting ready for the supermarkets.

When they were leaving, Beth turned to them, giving them a little wave and smile.

On the journey up the road, Kim turned to Vinny and said," Hey stud, what's it like to be admired by all the girls?"

"It's a burden I'll have to carry with me all my life."

Kim thumped him on the leg, almost making him lose control of the car.

The station worked on as normal, with no interference from Brian Lawson, and everybody's life got back to normal.

Epilogue

The final part of the restructuring lasted another five months. All stations, large and small co-operated without a murmur, but the team thought that word had got round. The hierarchy thought that the team had done a great job, and they wanted to speak to Vinny and Kim about the next stage.

Bob hadn't stayed till the finish. He didn't want to be in the force any longer than he had to be. Vinny gave him his blessing, and both he, and Kim did receive postcards from some obscure places in the North of Scotland. Occasionally, Bob would make a quick phone call to Vinny, asking how they were.

Brian Lawson was promoted to Detective Inspector, working out of head office.

Vinny and Kim would often sit up the hill looking at their favourite views contemplating their future. Occasionally Kim would snuggle in to Vinny and say, " Hey Hunter you're not being very attentive are you. I'm not wearing any knickers again."

One day Vinny checked the station answering machine at Innerleithen, and there was a message left, which made his heart sink.

"Hey, its Denny Foggerty, give me a call."